Beyond the Thistles

Special Edition

The Highlands Series
Book One

Samantha Young

Beyond the Thistles

A Highlands Series Novel

By Samantha Young

Also by Samantha Young

About the Author

Samantha Young is a *New York Times*, *USA Today* and *Wall Street Journal* bestselling author from Stirlingshire, Scotland. She's been nominated for the Goodreads Choice Award for Best Author and Best Romance for her international bestseller *On Dublin Street*. *On Dublin Street* is Samantha's first adult contemporary romance series and has sold in 31 countries.

ACKNOWLEDGMENTS

For the most part, writing is a solitary endeavor, but publishing most certainly is not. I have to thank my amazing editor Jennifer Sommersby Young for always, *always* being there to help make me a better writer and storyteller. Thank you for working with me to make sure Walker and Sloane's story fell as authentic and true as possible. You're my Rockstar!

Thank you to Julie Deaton for proofreading *Beyond the Thistles* and catching all the things. You have an amazing eye for detail and I'm always reassured my stories are going out into the world in the best possible shape.

And thank you to my bestie and PA extraordinaire Ashleen Walker for helping to lighten the load and supporting me through everything. I appreciate you so much. I love you, friend!

The life of a writer doesn't stop with the book. Our job expands beyond the written word to marketing, advertising, graphic design, social media management, and more. Help from those in the know goes a long way. A huge thank-you to Nina Grinstead, Kim Cermak, Kelley Beckham and all the team at Valentine PR for your encouragement, support, insight and advice. You all are amazing!

Thank you to every single blogger, Instagrammer, and book lover who has helped spread the word about my books. You all are appreciated so much! On that note, a massive thank-you to the fantastic readers in my private Facebook group, Samantha Young's Clan McBookish. You're truly special and the loveliest readers a girl could ask for. Your continued and ceaseless support is awe-inspiring and I'm so grateful for you all.

A massive thank-you to Hang Le for creating a beautiful cover that feels in keeping with the Ardnoch world but has its own stunning flavor to set this series apart. You are a tremendous talent! And thank you to Regina Wamba for the beautiful couple photography that brings Walker and Sloane to life.

As always, thank you to my agent Lauren Abramo for making it possible for readers all over the world to find my words. You're phenomenal, and I'm so lucky to have you.

A huge thank-you to my family and friends for always supporting and encouraging me, and for listening to me talk, sometimes in circles, about the worlds I live in.

Finally, to you, thank you for reading. It means everything to me.

For my beloved Scotland.

"Wherever I wander, wherever I rove,
The hills of the Highlands for ever I love."
—Robert Burns, *My Heart's in The Highlands*

PROLOGUE
SLOANE

Fourteen months ago

I f I told anyone I was sick of palm trees and sunshine, they'd think I wasn't in my right mind, especially since I was someone people described as having a sunny personality. However, I'd been sick of the monotony of endless summer since I was fourteen. My dad afforded me the sweet taste of travel as a kid, and it had made me long for something different. To be anywhere but in LA.

You know what they say—the grass is always greener. Literally. Grass in my part of town dried up. Not just because of drought, but because no one around here had time or resources for such things as lawn maintenance.

I'd never wanted to be anywhere else more than I did as I stopped outside my apartment door and saw the eviction notice posted to it.

"You've got to be kidding me," I whispered hoarsely, pinching my nose to stop the sting of tears.

An overwhelming powerlessness threatened to seize hold of me. I fought through the panic tightening my chest, thinking of the little girl on the other side of the door. Had she seen this? Or had Juanita shielded Callie from the truth? Dread settled in my gut. My Callie might appear shy and quiet, but she was sharp as a tack and missed nothing. It made trying to shield her from the crappiness of our circumstances extremely difficult. But I was determined.

Bracing myself, my stomach roiled as I snatched the eviction notice off the door.

Today I was fired from the receptionist job I'd lied my way into. A colleague who'd had it in for me from the beginning looked into my claim that I'd worked as a receptionist for another casting agency. She knew someone at said agency, and they told her they had no record of me ever working there.

So, I got fired, even though I was more than competent at my job. Yeah, I knew the lie was wrong, but when you're a single mom, you'll do just about anything to make enough money to put a roof over your child's head. The irony of being fired from a casting agency for lying on my résumé was not lost on me. The agency lied on people's résumés all the time.

I'd spent the rest of the afternoon using most of the gas in a tank I couldn't afford to refill, following up on ads I found on my phone for positions. Out of ten, one—for a receptionist at a beauty salon—offered me an interview. I took it, even though they paid way less than what I'd been earning, and I was already behind on my rent.

Exhibit A: Eviction notice.

Even renting in Crenshaw, in one of the cheapest studio apartments I could find, where my kid didn't even have her own bedroom, I was behind on my rent.

Because my useless, scumbag ex forgot we existed half the time.

In a perfect world, he would forget we existed, period. His

reputation preceded him, and the man I'd stupidly had sex with at sixteen and gotten pregnant by had become someone so dangerous, I barely recognized him.

I'd never regret my Callie.

I only wished her father was someone different.

Someone I didn't have to track down and beg for money, even though knowing where that money came from made me nauseous. But for Callie, I'd not only throw pride out the window, I'd throw my morals out too. I'd do anything for her.

So I called Stacie.

It was a short, snippy call. Afterward, I took a deep breath, opened the apartment door, and walked into the studio. During daylight hours, it was light and bright and airy. Even with our twin beds crowding half the space, we tried to keep it as nice as possible.

I buried my worries and grinned at my kid like I had none.

"Mom!" Callie dropped her book and launched herself off her bed, hurrying across the apartment to throw her arms around me.

Love and determination filled me as my daughter rested her head against my chest and I wrapped my arms around her. Bending, I pressed a kiss to the top of her blond head. When she was a baby, I'd felt overwhelming love for her, but I'd felt overwhelming terror too. I was only a kid myself. What did I know about raising a daughter? The love had grown to impossible depths over the years, and the terror became manageable, sharpening in moments like this.

Callie pulled away to stare up at me with the only beautiful thing her father gave her—big, gorgeous blue eyes.

I smoothed her hair off her face. "How was your day, baby girl?"

"I won the class spelling bee. Ms. Francis thinks I should join the school team."

My smart girl who, somehow, would be in the fifth grade

next semester. I didn't know where the time had gone. "Congratulations! I'm so proud of you." I took her arms and danced with her on the spot, making her giggle. "Does that mean I get to come see you in competition?"

"Yup."

"Sloane."

Juanita's voice drew my gaze. The best thing about this apartment building was that it came with Juanita. She'd seen us moving in on the first day and we got to talking. When I mentioned I was concerned about Callie taking the bus home from school and staying in the apartment until I got home, Juanita had offered her babysitting services. Her husband, Eli, worked nights and their kids were grown, so she said she had time. Though she charged less than other babysitters, I still couldn't afford her. But Callie's safety was all that mattered to me. Hence why I was behind on rent.

We shared a look, and she gave me a small shake of her head.

Relief filled me. Somehow, she'd kept the eviction notice from Callie.

"I know you've stayed longer than usual tonight, but could you give me another hour?"

"Where are you going?" Callie scowled up at me.

My smile was reassuring. "I promised a friend I would help them with something tonight. But I'll be back soon." I looked at Juanita.

She frowned and jerked her chin toward the door. "A word outside, mija."

Despite my tension, I offered Callie another kiss on the head and told her to return to her book. My daughter stared suspiciously up at me but did as I bid, and I thanked God for giving me a child as easy as Callie. She'd been the quietest, most chilled-out baby, and she was the sweetest kid. I often wondered if that meant she'd be a hellion as a teenager because no one could be that lucky with their child.

However, that was a worry for the future. I had enough to be concerned about in the present and was grateful Callie's behavior wasn't one of them.

As soon as we stepped outside, Juanita turned on me. "Everyone who has passed your door will have seen that eviction notice. You can't hide that from Callie for long."

"I know, and I don't intend to. I'm going to get the money."

She narrowed her eyes. "How?"

"I need you to watch Callie so I can pay her father a visit."

Alarm filled Juanita's eyes. She knew who he was because I'd told her. But she also knew who he was because he was now a high-ranking soldier in a gang that primarily traded in drugs and chopped cars. "You are not going after him at night."

"I called Stacie. She told me where to find him." Reluctantly. We'd been friends when I was still with my ex. But when I left him and tried to start fresh for Callie, Stacie called me out for thinking I was better than her, than them. For wanting to get away from that life. That I'd never really stopped being that spoiled rich girl from Beverly Hills.

"Where is he?"

"He's at some house party in West Adams. She texted me the address."

"You are not going alone at night to a house where that man and his thugs are. No way."

Though I appreciated Juanita's concern for my safety more than I could say, I couldn't back down. "I need to find him. And while I hate that I need to, the one upside to being his kid's mother is that he won't let anyone hurt me."

"No, he likes to leave that job to himself."

I flinched and looked away.

"I'm sorry, mija. I just worry. Wait for Eli to get off work. He'll go with you."

"I'm not dragging Eli into this. Please." I clasped her hands in mine. "I don't have time to argue. I need to find him, get the money, and get home to my baby girl. Will you please stay with her until I get back?"

Sensing my stubborn determination, Juanita reluctantly agreed.

A few minutes later, I was in my car, hands trembling as I clipped in my seat belt. Using the map on my phone, I slowly made my way toward the house in West Adams.

There were people sitting on hoods of cars parked curbside, others drinking in the yard, and music boomed so loud from inside that I'd heard it as soon as I turned onto the street.

I wouldn't give up Callie for anything in the world. She *was* my world. Every action I made was in service to loving her. But that didn't mean I wasn't angry at my past self. Furious with that hurting sixteen-year-old who wanted to punish my father for ignoring me and marrying a woman half his age who hated me and made me feel like a stranger in my own home.

I'd started partying at fifteen.

I met my ex at sixteen at a club where I'd used a fake ID to get in. He was eighteen, charming, from the wrong side of the tracks. All that cliché stuff that appealed to me because I knew my father, lawyer to the stars, would hate him the most.

I didn't intend to get pregnant.

Or get kicked out of my own home for refusing to give up my child for adoption.

Or end up with an abusive criminal.

That's why I left my ex. Though in his mind, I was still his.

One day, I'd save enough to get Callie and me as far away from him as possible.

Sucking up my courage, I got out and rounded the hood,

ignoring the catcalls from a couple of guys leaning against their car.

I stepped into the yard, and a tall guy with a gun tucked into the waistband of his pants blocked my way.

"Who the fuck are you?" he shouted to be heard over the music.

"Relax, Kai!" My ex's friend, Brix, clamped a hand on my interrogator's shoulder. "She belongs to Andros."

Nathan Andros. My ex. His family owned a Greek restaurant in Culver City. They'd disowned him a long time ago. Just like mine disowned me. But that didn't make me *his*.

I belonged to no one but Callie.

Yet, I curbed my tongue, because despite the way it made my throat close with impotent anger, that imagined ownership was the only thing keeping me safe.

Brix gestured with a bottle of beer and yelled, "He know you're coming?"

I shook my head. "It's an emergency."

"The kid okay?" he asked, as if he might even care a little.

"She won't be. That's why I need to see Nathan!"

"Shit, man, even I think the music is too fucking loud!" Kai turned on his heel and hurried into the house.

"This way!" Brix jerked his head toward the small porch.

It was like most homes in the neighborhood. Single story in the Spanish style. Bars guarded the windows and the front door.

As we entered the crowded house, the volume of the music lowered. It was still loud, but I couldn't feel it reverberating through my chest like before. It was stifling hot with all the bodies inside. Alert, wary, I glanced around as Brix led me through the sitting room and into the kitchen. I didn't see Stacie or anyone else I recognized from my old life. Brix turned left down a hall off the kitchen, leading to what I guessed were the bedrooms.

Crap.

"He's down here?" I asked, attempting to sound cool.

"He's in a meeting," Brix called over his shoulder. Then he stopped at the third door and knocked. "Andros, it's Brix!"

"I'm busy!"

"Sloane's here! She said it's an emergency!"

There was silence, then, "Let her in."

Taking a deep breath, I prepared to face my ex.

Brix opened the door and gestured me in, and as soon as I stepped inside, the door closed behind me.

We were in the main bedroom, but it was small. Two guys sat in armchairs near French doors that led into the backyard. Behind them, the yard was dark and empty, like the guests had been told it was off-limits. My ex stood near them. And on the bed, looking a little worse for wear, was a gorgeous brunette.

A way-too-young gorgeous brunette.

Nathan gave me a hard look. "What couldn't wait?"

I glanced at the two men, then back at him. "Can we talk in private?"

"It can't wait?" he pressed. "I'm in the middle of something here."

"I only need five minutes."

One guy gently tapped the other. "Let's give them a minute."

"What about her?" The other stared at the brunette like she was a piece of meat.

The girl tensed but said nothing.

"We'll talk," Nathan answered. "I'll be right out."

The two men were tall. They had a few inches on Nathan and plenty of muscle. The one who had excused them eyed me with a flirtatious smirk as he approached. "Hey." He jerked his chin as he leaned past me to open the door.

Stepping aside to let them out, I gave him a practiced friendly but platonic smile as I said hey back.

Once the door closed behind them, Nathan crossed the room to me. I tensed as he reached past me to lock the bedroom door.

Intimidation tactics.

Then he put his hands on my hips and yanked me into him. "My girl's looking tired. You should let me take care of you."

When I'd first met him in that club, I'd thought him the sexiest guy I'd ever met. His father was Greek, but his mother was Danish-American. That heritage had resulted in beauty for Nathan. Olive skin, dark hair, and striking light blue eyes.

He was all charm and humor, and he'd wrapped me up in affection and attention that I'd been missing at that point in my life.

I was too naive to realize that he got off on taking a good girl and dirtying her up. That I was some kind of prize to him. Something he owned, not someone he loved. Two years after Callie was born, I'd gotten the courage to leave him. He'd haunted my doorstep for a year after that, trying to cajole and threaten me. Thankfully, he'd grown bored. Now he appeared every few months to drop off cash and remind me who owned me. He'd even beaten up a guy I'd dared to date when Callie was five. I hadn't dated since.

Nathan thought that somehow meant I agreed he owned me.

Delusional asshole.

I was just biding my time until I had enough money to get Callie and me out of his orbit.

Now looking up at him, I saw the malice behind his beauty. Trying not to let it show in my expression, I stayed still in his hold and said, "I lost my job, and they're evicting me. I need money to get up to date on my rent and to tide us over until I get a new job."

His fingers bit into my hips as his gaze hardened. "Well,

you know the answer to that. You get your ass back in my bed, and you won't need to worry about that shit."

"Hey!" The brunette I'd almost forgotten was there jumped off the bed and shoved Nathan away from me. "I'm right fucking here, and you're trying to get with another girl!"

I was surprised she sounded so lucid, considering she looked like she'd been partying for days.

Nathan's face hardened. "Bitch, shove me again and you'll regret it."

Her expression turned mulish. "No one treats me like shit. And that includes offering me up to one of those miscreants who was just in here."

Miscreants?

My eyes narrowed on her. Why was she so familiar?

"Princess, you're in my world now. You do whatever I fucking tell you to do ... and right now, I'm telling you to SHUT THE FUCK UP!"

I flinched at his roar while the brunette barely moved. After a second, she spit right in Nathan's face.

My heart plummeted.

"Nathan, no––"

The crack of his hand across her face cut me off, and the girl fell back on the bed. Suddenly, Nathan was on her, straddling her, trapping her legs.

I got a flashback.

The first time I tried to leave.

Callie, a toddler, screaming in the living room from her playpen. Nathan holding me down on the bed, unzipping his pants. To prove who owned me.

His friends had thankfully interrupted us, bursting into the apartment before he could take what he wanted. I'd left him that evening while he was out.

Pulled from the memory and back into the room, I

watched in horror as he held the girl down with one hand and reached for the zipper on his pants.

"Nathan!"

He snapped his head toward me. "Want to see what you're missing?"

"Get off me!" the girl shrieked.

His shirt rode up as he hit her again, and I spotted the gun tucked into his waistband. Moron kept his loaded gun down his pants.

Fear thrummed through me as I zeroed in on it.

I couldn't let him ...

I took a step toward the bed, but my heart sank as Nathan yanked the gun out and pressed the muzzle to the brunette's forehead.

She stopped struggling, but glared defiantly up at him.

"That's a good girl."

Revulsion slithered through me.

That's what he used to say every time I capitulated to him. He'd never gotten the chance to rape me, but he had raised his fists to me and I'd pretended so many times to forgive him. To go along with whatever he wanted for a quiet life. Until that day he'd tried to take what I didn't want to give. That was the final straw.

"Wait for me out in the hall." Nathan shot me a look. "We'll talk when I'm done here."

My eyes flew to the girl. She stared at me.

Pleading.

"I'm not leaving. I need to get back to Callie. Let the girl go."

He sneered. "If you don't leave, we're gonna do this, anyway."

"It doesn't look like she wants to, Nathan, so let her go."

"Do you want to?" He pressed the gun harder against her head.

And even then, she hissed, "No."

I lunged at him. It distracted him long enough for her to bite the hand holding his gun so hard, Nathan cried out.

The rest of the scuffle was a blur. Nathan punched me in the head and stomach. But I thought between me and the brunette, we'd have the upper hand.

I don't know who had the gun, but when it went off, pain ricocheted through my upper arm, and I screamed.

"Shit!" Nathan bellowed.

The door to the bedroom rattled, but it was locked. "Andros!"

"Fuck, I'm okay!" he yelled back, and I blinked through my red haze of pain to see the girl was on her ass against the bed, staring at me tear-streaked and wide-eyed. Nathan wrenched the gun out of her hand.

Concern wrinkled his brow as he dropped to his knees beside me. I noted he laid the gun down even as I clasped my bleeding arm with my free hand and strained away from him.

"Shit, Sloane," he hissed, reaching for my wound. "Why the fuck did you do that?"

"She ... she needs an ambulance," the brunette whimpered.

"No fucking ambulance." He glared at her. "I'll take care of her. You know why? Because I actually give a shit about her. This is my kid's mom you just fucking shot!" He stood up, stupidly forgetting about his gun. And he began punching her.

Over and over.

And over.

Like he wouldn't stop until it was too late.

I pushed through the agony blazing through my arm, grabbed the gun, and aimed it at him.

ONE
SLOANE

Present day

Ardnoch, Scottish Highlands

T he aim of housekeeping at Ardnoch Estate was to be as invisible as possible. We didn't use the main stairwells, and we had staff elevators that took us from floor to floor. On most days, I only ever saw the grand entrance of Ardnoch Castle if I was walking past it on my way to club manager Aria Howard's office.

The members-only club in the remote Scottish Highlands was the last place I'd ever have imagined I'd end up working. But here I was, in my housekeeper's uniform, pushing my little cart with fresh towels and amenities down the plush carpeted hallways of the renovated castle. The coastal estate was enormous, and the elite membership was only open to film and television industry professionals who could afford it. Once the crumbling ancestral property of ex-Hollywood actor and local Lachlan Adair, he'd turned his family's estate into a lucrative haven for famous people seeking peace and quiet from their celebrity lives. Highly trained close protection teams and state-of-the-art security meant Ardnoch was one of the safest places on earth.

As soon as I stepped into my first suite of the day, I realized pretty quickly I'd forgotten the parcel of locally made biscuits I was supposed to leave in each room after I cleaned. At night, the turndown service left members hot toddies and chocolates in their bedrooms. Smiling to myself, thinking how much I'd love someone to bring me a hot chocolate each night, I pushed my cart off to the side so it wouldn't get in anyone's way. The staff elevator was at the end of the hall. It would take me only a few minutes to get to the housekeepers' storage room.

I'd just stepped into the staff elevator when I heard a familiar, deep, growly voice demand, "Hold the lift."

I knew that voice. It did *things* to me. Heart racing, I turned around and held the door open as Walker Ironside strode toward me.

No name could be more perfect for a man.

The first time I saw Walker, he should have intimidated me. He towered over most everyone, standing about six feet five. He had massive shoulders and thick biceps, a tapered, strong waist, and long legs. The man was too handsome for his own good, smooth and rough all at the same time. He kept his beard trimmed, but his brown hair was styled—shaved at the sides and longer on top. The first time I saw Walker, it wasn't intimidation I felt. I had the most visceral physical reaction I've ever had to a man in my life.

I wanted to strip him naked and explore every inch of his spectacular body. I wanted to climb him like a freaking tree while he murmured dirty words in my ear in that gruff Scottish accent.

Even his monosyllabic, steely-eyed manner didn't put me off. His utter masculinity enthralled me. Back in LA, I'd been surrounded by gun-toting thugs and gangsters ... but I'd never met a guy who was so truly a grown-ass *man* as Walker Ironside.

My physical response to him was unsettling. His lack of physical response to me was disappointing.

Correction: It was crushing.

My breath caught as I had to tilt my chin to meet his aquamarine eyes, stepping back to allow him entrance. He dwarfed the entire elevator. "Thanks," he muttered.

"No problem."

I let the door go and it shut. Heavy silence fell between us, and my whole body zinged with hyperawareness. Feeling all of thirteen with an infatuation, I tried to control my breathing so Walker wouldn't see how he affected me. I was already concerned there was a telltale flush to my tan cheeks.

The elevator moved downward, and I glanced at him out of the corner of my eye. He wore a black tailored suit that fit to perfection. All the security guards at Ardnoch dressed like the Men in Black. It was a good look for Walker. "What brings you to our level?" I asked in a teasing voice, referring to the fact that the guards spent most of their days monitoring the security perimeter, estate entrances, and escorting any members who required private security while they toured the Highlands.

Walker's expression was annoyingly blank. "We're considering alarming vulnerable areas of the castle in case the estate is ever breached."

My eyes widened. "I didn't think that was possible."

"It's very unlikely. As I said, it's only a consideration."

"Yeah, I don't think the members want to feel like they're in a fancy prison." I grinned.

His intense gaze flicked to my mouth before quickly returning to my eyes. He didn't smile. Not that I'd ever seen Walker smile. I'd never taken his gruff demeanor to heart, but lately he'd verged on cool and distant. He had come to Ardnoch with Brodan Adair, Lachlan's younger brother. While Lachlan might have retired from Hollywood years ago, Brodan was even more globally famous. He'd returned to Ardnoch last summer with his bodyguard, Walker, in tow. Brodan had infamously retired to stay at home in Ardnoch after he and Monroe—his estranged childhood best friend—rekindled their epic love story. Walker decided to stay, too, after Lachlan offered him a job as part of the estate's security team. Monroe shared all this with me—she was Callie's teacher last year, and the two of us hit it off and became fast friends.

I'd spotted Walker before I met Monroe. He's kind of hard to miss around the estate. And working in the same place meant I got to catch frequent glimpses of his gorgeous ass.

Anyway, working together and being in the same friendship circle meant I learned Walker was gruff with everyone and not to take it personally. Still, after watching the way he salivated over my baked goods (not a euphemism—we officially met at a school bake sale, and he practically devoured my table), it was disheartening to not have him acknowledge, much less reciprocate, my subtle flirting. I'd seen him weeks before the bake sale, working on the estate, and I'd hoped he'd notice me, but as a housekeeper, I was invisible. At least, that's what I'd been counting on. That once we met for real, he'd see me.

He didn't.

As far as Walker was aware, I was just a person with a knack for baking who was also friends with his friends.

Realizing he had no intention of saying anything else, I worried my lip with my teeth. Usually, I could talk to anyone, and I was pretty good at bringing the most reserved people out of their shell. But Walker reduced me to feeling like a teenager. He's older than I am—according to Monroe, in his late thirties, so he's at least a decade older. There was a worldliness about him, and he exuded a weary-eyed, *seen everything, done everything* attitude. But I liked that about him.

I opened my mouth to ask him how he'd been since we hadn't seen each other in a while and he was treating me like a near stranger when the elevator jolted, metal creaking and squealing as it stopped. It threw me off-balance, and I fell against the wall.

"Are you all right?" Walker reached to steady me, concern marring his brow.

Fear slivered through me. "Are we stuck?"

He hit the ground-level button, and nothing happened. His tone was grim. "It would appear so."

As I took in the small elevator, anxiety tightened across my chest.

Walker's eyes narrowed on me as he pulled a walkie-talkie off a clip on his belt. Holding it to his mouth, he said, "You've got Walker. I'm in the east wing staff elevator with housekeeper Sloane Harrow. It's stalled. We're stuck."

We're stuck.

"Oh, God." Black dots crawled across my vision, my cheeks tingling as my panic increased.

I was vaguely aware of the talkie crackling. "Got it. Maintenance is on their way."

"Sloane."

My chest rose and fell fast as I struggled to draw in sufficient breath.

"Sloane."

A large, warm hand settled on my shoulder, and I looked

up from my clenched fists to find Walker's head bent toward mine. His eyes were like staring into the waters of the Mediterranean on a sunny day.

"Are you claustrophobic?"

I nodded rapidly.

He squeezed my shoulder. "Look at me. Keep looking at me."

I did as he commanded.

"Breathe in." Walker took a slow, easy breath in and then released it. "Breathe out."

I copied him.

"Keep doing that and stay focused on me."

Up close, I could see every hair of his trimmed beard, and there were a few grays. Not a lot, but some. My gaze dropped to his mouth as I continued to slowly, calmly breathe. His lower lip was full compared to his top. His mouth was usually pressed into a hard line, so I hadn't noticed the plushness of that bottom lip. I wanted to nibble on it. My cheeks heated, and I glanced up at him to see if he'd noticed. To my shock, his fierce gaze was fastened on my mouth.

My breath hitched as tingles awoke between my legs and in the curve of my breasts.

Walker straightened as if he'd been shot. "Sit down."

His command was far blunter than I think he'd intended.

At my bemused expression, he moved to my side and opened his suit jacket so he could slide down with his back against the wall. His legs were so long. With his knees bent, his suit trousers strained against the heavy muscle of his thighs.

With his pure sexiness, the bastard had distracted me from my claustrophobia.

I felt a sharp pang of alarm that I forced away.

Okay, so not entirely distracted.

I hurried to sit beside him, my elbow bumping his as I

drew my knees to my chest. Though I wasn't short at five seven, I still looked tiny next to him.

"Better?" he asked.

"Yeah, thanks."

There was a beat of silence, and as if he had to force the question out, he asked, "Have you always been claustrophobic?"

Shaking my head, I tried not to wince as I remembered the day that would set off a lifelong fear of enclosed spaces. "I got trapped in a closet for five hours when I was six years old."

Walker nodded solemnly. "That will do it. Maintenance will fix this soon."

"Do you think we're close to the ground?"

"I reckon we're above the opening to the ground floor."

At least that meant if the elevator suddenly crashed, it wouldn't kill us. "I take it you're okay with confined spaces?"

"They don't bother me."

I studied his face as he turned it to me. "I suppose little does. Bother you, I mean?"

Walker shrugged and agreed. "Not much."

A man of few words. I tried to bite my lip against a smile, and his gaze dropped to my mouth again. A muscle ticked in his jaw, and he looked toward the door. "How's Callie?"

The question surprised and gratified me. The only people I'd seen Walker soften toward were kids, Callie being one of them. It made me wonder why he wasn't married with his own brood. Sure, I knew from Monroe, and from what I'd witnessed myself, Walker was a bachelor who seemed to like his life free of complications. Including complications of the female variety. The man seemed only to be interested in a one- or two-night stand.

Casual was his middle name.

My gaze drifted down his body, and my skin heated. I'd

like to know what it was like to do casual with Walker Ironside.

"Callie's good," I answered. "Wonderful, in fact. She spent most of the summer getting up at the crack of dawn with me to bake." After selling my cakes and pastries at a school fair and then the Christmas fair, I'd gathered a small group of loyal clientele in the year that we'd lived in Ardnoch. They regularly placed orders for special events, and word was spreading about my baking. I had a real hope that at some point, I might quit housekeeping to run my own bakery. Except for the small array of baked goods in Morag's the village deli, and a few of the cafés, there wasn't an actual bakery here. "She's my patient helper and way too understanding for her age."

"What do you mean?"

I shrugged. "Being a single mom ... I can't always get the balance right. We have to rely on each other and on friends. Some kids might be a brat about the fact that their mom needs someone else to pick them up from school, but she goes with it." I relied on Regan Adair, the wife of the second-eldest Adair brother, Thane, to pick Callie up from school and keep her at her house until I finished work. Regan's stepson, Lewis, was Callie's best friend, and the Adairs were the kindest people who offered help because they knew I needed it. As much as that pricked my pride.

Walker scowled at me. "You're not the only parent who has someone else collect their kid from school. You're doing fine, Sloane. Better than fine."

His words lapped over me like warm water on a chilly day. "Thanks."

He gave me an abrupt nod.

I nudged him, and he glanced at me sharply, almost suspiciously. So wary and bristly. It made me want to cover him in kisses. "Thanks for calming me down. I owe you cake."

Walker eyed my mouth again before he looked away.

Huh. Maybe he wasn't completely immune to me.

"You don't owe me anything," he grumbled. "But I won't say no to one of your cupcakes. Or that pie thing with the chocolate you made for the Christmas fair. Or your strawberry tarts. Hmm. What made you get into baking?"

I grinned, pleased he loved my baking so much. "I started as a cheap way to keep Callie entertained, and I got really into it. I loved how therapeutic it was and how the more I learned and got better, people reacted to it. Cake makes people happy, and I like making people happy."

The corner of his mouth turned up at that.

I wanted to kiss him so badly.

"I'll rustle something up for you as a thank-you for distracting me. Maybe I could bring it over on Saturday." It was pushy, I know. But I was getting kind of sick of lusting after the guy without doing something about it.

Before Walker could reply, the speaker mounted inside the elevator near the buttons crackled. "This is Bruce from maintenance. You folks all right?"

Walker stood in one fluid movement and pressed the button to reply. "All good. How's it going out there?"

"Good. Found the problem. You'll be out in less than a minute."

A strange mix of relief and disappointment that we'd been interrupted filled me. Relief won out, however, as I stood up as the elevator shook to life and we felt it pulling us downward once more.

"Thank God."

Walker glanced over his shoulder at me, but said nothing.

Then suddenly we slowed to a normal stop, and the doors opened.

Two smiling men stood outside it, one who I assumed was Bruce.

Walker gestured for me to step off first, and, no lie, I practically ran out. "Thanks!" I waved at the maintenance guys who grinned back.

Turning, I watched Walker step out and nod his thanks to the men before those intense eyes came to me. "You good?"

"Yeah. Again, thanks."

Walker studied my face for a second, as if weighing a decision. He must have made it, because he gave me another abrupt nod and marched away.

"Guess that was a no to Saturday," I muttered forlornly.

Two

SLOANE

The head housekeeper, Mrs. Agnes Hutchinson, asked after my well-being once I returned downstairs (reluctantly in that damn elevator with my cart) to have lunch. She then asked me, before I hit the staff cafeteria, to deliver a message to Mr. Ramsay, the maître d'hôtel, about a new stock of silverware that had arrived. Mrs. Hutchinson seemed to know all the goings-on at the castle, including the minutiae of everyone else's jobs. Having delivered said message, I was trying to stroll inconspicuously through the dining room as I headed toward the staff quarters to have my lunch.

All staff quarters were at the back of the first floor (or ground floor, as they called it here) of the castle. The rooms and hallways were utilitarian compared to the rooms dedicated to the members. Soft gray walls and wooden floors gave way to wood-paneled and wallpapered walls and hardwood floors covered in Aubusson carpets.

I hurried out of the dining room and glanced to my left. The grand reception hall of Ardnoch Castle was a thing of beauty. I saw the head butler, Mr. Wakefield, carrying a tray with cups and a teapot. He gave me a nod and swept into the grand hall in his butler's tailcoat and white gloves.

He strode across polished parquet flooring that was interrupted by an enormous Aubusson carpet in the center of the room. The décor was traditional, Scottish, timeless luxury. A grand staircase descended into the center, fitted with a red-and-gray tartan wool runner. It led to a landing where three floor-to-ceiling stained glass windows spilled sunlight. Then it branched off at either side, twin staircases leading to the floor above, which I could partially see from the galleried balconies at either end of the reception hall. A fire burned in the huge hearth on the wall adjacent to the entrance and opposite the staircase. The smell of burning wood added a coziness to an otherwise mammoth room. Tiffany lamps scattered throughout on end tables gave the space a warm glow too.

Opposite the fire sat two matching suede-and-fabric buttoned sofas with a coffee table in between. Mr. Wakefield moved toward it where a member sat reading on his phone.

Moving quickly past, I entered the staff area and got excited about lunch. The amazing estate chef served lunch to the staff. It was a definite perk of working at a five-star resort that we got to eat five-star meals. Even staff who worked in separate buildings farther out from the castle made the trek across the estate for lunch.

I grabbed my phone from my locker before I headed toward the lunchroom. There were no texts from Callie, though there were a couple of new cake orders from locals. I smiled at that and resisted the urge to text my daughter. I'd given her a basic cell phone because it made me feel safer knowing she could contact me whenever she wanted, but I also tried to deter her from using it unnecessarily. And definitely not at school.

I'd dropped her off this morning for her first day of primary six. It took some getting used to—the names for things. Callie would be a fifth grader if we were back in the States. Right now, she was dismayed because last year Monroe had been her teacher, and this year, Monroe was on maternity leave. Callie had Mrs. Hunter, who wasn't as warm and sweet as Roe. I was itching to know how my girl was. I hated the thought of her not enjoying school.

Before I could even step foot in the lunchroom, however, my phone rang. I stopped in the quiet hallway, concern flashing through me at the sight of Regan Adair's name. "Regan?"

"Hey." Her bright, American-accented voice sounded free of worry, and I relaxed a little. "Sorry to call you during your lunch break, but we missed each other this morning at the school gates, and I wanted to run something by you."

"Oh? What's up?"

"So, yesterday while Callie was at our place, Lewis was showing her the program for the tae kwon do school he starts next week. It's in Inverness."

Confused, I replied, "Okay?"

"Well, Callie got really excited about the idea of attending the classes too."

I frowned. "She never mentioned a thing to me last night."

"Maybe she thought you wouldn't let her."

Feeling defensive, I asked stiffly, "What does that mean?"

"Oh, no, you're an amazing mom, Sloane. I ... you're just super protective. Which I get."

Of course I was super protective. I'd given birth to Callie when I was seventeen years old. I was a scared kid, but I took one look at my daughter and she became my entire world in an instant. As terrifying as it had been (especially any time she got sick), it had been my job to protect her. Only mine. It was difficult to loosen the reins sometimes.

"Callie learning self-defense can only be a good thing," I said.

"Great! Agreed. So why don't you talk to her about it tonight because we'd have to get her signed up pronto. There are only a few spaces left."

What? Wait. "Inverness? Isn't that a two-hour round trip?"

"Yeah, but it's after school, so I'm happy to take them and wait. I can study in my car until class is over and then bring them back."

Regan was in business school, preparing to open her own preschool. That she looked after Callie on top of being a full-time mom and student meant a lot to me. Offering to take the kids to class was typical awesome Regan.

But still … "How much are classes?"

"It's £50 a month."

My jaw dropped.

Fifty pounds a month!

I know that didn't sound like much to some folks, but every penny I made counted. Living in a tourist spot in the Scottish Highlands meant the cost of living wasn't cheap.

"Plus, if she likes it, there's a uniform and equipment to buy. Oh, and the instructor said there's a fee every time they advance to the next rank, and there are entrance fees if they want to take part in competitions."

Panic rose. I wanted Callie to do whatever made her happy, but she'd never had a hobby that cost so much money before. Her paint-by-numbers phase was a lot cheaper. "Um … let me talk to Callie first. Like I said, she didn't mention it, so I want to make sure she really wants to attend the classes before we decide anything."

"Of course. We'll talk when you pick her up tonight."

I WAS STILL WORRYING about how I'd afford to send Callie to tae kwon do lessons two hours later as I cleaned Byron Hoffman's room. Hoffman was the youngest son of Henry Hoffman, owner of one of the largest TV and film production companies in the world. He'd only been granted membership and arrived on the estate two weeks ago. I had no idea who he was, but Mrs. Hutchinson liked to point out all the members and give me a rundown on their background.

Last week, I was dumping used towels from another guest's room into my cart outside the door when I felt the hair on the back of my neck rise. When I turned around, Byron Hoffman was strolling down the hallway, his eyes glued to my ass. Catching him in the act, he'd taken his time looking me in the eye. When he did, he winked at me like he was God's gift to mankind.

I looked away, but when I glanced up, he'd turned around so he was walking backward, staring at me in a lascivious way that made my hackles rise.

He was also a total slob. His room was always a mess. Clothes strewn everywhere, food crumbs in places that made no sense ... but the worst part was his sheets. Don't get me wrong, I'd had to pretend like I hadn't seen "dirty" sheets many a time in the year I'd been working at Ardnoch. However, Hoffman almost always had dirty sheets, and there was a part of me that wondered if the sick bastard was doing it deliberately.

Sometimes, I really hated my job.

However, there was also satisfaction in looking around the beautifully appointed room and seeing it returned to rights. Replacing shampoo bottles with new, I grabbed the old and walked toward the door to let myself out. Finishing up Hoffman's room meant I was almost done for the day. And I was excited to see Callie and find out how the first day of school had gone. I was also hoping she'd contradict Regan and tell me she didn't want to go to tae kwon do. Totally selfish, yes, but I really didn't know how I could afford it.

Mind elsewhere, I didn't even see him when I stepped out of the room toward my waiting housekeeping cart. But as I dumped the empty bottles into it, I felt the abrupt hard heat of a male body at my back, and my heart lurched into my throat.

I tried to turn, but firm hands on my hips stopped me.

"Working hard?" a male voice asked huskily in my ear.

Fear shivered through me, but I looked down the corridor, reminding myself we were out in the open, and there were security cameras all around the castle.

I glanced over my shoulder and, sure enough, it was Hoffman who had me pinned to my cart. "Just finishing up, Mr. Hoffman. Have a good day." I moved to push away with the cart, and his grip tightened.

Pulse racing, I opened my mouth to protest when two actors appeared at the end of the hallway. Hoffman released my hips, and I hurried away. The women, whose famous faces had graced the covers of magazines, barely even noticed me as I rushed past them and into the service elevator at the end of the hall. I didn't look up.

My heart pounded in my chest, and my legs trembled.

Summer at the estate was the busiest time of year, except for New Year. I knew from growing up in LA that Hollywood took time off around summer and returned to business as usual in September.

I was looking forward to a quieter estate.

And the departure of Byron Hoffman.

———

I CHOSE NOT to tell Mrs. Hutchinson about the incident. What could I say? He came up behind me and touched my hips. He was the son of a powerful man. I was a housekeeper. It would sound like nothing to most people. So I kept it to myself and decided to avoid Hoffman as much as possible.

The one thing I'd strived to do for ten years was to never let Callie see when I was worried or anxious. My mom died when I was young, but I remember her mood swings and how on edge they'd put me as a kid. The worst day of my childhood, other than her death, was the day she'd locked me in a closet for five hours because I'd had a tantrum. My dad had returned home from work and lost his ever-loving mind to find me locked away. He hired a nanny, and I was never left alone with my mother again. But I still had to endure her mood swings, and I never wanted that for Callie, not even in the smallest sense.

I pasted on a bright smile when I entered Regan and Thane Adair's home to pick up my daughter. Thane Adair was an architect, and he'd designed his and his siblings' fancy homes on a stretch of coastal land outside Ardnoch.

He had two children, Lewis and Eilidh, but he'd been widowed when Eilidh was a baby. When Regan visited her sister in Ardnoch, Thane hired her as his kids' nanny. They'd fallen in love, despite the thirteen-year age gap, and Lewis and Eilidh now called Regan *Mum*.

The auburn-haired beauty was a supermom. Seriously, Regan could multitask at inhuman levels. It was impressive. Usually, I adored her and all she'd done for me and Callie since we arrived in Ardnoch. But as Callie excitedly told me about wanting to go to tae kwon do two times a week with Lewis, I felt a teeny bit resentful toward Regan as she stood in her fancy big ocean-front house. Regan was normally considerate, but it hadn't seemed to occur to her that sending Callie to martial arts classes would be a strain on my resources.

Still, it wasn't her fault, I reminded myself. Callie had

jumped on the idea as soon as Lewis started talking about it. Regan had only encouraged it, thinking it was a good thing.

And it was.

I wanted Callie to have interests and passions, and being able to defend herself was an awesome idea.

It was just ... expensive.

"It's £40 for the first class to see if I like it. And then if I do, it's £50 a month. That's okay, right?" Callie asked as I drove away from the Adair homes down a narrow country lane toward the main road.

"Uh-huh." I grinned at her, not wanting her to see my internal anxiety.

Monroe had helped us get a steal on a rental property on the main thoroughfare of the village. Normally, the rent on such a place would be way outside my price range, but the cottage belonged to Brodan's brother-in-law. And since Brodan adored his very pregnant wife, Monroe, and she, thankfully, adored me and Callie, they'd hooked us up. However, since moving into the lovely cottage on Castle Street, I think Callie had gotten the idea that we were doing better financially than we were. I wanted her to think that. I wanted her to feel secure and safe.

But it had its drawbacks.

"Lewis said we'd start as white belts or at tenth gup. I don't know what that means yet, but he said the next rank after that is a white belt with yellow tips, and he wants to get that faster than anyone else. I never knew he was so competitive." She giggled. "He's gonna be so bummed when I get yellow tips before him!"

Hearing the joy and excitement in her voice, I realized there was no way out of this. I'd have to find more baking jobs every month to cover the extra cost. Or stop using the hairstylists on the estate. I got a mega staff discount, but not using them would probably cover the costs of the classes.

So lost in my thoughts, it took me a second to realize my car was jerking.

"Mom?"

I glanced at Callie to see her gripping the seat, her smile gone as the car jerked harder three more times.

Crap!

"It's okay," I reassured her calmly as I guided the car onto the side of the road seconds before it violently jerked a few more times and then hissed to a stop. "We're okay."

"I think we should get out."

Nodding, I remembered my purse as Callie grabbed her backpack and we bailed. I wasn't even going to pretend to look under the hood because I was clueless about cars.

"I'll call Regan," I said as an SUV coming toward us slowed.

"Isn't that Walker's car?" Callie asked. Her face lit up. "That *is* Walker!" She waved her arms, hailing him.

Great.

Two rescues in one day?

Wearing his perpetually handsome stone-faced expression, Walker slowly drove his SUV onto our side of the road and parked in front of my dead car. I tried to ignore the flutter in my belly as he stepped out of the vehicle with those long legs. While I liked the black suit that made him look more like a billionaire playboy than a security guard, I liked his off-work uniform of tees and jeans more. His T-shirts were always tight at the biceps, and I had a thing for his arms. Especially his forearms. They were all strong and veiny. He had great hands too. Long fingers, big knuckles. I'd imagined those hands on my body more times than I cared to admit.

God, I needed help.

Trying not to ogle him, I gave Walker a wide smile that I didn't feel like giving anybody. But for Callie's sake, I was going to pretend like our car dying was not a big deal. It was a huge deal. I did not know how I'd pay for repairs. The butter-flies Walker inspired turned to anxious knots.

"We meet again," I said breezily.

Walker's gaze drifted over me and Callie as if inspecting us for injury. "What happened?"

Callie shrugged emphatically. "It started jerking and then it died."

He looked at me.

I shrugged too. "What Cal said. I was going to call Regan, but you showed first. If you're on your way somewhere ..." Was he on his way to one of his casual dates?

"It's not a problem." He whipped out his cell from his ass pocket, hit a button, and held it to his ear. "Joe, it's Walk ... aye, look, I need you to send a recovery vehicle to the A949 just outside Caelmore. A friend's car has broken down." He gave Joe, whom I had a sneaking suspicion was Joe the head mechanic at Ardnoch, my car details.

Crap.

As soon as he hung up, I spoke before he could. "You didn't have to do that. I could have called for a recovery vehicle."

"It's done." Walker gestured toward his SUV. "Jump in. I'll take you home."

Being stuck in proximity again with him so soon after he'd basically rejected my offer for "cake" on Saturday did not appeal to me. "We really don't—"

"Sloane."

I clamped my lips shut at the stern way he said my name.

Fine. For Callie's sake, I wouldn't argue over accepting his help.

I muttered *thanks* under my breath as I passed him, and I could have sworn I heard him snort. But when I looked back at him, his face was expressionless.

As I climbed into the passenger seat of Walker's very nice

Range Rover, I glanced behind me at Callie to make sure she was settled. Walker got in and closed his door. "Everyone belted in?" he asked.

"Callie?" I grinned at her smile as she put on her seat belt and then shimmied in her seat.

"This is comfy," she declared.

I shot Walker a look and saw the handsome bastard was almost smiling. Why was it only my kid who could crack his hard veneer? Why did he never shoot that smirk my way?

"Uh, my backpack's zipper's stuck," Callie said as Walker did a U-turn.

"We'll unstick it when we get home."

"I need a drink."

"Now? You can't wait ten minutes?"

"Not really."

Sighing, I unclipped my belt and stretched between the front seats to look at her backpack.

"Careful," Walker murmured.

"Yeah, will be," I assured him as I huffed, trying to squeeze through enough to yank on the zipper. Unsuccessful, I released it back to Callie. "I'll look at it when we get home."

Please, please be fixable. I just bought that backpack.

As I tried to unwedge my shoulders from between the passenger and driver's seat, I caught my boobs against Walker's hard shoulder and sucked in a breath at the contact.

His eyes shot to mine for a few seconds, and there was a look of such heat in them, I froze like a deer in headlights. Blood rushed to my ears.

Then he looked away just as abruptly, and when he glanced at me again, the heat had been replaced by indifference. And there I was imagining things again, like Walker giving me sexy eyes.

Disappointed, I settled back into my seat and clipped myself in.

"I'll look at your bag," Walker said to Callie in the rearview mirror.

If I'd been a fanciful sort, I would've said his voice was gruffer than usual. But this was Walker Ironside. I was beginning to think I could walk around naked in front of him and he wouldn't even blink.

Thankfully, Callie kept up most of the conversation as we made the short drive into Ardnoch. My once quiet and reserved daughter had really come out of her shell. Because her father was a total asshole (and she'd never met her grandfather), Callie had never been comfortable around men. However, with Walker, she chatted easily. She told him all about her upcoming adventure into the world of tae kwon do. I tried to focus on her excitement about it again and not worry myself over the cost of that on top of car repairs.

"I'm gonna be as cool as Robyn when I'm older. Lewis says she's a martial artist and she, like, kicked some people's butts, and she's been shot and she saved her husband's life. She's like a real-life superhero!"

We'd all heard the stories about Lachlan's wife, Robyn, Regan's sister. Lewis's aunt was kind of legendary around these parts. The woman was truly badass. A part of me felt a prick of jealousy at Callie's hero worship, but mostly, I felt grateful I could surround my daughter with women who were such incredible role models.

As we pulled up outside our cottage on Castle Street, Walker turned to look at me as he asked Callie, "When is your first class?"

"Next Monday. Regan is gonna drive us there and bring us back 'cause it's in Inverness. We've only been to Inverness a few times, and I like the bridge we cross over to get to it, so even the car ride will be cool. As long as Eilidh doesn't hog the music."

The whole time my daughter rambled, I held Walker's

gaze, trying to give nothing away.

However, I sometimes wondered if the man could strip back my layers and see everything I was feeling.

If that was true, he now knew of at least five different sexual fantasies I had about him.

Shaking off that thought, I gave him a small smile. "Thanks for the ride. Can you text me Joe's number so I can deal with the car?"

"Don't worry about the car."

"Text me Joe's number," I reiterated with as much sternness as I was capable of. I jumped out, hurrying around the car to get Callie, but Walker was already out and opening her door.

"Let's see that backpack." He gestured to her yellow floral school bag.

Callie held it out to him, and the capable Scot unstuck it in seconds.

"Thanks!" Callie cried, looking up at Walker as if he'd saved her from something life-threatening. I did not want my kid getting attached to this guy unless he intended to get attached back. And all of Ardnoch knew that would not happen.

"Yeah, thanks," I offered quietly, because I was grateful. Really. I was.

"Can we talk a second?" Walker asked pointedly.

After this morning, I wasn't sure I wanted to talk alone with Walker again so soon. The incident with Hoffman had distracted my thoughts from Walker and the elevator, but now that Walker was in front of me, I felt rejected. We both knew I had put myself out there with my invitation. An invitation he'd ignored.

Ugh. It had been one crappy, crappy day. Handing Callie the house keys, I told her to let herself in.

She grabbed them, grinned at Walker, and waved adorably

as she called, "Bye, Walker!"

"Bye, wee yin," he murmured, wearing that tiny, imperceptible smile again.

Once Callie disappeared inside the house, I gave Walker a tight-lipped look, my eyes saying, "So, what is it?"

To my shock, he looked almost uncomfortable. He cleared his throat and scowled at me. "The tae kwon do classes are a good idea. A girl should learn to defend herself."

Not what I'd been expecting. "Okay."

"It's a lot, though. I train in jujitsu, and there's an investment involved."

Embarrassment heated my cheeks as I realized Walker *had* seen right through me.

"I'd love to sponsor Callie's training."

Gaping at Walker, I didn't know what to say. Usually, I'd smile and thank him and then tell him it was unnecessary. But I didn't feel like smiling. My pride stung. I'd had the day from hell. He'd already rescued us (me twice!), and now he was insinuating (correctly) that I might not be able to afford to send Callie to tae kwon do.

"That won't be necessary, but thank you." Even to me, I sounded cold.

Walker scowled. "Sloane, I meant no—"

His phone rang, and I glanced down at it clutched in his hand. He sighed in irritation and brought the screen up.

A woman's name flashed across it.

Of course it did.

"*Chloe* is calling, so I'll let you get that. See you around." I turned and took the two steps required to push open my front door. He didn't stop me, and I locked it behind me.

I didn't know what agitated me more: that he'd jabbed at my pride and need to take care of my daughter by myself.

Or that Walker might actually be *dating* that Chloe person.

THREE

SLOANE

Walker texted me later that night to tell me a Hyundai would be in my parking spot behind the cottage come morning, and he'd posted the keys through our letter box. He told me not to worry about insurance because I was covered. How he got my details to insure me, I'd rather not know.

And sure enough, there it was. When I asked him about my car, he said the mechanics were looking at it and he'd get back to me. When I asked how much I owed him, he said nothing.

Part of me wanted to seethe with misdirected anger and hurt pride.

But I didn't have time for that. I had to drop Callie off at school and get to work.

Callie had a ton of questions about the new car, none of which I could answer, except that Walker had left it for us. I could only assume the car was one of his and he'd added me as a secondary driver to his insurance while he loaned it to us. I refused to question that supposition or the fact that Walker probably didn't need a second car when he drove a Range Rover.

I also would not admit to myself how much I enjoyed driving the newer-model SUV.

Instead, I focused on getting my kid to school. Callie had assured me that her new teacher, Mrs. Hunter, seemed okay. She wasn't Monroe, but she wasn't as strict as rumor had implied. Mostly, Callie was excited to tell Lewis that she'd be attending tae kwon do classes with him. I had given it the go-ahead. My hair would have to suffer the consequences. And I'd need to increase the cake orders I fulfilled per month.

I'd left Callie with Lewis in the lineup outside the school, told Regan I'd get the money to her for the first class, and hopped back into the pretty blue SUV. My phone rang through the car as I drove away. Monroe's name lit up the cool screen in the middle of the dashboard. I hit the Answer Call button on the steering wheel, telling myself not to get used to the car and its modern stellar ways.

"Hey!" I answered brightly because we hadn't talked in a few days. "How are you feeling?"

"Like I'm fifty months pregnant," Monroe grumbled in her cute Scottish accent. "Otherwise all right."

I chuckled, remembering that feeling. "That means you're getting close."

"Eight months. I don't know where those weeks went, but I can feel them," she joked. "In all seriousness, I'm fine. Missing the kids. How was Callie's first day?"

I told her about her new teacher.

"Ellen Hunter gets a bad rap. It's unfair. She's a good teacher. She's just a wee bit less warm and fuzzy than I am."

Grinning, I nodded as I followed the long stretch of road toward Ardnoch Estate. "Well, my kid misses you, that's for sure."

"I miss her too. I know you'll be busy baking this weekend, but I thought I'd pop round for a visit."

"Of course, we'd love that."

We talked a little more about her pregnancy and then as I approached the staff entrance to show the security guards my ID, Monroe said, "So, Walker told Brodan that Callie wants to attend tae kwon do classes in Inverness."

I reached out of my car window and flashed my ID. The security guard, Jamie, tapped it and smiled at me. "New car, Sloane?"

Between Monroe's words and the reminder of my fancy borrowed car, I pasted on a smile to cover a frown. "Just a loan."

"A loan for Sloane," he teased. "It suits you."

"Thanks."

"Go on in." He waved at his companion at the guard station, and the gates swung open.

"Sloane?" Monroe asked.

"Hey, yeah, sorry, I'm at the estate·gates."

"So, tae kwon do?"

"Yeah," I answered, holding back my annoyance with Walker for telling people my business. "I think it's a great idea."

"It is," Roe agreed. "You know what's also a great idea ... to let Walker sponsor her. I don't know if you know this about Walker, but he's very protective of women. He'd love to see Callie learn self-defense and, as a martial artist, he'd make a great mentor and sponsor."

Since I knew Monroe wanted only to help ease my financial stress, I didn't snap at her. I'd accepted her help with the cottage because I was still paying rent and thus felt like I was paying my own way.

But accepting money from Walker for my daughter ... no.

The last time I'd forsaken my pride to get money from a guy to help raise Callie, it blew up in my face.

"I can handle it myself," I assured Monroe lightly. "We're all good."

"Are you sure, because Walker mentioned your car—"

"Roe, I'm late for work," I cut her off. "I'm sorry. I don't mean to be rude. Can we talk later?"

"Of course." She sounded unsure. "Call me?"

I promised her I would, but hung up feeling awful. Monroe had sounded worried, and I knew she was probably kicking herself for mentioning Walker. I'd have to reassure her we were okay.

Unfortunately for Walker, he was one of the first people I saw as I hurried in through the staff entrance. He stood talking with Jock McRory, head of security.

At my appearance, Walker turned that intense gaze on me. I held it as I strode toward him. But instead of stopping, I skirted him and Jock and said coolly as I passed, "I'd appreciate it if you'd stop telling people I can't afford to give my kid the things she wants."

His chin jerked in surprise, his eyes flaring, but I turned away and marched toward the housekeeping staff room.

"Sloane," Walker called after me, voice gruff, but I was already gone.

"I HOPE THOSE ARE FOR ME."

At my boss's teasing tone, I glanced up to see Mrs. Hutchinson staring at the Tupperware filled with madeleines. Agnes Hutchinson was a woman of indeterminate age, but I knew from talking with her she had a grown son and daughter and a gaggle of grandkids. There were laugh lines at her eyes and mouth, but otherwise, she had smooth skin most of the members here paid lots of money to maintain. Her blue eyes were bright with amusement as our gazes met.

I fastened the three gold buttons on the left upper chest of my black tunic. The housekeeping uniform at Ardnoch was simple and comfortable. It was a black tunic and black pants. The short sleeves turned up at the ends to reveal a plaid (or tartan) fabric detail. We could wear comfortable black shoes of our choosing, so I wore black sneakers. My hair was up in a ponytail most days. It was not the sexiest look, but staff were seriously discouraged from becoming involved with the members, anyway, so we weren't supposed to look sexy.

"They're for Ms. Howard," I told Mrs. Hutchinson before reaching into my locker to produce another Tupperware filled with small cupcakes. "These are for you and the rest of the team."

"I swear my uniform no longer fits," Mrs. Hutchinson commented with glee as she took the box. "Thank you, Sloane. I'll put these in the staff room ... after I pinch one for my wee morning tea." She winked.

Determined to shrug off my anger with Walker, I chuckled as I tightened my ponytail. My fellow employees had warned me that Mrs. Hutchinson was fair but stern. However, she'd only ever been super warm to me. "Do you mind if I drop these off"—I picked up the box of madeleines—"to Ms. Howard before I start my duties?"

"Be quick about it." She glanced at her watch. "Ms. Howard has a meeting in fifteen minutes."

The woman's knowledge of everyone's schedule was practically occult.

I nodded and hurried out of the room.

Aria Howard was the daughter of Hollywood director and Ardnoch Estate board member Wesley Howard. The family owned a large home on the estate, and that was where Aria was staying while she worked as the new hospitality manager. She was pretty much running the place, giving Lachlan more time with his family.

I stopped outside her office and knocked lightly.

"Come in," her familiar husky voice called.

Letting myself in, I smiled at her as I closed the door behind me.

Aria sat behind an intimidatingly large captain's pedestal desk. It even had a leather top. The office was like a smaller version of the estate library. Wall-to-wall dark oak bookshelves, an impressive, open fireplace, two comfortable armchairs situated in front of the desk. A floor-to-ceiling window adjacent to the desk let in light so it didn't feel too dark. Tiffany lamps aided in chasing off the gloom too. Luxurious velvet curtains at the window pooled on the wooden floors, most of which were covered in expensive carpets.

Aria was a tall, attractively curvy brunette with a Mediterranean dark beauty bestowed upon her by an Italian mother. Her mossy-green eyes were the only feature she'd inherited from her father. Aria was brusquely efficient, with a no-nonsense attitude that made her excellent at her job. However, I knew there was more to her than her aloof facade. She gave me a small smile as I approached her desk and placed the box of madeleines, her favorites, before her.

She shook her head but reached for them with elegantly manicured hands. Almost every one of her fingers was adorned with a barely there, delicate gold ring. Her long, dark hair was curled to perfection, her makeup soft, immaculate, her dark suit tailored and expensive. Even though I couldn't see her bottom half, I knew she'd be wearing a pencil skirt that hugged her curves, and high heels I'd break an ankle in. "I'll have to hide these from my mother." Aria sighed. "But thank you."

"Your mother's still here?" I knew Mrs. Chiara Howard vacationed at Ardnoch every summer, but I'd thought she'd have gone home by now. She'd insisted on meeting with me at the beginning of the summer. She was an intimidating woman compared to her easy-going husband, but I owed this family, even if they didn't think so. I'd meet with them any time, any place, whenever they asked.

Aria nodded, studying me. "She leaves in a few days."

"I'm sure you'll miss her."

She smirked like she knew I knew better. "I'm sure I will."

"I should have brought more madeleines for Mrs. Howard too."

"No, you shouldn't have." Aria tapped the top of the box of mini cakes. "I'm hiding them from my mother so she doesn't give me another lecture on how to maintain my Italian curves." She mimicked the Italian accent as she said, "They should be sleek like a Ferrari, Aria, not jiggly like a panna cotta."

I winced. "Sorry."

Aria waved off my sympathy. "I'm used to it. And she'll be gone soon and I can return to eating without wondering if she's watching and judging."

An awkward silence fell between us, so I cleared my throat. "How is she?"

She knew I didn't mean Chiara. Aria's expression softened. "She's doing really great. You haven't heard from her?"

I nodded. "She texts. I just ... sometimes people tell you they're okay because they don't want you to worry."

"She's more than okay," Aria assured me.

"Are you okay? Here, I mean?" The question had been bubbling in my mind for months and burst forth without thought. Though I didn't know Aria well, I was beyond grateful to her. She treated the staff fairly, and despite her reserve, there was kindness in her.

If she was surprised by my question, she didn't show it. "You're either someone who thrives in a place like LA or it drowns you. My mother thrives there. I'm thriving *here*. Are you?"

I smiled. "I really am."

"Good." Aria nodded and then glanced at her phone. "I have a meeting. Thank you again for the madeleines."

Dismissed, I let myself out of her office and almost ran straight into Walker. Before I could remember my annoyance, his familiar cologne wafted over me, making me weak at the knees. Okay, so maybe it wasn't that delicious combination of citrus and sandalwood that made me weak at the knees. It was the man wearing it.

I cursed Walker Ironside for making me so hyperaware of him. It would have been really nice to feel this physically attracted to someone who actually noticed me back and didn't go around telling people I was poor.

"Sloane." He blocked my way, scowling down at me. "About earlier—"

I pasted on a big fake smile and pushed open Aria's door so she could see and hear us. "Going in?"

"Ah, Walker, there you are. Come in," Aria called.

He narrowed his eyes at me as I moved out of his way. "We'll talk."

It sounded like a threat.

"Yeah, I'd like to know when I can get my car back," I said over my shoulder as I strutted away.

WHEN CALLIE and I first arrived in the Highlands, Aria had gone above and beyond by having a car pick up Callie from school and bring her to the estate. She'd wait for me in the staff room, doing her homework, until my shift was over and then we'd walk to our lodge on Loch Ardnoch. There was a high turnover of staff on the estate, but only because they hired seasonally. For instance, students could work for the entire summer and stay in the staff accommodation on the loch before returning to school. The lodges were great for them, but they were a temporary solution for us.

When Brodan's sister, Arrochar, and her husband, Mackennon Galbraith, offered their rental cottage in the village, I'd jumped on it.

Being a single mom was the hardest and greatest thing I'd ever done. But I don't know how I would have juggled parenting and being a mother if it hadn't been for the kindness of other people. For her safety, I'd never been able to tell Juanita where Callie and I disappeared to. But I'd let her know we were okay. I was grateful for what she'd done for us and for what Monroe and the Adair family were doing for us. Gratitude didn't scare me. The opposite, in fact. I felt nothing but sad for ungrateful people. Gratitude was its own kind of joy, and I pitied those who couldn't see that.

I was thinking about this, about why I was so mad at Walker when he was only trying to help. Where was my gratitude? Maybe it was because I was attracted to him? Or maybe it was because I finally felt like I was doing right by Callie. That I wasn't failing her. Walker knowing that the classes were a strain for me, knowing that I couldn't afford the repairs on my crappy car, felt like a slide backward.

As the working day wore on, the guiltier I felt for being cold to him when all he'd tried to do was offer help.

I was stewing over my remorse as I pushed the laundry cart toward the elevator at the end of the second floor. I still felt iffy about getting on the elevator, but I needed to use it every day, so I couldn't avoid it and let my fear win.

My shift was over. I just needed to deliver the dirty sheets to the laundry service and I could clock out. Except for my cool encounters with Walker, it had been an unusually juicy kind of day on the estate. I'd changed the sheets of an actor who had arrived alone but was definitely getting it on with someone here who liked to celebrate his release on her sheets. I'd spotted false teeth in a tray in the bathroom of an actor that surprised the heck out of me, and I'd accidentally walked in on a director screwing an actor who was most definitely not his husband.

Yet I was the utter definition of discretion. I didn't even text Monroe, someone I trusted, to share my gossip. Having been the butt of celebrity gossip since falling pregnant with Brodan's child, and then marrying the retired actor, Monroe wasn't interested in knowing people's business. That suited me fine. I didn't need to share what I knew about people, especially if I thought it could hurt them. Also, I'd signed an NDA when I took the job.

As I passed the staircase, I noticed movement out of my peripheral. Glancing toward the stairs, I caught sight of Byron Hoffman climbing the last step onto the landing. I'd pushed yesterday's encounter with him to the back of my mind, preoccupied with other disasters. But at the sight of him, I stiffened, my skin flushing hot with tension. I nodded a polite hello and kept walking toward the elevator, picking up my pace.

"Excuse me, miss."

Ah, crap.

I halted and looked back at the actor. My father had represented a lot of famous clients, and he'd thrown parties for them at our house. Famous people didn't faze me, which was one reason Aria was happy to hire me. But men like him, who thought they could own everything, made my skin crawl.

"May I help you with something, Mr. Hoffman?"

He smirked, gaze dipping down my body and back up again. "Please, call me Byron."

I didn't respond because it would be inappropriate of me to call him by his first name and I didn't want to encourage him. Yesterday was so far beyond inappropriate, it wasn't funny.

Maybe I should've told Mrs. Hutchinson, after all. Maybe I still should.

Hoffman sighed heavily. "Very well. *I* know *your* name now, though. *Sloane.*"

I stiffened. "Has something been amiss with your room, Mr. Hoffman?"

"Not at all." He waved his hand and took a step toward me. "Would you mind leaving me an extra little chocolate on the pillow tonight at turndown?"

"I don't do the turndown service, but I will pass along the request."

"So, you're the one who cleans my room and has it looking spotless for me when I return to it in the afternoon?"

"Yes, sir."

His eyes gleamed. "Well, you do an excellent job. What time do you clean my room? Just so I know when to skedaddle."

I hesitated, the equivalent of warning bells going off in my ears. "Uh ... Thank you. I usually get to your room after noon."

"Precise timing, please, sweetheart?" Despite the *please*, there was a hard bite to his words.

"Around two o'clock. Good evening, Mr. Hoffman." I dismissed him when I probably should have waited for him to dismiss me, but I wanted to get as far away from him as possible. Hurrying toward the service elevator, I hit the button and, thankfully, the doors pinged open right away. I got in with the cart and turned to hit the button for the ground floor.

Byron Hoffman still stood there, watching me.

A knot formed in my stomach as the doors closed. His question bothered me. Why did he want to know the exact time I cleaned his room?

So he could skedaddle.

Was it really, though? Maybe he wanted to trap me between him and my cart again.

Or was I being paranoid?

The elevator doors opened and I finished my shift in a daze. I couldn't shrug off the feeling of unease.

"SLOANE." A heavy hand landed on my shoulder as I stood at my locker, and I squawked in fright.

It felt like my heart had leapt into my throat as I turned to face the intruder.

Walker stood before me, a deep frown pinching his brows. "I said your name four times and you didn't respond. You okay?"

Trying to catch my breath, I pressed a hand to my chest and nodded. "Sorry. I was ..." I shrugged. Then I remembered my earlier confrontation with Walker. "Hey, about earlier—"

He lifted a hand to halt me. "Who do you think I've been talking to?"

"Monroe mentioned you told Brodan about Callie's tae kwon do classes. But I know you never meant anything by it. I'm just having a crappy few days, and I took it out on you. I'm sorry."

Walker continued to frown. "I'm sorry if I made you feel like a charity case. That was not my intention. That's not how I see you."

It was on the tip of my tongue to ask how he did see me, but Walker bent his head to study my face more intently.

"What's going on? Why are you so jumpy?"

"You startled me, that's why," I replied with a nervous laugh as I turned to lock my locker. Grabbing my purse off the bench in the middle of the room, I didn't meet his eyes.

"No, you were lost in your head about something, and you look ..."

"I look?"

"Something's wrong."

"Nothing is wrong." I tried to shrug off my worries about Hoffman. "When do you think I'll get my car back?"

Walker kept peering at me as if he could see right through me. "I'll keep you posted."

I huffed out a shaky laugh. "Shouldn't I know what's going on with *my* car?"

"Aye, and it's in the garage being looked at. I'll keep you posted. Now tell—"

"Great, fine." With a fake smile, I cut him off. "I have to go pick up Callie from Regan and Thane's." I moved to brush past without looking at him and was shocked when he wrapped a hand around my biceps to stop me. "Walker?"

He scowled at me. "Something's wrong."

"It's nothing."

"Sloane." Warning spiced his tone, even as he released my arm.

Glancing around to make sure we were alone before responding, I lowered my voice. "It's really nothing. I-I get a bad feeling around one of the members. It's nothing."

Walker gave a small nod but insisted, "Who is it?"

"Walker—"

"I won't tell anyone who it is."

Trusting Walker at his word, I shrugged. "Byron Hoffman."

His aquamarine eyes hardened. "Explain this bad feeling."

Hadn't I already decided I should tell someone what Hoffman did? Maybe it wouldn't be completely stupid to have at least one person know about it. "Yesterday, he came up behind me while I was at my cart and trapped me against it."

Walker's nostrils flared as he straightened to his full height.

"Nothing happened," I assured him. "Two members showed up and he let me go."

"Why didn't you report it?" he growled.

Indignation flared through me. "Report what, Walker? A powerful and well-connected club member came up behind me and touched my hips before letting me go. Not exactly reportable stuff."

"You know that's not true."

"I know nuance means nothing to these people."

Walker bit out, "Has he done anything else?"

I shrugged. "I bumped into him at the end of today's shift. He knows my name. And he wanted to know what time I clean his room because he wanted to make sure he wasn't in it when I do, but he's never asked the last few weeks, so why now?" I sighed. "Am I being paranoid? As if a member would give a damn about my comings and goings, beyond how it affects them?"

Walker responded sternly, "Always listen to your gut. If you have problems with Hoffman going forward, I want to know. I'm not just here to protect *them*."

Warmth filled my chest that he hadn't dismissed my feelings. "Thanks, Walker. For everything." I gave him a little wave and left to go collect Callie. There was nothing like my daughter's "happy to see you" smile to shrug off the strange disquiet the day had brought.

FOUR
WALKER

W hen I followed Brodan Adair to a tiny wee place in the Highlands for a job, I'd assumed I'd be parting ways as his bodyguard sooner rather than later. That the temporary position his brother offered me on the exclusive estate would be just that. Temporary.

I couldn't imagine that the village could hold me. That there would be anything here to appeal to me. Yet, to my consternation, I liked the slower pace of the Highlands.

At seventeen, I joined the Royal Marines and traveled in and out of the UK, eventually joining 43 Commando Fleet Protection Group based at HM Naval Base Clyde in Scotland. After a few years of protecting the UK's nuclear deterrent and conducting specialist maritime security tasks, I took up a friend's offer to become a bodyguard in California. I continued to travel the world and almost feel a part of it again. After twenty years of moving from place to place, I'd never imagined Ardnoch, population 1200, could hold any appeal, let alone so much.

I liked not moving.

I enjoyed knowing what to expect when I woke up each day.

Except for seasonal staff turnover on the estate, I had time to observe those around me. To learn them. Understand them. There was a security in it that unexpectedly worked for me. Perhaps because I'd spent so much of my life looking over my shoulder for the next threat.

There were a lot of good people here. A community. I hadn't had a community around me since leaving the Commandos. I had a group of mates I served with who I met up with once a year, and they knew a different version of me. But only Brodan was a constant, and one bloke didn't count as a community. That is until his family welcomed me in as one of them. With them I got to be the guy who protected their brother, who worked at the estate to protect others.

The guy who'd done questionable things in the name of God and country was buried where no one knew he existed. He only got to come out during sessions with Rich. After, he got stuffed back down again.

The Gloaming was the social hub of Ardnoch. A pub, restaurant, and hotel owned by Brodan's brothers Lachlan and Arran, a two-hundred-year-old building they'd renovated where the locals gathered within its aged walls every night. Their chatter suggested relief when tourists disappeared once summer was over. Tables and stools freed up in the pub again. Ardnoch apparently had a love/hate relationship with the tourist season. Ardnoch Estate drew folks from around the world, excited at the prospect of maybe spotting a celebrity. Local business owners' coffers were filled enough to see them through the entire year. But it didn't stop them from complaining about tourists parking in their driveways or in no-parking zones, of filling their beaches, and taking up all the tables at their few eateries.

I'd avoided the pub during the summer. Now I walked the

ten minutes from my rented bungalow to the heart of the village. To the Gloaming, built in the square with a large car park for visitors out front. The historical architecture and design of the village appealed to tourists as much as the celebrities staying on the village outskirts. Everything predated the mid-twentieth century, and dominating it all, near to the Gloaming, sat a medieval cathedral.

Shops, restaurants, and bed-and-breakfasts were scattered throughout the village on quaint row streets. Castle Street was the main road off the square that led out of Ardnoch toward Ardnoch Castle and Estate. It was an avenue of identical nineteenth-century terraced houses with dormer windows. Many of the homes had been converted into boutiques, cafés, and inns. There was Morag's, a small grocery store and deli that did fucking great sandwiches, and Flora's, the most popular café in Ardnoch.

Some of the row cottages, however, remained residential. Sloane Harrow and her daughter rented one.

Passing by Sloane's place, I resisted the urge to stop and knock on her door, to check she was all right. Her worries about Hoffman bothered me. She didn't need that shite on top of everything else. I'd fucked up asking her if I could sponsor Callie's training. Stung the woman's pride. I could respect her need to take care of her girl by herself. I didn't want her to think anyone saw her as a failure. She was a great mum. Anyone with eyes could see that.

I shouldn't have offered.

I was too curious about Sloane as it was. The urge to investigate why a single mum from California had ended up as a housekeeper at Ardnoch, with connections to a powerful family like the Howards, had seen me almost look into it. That I wanted to made me back off. I had no business being in Sloane and Callie's business.

Which was why it was stupid of me to have offered to pay for Callie's martial arts training.

And to fix Sloane's car.

And to get in her face about Hoffman.

No. The latter was too important not to know. I was glad she told me. Now I was on alert.

"You look angrier than usual," Brodan greeted me as I walked into the Gloaming and spotted him at the bar. I'd given the room my usual visual sweep. Beyond the low ceiling with its wooden beams and the typical dark warmth of an old pub, I catalogued which locals were there, where they sat, who was unfamiliar, and where they were sitting. I'd already memorized the exits the first time I'd visited the pub. It was a habit I'd never break, and I'd made peace with that.

Brodan's brother Arran wasn't bartending tonight. An older woman, Jess I think her name was, worked the bar.

I slid onto the stool next to Bro and asked Jess for a local ale I'd developed a taste for since moving here.

"I hate sitting with my back to the door," I grumbled.

"Is that what the dark look is?" Brodan asked.

"What?"

"You look like you want to murder someone. More than usual, I mean."

I'd sit with my back to the door if there was no other option. But there were options here. Knowing I couldn't get comfortable in this position, I got up and took the stool on the curve of the bar that faced all three entrance and exit points.

Brodan rolled his eyes but got up and sat on the stool next to me.

"How's Monroe?" I avoided his last question, knowing the lovesick fucker could talk for days about his wife. Brodan and I used to have more in common when he was a miserable bastard, but, to be fair, I only had myself to blame for his current happiness.

I might have manipulated him into spending time with Monroe when we first arrived in Ardnoch.

Don't get me wrong, I wanted happiness for Bro.

But I didn't understand why he was so smug about his state of romantic imprisonment. If I were the shuddering type, I'd shudder just thinking about it.

Brodan's brow furrowed. "She's tired a lot. I'm constantly worried about her. She told me I was mother-henning her this morning. Me?"

"I can see that."

He shot me a dirty look. "I've never mother-henned in my life."

"I can easily picture you clucking around Monroe. Bugging the shit out of her."

"You're in a pleasant mood."

"Maybe because someone told Monroe that I was worried Sloane couldn't afford Callie's martial arts classes."

Brodan frowned. "Did I relay the information like that? I'm not sure I did. Why is it a problem?"

"Because Sloane handed me my arse today for it."

"Sloane?" Brodan grinned. I contemplated smacking that grin off his face, but took a pull of the ale Jess put in front of me instead. "Are we talking about the same woman who goes around pissing rainbows and farting roses?"

I narrowed my eyes. "What does that mean?"

"She's nice to everybody. I can't imagine her handing you your arse. Though I would've liked to have seen it."

"Point is, you don't have to tell your wife everything we talk about."

"She likes to know that there's a person buried in there." He patted my arm. "That you actually string words together to form sentences. She never gets to see it for herself."

"Go fuck yourself," I replied flatly.

He grinned smugly. "I don't need to anymore."

Aye, like the bastard ever needed to before he settled down with Roe. "Brodan."

At my serious tone, Brodan stopped smiling. "Look, I'm sorry. I shouldn't have mentioned it. Monroe jumped on the idea. She wants to ease Sloane's stress, and she likes the idea of you looking out for her best friend."

Warning bells rang in my head. "I'm not interested in looking out for Sloane."

"You seem awfully upset that she handed you your arse today," he observed, eyes glinting.

"I'm upset that I can't tell you anything. You're like a gossiping auld fucking woman."

Brodan snorted. "Aye, you keep telling yourself that."

"Don't. You know I'm not interested in Sloane like that, and you better not be filling Roe's head with that shite."

His friend sighed. "Of course, I'm not. Just as long as you're aware that you're in denial."

"What does that mean?"

He leaned in so only I could hear. "Why don't you fuck her and get it over with? You know she's open to it."

Heat filled my groin at the mere thought of fucking Sloane Harrow. I knew she wanted me. Even before she'd subtly asked me if I wanted to have "cake" with her at the weekend, I'd caught her looking at me. Had adamantly ignored the way my gut clenched at the invitation in her eyes. Or the way time seemed to stop when she smiled that gorgeous bloody smile. Never seen a smile so sweet but sexy like Sloane Harrow's. It bothered me I was aware of her. Not merely aware, but ... like all the north-seeking poles of my atoms lined up in the same direction whenever she was near, trying to pull me toward her like a magnet. It made no sense. I barely knew her. And I intended to keep it that way.

She was too young, too complicated. Her daughter Callie was a good kid. Something had chased them here. I'd bet my life on it. There was no need for me to mess with a single mother. I didn't do commitment. Sloane and Callie deserved better.

I glared at my ale. "Talk about her that way again, Brodan, and I'll send you home to your wife with one fewer testicle."

My friend choked on a laugh. "No offense meant."

"She's not for me." I cut him a hard warning look.

His expression flattened. "I get it. It was a joke. Sorry."

Tension rippled between us for a few seconds. I was determined more than ever to keep my distance from Sloane. Get her car fixed and stay out of her life. Except for watching her back when it came to Hoffman. I cleared my throat. "What do you know about Byron Hoffman?"

Brodan went easily with the subject change. "Apparently, Lachlan heard a rumor that Hoffman sexually harassed costars and female members of the crew on several film sets. He didn't want to grant him membership. These days, that kind of behavior won't last before someone makes it public. However, until then, his father is a powerful man in Hollywood, and that swayed the other board members. Despite Lachlan's concerns, they gave him a membership. You having problems with him? Lachlan would like that. Give him reason to oust him."

My concern grew. This information only gave credence to Sloane's story about him trapping her against her cart. The thought of it made me want to rip the bastard's hands off.

"Get a feeling around him," I hedged, not wanting to share any more of Sloane's business. Especially not something that affected the job she depended upon. "I'll keep an eye on him."

For a while after that, Brodan distracted me, catching me up on the whisky venture he and Lachlan had undertaken. They were opening a distillery outside Ardnoch, something that would take a good few years to develop, but Brodan was enjoying the process. We talked about finding somewhere to watch the NFL kickoff game next month since we'd both gotten into American football while living in LA. It had been awhile since we'd caught a game. I told him about Chloe, a younger woman I'd hooked up with in Inverness. She was a hairdresser. She was also a mistake. I didn't know if it was that she was too young to understand the nuance of casual sex or if it was my fault for going back for a second round. Probably a bit of both. But now the lass was pestering me constantly, and not answering her calls and texts didn't seem to send the message it usually did.

Brodan was ribbing me about it when Monroe called. Like a puppy on a leash, he finished his pint and left me in the pub, happy to be called home. Part of me felt smug that I didn't need to deal with someone checking in on me, wondering where I was, what I was doing. But Brodan was a different man from the one he'd been when we arrived in Ardnoch. He'd been a haunted man back then. If I was honest, it wasn't just our Scottish blood that bonded us. We didn't talk about it, but we'd recognized something broken in each other. Confiding our secrets came later once we'd built trust. But Brodan had since faced his ghosts.

I might have been a soldier and Brodan an actor ... but which one of us was braver? The one who worked through his shit to make a life with someone? Or the one who pretended his ghosts had stayed buried?

The thought fucked me up.

As if on cue, my phone vibrated in my pocket. I pulled it out to see another text from Chloe.

> Hey, I dnt no if ur gettin ma texts bt am free
> 2nite. U up 4 it? xx

I sighed heavily. I wasn't one to pussyfoot around the truth, and I'd rather be cruel to be kind.

My thumbs flew over the keys.

> Thanks for the good times but not interested in anything more.

A few seconds later, she texted back:

> Bt I thnk we hve somthin good here xx

Irritation and guilt filled me as I replied:

> Sorry, don't feel that way. I won't be in touch again. Wish you well.

What followed was a stream of abuse that killed my guilt. She called me every dirty name under the sun, one quick, misspelled angry text coming in after the other, until there were twenty unread texts sitting in my inbox.

My fault for not reading the lass correctly. She was too young. I shouldn't have gone there. After throwing back the last of my ale, I blocked and deleted Chloe. Then I threw some cash on the bar for Jess, nodded at a local as I strolled out of the Gloaming, and tried to ignore the unease riding my shoulders.

I didn't know why I felt so out of sorts.

I could have done with the distraction of sex tonight. Someone to release my tension on. Instead, I had no choice but to go home alone and take care of myself in the shower.

As I was chasing release, I didn't think of Chloe. It wasn't a faceless woman or a past lover. It was someone real whose naked body I could only imagine, whose smile lit up the fucking room, who came with a scream of my name in my fantasies. *Her* name released from my mouth on a hoarse shout as I climaxed around my fist.

That name echoed off the tiles, and I leaned my forehead against the damp ceramic as I caught my breath.

Sloane.

I squeezed my eyes shut again.

Fuck.

Good thing I was an expert at compartmentalization.

Just because I fantasized about a woman didn't mean I wanted anything real from her. Fantasy and reality were easily separated.

I could force myself to forget coming to the fantasy of fucking Sloane Harrow.

And I knew I could because I'd been doing just that for the last nine months.

FIVE
SLOANE

A week passed. It lulled me into a false sense of security. Using money I'd saved from my baking venture to send Callie to her first tae kwon do class, I was excited for her, despite my financial worries, when she returned home filled with hyper chatter about it. She'd loved it. She signed up and was now officially in training.

Things were progressing nicely for me. Flora, the owner of the village's most popular café, had contacted me and asked if I'd be interested in baking cakes and pastries for her to sell every Saturday. She said she'd advertise my name. It was a no-brainer. Of course I said yes. We'd discussed what treats she was interested in selling, and I made plans on how to prepare everything in time to deliver early Saturday morning.

When my car didn't show up halfway through the week, though, I found Walker at work and he'd told me the garage had to order in a part so it might be another few days. Feeling agitated about the growing cost of this fix, I wanted to argue with him, but he made an excuse to depart and that was that. He was being extra icy around me lately. I'd apologized, so I didn't know what else I could do. Walker hadn't seemed to me the kind of person who held a grudge, but I didn't know him all that well.

Friday came around, and I was brimming with anticipation. Regan was taking Callie to tae kwon do after school, which meant I could get home and finish up Flora's orders. I'd already started prep at the crack of dawn and was trying not to yawn my way through work.

When I let myself into Byron Hoffman's room, I was a lot more relaxed than I had been. I hadn't seen the asshole all week, and Mrs. Hutchinson told me he was leaving tomorrow. The weekend housekeeping would give it a thorough clean upon his departure for the next guest.

Mind on my cake and pastry plans for the night, I cleaned his room on autopilot. I'd just pulled the sheets off the bed, bundled them in my arms, and was heading toward the cart I'd left outside when the bedroom door opened.

My heart jolted in my chest as I halted.

Hoffman stepped into the room and closed the door, leaning against it.

Fear rooted me to the spot as my instinct screamed the opposite.

Run.

He raked his eyes over me, nothing behind them except what he wanted.

I cleared the terror from my throat and said as forcefully as possible, "Mr. Hoffman, let me by."

His lips curled at the corners. "We both know these doors automatically lock once closed. There are no cameras in here. There's no one but you and me."

Nausea rose in my gut as my breathing grew shallow. "Let me out."

"I've seen the looks you give me." He took a step closer and I retreated, dropping the laundry. My eyes darted around the room, searching for escape, searching for a weapon. "You can't look at a man like that and then not follow through."

My attention whipped back to him, and I sneered. "You're delusional if you think for one second I want anything to do with you."

He bridged the distance between us and slapped my face so fast, I didn't have time to avoid it.

An explosion of light filled my vision as hot pain radiated across my cheek and down my shoulder. Discombobulated, it took me a second to realize I'd fallen against the bedpost before hitting the floor.

"On your back, just as you should be."

I blinked, clearing my vision to find Hoffman towering over me.

Unbuckling his trousers.

Rage and stunned horror tore through me.

This was not happening.

Not today. Not ever.

As he got to his knees, I drew mine back and slammed my feet into his chest with every ounce of strength within me. He cursed as I shoved him and scrambled to my feet. There was no space to pass him. He'd grab me.

"Fucking bitch!"

I crawled onto the bed, almost across, when a hand clamped down on my calf.

I screamed for help over and over as his nails dug into my leg, and I clawed at the bed for purchase, trying to pull away. But then he was over me, his hand on my head, crushing me into the mattress so I could barely breathe, much less shout. Panic suffused my entire being and I flailed helplessly, my mind split between trying to breathe, trying to free myself, and trying not to think about the hard body holding me down, the hands tearing at the waistband of my pants.

Black spots covered my vision.

Then there was a muffled bang.

A roar of fury.

The crushing weight disappeared, and I lifted my head, air rushing into my lungs as I panted. My vision cleared.

Two men grappled with Hoffman.

Walker.

I was safe.

Relief drained me, and I sagged against the mattress as I watched Walker and the other man pin Hoffman to the floor. Walker's face was a mask of icy rage as he asked his companion if he had a firm hold on him.

"I've got the fucker," the man snarled with a nod.

Recognition hit me.

The other man was a club member.

A Scottish actor. North Hunter.

What?

Walker stood, chest heaving as his eyes met mine, and his anger flared brighter.

That roar of fury I'd heard ...

It was him.

"Are you all right?" he demanded.

I sat up, feeling my pants loose around my waist and flinching. "I'm okay. He didn't ..." Nausea rose in me again, and I took a deep breath to shove it back down.

Eyes still on me, Walker unclipped his walkie-talkie from his belt. He held it to his mouth, button pressed so hard it was a wonder he didn't break it. I kept my eyes on him. Couldn't look at the monster pinned to the floor. "Jock, this is Walker. Code 12 in Room 21. Need immediate assistance."

Code 12?

I shakily swung my legs off the bed but couldn't bring myself to stand.

Walker looked down at North and Hoffman. "You still got him?"

North had his knee in Hoffman's back. "I've still got him. If you want, leave him in here with me." He pressed his knee deeper into Hoffman's back, and Hoffman yelled at North to get off. "I'd love a chance to teach the bastard some manners."

Walker seemed to consider this for a second before he gave a quick shake of his head. Instead, he turned. He cleared the rage from his face as he walked slowly toward me. I had to crane my neck to keep his gaze as he stood over me, his brow creased with concern.

Recognizing the question in his eyes, I shook my head as the rest of my body trembled with shock. "He didn't ... he didn't have time to ..."

He reached out to touch my cheek, and I instinctually flinched. His arm dropped. "Sorry," I whispered.

"Never apologize ..." Walker cleared his throat. "You need ice on your cheek."

I'd bruise.

How the hell would I explain that to Callie?

Tears burned my eyes, and I finally forced myself to look at Hoffman. I *hated* men like him. I despised them with the kind of hatred I didn't even know existed in me.

He'd planned to rape me.

The thought made the room sway.

Thundering feet out in the hall drew my spine up. I wanted to disappear, hide somewhere they couldn't see me.

But Jock was striding through the open door with another member of the security team and at their back ...

Lachlan Adair marched inside, expression thunderous, dangerous, as Aria hurried after him. Lachlan was a tall man with an intimidating aura, a presence that filled a space. Both he and Aria took in the scene, and Lachlan asked me hoarsely, "Are you all right?"

I nodded, embarrassed, even though I had nothing to be embarrassed about.

Aria stared at North pinning Hoffman, and wrath flashed in her eyes. "What the hell happened here?"

North jerked his chin toward Walker. "I was talking to Walker down the stairwell when we heard the housekeeper—"

"Sloane," Walker bit out. "We heard Sloane scream for help. I had a key to Hoffman's room, so we burst in and found him attempting to rape her. We got here in time."

I curled in on myself at his blunt retelling in front of all these people.

I wanted a sinkhole to open up.

"Perhaps, Ms. Howard, you could see to Sloane while we deal with Hoffman," Walker suggested.

Aria hurried over to me, peppering me with questions as I stood on shaky legs to leave the room. We were halfway down the hall when the vomit rose before I could stop it, and I bent over, hurling my lunch all over the expensive carpet.

I realized I was worrying about the stain out loud when Aria wrapped her arms around my shoulders and pulled me away, telling me not to worry in a soothing voice.

The next thing I knew, I was in her office, a throw blanket wrapped around me, holding an ice pack to my cheek and a mug of hot tea in my other hand. Lachlan and Walker, having dealt with Hoffman, found us, and I had to endure their questions.

I explained my previous run-ins with Hoffman, how I'd told Walker. Walker explained that's why he had a key to Hoffman's room, that he'd begun sticking close when I was cleaning the suite. He'd been late to the floor that afternoon, then North Hunter had distracted him, and that's why he hadn't seen Hoffman enter. He'd looked furious at that. At himself.

"It was a good thing North was there," Lachlan said. "It's one thing for Walker to witness it, but North's account is damning. Hoffman's gone. It also means the police will have more than enough evidence to arrest him."

Horror filled me. "No police. You didn't call the police?" I asked frantically.

Lachlan frowned, and I noted Walker stiffen out of the corner of my eye. "Not yet. We're holding Hoffman until you decide what you want to do."

"No police." I turned pleading eyes on Aria, who knew exactly why I didn't want the police involved.

She gave me a small, reassuring nod before telling Lachlan, "No police. We can't force Sloane to report this."

"And if he does this to other women?" Walker bit out.

I flinched, unable to meet his eyes as shame filled me. "I ... if he were anyone else, I would. But this would cause a media circus, and I have Callie to think of. She's what matters. And he didn't ... he didn't get to do what he set out to do. I'm all right. I'm sorry if that makes me selfish."

"Let's not shame a woman who's been assaulted, Mr. Ironside," Aria snapped angrily.

"I didn't mean it like that," Walker responded flatly. "But while he didn't rape Sloane, he intended to. He planned this. And she could barely breathe when we got to her." Emotion flooded his voice now as he growled, "He could have killed her."

A shiver raced down my spine, and I forced myself to look at him. "But you stopped him."

"Who stops him next time?"

I squeezed my eyes closed, clawing back the tears. He didn't understand.

"Walker," Lachlan warned. "You of all people should know what you're asking Sloane to do. The tabloids would descend and feast on her and Callie until there was nothing left. I have ways of dealing with people like Hoffman. Unfortunately, this isn't the first time one of my members thought they could get away with this shit. They were wrong then and Hoffman is wrong now. But nobody does this to a member of my staff, under my roof." He turned to me, eyes blazing with retribution. "I will find a way to make sure he never does this again."

Something eased in me at his vow. For some reason, I believed him. "Thank you."

"You should go home, Sloane. Get some rest," Aria suggested kindly.

"Okay." I nodded, still feeling like I wasn't quite inside my own body. She took the ice pack and mug from me, and I left the blanket on her chair. I skirted her table, not looking at Walker.

"Someone should see you home," Lachlan said.

I shook my head. "I'll be fine. Thank you again."

"You don't need to thank me," he answered. "I need to apologize to you. Hoffman should never have been here."

"Don't take that on. You're not responsible for his actions." At that, I slid out of the office, amazed that my legs were working.

"Sloane, wait."

I turned as Walker followed me out of Aria's office and glanced over the lower half of his face, not quite meeting his eyes. I was so incredibly grateful for what he'd done for me, and I felt like I was letting him down as repayment.

"I'm sorry," Walker apologized gruffly.

Finally, I looked him in the eyes. "What are you sorry for?"

The muscle in his jaw ticked. "I did not intend to make you feel bad for not wanting the police involved. I spoke without thinking beyond my need to see the bastard pay. But Lachlan's right. You'd end up paying for coming forward too. Fucked-up world we live in, such as it is. But I want you to know, if Lachlan doesn't find a way to make Hoffman pay, I will."

Relieved he understood, and grateful for his promise, I nodded. Did I wish I was in the position to exact retribution from Hoffman without dragging my daughter into danger and scandal? Yes. Did it make me furious to feel so powerless? *Yes.* But for Callie's sake, and my own, I had to let the anger go. I had so much to be angry at ... but I didn't want to live my life that way.

"Thanks. For getting it. And for ... for stopping him." I needed to thank North Hunter too. Yet the thought of finding him to do so made me cringe.

I wanted home. I wanted to bake in my little kitchen and forget this whole awful day had happened.

"You're handling this amazingly well," Walker said, but it sounded almost like a question.

Maybe it was exhaustion, disbelief, adrenaline, or all of the above, but I answered thoughtlessly as I replied, "It's not the first time I've escaped a bad situation." He opened his mouth to speak, but I cut him off. "I'm going home."

"Let me take you."

"No." I retreated. "I just ... I'm going home."

I could feel his eyes on me as I walked away.

Mrs. Hutchinson clucked around me, worried and angry, after I changed out of my uniform and gathered my stuff in the locker room. I tried not to think about the torn fabric on my uniform pants and asked Mrs. Hutchinson if she could order me a new pair. I'd never seen my boss look so enraged as understanding dawned. But she nodded quickly and told me she'd take care of it.

She wanted someone to escort me home, too, but I convinced her I was fine and made my way out of the staff entrance toward my parked car.

Fumbling in my purse for the keys, I became aware of my throbbing cheek and shoulder. I'd have to tell Callie I tripped and fell into the bedpost. The sound of him hitting me ricocheted through my mind. The fear of lying trapped beneath him, of being practically suffocated as he tried to—

A sob rose out of me like a wild animal set free, and I bent over, leaning blindly against my car as the cries wracked my body.

A hand touched my shoulder and I whirled in fear, dropping my keys.

Walker held up his hands between us, as if approaching a wounded animal, his eyes bright with more emotion than I'd ever seen.

Without thought, I sobbed harder and fell against him, arms around him, clutching the back of his suit jacket like he was a lifeline.

His powerful arms bound tight around me, and he murmured soothing words as I cried out the shock of the day, soaking the front of his shirt with my tears.

Six

WALKER

Part of my experience in the marines and as a bodyguard included learning to defuse situations as much as deal with situations that had already exploded. It was that training and experience that allowed me to rein in the fury at seeing Sloane pinned to the bed by that sick fucker. To detain him without beating his face to a bloody pulp.

For the first time in a long time, I regretted my ability to control my anger. Holding Sloane while she broke down in my arms, I'd wanted to march back into the castle, find Hoffman, and end the bastard.

The only thing stopping me was Sloane. I'd bundled her into my Range Rover and driven her home. During the entire ride, I kept glancing at her. She'd stopped crying. Her face was pale except for the bruise that bloomed on her cheek. My hands had tightened around the wheel at the reminder he'd hit her. The reminder that he had a chance to. I was raging at myself. All week I'd made sure I was on Hoffman's floor while Sloane was working it. Then today, Jock had called me in to his office to discuss an update to the current drone system we used as security around the estate perimeter. Our meeting had run late, and I'd been hurrying toward Hoffman's room when North Hunter stopped me to ask if I'd be interested in working as his personal security.

That's when we heard Sloane's muffled screams down the hall. It was a miracle we had. The castle walls were thick, the doors heavy.

The last time I'd felt that kind of fear was when Brodan called to tell me he was on his way to rescue Monroe from a madman, without backup. I could have killed Bro for doing that. But then I also understood why he couldn't wait, not while Monroe's life was in jeopardy. In the end, she'd been the one to save them both.

But who would have saved Sloane if I hadn't gotten there in time? And did I get there in time? She'd still been traumatized, even if the piece of shit hadn't raped her.

For that reason, I couldn't take my eyes off her even as Sloane moved about the small kitchen in the cottage, baking as if on autopilot.

"Sloane, you need ice on your face," I told her for the third time since we'd arrived back at her place.

She shook her head. "I don't want Callie to see me like this," she replied. She'd muttered the same thing a few times now, and I was getting worried about her emotional state, that she wasn't dealing with what happened. Not quite sure what to do for her, I'd called Monroe when we got to the house. Callie was in Inverness with Regan and Lewis for the tae kwon do classes and wouldn't be home for a while.

I took a step toward her. "Sloane, ice."

My tone stopped her in the middle of stretching a dough that she'd whipped together impressively fast. As I'd glanced around the kitchen that was too small for her to run her baking business from, I realized that she didn't even have a mixer. She mixed everything by hand.

"I will ice it," she replied with amazing calm. "Let me put

some cookies in the oven first. Callie likes the smell of them baking." She shrugged, sadness cascading down over her false smile. "*I* like the smell. It soothes me."

Understanding, I nodded. "Do what you need to do. Then ice."

Sloane's mouth curled at the corners, and I tried not to stare at it.

For the next ten minutes, I leaned against the door, watching her work. I catalogued the things she didn't have but reckoned a professional baker needed. She chattered as she baked, telling me about Flora's proposal, about Callie's excitement over her martial arts lessons. I listened and nodded so she'd know I was paying attention.

"I'm talking too much." Sloane threw me an apologetic look as she finally grabbed an ice pack out of the freezer.

"You're fine," I assured her.

"No, I know you don't like people chatting at you like that."

Where did she get that idea? I frowned. "Talk until you're hoarse. It doesn't bother me." I liked Sloane's voice. I liked her laughter best but didn't seem able to provoke it like others could.

"Coffee, tea?" she asked, ice pack on her face.

I pushed off the doorjamb. "I'll make it. You sit down. Tea?"

"You don't—"

"Sloane, I'll make it."

She gave me a grateful smile. "There's peppermint tea in the cupboard above the kettle. I'll have that. There's coffee there, too, but it's instant."

"Tea will do," I assured her.

Instead of going into the adjoining sitting room, Sloane hovered in the doorway, watching me.

I glanced up at her as I stirred milk into my tea and found her wearing a soft, genuine smile. "What?"

Her gaze moved to mine, and I tried not to think about how warm and dark and gorgeous her big brown eyes were. "You take milk in your tea."

Bemused, I nodded.

"No sugar."

I smirked, realizing what she was getting at. "Stopped taking it since you moved to town with your shit-hot baking. Have to curb the sweet tooth somewhere."

Sloane laughed. A small, breathy laugh. I felt about nine feet fucking tall as her eyes glittered, the sadness temporarily chased away. "You don't have to eat my cakes, you know."

I grunted at that and handed her the mug of peppermint tea. "And the earth doesn't need to orbit the sun."

She chuckled again, and I turned back to my tea, a smile of triumph pulling at my mouth.

Catching sight of the photos pinned to the refrigerator, mostly of Sloane and Callie, I paused. There was one from last Christmas. The Adairs had invited us to join them. The photo was of Sloane, Callie, Monroe, Brodan ... and me. I stood behind Brodan, beer in my hand, staring stonily at the camera. There were loads of photos taken that day. But she'd picked this one to hang on her fridge.

Feeling her attention, I looked and found her watching me, biting her plump lower lip.

I glanced back at the fridge and noted the other photo that stood out from the rest. Callie was with an older Latinx woman. Curiosity about their past life got the better of me. "Grandmother?"

Silence met me.

I looked at Sloane. She wore a wary expression. "An old friend."

Again, that annoying need to know who she was, where

she'd come from, agitated me. How the hell had she ended up in the middle of nowhere in the Scottish Highlands? Remembering Aria's defense of her today and the secret shared looks between them reinforced my theory that the Howards were protecting Sloane.

"I need to sit down."

At Sloane's tired words, I grabbed my tea and followed her into the sitting room. I watched her as she curled up on one sofa and I took the other. She sipped at her drink, those big dark eyes looking at me over the top of her steaming mug.

I stared back, trying to gauge her emotional state.

She returned my stare unabashedly, and we did that for a while, sipping our drinks and just looking at each other. Something tight twisted in my chest and gut.

I wanted to kill Byron Hoffman. But I wouldn't. Not in the traditional sense of ending his life. I would kill him where it hurt. I'd take away the power he hid behind. I'd take away everything that mattered. Somehow. I'd work with my new boss to make sure it happened.

"That's an awfully fierce look on your face." Sloane ended the silence. "What are you thinking?"

Sloane impressed me with how well she was handling today. Aye, she'd broken down in the car park, but that was to be expected. Her words from earlier bothered me. That she'd escaped bad situations before. I already sensed that. But having it confirmed disturbed me more than I liked. Still, I didn't need to pussyfoot around Sloane. "I'm thinking of the ways I can destroy Hoffman."

A savage glint lit her eyes, and I felt inappropriate heat rush south. "Good. I wish it were in my power to destroy him. I want him to pay for that too. My powerlessness. I'm so angry that I can't do anything without hurting Callie. I'm angry that men like him can make me feel that way." She shook her head. "But I won't let him leave me with that. I won't live my life angry. I can't. I have to live life in the light. With hope. With optimism. For Callie's sake. I won't be a bitter, unhappy mom."

"Then you have more power than you realize, Sloane," I assured her, awed. "Choosing to let go of your anger for the sake of your daughter ... that's powerful fucking stuff."

Her eyes flared, lips parting as she stared at me like I was worth something.

I wanted to disabuse her of that notion.

I didn't *ever* want to disabuse her of that notion.

A pounding at the door broke our moment, and Sloane moved to get up, but I gestured for her to stop. "Let me."

Placing my mug on the table, I stood and crossed the room to open the door.

Monroe and Brodan were on the other side. Brodan's small, redheaded wife glowered fiercely up at me. "Let me in," she demanded, pushing inside before I could react.

I stepped out of her way as her pregnant belly passed me first, followed by the rest of her. She'd had a neat little bump for the majority of her pregnancy and then suddenly, she was huge. Brodan told me she couldn't sleep because she was so uncomfortable and that she cursed him nightly.

Sloane stood at the sound of Monroe's voice.

"She okay?" Brodan murmured as he stepped in and closed the door. We watched as Sloane met Monroe and the two friends hugged around Monroe's bump.

I kept my attention on Sloane as I answered, "She's a fighter, so she will be." I glared as I turned to Brodan, knowing he'd see my wrath. "He could have killed her."

Brodan's expression hardened and he murmured, "But she doesn't want the police involved?"

I shook my head.

A dangerous look lit Brodan's eyes. "Then I suppose it's up to us."

Satisfied, I nodded. "Lachlan promised her he'd take care of it. But I want in."

"I'll talk to him. I want in too."

"What are you two whispering about?" Monroe asked.

We turned to find the two women staring at us in curiosity.

I answered honestly, for Sloane's sake. "Planning Hoffman's payback."

Monroe scowled. "Good." Then her face softened as tears lit her eyes. "Sloane says you saved her."

Before I could answer or prepare myself, Brodan's wife crossed the room and threw her arms around me, pregnant belly angled so she could get close enough to hug. There hadn't been a lot of hugging in my life over the last two decades, so I patted her back awkwardly as she sniffled against me.

Brodan snorted as he cupped his wife's head. "Sunset, remember Walk isn't a hugger."

Sloane shot me a bewildered look as Brodan pried Monroe away.

I knew what she was thinking.

I'd willingly held her in my arms.

No awkwardness.

It felt natural to hold Sloane Harrow against me.

And wasn't that a giant fucking problem?

"Sorry." Monroe wiped her tearstained cheeks. "I'm just grateful. And hormonal."

"It's fine," I promised her gruffly.

"Let's have some tea," Brodan suggested.

"Ice." I pointed to the pack Sloane had left on the coffee table. "You've barely iced your cheek."

"I want in on the payback," Monroe growled.

I looked down at Brodan's ferocious wee wife and not for the first time understood why he'd loved this woman his entire life. She had a fire in her. A determination. Life had not been kind to Monroe, just as I assumed life had not been kind to Sloane. I wondered if that was why she and Sloane were friends. If trauma had drawn them to each other ... and through that, their mutual fire and determination cemented their bond.

I wonder too much about Sloane. I needed to harden myself against the curiosity. Against her. The threat she posed to my peace.

She was safe now.

Her friend was here, Brodan was here.

"I better go," I announced abruptly.

Sloane's eyes widened slightly before she pasted on a polite mask. "Thank you for everything."

Giving her a gruff nod, I grabbed my keys off the sideboard. "I'll make sure your car is brought to you."

"You don't have to do that."

"But I will," I said, barely looking at her.

I nodded at Monroe and Brodan as I moved past them, avoiding my friend's searching gaze, and slipped out the door without saying another word.

SEVEN
SLOANE

W alker had disappeared.

  I knew it was dumb for that to be at the forefront of my concern only ten days after being assaulted, but his distance bugged me. I'd stubbornly refused to take more time off work than was suggested. Lachlan had offered me paid leave for as long as I needed. However, Callie would wonder what was going on, so I took two days off and told her I'd used some of my paid holidays so I could work on baking orders.

Then I got right back on that horse.

I hated that I was apprehensive the morning I returned to work.

I hated that nausea and fear had churned in my gut.

However, I returned to a new system for the housekeepers. While Aria and Lachlan wanted to assure me that the board would be much more cautious about who they granted membership, Aria had also insisted that each room be cleaned by two housekeepers. Safety in numbers, she said. It was an immense relief.

The first few nights after the attack, I'd woken from nightmares where Hoffman's assault and my past life in LA collided. The dreams were a confused mix of past and present. For Callie's sake, I didn't let the exhaustion of those night-mares show. My daughter had no clue what had happened to me, and she never would.

Mrs. Hutchinson teamed me up with Frannie, an older but jolly woman who started working on the estate when it first opened to members. She liked to gossip about what we found in the rooms, and she made me laugh. The days moved quicker with her, and I relaxed more and more with each one that passed.

For those first few days, I'd caught sight of Walker in the castle halls. He never looked my way, but I had the strangest feeling he was watching over me. Brodan had shown up to give me the bad news that my car was beyond repair, but that he was covering the rental costs of my new Hyundai (confirming the car was not Walker's), and he didn't want any arguments. It stung to take his charity, but I couldn't afford a new car. I needed to drive Callie to school, and I needed transportation for work at the estate and delivering baking orders.

I reluctantly kept the car but promised Brodan I'd get my own as soon as possible. He'd brushed me off, but I meant to keep my vow. I just didn't have a timeline for it. And I made the choice to find joy in my gratitude.

That it was Brodan, however, who'd delivered this news bothered me. I wanted to text Walker, but it was clear if he was sending Brodan in his place that he didn't want me getting any ideas about him being in our lives.

That hurt more than it should. Walker made me feel safe. I couldn't remember the last time anyone had made me feel safe.

The Saturday after my first week back at work, Callie and I took a trip to the library. When I was younger, I devoured all the words, but there had been little time for reading since Callie came along. However, I was determined to make sure she had access to all the books she wanted. The library at Ardnoch wasn't the best, but we could request books from other branches, and Callie's small order from a few weeks ago had come in. We collected those, as well as a few others, and then went food shopping.

I listened to my daughter chatter about Lewis, about her other friends, about tae kwon do, and about the writing assignment she'd had at school that week. One of her and Lewis's friends was having a birthday party that afternoon, and on top of all the baking I'd dropped off at Flora's at the crack of dawn, I'd made cupcakes for the party. It was a full day, and we were hurrying home from the grocery shopping so Callie could get changed.

I pulled the car up outside the cottage so we could drop off the shopping. As soon as Callie and I got out of the car, we heard the yelling.

A loud, screechy female voice echoed all the way down Castle Street from Morag's deli. Frowning, I turned that way and halted at the sight of Walker. He was standing in the middle of the sidewalk being yelled at by a woman.

Realization dawned as I picked up bits of what she was shouting. Monroe had mentioned that Walker was having a hard time with a woman he'd slept with. Apparently, he'd told her up front that what they had was just a casual thing, he didn't want to do it anymore, and he'd blocked her when she got abusive. She'd since used a different phone number to contact him, and when she couldn't get him, she even called the estate.

I'd known it wasn't my business, and a stalkerish woman was the consequences of Walker treating females like they were disposable. But harassment was harassment. And I understood too well how stressful that was.

Plus ... I owed him.

"Callie." I rounded the hood and held out my keys. "Go inside."

She scowled in Walker's direction. "Who's that lady hassling Walker?"

"Just go inside, please," I insisted with a tone.

My daughter frowned at me but took the keys and let herself into the cottage. I knew she'd have her face pressed up to the window, but I couldn't think about that.

Instead, I hurried down the street, adrenaline already pumping as I heard the woman shouting the same stuff over and over and using foul language that any kid in the vicinity could hear. I also heard Walker say her name. *Chloe.*

As I got closer, I noted that Walker certainly had a type with his women. I'd seen him a few times with one of his casual things and while hair and eye color changed, their tall voluptuousness did not. While I definitely had boobs and an ass, it was nothing on the women I'd seen him with. Walker liked *curves* for days, apparently.

Ignoring my dismay at that realization, I forced my face into a thunderous scowl, and Walker caught sight of me in his peripheral. He looked as taken aback as Walker could look— either from the sight of me or my expression.

Then Chloe shoved Walker, and he staggered, taken by surprise again.

The sight of big, strong, formidable Walker Ironside stumbling did something to me.

I saw red.

I pushed between them as Walker righted himself, and I shoved that stalker right back with all my might. "Back off!" I growled.

Chloe stumbled before quickly steadying herself, as if ready for a fight. It was entirely against my nature to have an embarrassing public showdown, but for Walker's sake, I'd draw on my best acting skills. The blond had a few inches on me and looked like she could pummel me into the ground. She also had crazy eyes, unsurprising for someone who harassed a guy because he didn't want to be with her.

And I'd always believed in fighting crazy with crazy.

"So, you're the asshole stalking my man!" I yelled.

Chloe's eyes flared. "Your man?"

I felt Walker step up behind me, his body brushing mine, clearly understanding my game. Needing not to feel the heat of him, I stepped into Chloe's personal space. "Yeah, my man. We got a kid together," I lied.

Chloe gaped at Walker over my shoulder. "You're married?"

He stayed silent while I shoved my face in hers. "Yeah, we got a kid. We were on a break. Now my man tells me you're harassing him. He told you he wants nothing to do with you." I jabbed a finger in her direction. "So, what? You think if you act insane enough, wear him down, he'll want you back." I pushed into her, and she stepped back, off the curb, looking wary. Hiding my triumphant smirk, I lowered my voice. "You think you're crazy, Chloe? Well, my man has a type. You ain't seen crazy ... but you will if you ever put your hands on Walker again. If you ever contact him again." My face was now almost touching hers, and I know I looked nuts as I whispered, "You ever shot someone, Chloe? Because I have."

Fear flared in her eyes, and I almost felt bad as she stepped back again, looking freaked out. "I didn't know he was with someone."

"Doesn't matter if he's with someone or not. A person tells you to leave them alone, you leave them alone. Harassment isn't fun. You want me to prove it to you? Because I got time. I can haunt your ass at your workplace, at your house, in your town. Everywhere you turn, I can be there. You want that?"

Chloe scowled but shook her head. "I don't want any

trouble." With that, she shot Walker one last wounded look and hurried down the street toward the Gloaming.

I watched as she got back in her car, aware we had an audience across the street outside Flora's, but I ignored them. Chloe whipped out of her space as if the hounds of hell were nipping at her exhaust pipe. She sped past us without looking our way.

Finally, I turned to face Walker.

Butterflies erupted in my belly.

Because Walker Ironside was full-on grinning at me.

I'd never seen him smile like that.

One corner of his mouth tugged up higher than the other, and his eyes crinkled attractively at the corners.

It was a sexy goddamn smile.

I flushed from head to toe but forced a smile back.

"Were you an actress in another life? Because I almost believed you were nuts," he joked.

Laughing, I shrugged. "I don't know where that came from. But it was fun."

Walker's shoulders shook with amusement, and I tried not to gape in wonder at the sight. His smile had softened, but his expression turned almost tender. An ache flared in my chest at that look. "Why did you do it?"

"Monroe might have mentioned a one-night stand was giving you a hard time. I guessed that was the woman in question, and I didn't like that she shoved you. She did it knowing you wouldn't hit back." I'd known that, too, with absolute certainty. "And I owe you."

Walker's trademark scowl slotted right back into place. "You don't owe me anything."

I grinned. "Now I don't."

His lips twitched again.

That warmth flooded me, and the distance I'd felt between us the past week was forgotten. "Callie is going to a birthday party this afternoon, and I have extra cupcakes. Do you want to come over for a coffee and some cake while she's gone?"

Just like that, Walker's entire demeanor changed. It was like a wall slamming down as his expression blanked and his body stiffened. "No," he replied bluntly. "I've got shit to do."

It took me a second to don my armor, to hide my wounded feelings. But I did it. I smiled through my hurt. "Of course. Well, have a good day."

While Callie was at the party that afternoon, I drove to Monroe's to tell her everything. Swearing her to secrecy. And she wanted to rip Walker a new one. But I told her I'd be no better than Chloe, then. Punishing Walker for not wanting what I wanted.

"Then maybe we need to find you someone new to crush on."

"Dating?" I sighed. "When will I have time to date?"

"You'll make time." Monroe proceeded to pull out her laptop and do a quick search. "There," she announced after a few minutes. "There's a speed-dating event in Inverness in two weeks. We could babysit Callie."

"And if your own little bump has arrived by then?"

Monroe flushed with excitement. "Then Regan can babysit Callie."

I laughed at her offering poor Regan's time, like she didn't do a lot for me already. "I'll think about it."

I don't know if I really meant it at that point.

On the Monday after the run-in with Walker and Chloe, there was no sign of Walker watching out for me. No sign of him at all on the estate. I finally gave in and asked Monroe about him, and she told me he was on vacation. She didn't know where he was, but he'd left Ardnoch on Saturday, and according to Brodan, he would be gone for two weeks. She also told me, with not a small amount of curiosity in her voice, that Brodan said Walker took the same two weeks off every year.

I wondered why but realized I'd probably never know. He hadn't told me he'd be gone from the estate. He didn't know that his leaving made me feel less safe. He didn't know because he didn't want to know. In fact, I suspected it would agitate him to know he made me feel safe.

He didn't want to be that person for me.

We weren't friends, me and Walker.

We weren't anything.

EIGHT
WALKER

I t was the end of the first week of September, and a heat wave had hit the country. Portobello Beach was fairly busy for the middle of a working day. I sat on the concrete wall of the promenade, feet dangling above the sand, staring out at the sky-blue water.

The cool breeze sweeping off the North Sea masked the heat from the sun.

People walked behind me, in front of me. Some ran. Some hurried after dogs. Others sat on the sand, enjoying the last of the summer sun before autumn hit.

There was no sign of turmoil here. Laughter lit the air, loud chatter muffled by the squall of seagulls above, the aroma of fish and chips prevalent and familiar.

My hometown shouldn't have been a place that hurt.

But, fuck, sitting there, I might as well have had a knife sticking out of my chest.

Every year, I took the same two weeks off work. Disappeared. I always went somewhere different. Somewhere I could hide. Somewhere safe I could be distracted. My head was not in the game, and in a job like mine, that could be a

danger to someone else. So I took off on this anniversary every
year.

But Rich had asked me to come here.

*"Are you taking time off work at the beginning of
September? Like always?" Rich asked.*

"Of course."

"This year I want you to go home, Walker."

*His suggestion made me instantly defensive. "I didn't
realize emotional torture was part of your process."*

*Rich's answering smile was patient. "You need to face the
past if you're ever going to move forward. Avoiding it does you
no good. I think this is a gentle first step toward processing what
happened there. You don't have to see anyone. I just want you to
explore Portobello. Spend some time there. If it's too much, you
can leave."*

And because I hadn't started seeing Rich just to ignore his
advice, I'd done as he'd suggested.

But I was starting to wonder if my therapist was a fucking
sadist.

Here ... *she* was everywhere. And they were here. It was a
wonder we hadn't crossed paths. Good thing I was leaving
tomorrow to spend my last week off catching up with some
lads from my military unit. This year we'd decided to meet up
in Perthshire to camp and fish and get drunk. It's what I
needed. It would hurt less than this shite.

A burst of giggles to my left drew my gaze, and I saw a
child with blond hair and blue eyes walking with her mum,
swinging her arm as she held tight to her hand. The mum was
blond, young. The sight of them miraculously drew my
thoughts of *her* to Callie and Sloane.

Before I'd left, I'd had a Zoom call with the Ardnoch
Estate board members along with North Hunter. We told
them what we'd witnessed. I was on my way down south when
Aria called to let me know Hoffman was out. Membership

stripped. Unsurprisingly. Lachlan had people looking into rumors about Hoffman's behavior, trying to find someone to come forward. I was doing the same, using what contacts I'd made while working as private security for the rich and famous.

North Hunter had reiterated his offer, but I'd turned him down. I liked Ardnoch.

I wished I was there now.

Wished I knew if Sloane was doing okay. She'd seemed better before I left.

Had shocked the shit out of me when she chased Chloe off. For good, I might add. Her strategy had worked. My lips curled in amusement, remembering the moment. Aye, Sloane Harrow had fire in her.

My smile dropped, remembering the hurt she'd tried to cover when I shot down her offer to have coffee.

Fuck.

That invisible knife in my chest twisted deeper.

"That's it. I'm done," I murmured before jumping off the wall onto the promenade. I'd come face-to-face with whatever it was Rich thought I needed to find here. I'd hovered around the coastal town outside Edinburgh for a week, haunting it like a fucking ghost.

Nothing was better.

Nothing was solved.

And worse, thoughts of another female I'd let down had chased me here.

I needed temporary oblivion. It was time to go find that instead.

NINE

SLOANE

Monroe knew everything about my life. Over the past year, we'd built trust and love and shared all of our deepest traumas with one another. It made carrying them easier, to have someone in our lives who knew what had shaped us. To have them care these things had happened to us, and to want a better life for us going forward.

Roe had become the best friend I'd ever had, and in her I fully trusted.

It was because of that trust I left the café in Inverness, feeling confused and more depressed about Walker than ever. *Go to speed dating*, Roe said. *It'll help you get over Walker*, she said.

The pepper spray I kept in my purse was now in the pocket of the light cardigan I wore, my hand clutched around it. Yes, life had made me extra cautious, even in the middle of a city when there were witnesses around. But it was a city I was unfamiliar with as I reoriented myself to where I'd parked my car. Out of the twelve guys with whom I'd just spent five minutes each—time I'd never get back—not one asked me anything beyond my name and occupation. The self-absorbed asshats spent the rest of the time telling me about their jobs, their likes and dislikes, and staring at my breasts.

To be fair, I was not physically attracted to any of them. Now that I knew I could physically react to someone the way I reacted to Walker ... that's what I wanted. I wanted butterflies and hot tingles between my thighs. I wanted to be aware of his proximity, to feel every touch like I was near a live wire.

I tried to relax as I followed the map on my phone back to my car. A few more people strolled along the high street, the area brick paved and designed for pedestrians. A mix of architectural styles suggested the street had been added to over many, many decades, maybe even centuries. Parts of it looked Georgian, while other buildings screamed the sixties and seventies. I'd only been to Inverness a few times but hadn't really taken it in because Callie was more interested in dragging me from store to store.

The high street gave way to a road, and I crossed it onto the sidewalk, passing a beautiful building that resembled a small castle. It was so out of place that it drew the eye. I knew from Monroe it had been built in the 1700s for a lord and was now Inverness Town Hall. I focused on it, lit up in the twilight, and clutched my pepper spray when I heard boisterous male laughter behind me.

I neared a pub, however, and a few sober adults stood outside smoking, so I tried to relax.

Tried being the operative word. I was more than a little jumpy these days, so I quickened my step, hurrying off the high street and up a steep, brick-paved hill that I now remembered walking down. I passed quaint brick buildings with large dormer windows that looked like they still might be residential and followed the narrow lane almost to the top.

A little out of breath from the climb, I was never more thankful to see the parking lot where I'd left my car. It was much busier than when I'd left it, and now that I wasn't rushing to get to the event in time, I took in the surroundings in the darkening light. Apartments. The parking lot was surrounded by two apartment blocks. I'd parked in a residential lot. No wonder there was no meter.

Ugh. I hoped I didn't have a ticket.

This night had been the biggest bust, and I needed to tell my best friend about it. Walking across the lot, I dug my phone out of my purse.

"How did it go?" Monroe asked without preamble.

The days were still long this far north, even in late September, but twilight was almost night now as I tripped over a grassy sidewalk that cut between the parking spaces for some bizarre reason. "Crap."

"You okay?"

"Yeah, tripped. Anyway, it was not worth the two-hour round trip." I pressed the phone to my shoulder with my ear as I used both hands to fumble for my car keys.

"Aw." Monroe sounded even more disappointed than me. "There wasn't even one bloke there you fancied?"

"Nope. And I parked somewhere I shouldn't have."

"That's rubbish. There was absolutely no one there that made you forget you-know-who?"

You-know-who.

Having an almighty crush on Walker had brought me nothing but an emotional roller coaster and distraction I did not need. Apparently, he was back from his vacation, but I hadn't seen him all week. The worst part of him distancing himself was that Callie even asked after him. She wanted to know where he was. Kids were more perceptive than we gave them credit for, and I think my daughter sensed I liked Walker. I think she liked that I liked Walker.

That was proof I should never let a guy into our lives until I was sure he intended to stay. And I had to be better at guarding my feelings. If Callie could sense them, then I knew Walker had too. Hence the distance he'd put between us.

Rejection stung.

"No. Most of them just stared at my breasts the whole time."

"Well, can you really blame them?"

I grinned as I stopped at my car. "Have I ever told you how good you are for my self—mmmughh!" Something suddenly covered my mouth, and it took me a second to register it was a gloved hand. A hard body pressed me against the car from behind, and I screamed behind the hand.

"Sloane? Sloane?" Monroe's muffled, frantic voice could be heard from where I'd dropped my phone on the ground.

I butted my head against my attacker and slammed my elbow into his gut. He grunted, not expecting the force of it, and I turned to find a man, a good few inches taller than me, wearing street clothes and a ski mask.

Eyes of indeterminate color beneath the streetlights glared ferociously at me. He lunged and I cried out, falling back against my car, the scream for help choking inside me. My hand dove into the pocket of my sweater and just as he reached me, I lifted and sprayed that crap into his eyes.

The smell stung my nostrils as he grunted repeatedly in pain and fell to his knees. I stupidly stood there, frozen, as he stumbled to his feet and ran away, weaving all over the place because I'd blinded him.

"Sloane!" I heard my name yelled as if from a distance, and it pulled me out of my moronic trance.

Scrambling for my phone and purse, I snatched them up and dove into my car, hitting the locks. I shook from head to toe, a cold sweat breaking out over my body as I floored it out of there. My phone automatically connected to my car, and Monroe's frantic voice filled it as I heard her telling Brodan something was wrong.

"I'm here, I'm here!" I shouted in my fear and shock.

"Oh my bloody God, what happened?" Roe yelled back angrily.

"Someone tried to mug me." Tears came now, and I knew she could hear them as I explained, "He came up behind me before I got in my car. I fought him off and sprayed my pepper spray in his eyes. Oh my God, oh my God, oh my God."

"What the ... Brodan ..." Her voice trailed off, and then I heard her husband's voice. "Sloane, it's Brodan. Are you safe to drive?"

"I ... I ... uh ... I'm in shock, but I can't stop." I shook my head as an image of stopping only for the attacker to appear again popped into it. "I want to come home."

"Okay. Okay. Stay on the phone with us, then. Come to us first before you collect Callie. Okay? It'll give you time to calm down."

"I smell," I said in realization. "I've got pepper spray on me."

"Then you can shower and change your clothes here. It's not a problem. Just... come here first, all right?"

"I can do that." I wiped the sweat off my forehead. "Someone tried to mug me. What the actual hell?" It was like I couldn't catch a break. "Is this for real? Who gets attacked twice in one month?" Anger I tried so hard to fight back won. "Fuck my life!"

I SAT on Monroe and Brodan's couch, clutching a hot mug of tea between my hands. I hadn't even let Monroe hug me when I arrived at their place. Instead, I'd jumped straight into the shower to scrub the smell of pepper spray off me. Then I'd changed into a dress of Monroe's that barely fit because she was so petite. Thankfully, Brodan had given me one of his hoodie to put on over it.

My clothes were currently in their washing machine.

Concern glinted brightly in my friend's eyes while I stared at her large bump, worrying about anything stressing her out.

Much less my bad luck.

"I'm just glad you're all right." Monroe stared down at me, wringing her hands.

As soon as I'd walked into the living room, fresh from the shower, she'd hugged me hard and burst into tears. I knew it was hormones for her, but when I cried, it was from shock and frustration.

I didn't want the anger to win. But someone had tried to mug me. "Do I have a target on my back?" I asked my friends. "Does it say 'easy pickings' on it?"

Brodan's brows pinched. "You are having a stream of bad luck lately."

"Lately?" I scoffed. "Try for the last twenty-six, almost twenty-seven, years. It started when I was born on Christmas Day. That's just bad luck." Seeing the worried look they exchanged, I sighed. "I'm sorry. I'm not myself right now."

"No bloody wonder." Roe paced up and down. "I mean, two attacks in one month is ..." She trailed off, turning pale as she stopped and looked at me. "What if that wasn't a mugging? Tell us exactly what happened."

"Not a mugging?" I frowned. "What could it have been?"

"Tell us exactly what happened. Every moment."

So I did.

"He never tried to take your purse?" Brodan quizzed.

"I didn't give him the chance."

"But why not grab the purse and run?" Roe insisted. "You'd dropped everything. He came at you again instead of stealing your purse."

Fear shivered through me as I understood what she was saying. "You think it was planned?"

"What if it was Hoffman?"

I shook my head. "He was too tall."

"Or someone Hoffman hired." Monroe shot a worried look at Brodan. "Do you think he might try to scare Sloane?"

Brodan squeezed his eyes closed as he rubbed his forehead. "It's always a possibility. Fuck ... why are the women in this family such danger magnets? If I die young, it will be from the stress of it."

Instead of his words eliciting fear, I felt warmth spread through me. Brodan considered me family?

"We could be jumping to conclusions here," I reminded them quietly. "There's a real possibility this is merely horrible luck."

"I don't know." Brodan shook his head, unconvinced. "He wore gloves and a ski mask. A ski mask, maybe ... but gloves? To mug you?"

"Okay, now you're freaking me out." What if it *was* Hoffman? Payback for getting him kicked out of Ardnoch? "Callie." My gaze met Roe's. "I can't have Callie in danger." *Not again.*

"Protection," Roe announced. "A bodyguard for you and Callie."

"I can't afford that." I stood, shaking my head at the suggestion. "And doesn't it seem a little overboard?"

"Maybe. But isn't it worth it to know Callie is safe?"

"Of course! But I can't afford that, Roe, and I am not taking any more handouts from you." My pride could only handle so many hits.

"Handouts?" She looked hurt.

"That's not what I meant. I'm sorry ... I'll just be extra vigilant. And something is less likely to happen here than in the city."

"I really think—arghh!" Monroe suddenly cried out, bending over slightly and clutching her belly.

Fear lanced through me as both Brodan and I reached for her.

She panted, wide-eyed, as she stared at Brodan.

"Roe?" He held her close, looking terrified.

Her gaze dropped to where a wet stain darkened the fabric of her wide-leg pants. She looked back up at him. "I think my water just broke."

TEN
WALKER

As soon as the ringing started, I was awake. My time in the military had trained me to be a light sleeper, to jump into consciousness at the drop of a pin.

Light filtered into the room through the cracks in my window blind, and I turned in my bed to grab my ringing phone off the nightstand. Brodan's name flashed on the screen. I noted it was five minutes to six, and my alarm was about to go off. I didn't work Saturdays, but I didn't like sleeping in for too long, and Brodan knew that.

"Morning," I answered, shoving my duvet off and sliding out of bed.

"Aye, and it's a good one," Bro answered.

I froze at the emotion in his voice. "Oh?"

"I'm officially a dad, Walk. My son was born this morning. We've called him Lennox."

I was sincerely happy for him as I wandered into my kitchen. "I'm chuffed for you, Bro. Congrats, man." But something occurred to me. "Isn't Lennox a bit early?"

"By a week. The doctors think stress caused Roe's water to

break, but they've assured me both Monroe and Lennox are doing well."

"What stress? Physical stress?"

"Ah ... no. Not exactly. It was Sloane."

My hand stilled on the coffee pot. "What about Sloane?"

"She was in Inverness last night, walking back to her car, and she was attacked by what she thought was a mugger. But he didn't go for her purse, Walk, so I'm worried this is a retaliation from Hoffman."

Anger churned low in my gut. "Is she all right? Did he hurt her? Where is she?"

Brodan was silent for too many seconds. Then, "She's fine. She pepper-sprayed him in the eyes and he took off."

"Good girl." I relaxed marginally.

My friend snorted. "I beg you not to say those words to her. No, on second thought, do it. Preferably in front of me."

"Short of entertainment these days? Is becoming a father not entertaining enough?"

"Aye, all right, you moody bastard. Sloane and Callie are fine. Sloane came to the hospital with us and stayed for the birth, but I had one of the men come from the estate to escort her home."

"Why didn't you call me to come get her?"

"Well ... she asked me not to."

I jerked back like the fucker had hit me. That stung. I didn't know why since I'd made up my mind to stay away from her.

"Anyway, she's fine. She's home. Lachlan is going to look into whether Hoffman might be behind it."

"Why do you think it wasn't a mugging?"

Brodan sighed. "Walk ... any other day, I'd want to discuss this, but Sloane is fine, my brother's dealing with it, and I want to celebrate the arrival of my wee boy for today. Just for today.

So I'm going to get back to my wife and son. He'd quite like to meet his uncle Walker soon."

Uncle Walker.

Fuck.

Agitated but touched, I replied, "Text me when Roe's up for visitors. I'll be there."

"Uh, wait a second. Roe wants to talk to you."

Frowning, I waited as Brodan passed his phone to her.

"Walker?" Monroe's voice filled my ear.

"Congrats, Roe. Happy for you."

"Thank you." I could hear the smile in her voice but also the exhaustion. "Lennox is eager to meet his uncle Walker, so why don't you pop by the house this evening?"

"You'll be home then?"

"Lennox and I are doing well so they said we can go home this afternoon."

"Are you sure you don't need rest?"

"No, I want my son surrounded by his family as much as possible. That includes you, you know."

Emotion thickened my throat. "Aye, okay. I'll be there."

"Great. We'll see you soon."

She hung up and I stared at my phone, my mind already racing to Sloane and Callie. If Hoffman had sent someone after her, I'd kill the prick. But maybe it was a mugging. What the hell was she doing in Inverness on a Friday night, anyway?

I itched to call her.

"Why didn't you call me to come get her?"

"Well … she asked me not to."

Fuck.

I COULDN'T REMEMBER the last time I'd held a baby in my arms, but there was no getting around it when Brodan planted his son in mine and left him there.

Lennox Adair was a big baby, and I wondered how Monroe could have been carrying him inside her wee body for so long. He had the chubbiest cheeks I'd ever seen and blue-gray eyes the size of marbles. He wriggled restlessly in my hold, his wee fists curled, arms stretching, his legs kicking beneath the blanket he was wrapped in. I bent my head to his and his eyes widened as I commanded gently, "Settle, wee yin."

He immediately stilled in my arms.

"That's some trick." Brodan snorted from where he sat on the arm of his sofa. Monroe was curled up on the couch under blankets, resting her head on his thigh as she watched me with her son.

"It's all in the voice," I said, holding out a finger to Lennox.

He grasped onto it and showed me his gums.

"He likes you." Monroe beamed. "He likes Uncle Walker."

"Well, who wouldn't?" I said dryly.

After a few more minutes of holding my "nephew," walking him around the large living room of my friend's home, the doorbell rang. Soon the room was filled with Adairs, and Lennox was slowly passed from aunt to uncle. I could admit only to myself that I'd hoped to see Sloane and was worried when she wasn't there.

Not long after the arrival of their family, I'd left the room to use the downstairs loo and when I came out, Monroe was blocking my way.

I frowned, concerned. "Should you be up?"

She waved off my worried question. "Forget about me for a second. I need a big favor from you."

"All right." I nodded.

"I need you to look out for Sloane."

I stiffened. "Monroe—"

"Last night wasn't a mugging. He didn't go near her purse. She dropped it on the ground and he still attacked her, Walker."

Anger rushed through me. "Hoffman."

"Possibly. She said he was too tall for Hoffman, but you know he'd hire someone to do his dirty work." Roe nibbled on her lip and took a step toward me. "But it might not be Hoffman. I … I can't go into it because it's not my story to tell, but there is someone else who might want to hurt Sloane."

"Who?" I demanded roughly.

Her eyes widened. "I can't tell you. But I need you to promise me you'll watch over her. She won't accept help. I wanted to hire someone to protect her, and she said no because she can't afford it. But she'd accept your help, Walker, if it meant protecting Callie."

"I can't protect either of them if I don't know who I'm protecting them from." Frustration churned inside me. I'd always known, hadn't I, that Sloane was running from something? That the Howards had something to do with it.

"I can't." Monroe scowled, her chin setting stubbornly. "I won't betray her confidence. But maybe she'll tell you. I just need to know you'll look out for her." She ran a shaky hand through her hair. "I'm going to be so exhausted and preoccupied with Lennox, and I don't want her to feel alone. I need to—"

I waved away her worries. "Stop stressing. Look after yourself and your son. I'll look after Sloane and Callie."

It was a dangerous promise. But I knew that I would have gotten involved even if Roe hadn't asked. I couldn't leave Sloane out there unprotected. Even if I also couldn't let myself dwell on the real reasons why.

ELEVEN
SLOANE

Perhaps the last few weeks had finally caught up to me, but when my daughter insisted I take a nap, I fell into a deep sleep.

I'd returned home to the cottage feeling a whole slew of emotions. Excited and overjoyed for Monroe and Brodan that their little boy had arrived safe and healthy into the world. That Monroe was safe and healthy too. Yet, the entire time I'd sat in that hospital waiting room for news of my best friend and her child, fear had slithered its way inside me.

Something had felt off about my so-called mugging. And could it really be coincidence to be attacked twice in one month? Or was it Hoffman exacting a little payback?

It couldn't be anything else.

Or could it?

While I waited for Regan to drop off Callie, I called Flora to explain why I couldn't deliver on this Saturday's cakes. She was perfectly understanding, but I felt awful that I was already letting her down.

Relief, however, soothed me when Callie walked through the door. I hugged her so hard, she teasingly complained.

"I love you," I whispered almost desperately against her hair.

Callie arched her neck to look up at me and grin. "Did seeing Monroe's baby make you mushy, Mom?"

Grinning, I smoothed my hands over her soft cheeks to cup her face. "Can you tell?"

Not even a few minutes later, though, when I stumbled into the sofa while attempting to walk to the kitchen, I found my way barred by my kid. "Mom, you need bed."

"I'm fine." I didn't want to leave her unattended today.

But Callie scowled. "Mom, you look like the walking dead, and you need to take better care of yourself."

"Gee, thanks."

She rolled her eyes. "You know what I mean. Take a nap. I'll be fine. I'm in the middle of a really good book."

Swaying on my feet, I knew I needed rest. "I'll nap if you snuggle with me. Bring your book."

Callie nodded. "I'll snuggle with you."

My kid was the best kid in the world. "Okay, grab your book and head on up. I'll be up in a second."

Thankfully, she didn't argue, and it allowed me to make sure the door and windows were locked without her asking questions. A few minutes later, changed into sweats and a tee, I climbed into bed beside Callie, who sat on top of the duvet reading what looked like a fantasy novel. I must have passed out as soon as my head hit the pillow.

―――――

CALLIE'S VOICE drifted into my consciousness. "She's sleeping, but I'll tell her you called ... Yeah, we're okay ... well, she was up all night."

I blinked out of the dark of sleep, feeling groggy and dry-mouthed. Callie sat up on the bed beside me, holding my phone to her ear. "Who you talking to, baby girl?" I asked, voice rasping.

What time was it?

"Oh, she's awake, Walker." Callie grinned and held out the phone. "It's Walker."

What the hell?

Why was Walker calling me?

Pushing up to sitting, I took the phone and glanced at the clock.

I'd been asleep for eight hours. Crap. Had Callie eaten? "Did you eat?" I asked her as I held the phone to my ear.

"I had a couple of snacks." She shrugged and returned to reading what looked like a new book.

"Sloane?" Walker's deep voice rumbled in my ear. "You there?"

Scrubbing at my face, I grumbled, "Barely."

"Callie said you were sleeping."

"Yeah. It was supposed to be a nap that apparently turned into a whole day of sleeping. Damn it."

"You obviously needed it."

I yawned, feeling like crap. "Right. What's up?" Something occurred to me and I was suddenly alert. "Are Roe and Lennox okay?"

"They're fine," he assured me. "I wanted to let you know that come Monday, I'll be driving you and Callie to school and work. I'll also drive you to Regan's on the days Callie isn't at tae kwon do to collect her, and drop you both off at the cottage. We'll wait to see if there are any more threats to your safety before we consider putting extra security on Callie when she's not with us."

The barrage of information was one of the lengthiest things he'd ever said, and I was entirely confused. "Uh … what? What is going on?" I shoved off my duvet, feeling hot and sweaty and yucky from my day's sleep.

Callie lowered her book, watching me with a frown. "What *is* going on?"

I waved her off to hear Walker as he explained, "The attack last night might have been deliberate, and until we know for sure, I will drive you and Callie wherever you need to go."

Was he nuts? "I can't ask you to do that." I mouthed at Callie to stay put and I hurried down the stairs for privacy while Walker insisted this was the plan. "What about Callie?" I hissed low so she couldn't hear. "How am I supposed to explain you driving us everywhere?"

"Tell her the Hyundai was a loaner. That I'm doing you a favor until you get a new car."

"I'm not leaving myself without transportation. I have a cake to deliver tomorrow to a client in Golspie."

"No, you don't. I'll deliver the cake. You stay put."

I didn't know what annoyed me more, his bossiness or the idea of being trapped in the cottage indefinitely. "I'm not living like that."

"It's just temporary."

A creak on the stairs had me whirling around. Callie stood a few steps up, arms crossed, worry all over her little face. "Mom, what's going on?"

"Callie, I'm talking to Walker. Go back upstairs."

Her expression turned mulish and she stomped down the last few steps. "No. Lewis and I overheard Regan tell Lewis's dad that something happened to you. Does it have something to do with the bruise on your face last month? What's going on?"

Oh. Crap.

I sighed heavily. "Did you hear that?" I asked Walker.

"Aye," he answered grimly.

"Then you know I need to hang up now."

"I'll be by tomorrow morning for the cake." He hung up before I could argue.

Lowering the phone, I stared at my daughter, feeling that terrifying, dizzying sensation I always felt when I wasn't certain what the right thing to do was.

"I'm not a kid anymore. You can tell me."

I smiled sadly. "You are ten, baby girl. That's still a kid. And I want you to stay being a kid for at least another eight years."

She tilted her chin stubbornly. "I know you don't want me to know things after what happened that night with Dad. But you think I don't know when you're upset, and I do. Everyone was weird when you came home with that bruise. And now Walker's calling and arguing with you. What is it?"

My gut churned. "All you need to know is that a bad person tried to hurt me. The key word being *tried*. Okay? Walker and another kind man stopped him before he could."

My daughter's eyes glistened, and her lips trembled. "But you're all right?"

Her fear and upset were exactly why I'd avoided telling her. "I am more than all right." I crossed the room to pull her into my arms, and she burrowed her head against my chest.

After a few minutes of holding her, soothing her, and hoping like hell I hadn't made a mistake in telling her even that paltry amount, Callie pulled back. "So, why is Walker calling you and making you act all weird?"

It was either tell her the truth and freak her out ... or give up my car. "I didn't want to tell you this, but I can't keep the new car. So Walker is going to drive us around for a while until I can find one that's more in my budget."

She narrowed her eyes. "Why would he do that?"

Not wanting her to get the wrong idea, I shrugged. "Because he works for Brodan, and Monroe asked him to make sure you and I are okay. So, Brodan asked Walker to chauffeur us around for a bit." I grinned, like it was no big deal. "Which means we better be cool people to chauffeur around or the poor guy might quit."

Callie flashed me a grin, and I relaxed marginally. "We're cool. Walker likes us. I don't think he'd have said yes to driving us around otherwise."

"Don't go getting all attached to him, you hear," I teased, but I meant every word. I ventured toward the kitchen, hungry. "I don't think Walker will stick around Ardnoch forever."

"Will we?"

I whirled at her quiet question.

"Well?"

"Do you want to?"

She nodded.

Fear of disappointing her rode my shoulders. "You know it was never meant to be permanent here, right? My work visa only lasts five years." The Howards had pulled off getting me a skilled workers' visa ... but I didn't know if we could get that extended. I said as much to Callie.

"But we'll stay another four years, for sure?" she asked.

"If it's what you want."

"I want you to be happy, too, Mom."

I beamed at my daughter. My kid was *the* best. "I'm happy too ... I'll be even happier with some food in my belly. How does mac and cheese and fries sound?"

"Uh, like a promise you better keep."

Laughing, I strolled into the kitchen, forcing myself not to think about Walker or protection or anything scary for a while.

TWELVE

SLOANE

Yesterday Walker showed up at the cottage in the morning to collect the cake and address to deliver it to. He asked what I'd told Callie, and I explained I felt horrible about feeding her the lie about the car. His answer was to ask for the keys, promising to have it removed so she wouldn't get suspicious. The thought of losing transportation tightened my chest, but it was better feeling stranded and reliant on others than telling Callie the truth.

I also handed over a lemon tart, Walker's favorite, as a thank-you to him, which he'd taken with a gruff nod and not much else. With one last piercing look at me, he asked if I was okay, and when I answered yes, he left, reminding me he'd be back in the morning.

And that was how I found myself, the next day, in the passenger seat of his Range Rover with Callie in the back, ready for school.

"You're a little early," I said.

"I like to stop at Flora's for a coffee. Want one?"

I would not say no to Flora's coffee. "Is it Monday?"

The corner of his lip curled up ever so slightly, and he

pulled away, only to slow to a stop less than a minute later outside Flora's.

"Uh, this is a no-parking zone."

He shot me a look. "I'll be quick. What do you want?"

"A latte."

"Callie?" He looked over his shoulder. "You want an orange juice or something?"

She grinned at him. "I'm good, thanks."

Once he was gone, I turned to look at Callie. "You cool with this?"

She nodded, smiling like a Cheshire cat. "Everyone at school thinks he and Mr. Galbraith are like superheroes come to life."

Mr. Galbraith was Arrochar's husband, Mac, and our landlord. He and Walker, both very tall and broad-shouldered, possessed an air of capability and calm mixed with a "you don't want to mess with me, motherfucker" vibe. Very compelling. It did not surprise me that even the kids picked up on that.

"They'll be so jealous Walker's driving me to school every day. A couple of the girls said their moms have a crush on him." She made a face. "He wouldn't like any of them."

I turned back around in my seat, wondering if he'd slept with any of those moms. My already confused mood soured, and I had to force myself to shrug off the feeling.

Just in time for Walker to return. He held the drinks out to me and I took them, watching the way he moved with impressive grace for his size. His seat was pushed back as far as it could go, which was why Callie sat in the middle of the bench seat.

Dragging my eyes off the strong thighs that stretched his black suit pants, I handed him his coffee and he took a sip before settling it in a cup holder.

"Thanks for the latte."

"No problem." He pulled away from the sidewalk.

"Walker, my tae kwon do teacher said I'm a natural," Callie told him as we drove toward school.

Walker glanced at her in the rearview mirror. "Of course, you are."

She beamed. "Will you come watch me at my first grading?"

A grading was when they were tested to move up to the next rank, and from what I gathered was like a whole big event we'd spend at least half a day at. "Uh, I'm sure Walker has other things to do, baby girl." I didn't want her trapping him into saying yes to socializing with us outside of this arrangement.

"I'll go," he replied. "Just tell me when."

I wanted to tell him not to promise her that, but I couldn't help the flare of gratitude that overruled my fear.

As we drove, I sipped at my latte and listened while Callie regaled Walker with the minutiae of her life these past few weeks in an impressively condensed five minutes. He listened patiently, nodding in the right places, and asking her questions, like how she felt when Michael Barr called her a name when she beat his mark on a math test. His lips quirked into a smile when she told him it made her want to beat all his marks from now on.

"Good girl," he murmured, approving, and Callie laughed.

The man was honestly a different guy with my daughter.

We got out of the car when we arrived at the school, Walker at our backs as we strode to meet Regan at the gates. There was a group of moms who were kind of cliquey and always stood together at drop-off. I could feel them watching us, probably wondering why Walker had driven us to school.

We waited for the bell to ring, for the kids to disappear inside, Regan and I engaging in conversation while Walker stood beside us, alert. Regan asked if I was okay, and I assured her I was before we moved on to talk about Monroe and Lennox. I'd chatted with Roe on the phone yesterday, and she seemed good. Tired but good.

Finally, once the kids were inside the school, Walker touched my arm. "Time to go. Regan, you'll call if there are any issues after school or at tae kwon do." It wasn't a question.

"Yes, sir. On it, sir." She tapped two fingers off her forehead.

He scowled at her, and she threw him a cheeky, dimpled smile.

Laughing under my breath, I let Walker lead me back to the SUV, ignoring the heat of his palm that didn't quite touch my back. He opened the passenger side door, and I climbed in.

"She needs to take this more seriously," he grumbled once he was behind the wheel.

"I don't think she's not taking it seriously." I smiled. "I think she was reacting to your bossiness."

Walker threw me a dark look. "Bossiness?"

"Yeah. You didn't ask her. You told her."

"How dare I?" he answered dryly.

"You were in the army, right?" I blurted, my curiosity about him brimming over now that we were alone. "You have military stamped all over you."

Walker didn't look at me as he drove out of Ardnoch toward the estate. "Not army. I was a Royal Marines Commando."

I blinked in surprise that he'd offered this information and also because I was pretty sure that was a special unit. "Aren't those guys, like, elite?"

"Special operations." He nodded. "We're part of the Royal Navy. Amphibious light infantry. Tell me what happened on Friday night."

I wanted to know more about his time in the Royal

Marines, but I knew by his tone that he was done answering questions. So I told him everything, observing him closely to see how he'd respond to the news I'd gone speed dating.

His face didn't move a muscle.

More proof he was not interested in me in that way.

I ignored the burn of disappointment and rejection and waited for Walker to respond to my tale. However, he remained annoyingly silent until we pulled into the staff parking lot behind the castle. Then he switched off the engine and turned to me. "Why are you in Scotland? Who are you running from? Could they have something to do with what happened on Friday?"

My blood ran cold at his out-of-left-field prying. It was scarily on target, and I stiffened. "I don't know what you're talking about." Then I shoved out of the car, furious. Just because he'd decided to stick his nose in to protect us, and I'd decided to let him for Callie's sake, didn't give him the right to know everything about me.

I was halfway across the parking lot when Walker wrapped his hand around my arm and pulled me to a stop. He glowered, holding tight to me as I tilted my chin to meet him glare for glare.

I didn't feel threatened or unsafe.

It was the opposite.

And that annoyed me more.

I yanked my arm out of his hold, and he released me immediately.

"I can't protect you if I don't know who I'm protecting you from." He pinched his lips together.

"This could all be a massive overreaction. You realize that, right?" I shook my head at him, irritated by so many things in my life right now. "I don't need you interrogating me like I'm the bad guy."

"You being evasive tells me there's something going on here."

"Yeah, you're interrogating me!" I threw my hands up in exasperation. "And you didn't even say thank you for the lemon pie yesterday." On that grand and ludicrous announcement, I whirled and marched into the castle.

Thankfully, Walker let me go. I changed into my uniform and told Frannie I'd catch up with her in our first room. A few minutes later, I knocked on Aria's office door and slipped inside.

Aria stared at me, brow furrowed. "Is there a problem?"

"I need you to call your dad," I answered grimly.

THIRTEEN

WALKER

I had a hard time believing that someone as easygoing as Sloane was annoyed because I hadn't verbally shared my thanks for the pie she baked me.

She could be pissed off about a multitude of things. Sloane had reasons. But my instinct told me she was pissed off because I was close to the truth when I asked her who she was running from.

Sloane Harrow was scared of someone.

And that caused a low rage in my gut that set me on edge.

The first person she'd fled to at work was Aria. What were those two women hiding? How did I get Sloane to trust me enough to tell me? The damn woman was a constant source of distraction, but I knew how to compartmentalize, to focus on work when I needed to.

As soon as the end of her shift came around, however, I let Jock know I was leaving. My boss and Lachlan had agreed to the change in my hours so I could protect Sloane.

Lachlan had called me that day, in fact, to let me know he was close to nailing Hoffman to the wall. He'd found two women who were willing to come forward to press charges against him and was working on a third.

Sloane wasn't in the housekeepers' locker room. Only the quiet housekeeper, Sarah McCulloch, was there, sitting on the bench typing on her phone. She glanced up at my entrance and dropped her gaze almost immediately.

Agitated by Sloane's absence, I turned to leave when she spoke up. "Are you looking for Sloane?"

I turned back. Sarah still stared at her phone, giving me her delicate profile. It was the first time I'd heard her voice, I realized. "Aye. Have you seen her?"

She nodded, without turning my way. "She said to tell you she's waiting at your car."

That she wouldn't look at me made me wonder if Sarah was afraid of me. Sometimes people were wary of me because of my size. And I wasn't exactly Mr. Smiley.

It bothered me, especially when it was a woman, but there wasn't a lot I could do about my height or my personality. Besides, from what I'd observed, Sarah seemed shy around almost everyone. "Right. Thanks, Sarah."

She looked up at me, surprise on her face. Shocked I knew her name? *I* was taken aback to notice she was attractive. The woman made a concentrated effort to be invisible, and it worked most of the time. "Y-you're welcome, Mr. Ironside."

"Call me Walker." I gave her a nod and turned to go find Sloane.

Sure enough, she leaned against my Range Rover, texting.

"Callie?" I asked.

Sloane looked up, those gorgeous dark eyes filled with wariness. Now that truly pissed me off. She should know by now she's safe with me. If my prodding this morning annoyed her, that was one thing ... but that it had put her guard up around me was another.

"What?" She stuffed her phone into her back pocket.

"Is Callie texting you?"

"No."

I unlocked the vehicle and Sloane jumped in without another word. Gritting my teeth, I got in beside her and waited for her to say something else.

Nothing.

She clipped her seat belt and stared out the window. I wanted to reach across the distance between us and trace the curve of her jaw. Instead, I turned on the engine and fisted the steering wheel against the urge to touch her. Usually, like her daughter, Sloane filled the silence with her soft voice. She'd tell me about her baking or pepper me with questions. Sloane never seemed bothered by my short answers, seeming to understand where others didn't that it was just the way I was. It wasn't my way of getting people to shut up. Most folks thought it was. That I was rude. It didn't bother me. I didn't have time for most people.

But I had time for Sloane.

Talk to me.

"Who was it?" I blurted, needing her voice to fill the emptiness.

"Huh?" She glanced at me with a frown.

"Who were you texting?" I meant it as a casual question, but it came out almost interrogative.

Sloane hesitated for a second. Then, "It was a guy on a dating app."

Sloane was dating.

It shouldn't bother me. I should consider it a good thing. She was moving on from whatever infatuation she had with me.

And yet the very thought of this faceless fucking guy touching her made me want to knock him senseless.

Or fuck Sloane senseless.

Keeping my face coldly impassive, I nodded as we

approached the gates of the estate. "Have you arranged a date?"

Sloane didn't answer as the guys at the gate let us out with a wave. As soon as we hit the road toward the village, she replied, "No. We've just started talking, but if we had, you're not stopping me from going on a date. I think we're blowing this whole thing out of proportion."

"We're taking precautions. If you'd tell me what you're running from, I'd know what to look out for, and we could plan your safety accordingly."

Silence.

Fuck.

"Sloane ... you can trust me." I glanced at her, and she gave me an apologetic curl of her lips.

"There's nothing. Just Hoffman."

Liar.

Disappointed and pissed off, I didn't speak again as we made our way to her cottage.

We drove in a thick, icy silence that didn't sit right between us, and I slowed as we came onto Castle Street, adhering to the twenty miles per hour speed limit. A quick glance at Sloane told me she was determinedly staring out the passenger window. Her fingers knotted together on her lap, though. Tension radiated from her. I hated it.

A sigh escaped me as I looked to my right as we passed her cottage. I indicated to pull over to park, but something drew my eye to her door.

What the hell?

"Stay in the car," I ordered as I cut the engine.

"Why? What's going on?" Sloane glanced around in fright.

"Just stay there." I got out and shut the door behind me, gently, trying not to freak her out even more. Blood rushed in my ears as I strode toward her front door.

"Fuck." Worry and dread filled me as I observed the surrounding street, searching for a threat.

Then I heard the car door slam, and I turned as Sloane rounded the bonnet. I bit out a curse as she marched toward me. Her eyes flew to the door and she stumbled to a stop.

Those pretty cheeks paled.

And I wanted to kill whoever had nailed a dead rat to her door.

"Is that a ...?" Her hand covered her mouth in shock.

"A rat." Gut churning, I stepped toward her. "So ... who did you rat on?"

Understanding widened her eyes, and her hand dropped. Her lips parted in realization and then pursed with fury. Without answering me, she pulled her phone out of her jeans pocket and, with trembling fingers, swiped at the screen.

A few seconds later, holding it to her ear, she said, "Did you hear from your dad yet?"

Annoyed and impatient that I didn't know whom she was talking to, I waited with my back toward the door, hiding the dead rat from sight.

If it was possible, Sloane's cheeks grew even paler. "He's out?" She ran a shaking hand through her hair. "Where is he? Does he know? ... I need to, Aria ... because there's a dead rat hanging on my front door!"

Aria Howard.

"Okay ... yeah ... please ... thank you. Bye." She hung up. Then shrugged in exhaustion. "If you help me get rid of the rat before Callie comes home from tae kwon do, I'll tell you everything."

I'd help her get rid of the rat without the information, but I needed to know who was trying to scare her. And once I found the perpetrator, I was going to make sure the very thought of terrorizing another woman made them piss themselves with fear of my reprisal.

FOURTEEN
SLOANE

I don't think I'd ever been more grateful to Walker than when he told me to wait inside the cottage while he disposed of the rat. First, he'd taken photographs, then he did his thing. As soon as it was gone, I scrubbed the entrance until the door shone.

One of my neighbors walked by, giving me a weird look as I cleaned. I smiled shakily, not wanting anyone to know the truth and hoping we were the first to see the rat. "Tripped and spilled my Diet Coke all over the door," I lied.

My neighbor gave me an understanding smile and walked on by.

By the time I'd finished washing and disinfecting and getting rid of the dirty sponge and water, Walker returned.

I heard the cottage door open and close as I removed the rubber gloves.

"Just me," Walker called in reassurance.

I hurried out of the kitchen. He stood staring, his vivid eyes searching my face. A powerful rush of longing swept over me. I wanted to run to him, to feel his strong arms around me. To feel safe.

Swallowing back the emotion, I asked, "What did you do with it?"

"Threw it into the woods for another animal to take care of." Walker gestured to the kitchen. "Need to wash my hands."

Our only bathroom was upstairs, so I stepped aside to let him use the kitchen sink. "Go for it."

When he strode past, I briefly closed my eyes against the urge to touch him, to whisper his name and plead with him to hold me. Instead, I watched as he stood at my kitchen sink, looking mammoth in the small room as he scrubbed his hands clean.

An ache spread through my chest, imagining him here because he wanted to be here with me. Not because Brodan had solicited him to protect me.

"Do you want a coffee?" I asked quietly.

"I don't drink coffee after noon," he shared, turning to look at me. "I drink tea."

That little slice of information made me smile, despite the circumstances. "Would you like tea?"

"I'll make it. You sit."

"No. I need something to do." I strode into the kitchen, sharing the space with him, scenting his expensive cologne, feeling the heat of him so close.

What was it about impending danger that made you want to jump the nearest sexiest guy for a little fun-time distraction?

Yeah, keep telling yourself that's all it is.

"Walker?" I asked, my back to him as I opened the cupboard where I kept the tea bags.

"Aye?"

"I'm going to tell you things only a handful of people know." At his silence, I glanced over my shoulder. Walker leaned against the opposite counter, arms crossed over his powerful chest, ankles crossed too. Waiting. Patient. "What's

your background? I'm not asking for super personal information. I just want to know ... how did you become a
bodyguard?"

With a slight exhale of breath, Walker pushed off the
counter and came to my side. I tensed as he reached for my
hands until I realized he was taking the box of tea from me. It
was then I noted how badly my hands trembled.

"It's all right," Walker reassured, eyes on me even as he
began making tea for us both. "I won't let anything happen to
you. Or Callie."

Tears burned my eyes. But I needed to know if that was
true. If he could truly protect us. And I know I had no right to
interrogate a man who offered his services without asking for
payment ... but I was scared.

As if he read all of that in my face, Walker gave me a small
nod as he filled the mugs with hot water. "Tea bag in or out?"

"Out."

A few seconds later, he handed me a hot mug. "Keep that
between your hands. It'll help with the jitters." Then he
gestured with a tip of his head toward the living room and
began speaking as I followed him toward the sofa. "As I told
you, I'm a trained martial artist. I started training in jujitsu at
ten years old. I was the Scottish junior champion at sixteen. At
seventeen, I joined the Royal Marines Commandos. I kept up
jujitsu through my service and still attend a class every week in
Thurso. In that way, I've known self-defense since I was a
child. Yet I consider that training basic compared to what I
learned in the marines.

"I was in for ten years. In the first six, after training in
simulated warfare in extreme conditions, I was deployed to
Afghanistan on operations." He spoke with matter-of-fact-
ness. No emotion. Like he hadn't fought in a freaking war.
"After those operations, I joined 43 Commando Fleet Protection Group. Its primary mission is to prevent unauthorized

access to the UK's nuclear deterrent. We also conducted specialist maritime security tasks throughout the world."

Holy crap. So, he was like ... super commando.

"Four years after I joined 43 Commando, an ex-marine friend recruited me to join his close protection security team in the US. We provided close protection for politicians and celebrities and high-profile businesspeople and their families. I've faced real-time threats to the people under my protection, and no one has ever been hurt or killed on my watch. Brodan hired through the company, but he and I got along, and he needed a permanent bodyguard. I've been his private security for the last six years." He sipped his tea, observing my reaction to all of this. "Sloane, I don't say this out of arrogance. There are very few people as well equipped to protect you as I am."

His confidence, lacking in arrogance, was the sexiest thing ever. It was shocking that I felt that little twist of need low in my belly when I was in the middle of a crisis. But there I was. All turned on by Walker's ... well, by everything that was Walker.

"So, you're a badass." I grinned, trying to free myself of the sexual tension I hoped he couldn't sense.

Walker's stony expression cracked a little. "I'm the biggest fucking badass out there, and anyone who thinks they can terrorize you is going to wish they were dead by the time I'm done with them."

It took everything within me not to jump him. To throw myself in his arms and start kissing that hard mouth into softness. I knew it wasn't particularly modern of me to get turned on by such overt masculinity, but I was a woman and he was *all* man ... and I wanted to taste what it was like to be with him.

Suddenly, in that moment, I wondered why I didn't go for it.

My body reacted to Walker like it had never reacted to

anyone, ever. Just because Walker was Mr. Commitment-Phobe didn't mean I shouldn't make a move on the guy. Why pass up the chance at what I was guessing would be incredible sex, because that's all it would ever be? That was more than most people got! Did I really want to go through my entire life not knowing what it was like to have sex with a man who turned me on like Walker did? Just because it would be temporary?

No. I didn't.

With rats being pinned to my door and whatnot, I actually didn't have time for a relationship.

I did have time for Walker to fuck the tension out of me.

Yup. I was going to do it.

I was going to seduce Walker Ironside into a casual sex arrangement.

His eyes narrowed. "You look flushed. Are you okay?"

Flushing even deeper, I squirmed in my seat. *Merely having inappropriate revelations in the middle of a threat to my life.* I semi-lied to cover my thoughts. "I'm preparing myself to tell you about my past, and, uh, I'm not proud of some of it."

Walker's expression softened ever so slightly. "Sloane, we all have shit in our past we're not proud of. I don't judge."

I believed him. My earlier thoughts of seduction dissipated under the reality of the moment, and my hand trembled as I took a sip of tea. Embarrassed by my shaking, I lowered the mug to the coffee table and squeezed my hands between my thighs. Staring straight ahead, feeling his probing gaze on my cheek, I took a shuddering breath. "I was sixteen when I got pregnant with Callie. Seventeen when I had her. I was only a kid. I was a rich kid in Beverly Hills, pissed off at Dearest Daddy for marrying a bitch who wanted to pretend like I didn't exist."

"Where was your mother?"

I looked at Walker. "She died. I was eight. She ... scared me a little. Her moods were erratic, and I couldn't trust her. One day she'd be all over me like I was the greatest thing that ever happened to her, and the next my dad would find her screaming at me to stay away from her, that I'd ruined her life. She's the reason I'm claustrophobic. She locked me in a closet for five hours."

"Fucking hell," Walker muttered.

I smirked sadly. "It was like another life, it was such a small part of mine. She died of an accidental overdose."

"I'm sorry."

"I have a lot of guilt about it." I shrugged, my gut churning at the thought. "Because things were better once she was gone. Dad was—is—a big-time lawyer to the stars. Busy a lot. We threw parties at our house. Celebrity never fazed me because of it. Even though he was away often, I never felt unloved. He was involved in every part of my life. Wanted to hear about everything, from stupid, petty arguments with friends to my academics." Pain twisted in my chest. "He was my everything. And I wanted to make him proud. I worked hard at school, I did extracurricular stuff, athletics. I did it all. Then when I was fifteen, he met my stepmom, Perry. She's half his age, and I thought she was a gold-digger." I looked at Walker for his reaction.

He nodded subtly for me to continue.

No judgment.

"Dad couldn't see it. He was head over heels. And when I tried to talk to him about my day or drama with friends, he didn't have time anymore. It felt like I was old news. I was hurt." Tears of frustration at my past self stung my eyes. "I acted like a stupid kid and started clubbing with my friends, getting drunk and high, having sex before I was emotionally ready. It pissed him off. But at least that was attention. Then I met Nathan."

I turned to Walker with disdain for Nathan, for myself,

blazing in my eyes. Walker tensed ever so slightly. "He's Callie's father. He was also a drug dealer. Told you I was an idiot."

"You were a teenager. Teens aren't exactly known for their rational thinking."

I chuckled humorlessly at that. "Oh no, they are not. Anyway, I got pregnant, and my father insisted I either have an abortion or give her up for adoption."

"And you didn't want to do either?"

I shook my head. "It might have been the smart thing to do. I mean, I was a kid myself, and kids shouldn't be raising kids. But I was alone and lonely." A tear slipped down my cheek, and I swiped it away. "I wanted someone to love and someone who would love me back. So I wanted to keep my baby. And my father kicked me out. I think he thought it would scare me into giving her up."

Walker sucked in a breath.

"You have to understand ... my dad came from nothing. His parents were dirt poor and he worked his ass off to get where he is. The idea of his daughter following a path he'd watched so many girls he grew up with go down because they didn't have the same opportunities that I did, it made him so angry. He'd given me everything he never had, and to him, I was throwing it all away.

"But I couldn't give Callie up. I had no one to turn to but Nathan. He promised to look after us. At first, I was naive enough to believe that it might work out. Callie came along and she became my universe. Everything I have done in my life since has been in service to that little girl."

To my shock, Walker reached for me, squeezing my arm in comfort. Reassurance. When I looked into his face, I thought I even saw admiration.

It steeled me enough to tell the rest of my story. "Nathan started getting in deeper with this gang that chopped cars and dealt drugs. He worked his way up the ranks. And he grew more abusive. So much so that I got up the nerve to leave him when Callie was a toddler."

Walker released my arm and asked, "How did he feel about that?"

"Oh, not good." I sighed. "In Nathan's mind, Callie and I belong to him."

"Belong, not belong*ed*?"

I grimaced but continued, "He got too busy after a while to keep up his threats to drag us back. He actually let us get on with our lives and dropped off money now and then. I took it," I admitted, ashamed, "even knowing where it came from. But I was a single mom with only a high school education."

"You did what you had to," Walker assured me gruffly.

That shame eased a bit. "I did," I agreed. "Nathan ... I tried dating when Callie was five, and he almost killed the guy."

At that, Walker straightened in his seat. Alert. Understanding where this story was going, no doubt.

"So, I didn't date again. I tried to get on with my life. We found a nice enough apartment that I could barely afford, and our neighbor, Juanita, watched Callie while I worked this receptionist job I'd lied my way into. Someone there had it out for me, and I got fired on the same day I got an eviction notice on my door. I was out of options. Callie would not be homeless under my watch."

"You went to Nathan?"

I nodded. "Last year. A few months before we came here. An old friend told me I could find Nathan at a house party. I went there to ask him for money, but I found him in a room with a young woman. When he asked her to leave, she got offended by my presence and she started arguing with him. He got violent fast. He was ... he was going to rape her right in front of me."

Anger hardened every inch of Walker's expression.

"He had a gun. I couldn't ... he'd tried with me, and I got away ... and I couldn't let that happen to this girl. I just couldn't. We fought ..." I shook as the memory played vividly in my mind. "And she got hold of the gun and accidentally shot me." Reaching for the sleeve of my shirt, I pushed it up and showed Walker the scar on my upper left arm. The memory of the pain flared, like searing nerve pain. A burn that was hard to describe.

Walker reached out, as if his hand had a mind of its own, his thumb sweeping gently across the scar. Goose bumps prickled in the wake of his touch. His eyes flew to mine, and my breath caught at the fierceness of his expression.

It took me a second to get my breath back, and even as I spoke, my voice was huskier. "Nathan has ... had a very twisted way of caring about me. I mattered to him, but only because he saw me as something he owned. So when he saw me shot, he wrestled the gun off her and he came to me." I patted the air beside me. "He left the gun at my side. Then he turned to her and he beat her. And beat her. And beat her. I knew, in here"—I punched my gut—"that he would not stop ... so I reached for the gun, and I shot him."

"Did you kill him?" Walker asked bluntly.

I gave him a quick swipe of my head. "Something very few people know about me is that my dad liked guns. Shooting them, I mean. It wasn't an interest we'd shared, but because I loved him and wanted his time and attention, I'd visited the gun range with him every month from the age of eight to fifteen. I could have shot competitively if I'd wanted. I have excellent aim. I shot to maim, not kill."

Walker raised an eyebrow. "I'm glad to hear it. About the excellent aim, I mean."

My lips twitched despite myself. "Anyway, Nathan had locked us in this bedroom at the back of the house. There were French doors going into the garden. The girl was a mess.

Nathan's thug friends were hammering on the door after hearing the second shot. And I guess adrenaline kicked in because I got my ass up, had the presence of mind to wipe down the gun, and I somehow got the girl to her feet and we escaped out the back door." My heart raced as if I was experiencing it all over again. "It felt like hours running through the neighborhood. She kept wanting to pass out, and I wasn't doing much better with a bullet in my arm."

Tears choked my throat. "The worst part was Callie. My whole life, I wanted to protect her from who her dad really was, and then I came tumbling into our apartment, shot, with a girl who was beaten to a pulp." I swiped at my tears. "Callie was so scared. I brought that into her life."

"No," Walker bit out angrily. "Her father did. Do not take that on. You saved that girl's life, and I'm sure Callie is proud of you."

"She was nine years old, Walker," I whispered. "She shouldn't have to be proud of me for something like that at nine years old. I never wanted her to experience being scared as a kid the way I was scared."

"You can't protect her from everything. You will drive yourself crazy trying. Sloane ... you are the best mum I've ever met."

I smiled tearfully at his words and tried to ease the tension. "I think Regan takes that award. I swear the woman has the ability to split herself in two."

Walker didn't smile at my joke. He pressed, "What happened next?"

"The girl"—I wiped my hands over my cheeks as I held Walker's gaze—"she was Allegra Howard."

Understanding dawned. "Wesley Howard's daughter. Aria's sister."

I nodded. "Aria's younger sister. She'd fallen in with the wrong crowd at school. She was only seventeen, but she'd developed a drug habit. That's why she was with Nathan. Anyway, Juanita was insisting we call the police and an ambulance, and I didn't know what the fuck to do because I'd shot Nathan. But Allegra came to and explained who she was, and she called her father. Wesley showed up with his security team, and he took care of everything." I huffed. "Money and power take care of everything. And he was grateful. So was Allegra. They paid my medical bills, and they got to Nathan. Wesley paid for his medical bills—even though he wanted to kill him —in exchange for his silence. They didn't want this splashed across the news about Allegra. They wanted to move on.

"But they also knew from Nathan's threats that I wouldn't be safe. Aria had taken the job at Ardnoch and offered me a place here. I jumped at the chance. We'd only just arrived when Nathan went back on his word. He started blackmailing the Howards for more money. I told them which clubs he dealt at and helped them set him up. He was arrested for possession, and the police weren't interested in his story about the Howards. Since it was not his first time being arrested for possession, Nathan got eighteen months." I sighed shakily. "But Aria just told me he's out early."

"And he knows you helped them put him away." Walker abruptly stood up. "We need to run a check on his passport to see if he's in the country." He pulled out his cell. "I need his full name and date of birth."

I didn't know what I'd expected after telling him a story I'd told so few people. In fact, the only people who knew about it were the Howards and Monroe. Now Walker. Who barely reacted and went straight into business mode.

Trying not to be hurt or disappointed by that, I stood and rifled through a drawer in the side table for paper and a pen. I was scribbling down Nate's full name and date of birth when I felt the heat of Walker at my back.

I glanced over my shoulder and grew still. The intensity

had returned to his eyes. Was it tenderness or awe or understanding or compassion ... or was it all of that? Did it matter? Walker Ironside looked at me like I was worth something, and it should frighten me how much his opinion mattered.

"Callie is the luckiest wee girl in the world," Walker uttered gruffly, "to have a mum like you. You're a warrior, Sloane. Never doubt it."

FIFTEEN
SLOANE

There was relief in confessing my story to Walker. To have him at my back. To have Monroe and alongside her, Brodan. For the first time, I felt like Callie and I might make it through whatever crap Nathan threw our way. It was selfish, but I was also relieved to hand over the burden of watching my back to Walker. To let him look into Nathan. To trust him to protect me and my daughter.

My burden was to keep it from Callie. I didn't want her to know unless it was absolutely necessary, and I didn't think, right now, there was any need to tell her that her dad might be tormenting me.

Instead, I could shove the fear to the back of my mind and concentrate on living my life. Yes, Callie was tailed by a member of the Ardnoch security team whenever she wasn't with Walker and me, and Walker was my constant companion these days ... but I wasn't really complaining about the latter.

I'd made up my mind about Walker Ironside and, for once, I wanted to be young, free, and a little selfish.

I wanted Walker in my bed, and I was determined to make that happen.

These feelings I had for him, this sexual chemistry I now knew had to go both ways because of its intensity, was the best distraction from the scary possibility that Nathan was back in our lives.

Callie was happy and oblivious.

We were protected.

Nothing else had happened since the rat.

Life was moving along as well as it could with this hovering over me.

It was time to take what I wanted.

When my mind wasn't on Callie or my baking or the thought of what Walker might discover about Nathan, I was thinking about how to seduce my bodyguard.

Thus, I was distracted. But apparently, I was making it obvious because Frannie complained as we walked down the halls toward the staff elevator. "All my jokes are falling on deaf ears. Where are you this week, lass, because you're certainly not here?"

I opened my mouth to respond with a vague answer but was interrupted.

"Sloane."

We turned to see Aria climbing the stairs onto our floor, her green eyes fixed on me. "Frannie, you can go on. I need a word with Sloane."

My coworker nodded and pushed our cart onto the elevator as I turned fully to face Aria.

She gave me a small smile and waited for the doors to close on Frannie before speaking.

"A member complained of a leaky faucet in the bathroom of a suite, so I'm on my way to check it out."

"Is that your job?"

"No. But maintenance is denying said leak, so management"—she gestured to herself—"has been dragged into it. Anyway, how are you? I spoke to Mr. Ironside, and I know he's looking into Andros, but you should know my father will be too. He wants nothing coming out about Allegra."

"Of course. He's not ... upset that Walker's looking into things, is he?"

Aria shook her head. "He's glad someone is looking out for you. As am I."

"Thank you."

"I know it's none of my business, but are you two ...?"

I gave her a rueful smile and shook my head. *Not for want of trying.* It had been a week since I told Walker my story. I'd spent any chance I had with him making it clear I was his for the taking. Touching him whenever the opportunity arose. Bringing him coffee at work, tea in the afternoons. And, as always, showering him with baked goods.

And nothing.

Nada.

Aria gave me a small, knowing smile. "I can see he might be a tough nut to crack."

"The toughest. But I imagine someone might have fun trying."

She laughed loudly, and I was a little surprised by her amusement. Aria was usually so contained.

"Well, wonders never cease," a voice cut through our moment.

Aria turned as I looked past her to see North Hunter striding up the stairs toward us. The Scottish actor hadn't been around since my encounter with Hoffman, and this was the first time I'd seen him since.

His gaze fixed on Aria as he came to a stop beside her. "I didn't know you could crack a smile, never mind laugh."

Aria shocked me by sneering at the member. "Oh. You're back. Yippee for us."

I covered a snort, pressing my lips together tightly to smother it.

North Hunter had dark blond hair and intense, light gray eyes that could pierce right through you. He was an actor mostly known for playing a serial killer in a huge thriller drama that won a ton of awards. But before that, he'd been typecast as the cocky, playboy Scot in more lighthearted movies because he was freaking gorgeous. His intensity, however, suited serious acting better.

Right now, all of his smolder focused on Aria. "I informed you I was arriving."

"I must have bleached that information from my brain in the hopes it wasn't true."

What on earth?

He narrowed his eyes. "Aren't you supposed to be hospitable as the hospitality manager?"

"Aren't you supposed to be charming as a Scot?"

North flashed her a wicked smile. "I can be charming if motivated."

"You mean, if someone's paying you?"

His smile dropped, and he glowered at her.

Aria glowered right back.

Tension so thick sparked between them, I felt like a spare. What had happened between them to cause such sizzling dislike?

I cleared my throat, and North seemed reluctant to drag his eyes off Aria's face. Recognition lit them. "Sloane ... right?"

"Right."

He straightened, his brow furrowed. "How are you doing?"

"Much better. I'm actually glad that I ran into you, Mr. Hunter. I never got a chance to thank you."

"It was my pleasure." There was an attractive growl to his words. "I hope Lachlan nails Hoffman's balls to the wall."

"And then skins him alive," Aria muttered.

North cut her a look. "Bloodthirsty wee thing, aren't you?"

"I've never been called 'wee' in my life, Mr. Hunter, and we both know it." She looked at me. "Keep me posted, and I'll do the same," she said, referring to Nathan.

I nodded. "I will."

Then she brushed past North without another word.

The actor turned his head to watch her go, and, if I was not mistaken, his eyes were on her curvy ass. When Aria disappeared, he looked back at me. "She's a tough nut to crack."

I tried not to laugh at him using the same phrase Aria had used regarding Walker.

ANTICIPATION FLUTTERED in my belly as I strode out of the staff entrance toward Walker's SUV. I'd started paying attention to what I was wearing on trips back and forth to work and taking my hair out of its ponytail once my shift was over.

Today I wore yoga pants that did excellent things for my butt and a sweater that hung off one shoulder. I'd fluffed out my hair before leaving the staff room and pinched my cheeks to add a flush of color.

Walker leaned against the Range Rover, arms crossed, long legs crossed at the ankle, and for the millionth time since we met, I longed to climb that man.

I didn't know why Walker was so against my advances. My instinct told me it was because he was allergic to commitment and he thought I wanted more. I was trying to show him through my actions that I didn't.

Grinning as I approached him, I watched his eyes flicker down my body and back up again. A thrill ran through me at the slight heat that filled his expression before he banked it. I'd noticed a shift in Walker. There were times I caught him looking at me in a way a man looked at a woman he wanted. His eyes would linger on my breasts or my mouth.

Yup, I was pretty sure he wanted me too. I hadn't been certain before, but now I was.

"Good day?" I asked with cheer as he pushed off the vehicle.

"Usual. You?"

I nodded as he opened the passenger door for me like a gentleman. "Thanks."

Once he was in the driver's seat, I told him about the encounter with North. "It was good to finally say thank you. He and Aria seem to have issues, though. Do you know what that's about?"

Walker shook his head. "No clue. He seems like a decent guy. He offered me a job."

My heart practically stopped. "Oh?"

"I turned it down. I like it in Ardnoch."

More relief than was healthy flooded me.

I reached over and placed a hand on his thigh. "Good. We'd miss you around here."

Walker glanced down at my hand as I slowly removed it ... but he didn't respond.

Stubborn, stubborn man.

"How's Callie's tae kwon do classes coming along?" he asked instead.

"Good. She's still loving it." I pulled down the mirror above my head as I stared at my roots. I had dark blond hair with lighter blond highlights, and they were growing out on me. "My hair is not. I'm using what extra I have, including my salon money, on the classes. Does it look bad?"

Walker shot me a quick glance. "You look fine. I told you I'd mentor her."

I look *fine.*

Ugh.

"We're good. But thanks. Better my hair than Callie's ability to defend herself. Plus, she's getting extreme enjoyment from whooping Lewis's butt."

Walker's lips twitched.

I wanted to kiss those lips until we couldn't breathe.

"Do you want to come in for tea before I go see Monroe and Lennox?" I asked a little while later as we drove onto Castle Street.

"I have to get back to the estate." He frowned. "Is Jamie taking you to see them?"

"Brodan's picking me up in an hour. He cleared it with Jamie," I explained, trying not to be disappointed by Walker's rejection. "I haven't seen Roe in a while, and I'm feeling like a terrible friend."

"You're not a terrible friend. Is Jamie watching you until then?"

"I'll be fine for an hour," I insisted as we slowed to a stop outside the cottage.

Walker gave me a cool look as he switched off the engine. "I'll call Jamie to come watch over you. Is Brodan bringing you home?"

"Yeah. We'll collect Callie from Regan's after dinner."

He nodded and then stared at me. Wanting me out of his SUV.

As anyone could see, my seduction of this stubborn Scot was going *so* well.

Smiling through my frustration, I leaned across the console and pressed a quick kiss to Walker's cheek. "Thanks for watching over us." Then I slipped from the car before he could scowl me out of it.

Less than an hour later, I heard a car pull up and went to check if it was Brodan. When I opened the door, I saw not only Brodan but Walker driving away from a parking spot across the street.

He'd sat outside, watching the cottage, protecting me from a distance, rather than join me for tea.

Damn the man.

Maybe it was time to give up.

Crushing disappointment followed me to the passenger side of Brodan's SUV.

AFTER I'D GOTTEN my fill of baby cuddles with Lennox, Brodan took his son from me. "I'll put him down for a bit. Let you two ladies catch up."

I reluctantly released the warm bundle of adorableness as Monroe stared at her husband and son with such love and tenderness, it made my chest ache.

"Would you want another one?" Roe asked as she watched me watch Brodan climb the impressive staircase in the center of their living space.

Their house was spectacular, much like the rest of the Adairs. I'd been in all but the youngest brother Arran's, and Brodan and Roe's had a splash of extra that made your breath catch. There was a lot of glass to capture the views of the North Sea beyond their windows. Their kitchen was a kitchen of dreams—lots of counter space, a huge island, a farmhouse sink, an Aga range, and the biggest integrated fridge and freezer I'd ever seen. The space had been designed with Roe's more traditional tastes in mind. The whole place was a wonderful, eclectic mix of modern and traditional. It amazed me that Brodan had pulled off the build so quickly, in time for Lennox's arrival.

"Hmm?" I turned to Roe.

"I asked if you'd want another one. Another baby?" She

eyed me thoughtfully, and I noted the dark circles under her eyes. She was also a little pale. But I knew that was because Lennox wasn't sleeping very well. Callie had been the same. I didn't get a full night's sleep until she was about two years old, and even then, those nights were sporadic until she was around four.

"It would be nice to do it all over again as an actual grown-up," I said with a wry smile. "But not right now. I'd have to find the right guy first, too, you know."

"Haven't you?" Roe gave me a knowing smile.

I rolled my eyes. "Walker Ironside is not the right guy. He's just a guy I want to climb like a tree and do very wicked things to."

My friend chuckled. "Well, why haven't you?"

"Oh, I've been trying," I insisted, leaning forward in my chair. "This past week I have been putting it out there that I want him. And I think he finds me attractive—"

"Of course he does."

I smiled at her loyal, quick answer. "But I think maybe he must think I would want commitment."

"And you definitely don't want commitment?"

"I want ... would it be awful if I said I just want an escape right now?"

"An escape?"

"Something exciting and thrilling that isn't serious. Two people taking what they want from each other. Roe ... I haven't had sex in five years."

She nodded in sympathy. "Been there. Trust me. I know that dry spell, and it is not fun."

"Right? The last guy I had sex with, it was in his car on a date—before Nathan threatened to kill him—and it was quick and satisfactory, but not much else. I ... I have never been as attracted to someone as I am to Walker, and ... I don't want to miss the chance at great sex. I'll take it without the relationship stuff. And if I were to develop feelings, I'd stop."

"You seem pretty certain. Why not go for it?"

I chuckled unhappily. "Didn't you hear me? I've been trying. I've been touching him and batting my freaking eyelashes at him. The man is immune. He would rather sit in his car watching my cottage than have sex with me." With a disappointed sigh, I flopped back in the oversized armchair. "I think it's time to give up. I'm ... I'm making him uncomfortable, and if it was the other way around, you'd call that sexual harassment."

"Then tell him the truth." Brodan's voice broke through the living room, startling me so much, I jumped in my seat.

"Brodan," Monroe huffed. "Were you listening?"

He snorted as he took the last of the stairs down. "You weren't exactly whispering, my love, and Lennox's room is at the top of the stairs." Brodan strolled to Monroe's seat and sat on the edge to slide his arm along her shoulders. His gaze fixed on me. "Might want to turn the volume down if you'd like private girl-talk time."

My cheeks flushed as my heart raced a little. "You heard all that?"

He grinned boyishly. "Almost every word."

"Oh, God.

"Brodan." Roe slapped his thigh gently. "Stop it."

"I found the whole thing very enlightening. So would Walker."

"Brodan."

"No, no, hear me out." He held up a hand, looking at me. "Sloane ... just tell him."

My pulse stuttered. "Tell him ...?"

"Walker does nothing but a casual one-night stand, maybe the occasional one-month stand. He probably thinks that you, with your whole situation and being a single mum, are looking for serious. That's why he's ignoring your come-ons."

My come-ons. Ugh. "Right."

"But if you lay it out for him that you want to use his body for your own pleasure, I'm sure that will do the trick."

I glowered at him. "Don't say it like that."

"What? Like the truth?" He chuckled. "Don't worry, sweetheart. No man has ever complained about a gorgeous woman wanting to use his body for pleasure." His grin softened to a tender smile as he looked down at his wife. "Unless he's in love with her, of course."

Roe's lips twitched as she shook her head at his flirtation. A strange mix of delight and longing scored through me at the way Brodan gazed at Monroe. One day, I wanted a man to look at me like that.

For now, I'd take multiple orgasms with Walker Ironside. "So, put it out there, huh? You really think that will work?" If anyone would know, it would be Walker's best friend, right?

Brodan looked back at me. "Oh, aye. It'll definitely work."

Sixteen
WALKER

I was agitated.

Taking a day off from guarding Sloane, it agitated me.

There had been times in the past with Brodan that I'd double- and triple-checked that the bodyguards replacing me temporarily on my days and holidays off were the absolute best. But it had never disgruntled me to let someone take over protecting him.

I drove back toward my bungalow after visiting Bro, Monroe, and Lennox. I had seen little of them these past few weeks as I guarded Sloane and upped their protection.

As for Sloane, she seemed fairly relaxed after telling me her story. I'd kept my finger on the pulse of her mood, and she was dealing with the stress well. Apparently, she was used to it at this point. She'd dealt with a lot in the past, but she was a fighter. I admired her even more now after hearing it.

And I'd love some time alone in a room with her ex, Nathan Andros, to teach him a fucking lesson. Hoffman too. Lachlan was making headway with Hoffman. It looked like there were several victims willing to band together to take him down, with Lachlan's help. Lachlan had done something similar in the past to another actor, and he was still rotting in prison for his crimes. It assured me knowing my boss would take care of Hoffman.

That left me to deal with Andros. I'd had my contacts run a check on Andros's passport, and the prick didn't have one. We'd also hired a PI in LA to follow him, but in the two weeks since, the PI hadn't been able to obtain security images of Nathan. That made me uneasy because it probably meant he wasn't in LA, but there was no history of him leaving the state, let alone the country.

Exceptional falsified passports cost upward of $15,000, and Andros didn't have that kind of money in his accounts. But that didn't mean he didn't have a stash of cash somewhere. The question was whether he'd be willing to drop that kind of money to get revenge against Sloane. Usually I'd order a lock on his mobile phone so we could locate him through that, but Andros must use burners because of the nature of his job.

We were blind, and I didn't like it. It meant keeping men on Sloane and Callie indefinitely until we could locate the fucker.

And I was agitated when that man wasn't me.

That was a warning. Proof that I should definitely take a day off from guarding Sloane.

Jamie, a guard at the estate, was on Sloane and Callie duty today. Sloane and I needed some distance.

She'd started touching me casually again in that way a woman did when they're interested. I couldn't react to it without leading her on. And ignoring it was a test of my bloody willpower.

Here I was, my day off, and I was still thinking about the woman.

I needed to go home, crack open a beer, and stick on an NFL game. I was behind on the season. Watch that. Relax.

Not think about the sexy, too-young-for-me, single mum who was off-limits.

There you go, thinking about her again, you fuck, I growled under my breath as I swung my SUV onto my street. The black Range Rover sitting outside my bungalow alerted me.

That was one of the estate fleet.

I drove past it and up onto my drive and as I jumped out of my own Rover, Sloane got out of the passenger side of the other. Jamie was in the driver's seat.

Tensing, I watched as she strolled toward me in a summer dress, cardigan, and ankle boots. She wore that glamorous smile that did things to me. There was a Tupperware box in her hands. And the dress was low cut, I noted as she neared me.

What the hell was she doing here?

"Everything okay?" I bit out more abruptly than I meant.

Sloane blinked, startled at my bark. "Uh, yeah. You okay?"

I gave her a lift of my chin.

She grinned at that for some reason and moved toward me until only the Tupperware was between us. Her perfume carried toward me on the cool breeze. My fist tightened around my car keys, the metal biting into my palm.

"Callie is with Lewis today—don't worry, so are three of the Adair men, so she is perfectly safe. And I thought I could pay you back since you won't let me pay any other way." She started walking backward toward my house, the curve of her breasts trembling slightly with the movement.

Images of her tied to my bed while I fucked her filled my mind, but I quickly shut them down. "How so?" I choked out, marching toward where she now waited by my door.

"Well, you're a bachelor, so I'm assuming your place needs cleaning. I'm a professional. Plus, I brought a collection of baked treats for your eating pleasure."

Eating pleasure.

What a choice of words.

Steeling myself, I unlocked the door and gestured for her to go inside. "I think you'll find I don't need your cleaning services." *But I'll eat you for pleasure.*

Groaning inwardly at the escaped thought, I ran a hand over my hair and watched her as she strolled through the large, tidy front hall into the even tidier living room. Following her, I tried not to like the adorable look of consternation on her face as her gaze swept over the place.

"It's clean and tidy. Like ... really."

When I realized I was going to be staying in Ardnoch indefinitely, I decided against pissing my money away on rent. The property market here made buying the wiser decision. I'd bought the bungalow from a couple who'd renovated it. There was no trace of its 1960s origins. The walls were a light gray, the flooring hardwood, my sofa a comfortable leather corner unit, my furniture choices in a darker gray wood.

Sloane made a small huffing noise and wandered through the living room and into the adjoining kitchen. The rooms had once been separated by large doors, but the couple had removed them and widened the wall opening so the living spaces felt like one. The kitchen was modern with flush cupboards in a gray so dark, they almost looked black. There was a contrasting island in white quartz with waterfall edges, and the flooring tile was white and gray. Modern steel lighting hung above the island.

I liked to cook, so I bought the house because of the kitchen.

"Wow." Sloane spun around to face me. "This is gorgeous."

Aye, she could bake many a cake in here.

"And clean." She wrinkled her nose. "Your house is so clean."

My lips twitched at her disgruntlement. "I have a house-keeper. And I like things tidy. Ex-bootneck," I reminded her.

"Bootneck?"

"Marine."

"Ah." She nodded in understanding. And then smiled that gorgeous smile again as she lifted the Tupperware. I was relieved to see her smiling more and more these days. As if telling me about her past had lifted some of the burden. "We can still indulge together. I've got some of your favorites in here."

Shit.

She laid the box down on the island and reached out to touch my arm. "Where are your plates?" Her fingers lingered for a few seconds too long, brushing my bare forearm.

I knew what she wanted. Where this would go. The problem was, she was far too tempting for my peace of mind. So I did the only thing I could think of to get her out of my house. "I actually have *company* coming over."

Despite my emphasis on the word *company*, she took the top off the Tupperware to reveal a collection of cakes and pastries. The woman was going to be the death of me in more ways than one. "There's plenty here. Who's coming over?"

Really? "A woman, Sloane. I have a woman coming over."

She tensed, then looked up at me with those velvety eyes a man could drown in. She searched mine, and I tensed as she didn't react at all like I'd expected.

In fact, she shocked the hell out of me.

"What if I suggested you cancel on her?"

My blood heated at the huskiness in her voice, at the invitation in her eyes. "Sloane ..."

She turned fully toward me, her gaze moving down my body and back up again in a way no man could misinterpret. "Callie won't be home until this evening. I'm yours all afternoon. If you want."

I wanted.

I really, really fucking wanted.

"It's not a good idea," I practically snarled, turning on my heel and striding back into the living room.

She followed. "Why?"

Jesus, woman!

I admired her gumption, but she was killing me. Turning to face her, I replied, as gently as I was able, "Because I'm not interested in a relationship, and anything less with you would be too complicated."

"But—"

"Sloane. Don't."

She was silent a moment, searching my face as if for answers. Then she shrugged, her cardigan falling off her shoulder with the movement, baring perfect olive skin. "Do you not find me attractive?"

No, I'm just a thirty-eight-year-old man fighting a hard-on like a fucking teenager because your cardigan fell off your shoulder. I scrubbed a hand down my face, gritting my teeth. "It's not that."

The cruel woman took a step closer. "I'm not looking for serious, Walker."

Aye, all women said that. Look at Chloe. "It's too complicated. We're friends. And you're too young for me."

Her cheeks flushed. "I'm twenty-seven this year. I have a child. I'm not exactly a baby."

"We're friends," I repeated sternly. "So drop it."

Hurt flashed across her face, and it punched me in the gut.

"I'm sorry if this was ... Sorry for bothering you." Sloane suddenly bolted past me.

Fuck. I should let her go.

My front door opened.

"Sloane." I hurried after her, only to find her halted on my front walk, staring at the space where the Range Rover had been. Jamie had left. Obviously, he thought I had her.

"Just so typical," Sloane muttered under her breath and started marching down my path toward the street.

"Where the hell do you think you're going?" I went after her, my long strides eating up the distance between us.

"I can walk," she threw over her shoulder. Her hair blew back from her face in the chilly breeze. Dark clouds above signaled rain.

"You are not walking." I caught up to her and gently took hold of her biceps. Sloane tugged a little as she turned to face me. She wouldn't look me in the eye.

Goddamn it.

"Get in the car. I'll take you back to the cottage, and we'll phone Jamie."

She shrugged out of my hold. "What about your booty call?"

I'd already forgotten my lie. So I didn't answer. I just gestured to the car and waited for her to get in it.

SEVENTEEN
SLOANE

A woman should admit defeat when rejected by the man she wanted.

I flicked a hurt look at him as we drove through the village back to my cottage. The day had turned dreary like my mood. Drizzle speckled the windshield and clouds above had darkened the interior of the SUV.

Walker hadn't called Jamie yet.

Brodan had been so sure Walker would say yes that I hadn't expected this to backfire. Didn't Walker believe me when I said I wanted it to be casual? Was that the issue? Because I'd caught him looking at my breasts several times in the past half hour. Walker wanted me. Right?

The SUV pulled up outside my empty cottage.

Despondency threatened, but determination edged it out.

One last shot. That's how much I wanted the brooding bastard.

"I really meant it." I stared into those aquamarine eyes with resolve. "I don't want anything serious from you, and I'm not asking for a commitment. Just sex."

The muscle in Walker's jaw flexed, and it was a few lengthy

seconds before he replied, "I'm not crossing that line with you."

"Then give me a real reason why."

His eyes flashed with frustration. "Because I'm not ... I don't do sweet and gentle, Sloane. I *fuck*. And I doubt, somehow, even if you say you only want casual, that you're looking for what I'd give you."

Hurt, worse than his rejection, scored through me. Was that how he saw me? As a tepid, lights-off, under the covers, single mom who needed to be gently made love to? But those other women ... oh, he'd *fuck* them.

I felt not rejection, but indignation. He might find me attractive ... but Walker didn't see me as a truly sexual woman. He didn't see me, period.

I scoffed, the sound bitter even to my ears. "You don't know a thing about women, do you, Walker?" It was a rhetorical question.

But he looked annoyed. And confused. "I know enough."

"Yeah?" I unclipped my seat belt. "Let me ask you a question ... all those women you see as sexy enough to *fuck* ... how many of them afterward suddenly wanted to date? Like Chloe, for example?"

Walker's eyes narrowed. "Sexy enough?"

"I bet it's a fair few. Because while you're so sure those gorgeous, childless women are the ones who want to be wild and free in bed with no strings attached, it's actually the opposite for many of them. They're all out there desperately looking for love and lying to you about what they want in the hopes that while you're *fucking* them, you'll fall for them.

"But my priority is my kid. And while you might look at me and see an exhausted single mom who needs to get gently laid and have a so-so, satisfactory orgasm, it's us single moms who genuinely want a guy to fuck them wild and hard and give us multiple orgasms. And then go home so we don't have to explain you to our kids or deal with you on top of the millions of other things we have to deal with on the daily.

"But thank you." I opened the car door, my expression disdainful. "For making me feel as attractive as a wet towel and proving once again that even the most perceptive males are clueless when it comes to women." With that, I jumped out of his car and slammed the door behind me.

WALKER

STUNNED, I stared after Sloane as she disappeared inside the cottage.

Go home.

Call Jamie and go home.

I didn't move.

My blood was up.

I'd hurt her.

I couldn't have said a worse thing to her.

But she got me, didn't she? She put me in my place.

Go home.

I'd never heard her swear before, not like that. I wanted to hear it again. I wanted to hear her beg me to fuck her.

Go. Home.

SLOANE

How dare he?

Skin hot with indignation, I'd thrown my cardigan off and paced my living room, heart racing with the confrontation, trying desperately to focus on my anger and not my rejection.

No one ... no one made me feel like Walker did, and to have him look at me and see me like a mousy, sexless, single mom ...

Don't think about it.

It was crushing to think about.

Ugh. I thought I was being so brave putting myself out there, and I'd just screwed everything up. How would I look at him again?

A small cry startled out of me as the cottage door flew open and Walker strode in like a freaking avenging Viking warrior. His expression was hard as he slammed the door shut and locked it. "How many times do I need to tell you to lock your door?" he demanded, his voice guttural. Walker's hands fisted at his sides, his body tense.

But it was the look on his face that made my belly clench low and deep.

Hunger.

Pure, unadulterated hunger etched a harshness into his handsome face.

"If we do this, there are rules," Walker stated.

My heart leapt, but his words from earlier still burned. "I don't need a pity fuck."

He bared his teeth, a wicked half smile, half snarl as he stepped toward me. "No, you need it wild and hard. Is that not what you said?"

Yes, yes, YES! My breathing grew shallow as my body reacted to him. This man was sexual radioactivity.

"Yes," I whispered.

His nostrils flared as if he could see how turned on I was.

"Just sex. No strings. When one of us wants it to end, it ends without harm or hurt. Or we don't do this."

"Agreed." I nodded. "I promise."

Decided, he lifted his chin toward the staircase. "Then get upstairs."

Thrill filled me even as nervous butterflies fluttered wildly in my belly. "Are you going to be this bossy all the time?"

"Did you think I would be anything but in charge when we fuck?"

No.

No, I guessed not.

The man was a dominant, sexy bastard.

And I realized that was part of his appeal. I'd spent my whole life making decisions for my daughter, for myself. Everything came down to my choices, my actions. It was exhausting.

But with Walker ... I trusted him to take charge in the bedroom and make me feel good doing it.

In answer, I bit my lip against a smile of anticipation, and his eyes darkened with heat. Then I turned on my heel and walked as calmly as I could up the stairs. My heart lurched into my throat as I heard his heavier footsteps behind me.

I didn't know what I expected once I reached my bedroom. I crossed the room to lower the blinds and when I turned, Walker stood in the doorway, staring at me like he wanted to devour me.

I was absolutely ready for that.

However, I'd expected it to be a controlled seduction. Because that was Walker. Always in control.

So when he rushed me like he had lost all control, my entire being ignited.

Our bodies collided seconds before our mouths did, Walker bending to steal the breath from me. His kiss was ravaging. Possessive. Dark, deep, and sexual. His beard prickled softly against my skin.

His hand fisted in my hair as he held me to him, and I grasped onto him as he plundered my mouth as if he couldn't taste me deep enough.

I knew it.

I knew it would be like this between us.

I whimpered against his tongue as his other hand gripped my ass to pull me into the hard-on straining the zipper of his jeans. The whimper turned to a moan, reverberating into his mouth. Walker ground his hips harder into me, squeezing my ass. I slid my hands under his tee in answer, shivering at the delicious feel of his smooth, hot skin, the dips and curves of his muscles beneath my fingertips.

He grunted as I touched his nipples. The sound rumbled in my mouth as we kissed harder, bruising each other's lips.

I needed him inside me. I needed that thick drag and pull. I needed him to obliterate my emptiness.

Fumbling for the button on his jeans, I made that very clear.

But Walker stalled my movement by lifting me into his arms. I was in the air for a second before I landed on my bed with a startled gasp. I gazed up into Walker's face, etched with the harshness of uncontrolled desire.

I'd never felt sexier.

Then suddenly I was overwhelmed by him, his heat, his scent, as he covered me with his large body and stole my lips again. He cupped my breast through my dress and squeezed, and lust exploded through me. I became frantic, pulling at his shirt.

"Walker, inside, inside." I broke the kiss to whisper mindlessly.

"Tell me what you want?" he demanded against my lips.

I looked deep into his beautiful eyes, confused. "I just said it."

"Give me the words. Tell me you want me to fuck you."

Understanding dawned and, if possible, my skin flushed hotter. "I want you to fuck me. Hard."

With a growl of satisfaction, Walker sat back, straddling me. His erection strained against his jeans as he took hold of the hem of my dress. I sat up to help him as he whipped it over and off. Before he could, I unhooked my bra and removed it. Walker's fiery eyes devoured my naked breasts.

"I've fantasized about sucking your nipples more times than I can count," he admitted.

Wet slickened between my legs. "Suck away, my friend."

Walker reached for my breasts, caressing them, plucking at my nipples as they tightened into hard points. "You've been driving me fucking nuts, you know that."

"Only fair, since I've been permanently turned on since we met."

Walker's lips twitched. "Is that so?"

"I think I might have used the term 'I want to climb that man like a tree' several times."

This time he grinned, and a whoosh of feeling fluttered through my belly. He was so sexy. Why was he so goddamn sexy? "I'll let you climb me later. Maybe."

He whipped off his shirt. Holy ... "Oh my God."

Walker didn't seem to be aware of how beautiful he was. His broad shoulders, his muscled, hard pecs, and a six-pack. A few scars marred his smooth skin, what looked like a healed long, deep gash at his ribs and a scar that looked very similar to the one on my arm. He'd been shot. And there was another on his belly. A cluster of smaller scars on his side.

I wanted to ask him what happened, but I knew from his expression that now was definitely not the time.

Instead, I reached for him, trailing my hands over his chest in awe at the power straddling me.

He grabbed my wrists and pinned them above my head,

holding me down as he hovered over me. "Keep your hands on the bed."

I nodded, anticipation tingling through my limbs.

He released my wrists to curl his fingers into my underwear before he moved down my body, peeling the fabric down my legs. They hit my boots and Walker removed those first before my panties disappeared.

I laid bare, arms above my head, as Walker Ironside stood, taking in every inch of me.

Shivering under his fiery stare, I felt everything tighten and swell, including my nipples.

"Spread your legs," Walker demanded as he took his wallet out of his back pocket.

My womb clenched, and I knew he heard my excited gasp by the way his nostrils flared. Then I did as he asked and raised my knees and spread them.

It had been a long time since anyone had seen me this naked and vulnerable.

I only had a second to wonder if he liked what he saw before Walker's chest began to rise and fall with quick, excited breaths. He yanked down his zipper and then shrugged off his jeans and boxer briefs.

I moved to sit up, to take him all in, and he commanded, "Don't move."

My belly trembled with need.

Walker's eyes remained focused on me as he rolled a condom up his impressive, thick length.

"Oh my God." I practically squirmed with need. "Come inside me. Please, Walker, now."

In answer, he grabbed hold of my ankles and yanked me toward him.

I cried out as I slid down the bed and then he was on his knees, his head between my thighs. "Walker."

"You said something about 'my eating pleasure' earlier," he

murmured wickedly, and then his mouth was on me. His beard scratched against my sensitive skin, and his tongue pushed inside me.

Another cry fell from my lips as I arched into him. His grip was bruising on my thighs as he held me open wide for his mouth, for the sinful things he could do with his mouth.

He fucked me with his tongue before sliding it up and over my clit.

"Walker!" I gasped, pushing into him. Then he sucked my clit hard and I was lost. Everything but the heat and tension swirling in my gut disappeared. It was coiled so tightly already, it took little to snap it.

For my orgasm to explode through me.

White-hot heat filled my vision as I came, my inner muscles clenching and unclenching, desperate for something to squeeze around.

My eyes flew open as I felt Walker come over me, his hands under my arms as he shifted me back up the bed with ease. He looked almost angry, his face was so hard with want. I invited him between my thighs as he gripped my wrists tight in his hands and held me down.

My panting filled the room as Walker nudged against me. Then he captured my mouth once more as he pushed into me. Hard.

My desire eased his way considerably, but he was big, thick, and that overwhelming fullness I'd been desperate for caused a pleasure pain to zing down my spine. I groaned into his mouth, and he released my lips to demand, "You good?"

I nodded, staring up into his eyes, feeling so filled by him, so connected. I clenched around him, and Walker squeezed his eyes shut. "Fuck, Sloane. You good?"

"Fuck me," I commanded hoarsely.

His eyes flew open, fire in them.

And then he let me have it. Have him. I'd never been so

consumed by another person. Everything was about the hot drive of him inside me. He didn't hold back. He drove into me in slow but powerful thrusts that my hips rose to meet.

My gasps grew into cries, loud, pleasured sounds I couldn't contain.

And I couldn't touch him, could only take what he had to give as he held me down, and it was so goddamn exciting, I knew I was going to come too quickly. The tension inside me tightened, tightened, tightened every time he pulled out and slammed back in.

"I'm close," I panted.

He released one of my hands to grip my thigh and pulled it up against his hip, changing the angle of his thrust. I reached for him blindly as the tension inside me shattered and I yelled his name.

My orgasm rolled through me, my inner muscles rippling and squeezing around Walker.

His eyes widened at the first tight clench and he bit out a guttural, "Fuck." He stared as if he'd never seen anything like me. With a gruff grunt, his hips pounded faster and then momentarily stilled.

"Sloane," he bit out between clenched teeth, his grip on my thigh bruising as his hips jerked with the swell and throb of his release.

As his climax shuddered through him, he let go of my thigh and slumped over me. "Sloane," he murmured, grinding into me as if he wanted to prolong his orgasm.

Walker's warm, heavy weight surrounded me, and I slid my free hand across his back. His skin was damp with exertion, his back so broad and muscled.

Our labored breathing rasped in my ears as he laid over me. Covering me.

I wasn't a small woman, but I felt tiny beneath this mountain of a man.

I felt claimed.

The feminist in me should be appalled. But my inner cave-woman exalted because I'd just had the best sex of my life.

"I want more," I said, wrapping my legs around his back. "I need you to do that again."

Walker lifted his head, his face relaxed in a way I'd never seen before. Pleasure and amusement glimmered in his eyes. "When does Callie come home?"

"Not until tonight."

"Then we have plenty of time." He pushed up, off, and out of me. "I have some more condoms in the car." Walker's gaze dragged down my body as he got off the bed and sauntered out of the room. I rolled onto my side to watch him go, squeezing my legs together at the sight of his muscular ass and long, strong legs. When he came back from obviously dealing with the condom, I sucked in a breath at the sight of his cock.

No wonder he'd felt so freaking awesome inside me.

So full and overwhelming.

"I'll be a minute," he said, shrugging into his jeans without bothering with his underwear. "When I get back, I want you on your hands and knees, arse facing the door."

A shiver rippled through me at the command. "Bossy," I whispered huskily.

The corner of his lip pulled up. "You're about to find out just how bossy I can be."

Eighteen
Walker

I couldn't regret it.

Maybe that made me a selfish bastard.

But as I watched Sloane pull on a fresh pair of underwear beneath the dress she'd redonned, I couldn't regret my afternoon with her. Or the decision to have her whenever she wanted me to. The woman had zero hang-ups in bed, and she got off on what I gave her.

Big-time.

Fuck, I could still feel her coming around my dick.

"You keep looking at me like that, and I'm going to take this dress off again," Sloane teased as she smoothed said dress. It clung to her pert, full tits, and I crossed my arms over my chest to stop myself from reaching out to her.

We'd just gone three very long rounds, followed by a shower, and Callie would be home soon. I needed to leave before she returned. At least Sloane seemed to stay true to her word. There were no longing looks or asking me to stay awhile. No "when will I see you again."

In fact, she turned to me upon her last orgasm and said, "This was awesome, but Callie will be home soon."

"See, standing there looking all GI Joe with that steely expression of yours," Sloane said with a smile in her voice as she halted in front of me, "makes me want to ruffle your feathers, and I don't have time. So stop looking all sexy and get moving, soldier."

Without thinking, I wrapped my hand around the back of her head and pulled her up into me for a thorough kiss that had her panting and rubbing her body against mine. Problem was, I could feel my blood heating again and shooting straight for my dick.

Woman had me acting like a teenager.

I released her, feeling smug at the dazed look in her eyes, at her swollen, pretty mouth. "I'll go, but I'm waiting out in the car for Ed to show up." Ed was one of the security team from Ardnoch. "It's his turn to watch over you tonight."

"I hope these guys are getting a bonus for doing this," Sloane murmured as she pulled away and then edged around me to head downstairs. "It must be boring as hell."

I followed her downstairs. "It's their job."

"Hmm. Well, nothing has happened in two weeks, so I'm not sure there is a threat."

"Until I know where Andros is, so I can or can't eliminate him as a suspect, security stays on you."

Sloane stopped by the couch and looked at me with a glimmer in her eyes. "Let's hope you don't find him for a while, because I thoroughly enjoyed having security on me. I mean, *in* me."

Amusement curled my lips. "Cute."

Her light laughter hit me in the gut, and it was time to go. Now. "I'm off."

She nodded and, still grinning, replied, "After getting me off. Just as we agreed."

"What are you? The innuendo queen?" I asked as I passed her, rejecting the urge to kiss her again before I left.

"Oh, yeah, I can make anything sound dirty."

It was nice to see her in such a good mood. Relaxed in a way I hadn't seen her in a while. I couldn't regret that either. "Evenin', Sloane."

Her smile softened, her tone sincere now. "Evening, Walker. I had a *lovely* time."

"Me too. Talk soon." I gave her a nod and then stepped out of the cottage, closing the door behind me. I waited to hear Sloane locking it before I crossed the street to where my SUV was parked illegally. Half expecting a ticket, eyes on the front window, it took me a second to notice the tires.

"What the ..." I reached the car and lowered to my haunches to inspect the front driver's side tire.

A very obvious slash cut through it.

Alert, I stood and looked around the street. A few people milled around farther down near the cafés and shops. No one was looking in this direction. No one suspicious was hanging around.

I quickly checked all four tires.

All slashed.

I whipped out my phone and sent a group text to the small security team I'd gathered to help watch over Sloane. The group included Lachlan, and the message I sent updated them on the situation. I told Ed he didn't need to show because I'd watch over Sloane and Callie tonight. Lachlan called me and said he'd send a recovery vehicle. After explaining there was no sign of the suspect, we agreed we'd ask around the village later to see if anyone had seen anything.

That decided, I hurried back across the street and pounded on Sloane's door. "It's me!"

A few seconds later, the door swung open. Sloane stared up at me, wide-eyed. "What's wrong?"

"Looks like I'm staying for dinner," I bit out, striding

inside and shutting the door behind me. I locked it and peered out the window onto the street.

"Walker, what's going on?"

At the fear in Sloane's voice, I turned. "Someone slashed my tires."

Her face paled. "In broad daylight?"

"Aye."

"Surely, someone saw something, then?"

"We'll ask around in the morning. For now, you're stuck with me, I'm afraid."

———

"HE'S BEING A LITTLE SKUNK!" Callie huffed in frustration as we sat eating dinner, plates on our laps.

Sloane's daughter hadn't overanalyzed my being here. She was too busy being mad at her best friend because he was annoyed that she kept beating him at things. I wondered if life was ever that simple for me. It probably had been at one point.

"Cal," Sloane admonished after swallowing a bite of the pasta we'd poured out of a packet. "Don't call Lewis a skunk."

"He is." Callie gestured with her fork. "He can't stand that I'm good at tae kwon do and video games. I beat him once in class, and I beat him today on the Nintendo, and suddenly it's a problem? He beats me all the time!"

Sloane flinched comically. "Bad choice of phrase, baby girl."

I tried not to smile around a bite.

"He refused to play for the rest of the day and holed up in his room. I ended up playing Nintendo with Eilidh because she isn't a little skunk. Do you think I should have let him win?"

"No," Sloane and I answered in unison.

She shot me a grin before she turned to Callie. "You won fair and square. Lewis needs to learn to lose."

"He loses easily enough to boys. It's because I'm a girl." Callie looked at me. "Would it annoy you if a girl beat you?"

"No."

Her eyes brightened. "So I did the right thing?"

"Aye. Especially in tae kwon do. Never let anyone beat you when it comes to self-defense."

She nodded, her agitation seeming to diminish somewhat.

Sloane frowned. "Why didn't you come home if Lewis was acting up?"

Callie shrugged. "It was your day off."

"From work, not you. I don't need a day off from you, kid. Believe it or not, I kinda like having you around."

Callie smirked. "I know." Then she glanced at me. "Anyway, you were hanging out with Walker."

I dared to look at Sloane and found her staring determinedly at her plate. Her cheeks were a wee bit pink, and I knew she was replaying exactly how we hung out today.

"Still, you don't have to stay somewhere you don't want to be. Call me next time."

"It was cool," Callie promised. "Eilidh and I ended up playing board games with Regan and Mr. Adair." She wrinkled her nose. "They're kind of lovey-dovey, though."

"Lovey-dovey?" Sloane grinned. "Where did you hear that phrase?"

"Eilidh."

"Of course."

"Is it normal for grown-ups to kiss as much as they do?" For some reason, Callie asked me instead of her mum.

I swallowed a bite of food. "If they love each other, aye."

"I can't see you doing that, Walker. You're too cool for that."

"I appreciate it," I replied, trying not to laugh.

Sloane, however, smirked at me with a knowing look in her eyes. Probably because I'd spent the afternoon kissing every fucking inch of her perfect body.

"Mom would do it." Callie wrinkled her nose at Sloane.

Sloane looked affronted. "So, I'm not cool?"

"You're kind of lovey-dovey with me, Mom, admit it."

I coughed, covering my chuckle.

"So, I'm not cool?" Sloane repeated indignantly.

"You're a mom." Callie shrugged.

"Your mum is cool for a mum," I opined.

"She is?"

"Very."

Considering this, Callie finally nodded. "Okay."

"Oh, so if Walker thinks I'm cool, I'm cool?"

"Pretty much."

Sloane gaped at her daughter. "Lewis has you all sassy today, huh?"

She grinned around a mouthful of pasta, and Sloane rolled her eyes.

As they continued to tease each other, I watched mother and daughter interact, trying to imagine Sloane as a scared seventeen-year-old with a baby girl. I'd been in scary situations throughout my life, but none as scary as that. To be responsible for a child when you were still a child yourself. It was amazing she'd not only done it, but she had a good relationship with her daughter. Anyone could see how much Sloane loved the kid, and despite Callie's teasing, anyone could see the kid thought the sun rose and fell with her mum.

We ate dessert (a piece of bloody delicious birthday cake from an order that got canceled) as we watched some bullshit UK talent show on TV. Sloane and Callie talked through it so much, I asked why we were watching it. They looked at me as if I were nuts, so I shut up.

At eleven, Sloane switched off the television. "Okay, time for bed."

Curiosity crossed Callie's expression as she looked between us. "Is Walker staying?"

"I'm heading out soon," I promised. Though I'd already told Sloane I'd be out in the car Lachlan had someone leave for me after mine was recovered. I'd stay in it, watching over them. I didn't trust anyone else to take night shift tonight.

"Oh. Okay. It was nice to see you, Walker." She yawned my name.

"You too, wee yin," I replied honestly.

Sloane took Callie upstairs, even though she was old enough to go to bed unescorted, and I stood, waiting for her to reappear. When she did, Sloane had a blanket and pillow in hand.

"Sleep on the couch," she ordered, handing them to me. "It's better if you're in here with us than out there. Right?"

At my hesitation, Sloane rolled her eyes. "It doesn't mean anything, Walker."

I could guard them better from inside the house. "All right."

"Do you think it's Nathan, not Hoffman?" she asked me abruptly.

"I don't know." I looked her straight in the eyes. "We can't find Andros, Sloane. Lachlan is keeping Hoffman busy right now. That makes me think it's likely your ex behind this."

"So he knows you're watching over me?"

"Obviously. I'll be keeping more of an eye out for familiar vehicles. Anyone tailing us back and forth from work."

"Two weeks." She ran a hand through her hair. It had dried naturally after her shower and was a thick mass of waves that made me think of sex. "It's only been two weeks of this, and I'm already losing my mind. I want my car back. I want Callie and I to do as we please."

"I know."

"I ... if something happens to Callie, I will kill him, Walker." Fear raged in her eyes.

My chest tightened. "It won't come to that. I won't let him near Callie. Or you."

She nodded, but I could see the tension still riding her shoulders. "I better go up. Give me a shout if you need anything."

"Wait." I dumped the blanket and pillow on the couch. Then I took her by the hips and walked her back into the wall between the kitchen and stairwell.

Her breathing shallowed, even as desire darkened her eyes. "What are you doing?"

"Helping you relax so you can sleep," I murmured against her mouth as my hand slipped under her dress. My fingers trailed across her belly, and she sucked in a breath. "Remember to be quiet."

"Walker—"

I hushed her with a kiss and slid my fingers beneath her knickers. Prodding at her opening, I watched as her cheeks flushed and she spread her legs a little wider for me. Then I pushed two fingers into her tight, wet heat as my thumb circled her clit.

Sloane bit her lip against a cry as she undulated against my touch.

I kissed her, swallowing her pants and gasps as I thrust my fingers in and out of her, all the while increasing the pressure on that bundle of nerves at her apex.

She clung to me, her fingernails biting into my arms.

A few seconds later, Sloane cried into my kiss. She shuddered hard as her inner muscles clenched and unclenched around my fingers, wet soaking them. Then she was limp against me, breaking the kiss to catch her breath.

I'd never seen anything as fucking gorgeous as Sloane Harrow flushed from coming.

Gently, I released her, smoothing her dress back down. I straightened the straps that were already straight and then caressed her tits, my thumbs catching her tight nipples. With an inward groan, I dropped my hands to her waist, squeezed it, and then stepped back.

Confusion furrowed her brow. She whispered, "What about you?"

Despite the pressure on my dick as it strained against my jeans, I answered honestly, "I'll be fine. That was for you. To help you sleep. You can make it up to me when we're alone."

"Oh." She bit her lip against a pleased smile. "Okay. I can do that."

The wicked mischief dancing in her eyes amused me. I wondered what she imagined doing to me and looked forward to the day it played out. "Good night, Sloane."

"Good night, Walker."

As I watched her climb the stairs to her bedroom, I wished like fuck I was following her up.

But that was a dangerous thought.

I threw it out and turned to the couch to stare at my bed for the night. Then I scrubbed a tired hand down my face and regretted it because I could still smell Sloane on me.

It was going to be a long night.

Nineteen
Sloane

It was strange. I knew I should be more upset because someone had been close enough to us to leave a rat on our door and slash Walker's tires while he was inside the house with me.

I *was* unsettled.

But not as much as I was distracted by the fire he'd lit in my belly. It was like Walker had pulled out the stopper on all this sexual tension I'd bottled up over the years. I couldn't stop thinking about him, about us. It was beyond distracting.

He'd left on the Sunday to investigate the car incident, but no one had seen a damn thing, which meant the perpetrator had been sneaky. Jamie watched over the cottage during the day while I baked a few cake orders for the week. Adam relieved him at night.

But Walker was there, Monday morning, to collect Callie and me. If I was aware of the man before, now I was hyper-hyperaware. For instance, the way his fingers brushed my lower back as I climbed into the passenger seat. School was on a mid-term break for the week and Callie was spending the day with Lewis. Regan was driving them to tae kwon do later that evening so the kids had asked if Callie could sleepover too. When we dropped Callie off at Lewis' and got back into the SUV, Walker had reached over and squeezed my thigh, and I felt it right between my legs.

Except for the touching, Walker was his usual self. Blunt, short sentences as he asked me how I was and updated me on the situation. They were still struggling to find Nathan in LA.

I wanted to kiss him, but except for the thigh squeeze, Walker's demeanor was a little standoffish. It was surprising, then, when we entered the castle together that he pulled me into a shadowed corner to kiss me breathless.

Then he'd released me, brushed his thumb over my mouth, his expression as tender as I'd ever seen it, and told me to have a good day.

At that moment, he reminded me of that Scottish flower —the thistle. There were all these prickles on the stem and leaves before you could get to the pretty flower. That was Walker. You had to look beyond his gruffness to see he was a caring, good man.

The thought panicked me a little.

I could not get attached to him. I'd promised Walker no-strings sex, and I intended to keep that promise.

Which I did when he drove me home from work that night. Callie wouldn't be home all night, so I invited Walker in, and we didn't even make it upstairs before the man was inside me.

The next day at work, I couldn't stop thinking about the way he'd bent me over my couch and ...

By the time the end of my shift arrived, I was revved up and wanting more. Problem was, there was no tae kwon do or sleepover tonight, and Walker and I were heading from the castle straight to Regan and Thane's to collect Callie.

There were only two nights out of the week where we'd

definitely be able to sneak in some time together and, honestly, that just didn't sound like enough to me.

"You all right?" Walker asked as we settled into his SUV after work. "Is it Andros?"

"What?" I asked, confused.

"You haven't said a word since I came to the staff room to collect you."

"Oh." I stared at his strong profile as he drove toward the staff exit. "No, I'm just preoccupied with other stuff."

Walker frowned. "Anything I can help with?"

Laughter trembled on my lips. "Actually, yes."

He glanced at me, one eyebrow raised. "What's up?"

Instead of answering, I waited until we'd driven through the gates and onto the main road that led toward the village.

"Sloane?"

"Is there anywhere private you could pull off? I ... there's something we need to discuss."

Walker's hands tightened ever so slightly around the wheel. "I can't think of anywhere. Just tell me as we drive."

"There." I pointed to a dirt road that cut into the trees.

"That's a private road for the estate."

"So no one will be in there, right?"

With a quizzical look and a sigh, Walker slowed and turned onto the dirt road. It disappeared into the trees, and he slowed the car to a stop a few seconds later. "We drive any farther, and we'll trip the CCTV system."

I most definitely didn't want that.

Glancing behind me, I was happy to see the road was hidden, which meant we were hidden.

"What's going on?" Walker turned to me.

In answer, I bit my lip and unclipped my seat belt, my eyes hot on him.

Understanding darkened Walker's expression. "Here?"

Instead of answering, I unclipped his seat belt and reached for the waist of his suit pants. His breathing grew shallow, and I locked eyes with him as I freed him from his pants. Eyes low-lidded with want, he studied my face, waiting to see what I'd do next.

So I wrapped my lips around his cock and took as much of him as I could into my mouth.

"Fuck!" Walker barked out as his hips jerked, thrusting deeper into my mouth.

Then he brushed the hair off my face so he could watch me suck him.

I watched him, too, as I sucked hard and licked, while I pumped the root of him with my fist. I rested my free hand beneath his now untucked shirt. The color rose in Walker's cheeks as his chest rose and fell in rapid breaths. While one hand held my hair back, the other grabbed the headrest of his car seat, his fingers biting into it. His biceps bulged, straining his black shirt. A sheen of sweat glistened on his forehead, and I felt his abs ripple beneath my hand. My jaw ached a little, and I sucked harder.

Walker huffed out my name in pleasured pants, and my underwear grew damp with my excitement. It thrilled me I could make this big, stoic man lose his mind.

Then his jaw clenched, his nostrils flaring, and he hissed, "Stop."

I was confused, but I released him immediately. My lips felt swollen and, by the way Walker's gaze zeroed in on them, I guessed they were.

"Jeans and knickers off," he demanded as he pressed the button on the side of his seat that pushed it back.

I didn't waste a second. With very little grace, I shimmied out of my jeans and panties as Walker donned a condom. Then I was straddling him, my thighs trembling with anticipation as I rested my hands on his big shoulders.

He gazed up at me with a fierceness that I now knew meant I was about to be thoroughly fucked.

"Top and bra off too," he commanded.

Impatience rode me, but I quickly drew my sweater up and off and unclipped my bra. When my breasts bounced free, Walker cupped them, and I arched into his touch.

"Ride me. Hard."

The man didn't have to ask me twice.

I took hold of his erection and guided him where I needed him. Then I pushed down onto Walker and gasped against his lips as his thickness filled me.

"Yes," I panted, bracing my hands on his shoulders again. "Walker, yes. Feels so good."

"Aye," he grunted, squeezing my breasts, massaging them, plucking at my nipples. "Fuck me, Sloane. Take what you need."

What I wanted was a mind-blowing orgasm, and my body seemed determined to get it immediately. But I forced myself to take it slow, to enjoy him. When I twisted my hips at a certain angle, he hit me exactly where I needed him. My fingers bit into his shoulders as I grew more desperate for the exquisite tension building inside me.

"Sloane," Walker groaned, squeezing my breasts harder as his hips flexed under me, his movements constrained by his clothes and the car.

It made me hotter. He'd been the boss so far, and was still topping from the bottom even now, but I enjoyed knowing I could do whatever I wanted to him.

As if he sensed my thoughts, Walker's eyes narrowed and he sat forward before he roughly pulled my hair back so he could clamp his mouth over my breast. His lips pulled at my nipple, and sensation scored down my belly to the apex of my thighs.

"Walker," I keened. My fingers scraped through his hair as

his mouth tormented me, and my hips picked up pace. Walker released me to lift his head, and we stared into each other's eyes as I rode him. We held each other's gaze, mine low-lidded with building tension and his intense with lust.

"Fuck me," he growled against my mouth.

I increased my pace, the pleasure building higher, higher, our breaths mingling as we panted against each other's mouths.

And then that tightening coil inside me snapped, and I arched my neck, crying out my release, Walker's lips pressing between my breasts seconds before he groaned in climax.

I shook, trembling as the orgasm melted through my limbs.

"Sloane," Walker grunted as I throbbed around his pulses. He tugged on my hair again and then his mouth was on mine. He kissed me thoroughly. Deep, possessive, wet kisses that lit me on fire all over again. He broke it to pant harshly, "The way you come ... fuck ..."

I took his awed tone to be a good thing.

Smiling, I leaned back. Despite the cooling weather outside, sweat dampened my skin. I moved to get off him, but Walker's grip on my hips tightened.

"Give me a second," he said, his gaze roaming over my face and then my chest.

As if he couldn't help himself, he bent his head and took my nipple in his mouth. Aftershocks of pleasure rippled through me, and I groaned as Walker took his sweet time licking and sucking at my breasts.

Finally, he kissed my breastbone and sat back. Satisfaction had softened his harsh features and he patted my bare ass. "We better go get Callie."

For a moment, I felt a flicker of shame that I was going to be late to pick my daughter up because I'd wanted to have car sex. It was unlike me to be so selfish.

"She's safe with Regan and Thane," Walker said, as if he read my thoughts. "We're not that late."

I gave him a grateful smile and climbed off him to get dressed.

He dealt with the condom and put it into a little plastic bag he'd kept in the back of his seat. "Remind me that's in there," he joked.

Chuckling, I nodded as I buttoned up my jeans and clipped my seat belt on.

"Better?" he asked.

"I still want you," I admitted with a wry smile. "I guess my body is making up for that five-year dry spell."

"Five years?" He raised a brow as he reversed expertly back to the road.

"Did I not tell you that?" I chuckled to myself. "Yeah, the last time I had sex was with that guy Nathan chased off, and it was only a quickie. Nothing to write home about. So I guess I have a lot of pent-up sexual tension."

"More than happy to help you with that," Walker assured me with a quick grin that did wicked things to my insides.

My ringtone suddenly blared through the car, and my heart jolted. Mom guilt immediately filled me, thinking it was Callie calling to ask why I was late. Fingers trembling, I grabbed the bag off the floor and riffled through it until I found the phone.

It wasn't Callie.

It was Flora. I told Walker so before I answered, "Hey, Flora."

"Sloane ..." Flora's voice held an edge I didn't understand but knew I didn't like. "There's something going on at your cottage, lass. Mrs. Fairley said she passed it and the door is open. She said it looks like someone has been in and vandalized it."

"Oh my God." My heart raced. "Okay, I'll be right there. Thanks for letting me know."

"Of course. We haven't called the police, but we can if you'd—"

"No, no police." I could feel Walker glancing at me constantly. "I'll be five minutes."

We hung up, and before Walker could bark orders at me, I relayed, "Flora said the cottage has been broken into."

"Fuck," Walker muttered under his breath and put his foot down.

We arrived at the cottage five minutes later, skidding to a stop outside it to see Mrs. Fairley, a neighbor, and Gordon, a retired villager who owned a bunch of property here, standing guard.

Walker asked them what they'd seen, and they answered him as if he were the police. All the while I stood there, afraid to peer inside.

Unfortunately, they hadn't seen the actual break-in.

"We should call the police," Gordon insisted.

"No police. This is a private matter." Walker stared him down, and Gordon, a large man not easily cowed, nodded carefully.

It was my fault. I knew Walker wanted the police involved, but I couldn't subject Callie to that.

"Thanks for watching over, but we've got this." Walker not so subtly suggested that they leave. Mrs. Fairley frowned at me in worry, but nodded as Gordon led her down the street to her own cottage.

My hands shook as Walker turned to me. "Wait here."

It seemed like an age that I stood on the sidewalk waiting for Walker to reappear. Eventually, he did.

"There's no one here." His face was hard with checked anger. "But prepare yourself."

I knew as soon as I stepped in what I was supposed to prepare myself against.

It wasn't the ripped cushions and couches that had been shredded. It wasn't the broken picture frames of me and Callie and the Adairs and Juanita. Nor the trashed kitchen or the cakes that had been smashed against the walls.

Later, I'd know it wasn't even because of the dead rat that had been left in my bed.

I was supposed to prepare myself against the threat spray-painted across the living room.

YOU CAN RUN BUT YOU CAN'T HIDE

Nausea rolled up my stomach. Nothing could distract me from the evidence of fury in the cottage. Pure and utter rage had been set off like a bomb in our home.

I hurried outside and threw up my lunch on the sidewalk.

TWENTY
SLOANE

W hen Brodan walked through the door of the cottage a little while later, my immediate feeling was guilt. He and Monroe had just had a son. They didn't need to deal with my crazy life. However, Walker had insisted on calling him after he called Thane to ask him to keep Callie with them until we'd dealt with this.

Honestly, thank God for Walker, because I think I was in shock.

Until this point, even with Hoffman's assault and the attempted kidnapping in Inverness, I think my mind had diminished the danger in order to cope with it. Yet, seeing the fury that had devastated our beautiful little cottage finally drove it home that my daughter and I were in trouble.

"Jesus fuck," Brodan said a few minutes later as he came downstairs from touring the upstairs. I hadn't gone up, but Walker told me about the rat on my bed and that someone trashed both our bedrooms. "We need to deal with this bloke now."

"We need to call the police," Walker insisted, his expression stern. "This has gone too far without reporting it."

My racing heart pounded. "I have a deal with the Howards. If we call the police, then we have to explain why Nathan is coming after me."

"No, you don't." Walker shook his head, leaning against the damaged sideboard. "All you need to tell them is that he's an abusive ex. We need them to dust the cottage for prints because Andros will be in the US system, and we can cross-match them to rule him in or out."

"Walker ..."

"Run it past the Howards first, but you have to protect you and Callie, too, Sloane. The Howards have enough money and manpower to protect themselves."

Knowing he was right, I waved my hand toward the door. "My cell is in your car."

He nodded and left to retrieve it.

"How are you doing?" Brodan asked.

"I feel bad for dragging you into this."

"You're not dragging me into anything. Sloane, you're our friend. You and Callie have become like family. We take care of our family."

Tears burned my eyes. It had been such a long time since anyone had wanted to take care of us. "Thank you."

"I don't know what to tell Monroe." Brodan stared grimly around the cottage. "She'll be worried sick if I tell her the truth."

"Then don't. I don't want her stressing about this."

He grimaced. "As much as I'd love to protect her, she'd be angry if I didn't tell her the truth. Roe can handle it."

That was true. The woman had been through more than most in her life. "She should concentrate on her new son and husband, not her best friend's crazy-ass life."

"She can do both," he assured me with a small smile that didn't quite reach his eyes.

Walker returned with my cell, and I took it with trembling hands.

I called Aria first to explain, and with her usual blunt efficiency, she took charge and told me she'd call her father right away.

Five minutes later, my phone rang.

"It's Wesley," I told the guys before I answered. "Mr. Howard."

———

AFTER I EXPLAINED what was happening, Wesley informed me that his people couldn't find Nathan, either, and he insisted I call the police. I promised to keep any mention of Allegra out of my story, and he seemed relieved to hear it.

Walker called the police immediately.

We only had to wait in my broken cottage for about fifteen minutes before two constables arrived from the police station in the nearby town of Tain. Ardnoch was too small to have its own station. They took my statement while Walker stood at my side. Brodan had gone outside to call and update Lachlan. I was careful about what I told the police, explaining my past with Nathan, minus the incident with Allegra. That he'd recently gotten out of prison, etc. We had no proof, however, that it was Nathan.

Thus, the police informed us the cottage was now a crime scene. Until detective inspectors and a crime unit could arrive from Inverness, I had to move out. Not that Callie and I could stay while it was in its current state. The female constable escorted me upstairs, and I packed an overnight bag for me and Callie. The intruder had destroyed some of our clothes. The bastard. Like I had money to buy a new wardrobe.

Upon returning downstairs, wondering where on earth we'd stay and how much it would cost, I followed the constables and Walker out of the house as they locked it up. They told us they'd be in touch and departed.

I stared after them in a daze, wondering why life continued to throw this kind of mess at me. Had I done something bad in a past life? Had I done something in this life? Yeah ... I'd been a stupid kid who had sex with the wrong guy. I didn't think that was worthy of punishment, though.

"Sloane."

At Walker's hard voice, I unglued my eyes from the retreating police vehicle and noticed faces peering out of windows, a few stray folks walking past us, staring and whispering.

I flinched inwardly.

"Sloane."

I looked at Walker, who kept his distance from me. After I was sick, he helped me clean up and hugged me. But since then, we hadn't touched.

"I spoke with Aria," he said. "We agreed you're safer on the estate for now."

Great. Back in the tiny staff lodge where we stayed before Monroe got me the deal with the cottage. I knew I shouldn't be ungrateful, but I had orders to fill and I needed money more than ever. And the lodge didn't cut it for baking.

"We know you need a kitchen, so you're staying with Aria."

That news shocked me out of my stupor. "With Aria?"

"At her house on the estate. No arguments. We'll collect Callie now, and I'll drive you over."

Brodan stepped forward to hug me good night. I squeezed him and said, "Tell Monroe I'm fine. Please. I'll call her later."

He looked like he didn't believe me, but he agreed.

Then it was just me and Walker, driving toward Caelmore to pick up my daughter. I barely even noticed his quietness. Butterflies raged in my belly—what would I tell Callie?

My daughter was ten years old. She'd already been traumatized by what happened that night with me and Allegra. I did not want to have to tell her that her dad was possibly terrorizing me.

I felt like I was outside my body as we pulled up to Regan and Thane's. My legs seemed to move without my permission, taking me to the door. Regan opened it before I could knock and pulled me into a tight hug.

"Where is she?" I asked softly.

"In the living room. She knows something is going on."

Those butterflies went wild, and I sucked in a breath to tamp down my nausea. Walker was at my back as we followed Regan into the living room.

Eilidh called out *hi* and Thane shot me a worried look.

But my eyes drifted past them both to where Callie sat with Lewis on the couch.

She hopped up at the sight of me and flew across the room to wrap her arms around me. "What's going on?" Her little voice trembled.

"Come with me," I urged, leading her into the laundry room for some privacy.

I saw Walker in my peripheral, standing in the doorway. But my focus was on my daughter as I smoothed her hair off her face. Her cheeks were pale, eyes so filled with worry.

No ten-year-old should ever look like that.

Rage burned through me. I wanted to hurt Nathan.

"We had an issue at the cottage. A ... a flood." The impromptu lie slipped out. "So, we're going to stay with Ms. Howard in her house on the estate for a few days."

Callie scowled up at me, her blue eyes bright with anger. "You're lying. You're lying!" She pushed away from me, her little mouth trembling as tears slipped down her cheeks. "Stop lying to me!"

When Callie cried, I cried. Our connection was so deep.

Everything she felt, I felt too. I sobbed as I reached for her, but she kept batting my hands away and screaming that I was a liar.

I glanced helplessly through my tears at Walker, noted his expression of distress, before he turned on his heel and walked away.

For some reason, watching him walk away gave me strength.

I got down on my knees and gripped Callie's arms to pull her to me. "You're right, you're right."

It took her a second, but she calmed, her chest rising and falling with her softening sobs.

"Baby girl, I'm so sorry. I was ... I just want to protect you."

"From what?"

"Someone ... someone broke into the cottage and vandalized it."

She grew still in my arms. "Why?"

"We don't know."

Her eyes narrowed.

I hurried to say, "It might be your dad."

Callie stiffened, fear entering her expression.

I hated Nathan.

I loathed him with every inch of my being.

"He's out of prison?"

Nodding, I pulled her closer. "But we don't know for sure it's him. Okay? We just ... we're taking precautions. So we're going to stay on the estate, and Walker and his team are going to look after us."

My daughter slowly relaxed, and she nodded calmly. "Walker won't let anyone hurt us."

"No, he won't," I promised. "Neither will I."

"I know." She threw her arms around me, and I hugged her tight, probably squeezing too hard. "Sorry I yelled at you."

"It's okay, baby girl. I'm sorry for lying."

"I understand."

She shouldn't have to understand. I took a deep breath to bury my seething. He wouldn't do this to me. He wouldn't make me bitter and angry. I'd worked too damn hard to make sure of it.

When we walked back into the living room, Callie burrowed shyly into my side, embarrassed the Adairs had heard her outburst. Lewis hovered near the island, concern marring his face as he watched Callie like a hawk.

"We better get going."

"Call if you need anything," Thane insisted.

"Thank you. We will."

Regan looked like she wanted to rush Callie and hug her, but Thane held her back, which I thought was for the best. Even Eilidh, who was not known for her tact, remained quiet, her expression troubled.

"See you later, Cal?" Lewis asked quietly, gaze questioning.

She nodded. "Yeah."

He nodded back, still not taking his eyes off her.

"Let's go," Walker said from the doorway.

In answer, Callie left my side to hurry over to Walker's. She looked up at him and reached for his hand.

Tears choked me as Walker took it without hesitation. He made her feel safe. And I knew it should make me happy. But it scared the crap out of me.

I murmured my thanks to the Adairs again as Regan handed me Callie's overnight bag and then I followed my daughter and Walker out to the car. Callie held tight to his hand the entire way, and I heard him murmuring reassuringly as he helped her into the back seat.

We didn't speak on the drive to the estate. I'd never been as far as the Howards' home. The road led away from the castle, passing the building that housed the spa, and then turned left. Soon the woods cleared and we were driving down a private lane. I could see the shadowed outline of four large homes sitting on the coast overlooking the North Sea.

We pulled up outside the biggest of them all, and I stared numbly at the New England-style house with its wraparound porch. Exterior lights lit it up in the dark.

A shade of embarrassment warmed my skin as I realized we were taking charity from my boss.

"The house is protected by the drone perimeter around the estate. An intruder would need to bypass security on the estate side or the massive dune cliffs on the beach side, neither of which is possible. So you'll be safe here," Walker announced matter-of-factly before he jumped out of the car and helped Callie. He took hold of our overnight bag, too, and I fumbled with my seat belt.

As I slid out of the car, the house's huge front door opened and Aria stood in the doorway. She wore jeans and a sweater, looking casual and so unlike herself. We were intruding on her privacy. To my surprise, she walked down the porch steps to give me a hug. She enveloped me in her warmth and expensive perfume.

"Are you okay?"

"I think so," I whispered.

Aria released me, her gaze assessing, before she turned to where Walker stood with Callie. She gave Callie a beautiful smile and held out a manicured hand that was, for once, bare of any jewelry. "It's nice to see you again, Callie."

Callie gave her a small, tired smile as she took her hand. "You too."

Aria tugged on her gently. "Come on in. I was just making hot chocolate. You want one?"

"Yes, please."

Aria shot me a look as if to say "your kid is adorable." It almost made me smile.

"Go on inside," I urged Callie. "I'll be in, in a minute."

She gave me a reluctant nod and looked up at Walker. "Night, Walker."

"Night, wee yin." He squeezed her shoulder, and then she followed Aria into the house.

I waited for Walker to say something reassuring. To hug me.

Instead, he stared stonily at me as he handed over the overnight bag. "We'll talk in the morning." With that, I got an abrupt nod, and he jumped into his SUV.

Hurt scored through me.

Stupid freaking hurt.

Steeling myself against it, I walked into the house without looking back.

TWENTY-ONE
WALKER

I stormed into my house, not bothering to switch on any lights until I reached the back bedroom I'd transformed into a home gym. Beyond the expensive workout machines, hanging from the ceiling in the corner was a boxing bag.

I palmed the light switch, illuminating the room and my destination. Pulling my sweater off, I dumped it on the floor and didn't bother wrapping my hands before fury exploded out of my fists.

The bag swayed and jolted brutally with my assault as I slammed into it in a flurry of impotent fucking rage. Sweat dripped down my face, my arms ached, and I didn't know how much time had passed until one particular brutal punch caused a worrying crack above me.

Panting, I looked up at the ceiling. "Fuck." I'd knocked the fixing loose, and it was tearing at the plasterwork.

Glancing down at my hands, I noted my swelling knuckles.

It was worth it. I felt marginally better.

Striding into the kitchen, I pulled out ice and threw it into a bowl large enough for my hand to fit. Then with one hand in it, I used the other to pull my phone out of my pocket.

I hit the number for my mate Dexter who I worked with back in LA and who didn't mind doing a bit of dirty work. With the time difference, I wasn't worried about waking him. I wouldn't have been, anyway. This couldn't wait.

"Walk, how you doing, man?" Dex answered, sounding relaxed.

"I need a favor."

"Tell me." His tone sharpened.

"Name is Kyle Brixton. I'll send you what details I have on him when we hang up. I want him found, and I want you to do whatever it fucking takes to get information out of him on the whereabouts of Nathan Andros. Whatever it takes, Dex."

"Understood."

TWENTY-TWO
SLOANE

Ignoring Frannie's worried glances, I pushed on with my work that morning just as I had done every day since the cottage was trashed. Some people might think me crazy, but I felt trapped on the estate. I was living in a beautiful coastal house with incredible views, yet all I wanted was our cottage back.

The police had taped off the house and dusted it for prints. We were still waiting on word if they'd found anything. Two detective inspectors interviewed me again. They also interviewed Walker and Brodan. I only knew that because of a quick exchange of words with Walker when he collected the cakes I needed delivered. Callie was still on mid-term break for the rest of the week but Walker thought it was better she stayed on the estate. That meant no tae kwon do until this was over.

I hated that.

I hated how trapped we both were.

Even if Aria was being super cool about it all. She wasn't around a lot because she worked long hours, but when she was, she was extremely sweet to Callie.

One person who was not being sweet, at least not to me, was Walker. Other than the cake delivery, he was avoiding me. His texts were blunter than usual and did not encourage conversation.

It made me furious. Hadn't we agreed that if one of us didn't want to do this thing anymore, we'd talk about it? Also, why did he suddenly not want to? Was I proving to be too much of a hassle? If so, why continue to protect Callie? Why not let someone else do it? I knew Brodan and Monroe would have someone watching over us in a heartbeat. My best friend had driven out with Lennox to see me last night, and the baby cuddles made me feel a little better. Seeing Monroe had, too, of course. I tried to paste on my brightest smile to prove I was doing okay, but the woman saw right through me.

"I wish there was something I could do," Monroe had said, worry written all over her.

"You're doing it," I'd promised her. "Callie and I were so alone until we came here, Roe. You changed that. *You* gave us a family again."

"Oh, God, I'm so hormonal, and that was so sweet," she sobbed, and it was so adorable, she actually made me truly laugh for the first time since the break-in.

Monroe's boost to my spirits didn't last. The following Monday morning when Walker arrived to collect Callie to take her to school, he wouldn't meet my gaze when he gave me that annoying chin lift before bundling my daughter into his SUV.

He didn't want me anymore? Fine. I wanted him to be a man and freaking admit it.

It seemed the universe did, too, because as I left Frannie in the staff room to make my way toward the cafeteria for lunch later that day, I bumped into Walker.

His expression was granite as he went to veer around me with a nod. As if we were merely strangers passing in the hall.

"Are you kidding me?" I snapped at him.

Walker stopped and looked back at me. "Problem?"

Glancing around to make sure we were alone, I stepped toward him and hissed, "You're really going to treat me like you've never been inside me?" I didn't care if it was blunt. I was past diplomacy.

His expression remained impassive, but I was learning Walker's tells. His hands had clenched into fists at his sides. "What the fuck does that mean?"

"It means you've treated me like I barely exist since the night at the cottage. If you don't want to do this thing anymore, fine by me." Lie, lie, lie. "But at least have the goddamn decency to tell me instead of treating me like I have the plague. In other words, grow the hell up."

Anger flashed across his face, and he leaned into me with a growl. "Does it not compute with you that you're in danger?"

"It's pretty much turned my life upside down, so yeah. What the hell does that have to do with us?"

"I am supposed to be guarding you. And Callie." His glower was ferocious. "I cannot be distracted by sex with you when I'm supposed to be protecting you. So, aye, we're not doing this *thing* anymore."

Disappointment crushed my chest, making it slightly hard to breathe. Being with him was the only time I felt free of all the darkness surrounding my life at the moment. And he was ripping it away? "What about what I want?" I hissed. "Because the only time in the last few nightmarish weeks that I haven't thought about the danger we're in is when we're having sex."

Walker's lips pressed tight as he searched my face, almost frantically. As if trying to determine the truth in my words. His fists clenched tighter. "I won't fail you because I can't keep my hands off you."

So he cared more about doing what he thought was his duty than being with me? I huffed bitterly. That said a lot about how much he wanted me, right? Rejection stung, and I lashed out immaturely. "Fine. I'll find someone else to get me off."

Walker stepped toward me, eyes narrowing. "Don't make this ugly between us, Sloane."

"I'm not making it ugly," I replied flatly. "I'm being honest. You're not the only one with a working dick, Walker. You were just convenient." I turned on my heel to march away, but I'd caught the flicker of something awful in his eyes before I did.

Guilt slammed through me, and I stopped with the force of it. He was still standing there. "I'm sorry," I said over my shoulder without looking at him. "I didn't mean that." But I walked away before he could respond.

TWENTY-THREE
SLOANE

The rest of the week passed in a numb blur. The days meshed into each other and felt like the same day over and over. I hadn't left the estate in almost two weeks. A security guard drove to the house to collect me for work and drove me back. Callie came home, I cooked for her and Aria, and left Aria's in the oven for her to reheat when she eventually got home. Callie did her homework while I baked. Walker collected my baking orders when he collected Callie, and he delivered them for me. We didn't even talk beyond the delivery instructions now.

Callie noticed and asked if we were okay. I lied.

Then we repeated the day over.

The only moments I felt truly awake were when the detective inspectors called to let me know they had found no prints in the cottage. The case had hit a dead end, but I was to call if any more incidents occurred. They'd let my landlord, Mac, know that the cottage was no longer a crime scene. Not that we were getting back in it soon.

The Howards' home, however, was nothing to complain about. It was surprisingly cozy for its size, with the large kitchen and island in the center of the living space that looked out over the North Sea. There were two large picture windows overlooking the water at either end of the space, and in the middle were French doors that led out onto the wraparound porch. One window had a cute breakfast nook built into it, while the other was in the living area. You could sit on the massive, deep-seated corner sofa with the wood-burning fire on, watching the sea. It was peaceful.

If we had to be trapped anywhere, I guess it was the best place for it.

I'd talked to Brodan that morning about letting Callie stay with Lewis. He was now my go-to guy since the harsh exchange with Walker. I'd explained that Callie needed some normality, and remembering how worried Lewis had been, I think he needed it too. So Brodan arranged for Walker to drive Callie and Lewis home after school, Callie with her overnight bag. Thane had a top-of-the-line security system in the house, and he promised to stay close if they ventured out for anything.

I didn't know how Walker felt about it, but it wasn't up to him, and my daughter shouldn't feel how I felt.

Flora, the sweetheart, had asked me to continue baking treats for her Saturday morning customers, so that night, alone in the house, I got to work on her order.

When Aria walked through the door, I was in the kitchen, my apron covered in flour, my cheeks and hair, too, because I'd dropped an entire bag of flour on the floor and had to clean it up. Thankfully, I had plenty more because it wasn't exactly easy to do a supply run.

Aria gave me a bemused smile as she dropped her purse on the dining table. "Accident?"

"You could say that."

"Well, the house smells amazing. Have I told you how much I love coming home to it smelling like cake?"

I smiled. "I'm glad because I'm worried we're cramping your style."

Aria raised an eyebrow. "What style? If you hadn't noticed, I kinda work a lot."

"I did notice. Is that your doing or Mr. Adair's?"

"Uh, definitely mine. Lachlan has asked me many times to stop working over my hours. But ..." She shrugged and headed toward her wine fridge. "I enjoy working. Red?" she asked.

"Yes, please."

"Okay. Give me a minute. I'm gonna change into my sweats and then you are going to let me swipe one of those cupcakes, yeah?"

I turned to see her pointing to the cupcakes I'd decorated for fall. They had rust, red, and orange buttercream piping, and I'd accented them with edible, gold-dusted leaves. "Of course."

True to her word, Aria came back downstairs a few minutes later. I marveled at her ability to make comfy clothes look chic. She was one of those women who always looked immaculate.

She poured us both a giant glass of wine and then grabbed a cupcake.

"I have dinner in the oven for you," I told her.

"Thank you. I'll have it after my cupcake."

I chuckled and nodded before clinking my glass against the one she held up to me. "What are we drinking to?"

"You. For handling all of this so amazingly."

"Then we're drinking to you, too, for giving Callie and me a place to live while this is going on."

"You never have to thank me for that." Aria sat back on the island and gave me a soft smile. "It's been nice, actually. Coming home to a warm house, seeing Callie's homework on the dining table, and all your baked treats stacked and tormenting me in the kitchen."

I snorted. "Yeah, Callie and I are so used to all the treats, it doesn't bother us now."

She rested her chin in her hand and watched me as I grabbed the puff pastry I'd made the night before for cinnamon swirls. "I have noticed a difference in you, though."

"A difference?"

"You seem ... sad. And I also noticed a little friction between you and Walker. You can tell me if it's none of my business."

Aria was technically my boss. Her title was hospitality manager, but she was doing Lachlan's job. So I knew I should probably watch what I said. However, I hadn't had a chance since my encounter with Walker to talk to Monroe. And I was worried about my reaction to him. How much the disappointment and rejection affected me. How cruel it had made me.

So I told Aria everything as we sipped our wine and she watched me bake.

"It wasn't me," I groaned, halting what I was doing. I'd just told her about what I'd said to Walker in the hall at work. When I looked at her, tears burned my eyes. "I don't treat people like that."

Aria considered this. "We all say things we don't mean when we're hurt. It's called being human. We're not perfect. And you said you were sorry two seconds after it. Walker will get over it." She frowned. "He really takes his job seriously if he's willing to put aside what you guys have to protect you."

"Well, we didn't have much but great sex." Longing gutted me. "Awesome, amazing, life-affirming sex."

Aria raised an eyebrow. "Wow."

"Yeah." Renewed annoyance flooded me. "And okay, I shouldn't have said what I said and I feel bad about it, but it's kind of crappy that I thought the sex was incredible while he would prefer to treat me like a job."

"Men suck." Aria threw back the wine and then poured more into each of our glasses. "They really suck."

My nosiness got the best of me. "Did I sense a little friction between you and North Hunter?"

Aria rolled her eyes. "Oh, please. That asshole wishes. He's just ... he reminds me of someone I don't like very much. It tends to make me act a little unprofessional around North." She grimaced. "Thankfully, he hasn't complained about me. I think the sick bastard gets off on it."

I smothered a laugh because I'd gotten that impression too. "Does he remind you of an ex?"

She tilted her head in thought. "Maybe a few exes. I don't have a great track record in that department. The last betrayal was a doozy, and I decided to take a break from dating. A long break. In the Scottish Highlands." She raised her glass in the air. "To long breaks in the Scottish Highlands."

"You came here to get away from a guy? Huh. We have more in common than I thought."

"Well, partly." Aria heaved a sigh. "I told you before that LA is not a place that makes me happy."

"Then this isn't really a break, right? You're living here."

She smiled. "Yeah, I live here now."

I lifted my glass toward her. "Then to *starting over* in the Highlands."

Aria clinked her glass against mine. "And to not letting men control our choices."

I repeated those words to myself, hoping I could make them stick.

TWENTY-FOUR
SLOANE

W alker being Walker, he got out of the SUV early the next morning to round the hood and take from me the bakery boxes I couldn't see over. He laid them carefully in the back seat and then opened my door for me. I tried to meet his eyes as I brushed past him to get in, but he stared stonily ahead. It was just like him to open my freaking door like a gentleman even when he was pissed at me.

It made me want to kiss him.

And it didn't seem possible that the last time I kissed him was the last time.

When he got into the driver's side, I opened my mouth to speak, to clear the air, but he spoke first.

"I had someone talk to one of Andros's friends. Kyle Brixton."

Startled, I nodded as Walker pulled away from Aria's. "I remember Brix."

"They got Andros's whereabouts out of him."

My heart raced. "And?"

Finally, Walker shot me a look before returning his eyes to

the road. "He's in Scotland, Sloane. On a fake passport that cost him thousands of dollars."

Fear thrummed through me. Nathan had dropped a ton of cash for his revenge. My stomach churned. "This is for real?"

"Well, we can't know for certain, but my guys put the fear of God into Brixton. He didn't have any more details other than Andros bought a fake passport to come find you. If he's telling the truth, and we're going on the belief that he is, we know now. We can cross Hoffman off the list of suspects and focus on finding Andros."

I let loose a shaky exhale. "I guess that's good."

"I won't let anything happen to you," he promised again.

That pricked my pride. He was so set on protecting me, above all else, that he'd forgotten one crucial bit of information. "Neither will I. *I* beat him last time, Walker. *I* did. And I will beat him again."

Walker's hands tightened around the steering wheel, but he said nothing. We lapsed into a tense silence as we drove off the estate and into the village.

Walker pulled up outside Flora's, and she spotted us and walked across the café to open the door. Walker insisted on carrying in the boxes of baked goods. Then he strode away to stand guard at the door. I moved to the counter to explain all the treats to Flora as she unboxed. Pride cut through my fear as she oohed and aahed over my fall cupcakes and decorated biscuits. She smelled one of the cinnamon swirls, and I swear her eyelashes fluttered.

"These will go in the first two hours," she said, gesturing to the baked goods. "Sloane, they're proving to be such a hit with my customers."

"I'm glad."

"You know, I was talking to Gordon, and he said it might

be possible for you to get a permit for a stall that could sit on the square."

Confused, I wrinkled my brow. "A stall? Like at the Christmas fair?"

"Aye, but this would be permanent. There are stalls that look like wee buildings. Gordon said, depending on the design, you should be able to plonk one down near the square. You know, instead of renting a shop to run your bakery from. It would be cheaper to have a bakery stall, hut, whatever you want to call it. You'd have to do most of your baking off-site, but it would get you up and running quicker."

Excitement cut through my nerves. "Gordon thinks this is possible?"

"Yes. You'll have to apply to the council for a permit and possibly planning permission, depending on the stall design, but he seems pretty confident they'd be open to reviewing it."

I didn't know how much a thing like that would cost, but I smiled brightly at Flora. "Thanks. I'll definitely look into it."

She asked me how I'd feel about baking two large cakes for next Saturday that she could sell by the slice. We were chatting about flavors when her shop phone rang.

"One second." She pulled it off the wall and answered it. I glanced back at Walker to see if he was getting impatient, but his back was to me, his eyes to the street outside. I took in the strong breadth of his shoulders, remembering the feel of his naked back beneath my hands.

Longing and hurt flashed through me, and I turned back in time for Flora to hold the phone out to me with a frown. "It's for you."

"Me?" I started around the counter, thinking perhaps it was Callie. "Who is it?"

"He didn't say."

That knot in my gut intensified as I took the phone from Flora. "Hello."

"Well, if it isn't my rat of an ex-bitch," Nathan's voice drawled down the line.

The fluttering rapidity of my pulse nauseated me. "Nathan? How ..."

"You think I don't know every move you make, you cunt?" He chuckled darkly. "I've spent the last few weeks watching your every move. You come to this bitch's place every Saturday before eight. You're fucking that asshole who won't let you out of his sight. And I know he got some guys to break Brix and that you know I'm here. So I thought I might as well say hello."

"Nathan ..."

"I used to love the way you said my name, you know. Now you're going to say it pleading for your fucking life. You know how I know that? Because I know everything. I know our kid spends way too much time with people that aren't her daddy. Like right now. Got my eyes on sweet Callie as we speak. When did you see her last, slut? Think about it, treasure it ... 'cause it was the last time." He hung up.

Callie.

Fear and rage unlike anything I'd ever felt froze me to the spot.

"Sloane. Sloane?"

Suddenly, hands gripped my shoulders and Walker's face was in mine. "Talk to me," he demanded.

Flora's phone slipped out of my hand as I stared into those aquamarine eyes. "Where are your keys?"

"Sloane?"

"Where are your car keys?!" I screamed in his face.

Walker's expression tightened with alertness. "Talk to me."

"Give me your keys!" I lunged for his pockets.

He grabbed hold of my wrists as gently as possible and drew me up against him. His voice was soft, calming. "Talk to me."

Fear was making it hard to breathe. I panted, "He ... he's near Callie. He's going to get Callie."

"Nathan?"

"We have to go, we have to go."

"Sloane, baby, I need you to take a deep breath. In and out." Walker demonstrated. "Like this. Come on."

"Callie."

"We're going to get Callie, and nothing will happen to her. But I can't have you passing out on me right now. You try to calm down, and I'll call Adam. He's watching over Callie today."

I didn't know that. Why didn't I know that?

As Walker called Adam, I attempted to breathe slowly, but I couldn't stop shaking. Flora wrapped her arms around me and tried to help, murmuring soothing, reassuring words even though she probably had no idea what the heck was going on.

"Where are you?" Walker barked at his phone.

Adam's voice came through the speaker. "Mrs. Adair got up early and took the kids to a morning market in Golspie," Adam replied instantly. "Got my eyes on them now. Problem?"

"Get to them. Andros is there. He just called in a threat."

"On it. I'll let you know when I have them in hand."

Adam had barely finished talking when Walker took my arm. "Flora, appreciate it if you kept this to yourself."

"I'm not really sure what I'm keeping to myself, but okay. Let me know Callie's all right, please."

He nodded and I followed him out of the café, my legs like jelly even as I powered toward the SUV's passenger side. Though I knew Adam had Callie in sight, it didn't matter. My fear and panic wouldn't dissipate until I had Callie in my arms.

Nathan was definitely here.

He was trying to hurt me. Us.

Would we never be free of the bastard?

Walker did a U-turn and then sped out of Ardnoch way above the speed limit. I braced my hands on the door, willing him to go faster even though he was already going way too fast. Not surprisingly, he handled the road like a professional, slowing into the bends so the SUV didn't topple, and then accelerating on the straight.

Neither of us said a word, the tension thick and excruciating.

My daughter's face remained a fixed image in my head, and I tried not to think about what I'd do if anything happened to her, but failed.

It would end me, I realized. All of my strength was in Callie. If someone took her from me, there would be nothing left but unfixable, broken fragments.

"Callie," I whimpered.

"She'll be fine," Walker promised.

Then, as if he was a prophet, his cell rang through the car. His thumb hit the Answer Call button on his steering wheel. "Adam?"

"I've got them. Callie is secure in the car with me, and we're heading back to Ardnoch. Mrs. Adair, Lewis, and Eilidh are in their vehicle following us back."

"Where's Mom?" I heard Callie cry in the background, frightened tears in her voice.

A sob burst out of me, and I smothered it with both my hands.

Walker reached across and squeezed my shoulder as he replied, "Callie, we're coming. Thanks, Adam. We're on our way. We'll meet you and transfer Callie to us so you can escort Regan and the children safely back home."

"Got it."

They hung up.

"Callie's fine," Walker reiterated. "She's fine, Sloane."

I nodded, sucking back my tears and the nausea that had come in the wake of relief.

A few minutes later, Walker said, "That's them."

A desperate need to get to Callie overtook me, and I rested my hands on the dash, leaning forward as Walker safely executed another U-turn and pulled off to the side of the road behind Adam.

I unbuckled my belt before he'd even stopped, and he'd barely drawn to a halt when I launched myself out of the car.

"Sloane!" Walker yelled, but I was already racing down the side of the road, past Regan's car to Adam's. I'd almost reached it when the back door flew open and Callie jumped out.

Sobbing hysterically, she ran to me and we slammed into each other so hard, I had to hold tight so she didn't fall over. "Mom!" she cried, her fists knotted tight in my T-shirt.

"I've got you, baby girl. I'm sorry. We scared you, and I am so sorry. But we're okay. We're okay."

"What's going on?" She hiccupped, lifting her tear-streaked face to look up at me.

"We can't do this here." Walker was suddenly at our sides. "Get to the car."

"Walker?" Callie's face crumpled.

Without a word, he lifted my daughter into his arms and she wrapped herself around him like a monkey. His face was grim as he ran a soothing hand down her back and jerked his chin. "Sloane, get to the car."

He glanced at Adam, who stood by his SUV, expression hard. "Follow Mrs. Adair home. Let me know she's safe."

Adam nodded and approached Regan's car to explain.

I turned to Callie in Walker's arms and ran a hand down my daughter's back before I followed them to the SUV to open the door for Walker. He murmured soothing words to

Callie, who unlatched herself from him long enough to climb into the car. Then we both hurried inside too.

For the first time since we'd moved onto the estate, I couldn't wait to return to the safety of one of the most secure places in the country.

Twenty-Five
Walker

I'd heard the yelling. Her scream. The way it changed from anger to terror. The door was before me. She was behind it. With him. Why was I waiting?

Last time I barged in. Didn't I?

Now I was frozen like a fucking deer in headlights.

Throw the damn door open! I roared at myself.

You're going to be too late.

Open the fucking door!

I brought my knee up and leg out, putting all my force into it.

The door swung open, crashing into the wall.

She lay there on the floor, eyes glassy and unseeing. Blood saturated her torso, pouring from the wounds at her neck.

Despair and grief like I'd never experienced brought me to my knees beside her. "Iona," I whispered, my hands reaching for her.

They were already drenched in blood.

What?

Confused, I turned them over, watching the blood, her blood, drip from my fingertips.

A snarl cut through the room, and my gaze jerked up to find him, feral and teeth bared, coated in blood and gore, glaring at me as he knelt over her. "You did this too. This is your fault too."

Then he lunged at me with a mouth filled with sharp teeth.

I jolted awake, blood rushing in my ears.

The nightmare faded as I took in the ceiling of my bedroom in the dim light of the dark night. I sat up, scrubbing a shaky hand down my face.

My body was damp with sweat.

Fuck, it had been years since I'd had that nightmare. Others from my time in war haunted me whenever I was stressed. But that dream ... I'd thought I'd seen the last of it.

Groaning, I willed myself to shake it off, but I felt sick. Getting out of bed, I glanced at the clock—just past one in the morning. I'd only been asleep for a few hours.

"Bugger," I muttered as I wandered into the kitchen to get a glass of water.

As I drank it, I stared at the clock on the kitchen wall. My mind discarded the last remnants of the dream as I returned to reality and immediately remembered Sloane and Callie.

I'd hated leaving them at Aria's. I'd stayed as long as I could while I called Lachlan, Brodan, Thane, and the security team. We knew for certain Andros was in the area, so Lachlan had offered a generous bonus to anyone on the team who brought him in. That meant we had men out there right now, searching for Andros.

I'd hoped it would make Sloane feel better, but I knew when I left her and Callie that they were both shaken. I could kill the bastard for putting them through this. For putting his own daughter through this. She was only ten years old.

Throwing back the last of the water, I dumped the glass and headed into the shower. After a quick one, I dressed and got in my car.

Ten minutes later, I was outside the Howards' home on the estate. I pushed my seat back and settled in for the night. I knew no one could breach the security at Ardnoch. We had state-of-the-art drone perimeters, silent trip alarms, CCTV, and highly trained guards. But I needed this.

I stared up at the house. There were no lights on, so I assumed everyone was asleep. Restless, I got out of the SUV and leaned against it, eyes to the house. It was hard to hear anything over the crash of the waves against the beach below the dunes. The sea air was freezing, but it felt good on my fevered skin. The weather had changed. We were deep into Autumn. I'd barely noticed the passing of the season, my mind elsewhere these past few weeks. On the woman behind the door in front of me.

As if I conjured her, the door opened and Sloane appeared beneath the moonlight. I pushed off the SUV and took the porch steps in two giant strides. She stepped out, closing the door behind her, shivering in her nightdress and oversized cardigan.

"You should go back to bed," I said quietly.

She stared up at me, her eyes like the black of night in the darkness. "I saw you pull up."

"I didn't mean to wake you. Just couldn't sleep."

"You didn't wake me. I couldn't sleep either."

Without thinking about it, I gave in to the urge to touch her, caressing her cheek with my thumb.

Sloane studied me, and I couldn't read her expression. I didn't like it. Usually she was an open book.

I didn't have to wait long to understand what was going on inside her, though. She reached for my hand, wrapping hers around it. Then she turned and walked along the porch, pulling me around the corner onto the side of the house that had no neighbors. Only woodland stretched along the coast beyond toward the castle.

She shrugged out of her cardigan and braced her back against the house, before drawing my hand up to her breast. Heat and hunger and a desire to fuck every good and bad feeling into her destroyed any rational thinking.

Control went out the window.

I covered her mouth with mine, needing to taste her, groaning at the way she kissed me like she was starving. Her tits were perfect in my hands, and I squeezed them, my dick straining against my zipper as I captured her excited gasps in my kiss. I tugged down the loose neckline of her nightie as I released her mouth to kiss my way down her neck to her right nipple. Her skin was hot despite the cold, her perfume light, summery. Like Sloane.

I needed inside her more than I needed anything.

Her nipples pebbled hard in the cool air, and I took turns pulling them into my mouth, sucking and laving the sweet buds until Sloane was writhing and clawing at me. Sliding my hand between her thighs, I slipped my fingers beneath her knickers and found her wet and ready. Just the touch of her heat sent me off the edge.

I tore down her underwear and she stepped out of them before reaching frantically for my jeans, unbuckling my belt and unzipping me. When she wrapped her hand around my dick and tugged, I fell into her, kissing her as I ground into her hand.

The edge was too close, though, and I wanted to come inside her. I almost dropped my wallet, trying to get a condom out, fumbling like a fucking teenager.

Shoving my jeans and boxers to my ankles, I wrapped up and lifted Sloane into my arms, sliding her back up the wall of the house as her thighs clung to me.

I prodded until I found her and then I surged up into her. She whimpered to bite back her cry as I gritted my teeth against the groan of pleasure. Fuck, nothing felt better than this woman. So tight and hot, her pussy gripping my dick like she never wanted to let go.

I pulled almost all the way out, bent my knees, and thrust back in.

She clung to me, fingers biting into my shoulders as I fucked her against the side of the house, staring into her gorgeous face, watching her struggle to contain the sounds of her pleasure. There was a part of me that wanted to bury my head in her throat and fuck her as hard and as fast as I could.

But I wanted to watch her more.

Wanted to watch the way all the fear and trauma of the last few weeks disappeared and the only thing that mattered was this. Lust. Need.

I could hear her breath quickening, her grip on me becoming fiercer, and I knew she was about to come. She choked on a cry, her mouth wide, eyes bright in the moonlight as her hips tensed against mine seconds before I felt the hard tugs of her pussy around my dick.

There was barely a chance to watch her face before the sensation was too much and I came in a long, throbbing release that shuddered through every fucking inch of me. I buried my face in Sloane's neck as I ground my hips into her, my dick still pulsing inside her even after I'd emptied myself into the condom.

Fuck, it felt never-ending. And yet not enough.

Finally, our breathing calmed, and I felt her body go pliant against mine, her thighs slipping as she struggled to stay up.

Reluctantly, I pulled back and out of her as I lowered her gently to the ground. Need for her still tightened in my gut as I watched her tug her nightdress up.

I wanted her in my mouth again.

I wanted to make her come so many times tonight so she'd have nothing to fear or worry over for hours.

But I knew I couldn't. Not here.

She knew it too.

Sloane reached up and tenderly stroked my face, her fingers rasping over my beard. "Go home and sleep, Walker. We're all good here."

I nodded.

We walked in silence back to the front door, and I waited as she disappeared inside with a wave and a soft, satisfied smile.

When I got back in the car and drove away, I tried not to think about my disappointment that I couldn't stay with her. That she hadn't asked me to stay. If I let myself think about it, it would scare the shit out of me.

TWENTY-SIX
SLOANE

Monday came around, and I hadn't wanted to let Callie out of my sight. My instincts screamed at me to keep her home, but the security team convinced me she would be fine and protected at school.

I, however, was not fine. Even though I wasn't supposed to, I kept my cell on me all day in case Callie needed me. And also in case the police called. We'd updated the detective inspectors about the phone call at Flora's on Saturday, and they had an alert out with Nathan's description. I knew I wouldn't rest easy until they caught him. It had to happen soon. The villages in this part of the country were close knit. Yes, Ardnoch had a ton of tourists, so it made things more difficult, but this was a quiet time, and outsiders stood out. For a start, Nathan had to be staying somewhere. The first thing the police did was start checking accommodation—B and Bs, hotels, holiday parks.

One of the worst things in the world is waiting by the phone for someone to bring you good or bad news.

Sometimes my mind would wander from it to Walker. To the early hours of Sunday morning when we'd lost ourselves in each other. That night, I'd tried to fall asleep, but I kept popping my head into Callie's room to check she was okay. She'd been pretty shaken up, and it had taken a bunch of Disney movies and pizza with Aria to get her to relax. She fell asleep on the couch, and I carried her up to her bed for the first time in a long time. When I checked in on her a fourth time, she woke up, said, "Mom?" and then fell back asleep. Realizing I was going to wake her, I'd forced myself to stop going into her room and instead paced in mine. That's when I saw Walker. The moment I saw him standing outside, guarding us, I needed him. And my instincts told me that's what he needed too.

I was playing a dangerous game with Walker Ironside.

"Sloane."

Turning from dumping dirty laundry into the bag attached to my cart, I found Aria hurrying along the carpeted hall toward me. She wore a deep frown.

"What's wrong?"

Aria waited until she'd reached me. "I don't want to alarm you, but there's been an attempted breach of the estate. The security team are out checking it, but Jock has asked me to bring you to my office to wait there until we can be certain."

My heart raced. "To be certain ... that it's not Nathan?"

She nodded.

"Oh." Frannie opened the door of the bedroom we were cleaning, carrying a refuse bag. "Ms. Howard."

Aria gave her a tight smile of acknowledgment. "I need to steal your colleague away for a moment. Will you be all right finishing up here by yourself?"

Frannie's gaze filled with curiosity, but she nodded. "Of course."

And that's how I found myself in Aria's office a few minutes later, jittery and hopeful that Nathan was stupid enough to attempt to breach the estate. He'd be arrested, and this could all be over soon.

Seated in the chair across from Aria's desk, I tried to stop my knee from bouncing but couldn't. Aria leaned against her desk, watching me with concern, but neither of us said a word. When her cell phone rang, we both jumped a mile.

She fumbled for it, cursing under her breath, and then her expression tightened. "It's my mother." She answered. "Mamma, can I call you back?" Aria's lips pursed. "I'm sure that's not true." Casting an apologetic look, Aria pushed off the desk and held up a finger to me. She mouthed, "One minute," and I nodded in understanding as she strode out of the office, gesturing that I should lock the door behind her.

Not even thirty seconds passed when *my* cell rang. Hoping it was Walker with some good news, I yanked it out and saw it was an unknown number. Usually, I'd ignore it because of spammers.

However, for whatever reason, my gut told me to answer.

As soon as I said hello, his voice grated down the line.

"If you ever want to see Callie again, you'll come meet me."

My heart raced, but this time I wouldn't let fear win. He couldn't get to Callie on Saturday, and he couldn't now. "Callie's in school."

"School's out, bitch." There was a rustle and then ice flooded my veins at the sound of my daughter's voice.

"Mommy," she sobbed.

She hadn't called me *mommy* since she was six years old.

"Callie!"

But then Nathan's voice was back in my ear. "Proof enough."

I stood, rage seething through me as I hissed, "You listen to me, you son of a bitch. If you do anything to hurt my daughter, I will put the next bullet in your fucking head."

"Ooh ..." He laughed softly. "I always knew you had wild in you, Sloane." His tone hardened. "And she's *our* daughter. Got my eyes. Look, I just want to talk without your bodyguards in our way. So here's the deal: I'm going to give you instructions, and you're going to tell no one because if you're followed or I end up back in prison, the next time I get out, Sloane, I'll kill our daughter right in front of you."

I heard Callie's frightened cries, and pain and terror unlike anything I'd ever known winded me. Silent, screaming sobs tried to burst forth, and I bent over, clutching my stomach.

"You got that? Sloane, you got that? Sloane!"

I fought through my panic at his agitated yell just as my phone screen showed Regan was trying to call. Probably to tell me Callie was missing. How did he take my girl?

"Fuck, Sloane?!"

I had to choke out the words. "I got it."

"I'm going to send directions to your cell. You're going to follow them. And you're going to tell no one."

"I'm on the estate. I can't get out without the guards knowing."

"Then do what you have to, to get out without them noticing. For Callie's sake." Nathan hung up.

I felt sick to my stomach, but I shut it down. I shut down everything so I could think.

Think, think, think.

My phone beeped with a text with the directions Nathan had promised. He was about thirty minutes south of Ardnoch.

Aria's SUV. Unlike everyone else here who drove around in the estate fleet of Range Rovers, Aria drove a BMW X7 with tinted windows. Perhaps the guards would realize too late it was me driving out of the gates.

Perhaps it was stupid.

In hindsight, it was definitely stupid.

Not to call for help.

Not to tell Walker.

But I believed Nathan when he said he'd never leave Callie alone if I didn't do this. And I had to believe that it was me he wanted, not our daughter. A sick part of me, that raging, exhausted part, wanted to fight him. Wanted to be the one to hurt him. He unleashed a savagery in me I hated him for too.

Rounding Aria's desk, I yanked open the drawers until I found her car keys. Grabbing them, I hurried out of her office, glancing left and right, relieved to see she was nowhere in sight. Never had walking through the castle been so nerve-racking as I tried to keep my steps slow and calm. I passed Wakefield, who gave me a nod of hello, but otherwise didn't stop me, and then I was out through the staff exit.

Aria's BMW gleamed under the fall sun. As soon as I got in, I drew up the navigation map and figured out where Nathan was from his directions.

Storm's Bluff. I'd never heard of it, but it looked like it was in the middle of nowhere.

The urge to drive like a maniac was real, but I drove steadily, my hands trembling around the wheel as I kept glancing in the rearview mirror, expecting someone to come racing out of the castle, demanding where I was going.

No one came.

As I approached the guarded exit out of the estate, I thought I might throw up, my heart raced so hard. Sweat dampened my armpits and along my hairline as the SUV pulled up toward the exit.

The gates swung open before the guards could even see my face.

They thought I was Aria.

As soon as the opening was wide enough, I floored it.

I sped onto the main road, too fast, afraid to look in the

rearview. Instead, I drove toward Ardnoch. When I was supposed to slow inside the village, I didn't.

My cell rang again, and I glanced at where I'd put it on the passenger seat and saw it was Walker. The entire drive, my phone didn't stop. Walker, Regan, Aria, Brodan, Walker, Walker, Walker. Call after call.

They knew.

I reached over with one hand and put my phone on silent. They were all probably frantic, and I hated to put them through that, but I knew Nathan. He'd keep his word. We would never be free of him if I didn't do what he said. My daughter would never be free of him.

And yet he'd underestimated me. He thought that I'd go to him and let him do what he wanted.

He didn't know that a mother would kill to protect their daughter.

That I would kill to protect Callie.

My fury drove me to him. It kept me calm, focused, despite the trembling in my limbs.

When the GPS brought me to coastal land, I realized it was some kind of parking lot. There were two trailer homes on it. Beside one of them was an old blue car. But nothing else. No one. No witnesses.

As I stopped the BMW, the door to the trailer nearest me opened.

Nathan came out of it, dragging Callie down the steps.

Grabbing my phone, I stuffed it in my pocket and then jumped out of the SUV, almost falling in my hurry to get to Callie.

Nathan whipped out a gun and pointed it at me. "Ah, ah. Stay there."

Raising my palms outward, I halted.

Callie stared at me, pale and tear-streaked.

"It's going to be okay, baby girl," I promised.

"Were you followed?" Nathan asked.

I finally looked at him.

He was thinner, his cheekbones sharper. His features harder. Maybe it was because I hated him now, but I couldn't see any remnant of the beautiful boy I'd made Callie with. His insides were finally becoming his outsides. "I don't think so." I didn't tell him about the cell in my pocket, the one I'd had to silence because it was filled with calls from people who knew we were in danger.

"Time we had a little chat, then." He gripped Callie harder, and my daughter winced.

I'd hurt him for that.

It took everything within me to keep my expression impassive. "We talk if you let Callie go."

"You think I want to hurt my kid?" Nathan sneered at me. "You drove me to this, Sloane. Anything that Callie's feeling right now is your fucking fault! You turned her against me!"

Our daughter whimpered in his grasp, eyes pleading with me.

"Nathan," I said calmly, taking a tentative step toward him. "You're right. And that's not Callie's fault. It is my fault," I lied.

That seemed to ease him a little.

"So let Callie go, and you and I will talk."

"Mom!"

I shook my head at her, begging her silently to be quiet.

Her lips pressed together as tears fell down her cheeks.

I'd hurt him for every one of those too.

"Callie can stay here, and we'll go for a drive. Like I said, I ain't got no beef with my kid just because her mom's a cunt. But I will have a problem with her if you don't do everything I say."

"I can't leave her here alone," I told him gently. "She's only ten, Nathan."

"Then leave your cell with her, and she can call someone after we leave." He gave her a shake. "But you don't call them until five minutes after we're gone. You hear?"

Callie shot me a look.

Trust me.

She nodded and turned back to Nathan. "Okay."

"Okay, what?" He shook her again.

"Okay, Daddy," she choked out.

"Damn right." He grabbed her arm and dragged her past me toward the BMW. "You wait in there." Once she was inside the car, he turned to me, gun pointed in my face. "Cell."

Tugging it out of my jeans pocket, I handed it over, but my gaze was on my daughter.

I didn't need to ask to know who she'd call, and I just hoped he'd get to her in record time.

"I'll be okay," I promised her.

She cried quietly again as Nathan handed her the cell. "Don't call anyone until five minutes is up."

Callie nodded, but I knew as soon as Nathan and I drove away, she'd make her call.

"Lock the car, baby girl," I instructed as soon as Nathan closed the door on her.

She immediately hit the button on the driver's door, and I heard the BMW lock her in, safe. From him.

Nathan gestured with his gun. "Get in my car."

It was like severing some integral connection inside me to walk away from Callie and get in his vehicle. But I'd do it. I'd do anything to get this crazy bastard away from her.

With one hand still holding the gun, Nathan drove us away from the bluff and toward Inverness.

I had no intention of letting him get too far. Just far enough away from Callie.

Eyeing the gun, I listened as he spewed his bile at me. "I

know it was you who told that bastard where I trade. Everything I did for you, and you stab me in the back like that?"

"Everything you did?" I asked numbly.

"You fucking shot me! I could have put you away for doing that!"

"And put yourself away for your troubles."

"Shut up! Shut the fuck up, you dumb bitch!" He waved the gun at me, the car veering across the road before he pulled it back under control.

"You think because that fucker has money that you're protected? You think a cunt I own—I OWN—can run from me? No! No fucking way! I'm gonna show you what it is to betray me, bitch." He shoved the gun into my temple, spittle dripping down his chin, his cheeks flushed with rage. Blue eyes filled with madness. I flinched as he dug the gun into my head. "First, I'm gonna fuck you into the next century and remind you who owns you. Then I'm gonna watch the light go out in your eyes, all the while you know that I'm not gonna stop until Callie's home with her daddy, where she's supposed to be."

A cold understanding crawled through me.

This would never end for Callie.

"How do you expect to get away with killing me?" I asked calmly.

My tone seemed to gentle him.

Nathan lowered the gun to his lap. "You're not the only one with connections."

Heart racing harder as I noted the empty road in front of us, I braced myself for two seconds, and then I lunged for the wheel. Nathan yelled as I twisted it toward the other side of the road and he dropped the gun, trying to grapple for the wheel.

But I held tight until we crashed down the embankment,

heading for a tree. I let go, forcing myself back in my seat seconds before impact.

If it hurt, slamming against the dashboard, I didn't know at the moment. I could feel the burn of my seat belt cutting into my neck, and my ears rang.

Dazed, I checked myself for injuries before urgency kicked in. I gasped as I looked to Nathan.

He was out cold. His forehead rested on the wheel, blood trickling down the side of his temple. The airbag hadn't deployed.

The gun. The gun!

I unhooked my seat belt as quietly as possible and leaned over to see the gun had fallen at Nathan's feet. Blood rushed so loudly in my ears, I could barely hear a thing over it. Praying he didn't wake, I squeezed my arm into the gap between the dashboard and Nathan's leg.

My fingertips touched the cool metal just as I heard him groan.

Oh my God. Oh my God.

Sucking in a frightened whimper, I pushed harder into the gap and my fingers curled around the gun. As I pulled it up, my eyes went to Nathan, and he was staring right back at me.

I cried out, falling against the passenger door as he started to come to. Scrambling for the door handle, I pushed it open and he said my name in a hoarse yell.

Falling out of the car, gun still in hand, I crawled away, desperately clambering to my feet as the sound of the driver's side door opened.

In my panic, I did something stupid.

Instead of running for the road, I ran into the woods.

"SLOANE!" Nathan yelled.

Bracken and leaves crunched under my feet as I ran back the way we came. My ribs throbbed with the movement, and I could feel a pulsing pain in my shins where they'd hit the dash on impact. Ignoring it, I ran as fast as I could.

I still don't know how he did it.

How he circled me so quickly.

But suddenly, Nathan ran out from behind a tree in my path, and I raised the gun as I startled to a halt.

He sneered at me and raised his arm.

There was a gun in his hand.

"You think I only carry one?" He curled his lip, blood dripping into his left eye.

"Stop," I demanded. "You can't get away with this, Nathan."

"It's amazing what people can get away with. I've seen it. I could have let this go"—he gestured between us with his free hand—"let you live your life here while I got on with mine back in LA. But it's just not in me. The thought of you walking around, living your life with my kid, like you didn't shoot me and then betray me ... I haven't got it in me to let it stand, Sloane." He laughed grimly. "It's fucked up because a part of me loves you for your fight. I admire it. I admire you. I even love you for it. But I hate you more." Nathan's arm was steady as he pointed the gun. "People will think I'm a pussy if I let you get away with it."

Disgust was clear on my face. "You're a psychotic son of a bitch."

Nathan sniffed, wiping the blood out of his eye without his gun hand wavering. "Maybe. But you had a kid with me, so I don't know what that says about—"

I pulled the trigger, shooting him in the shoulder.

It shocked him enough to give me time to dive behind a thick tree trunk.

A bullet clipped the bark close to my ear as he screamed vile words at me.

His voice grew closer as another bullet hit the tree. Another bullet. Another.

My pulse was racing so hard, my breaths were short and sharp and fast.

But then the sound of a click.

And, "FUCK!"

His gun wasn't fully loaded.

I jumped out from behind the tree, gun clasped in both hands, and shot him in the thigh before he could lunge for my weapon.

Nathan dropped to the ground instantly, clutching his thigh as blood spurted out of an artery. "Call an ambulance, you fucking bitch," he growled up at me, his skin pasty and chalk white.

Gun trained on him, I shook my head. "We're not going anywhere."

"I'll bleed out!"

"Walker will be on his way."

"No one knows which way we came!"

"He'll find us," I said, believing it.

And if Nathan bled out while we waited, I wouldn't cry about it.

TWENTY-SEVEN
WALKER

A ndros couldn't know it, but he timed his move well. What were the chances that he'd take Callie the same day two celebrity fangirls tried to break onto the estate? Being on such high alert, it distracted us long enough for Sloane to take off with Aria's vehicle.

The pieces fell into place with a frantic phone call from Regan to inform me Callie hadn't come out of the school gates with Lewis. When school ended, the teachers and students had been distracted by a fight that broke out between three of the older boys, and a parent saw a man of Andros's description talking to Callie outside the gates. No one had seen her walk off school grounds because of the fight. They'd spoken before they walked away together hand in hand. Callie had gone willingly. Regan hadn't known Callie was gone until almost everyone else had cleared out.

An alert from the guards that someone had stolen Aria's BMW followed that call.

Sloane.

When she didn't answer her phone, I felt fear like I hadn't felt in a long time.

It had been years since I'd felt that close to losing my fucking mind.

We followed Sloane's phone, and Callie called me from it. The relief of finding her safe inside Aria's vehicle barely tempered me. Facing that wee girl as she begged me to save her mum ... I honestly hadn't known what I'd do if I failed her.

Callie went willingly with Jock after explaining Andros had threatened her mum's life and that's why she'd left with him at the school gates. She pointed us in the direction they'd gone but could only tell us the color of the car and that it was old.

"We'll find her," Jamie had said as I drove us toward Inverness.

We had to find her. There was no other option.

The last time I saw Sloane couldn't be the last time.

As it turned out, finding her was easy. Two cars had pulled off to the side of the road about ten minutes from where we found Callie. There were people climbing up from the embankment after inspecting a blue car that had crashed.

I swung the SUV in behind them and ignored the drivers who had stopped to investigate as Jamie and I hurried down the slope to check it out. The vehicle was empty.

We shared a worried look, and then I rounded the hood and saw the footprints in the mud. Smaller and larger. "They went into the woods." Fuck! Why had Sloane run for the woods instead of the road?

Guns out, we moved swiftly into the trees and followed the smaller footprints. Soon we heard a male voice and ... Sloane.

I picked up the pace until I saw her.

Standing over Andros with a gun in her hands while he clutched his bleeding thigh.

Relief and pride rushed through me.

"Sloane," I said quietly, trying not to startle her.

She glanced sharply over her shoulder without moving her gun off Andros. As soon as our eyes met, she burst into tears.

My gut knotted, and I moved to her side as I murmured, "You can lower your gun, baby."

Jamie stood over Andros, gun trained on him, while he called for an ambulance and the police.

Sloane lowered her gun, slumping into me. "Callie?"

"She's fine. She's safe. Are you injured?"

"I don't know," she whispered.

I wrapped an arm around her as she rested her cheek on my chest. Her body trembled like she was in shock.

"Is he going to die?"

Looking down at Andros, I noted he'd passed out. Blood saturated his leg, and I realized he had a second gunshot wound in his shoulder. Sharing a glance with Jamie, I waited as Jamie kneeled on his haunches and checked Andros's pulse. He looked up at me grimly. "Pulse is faint."

"I think I hit an artery," Sloane observed flatly and repeated, "Is he going to die?"

"I don't know." I held her tighter as Jamie took off his tie and made a tourniquet around Andros's thigh to stop the blood flow.

"Is Callie all right?"

Her trembling wouldn't desist and between that and her repeating herself, I was worried she was definitely in shock. "Callie's fine." I slipped my gun back into its holster and drew off my jacket to cover Sloane. I rubbed her arms as she stood impassively against me, cheeks chalk white, eyes too big. "Jamie, go flag down that ambulance," I ordered, not taking my attention off Sloane. "We'll be fine. Andros isn't going anywhere."

Once Jamie left, I cupped Sloane's face and forced her to meet my gaze. "Sloane, stay with me, baby, okay?"

She nodded, but her eyes were glazed. "I think I killed him. What will happen to me?"

"Nothing is going to happen to you," I vowed fiercely. "Do you understand me? It was self-defense."

"Self-defense," Sloane murmured.

I crushed her to me, holding tight, trying to keep her warm. But really, the embrace was for me too. How many times had I promised I wouldn't let anything happen to her? I'd failed her by not protecting her from Andros's attack, and if he died at her hands, I'd have failed to protect her from the trauma of taking someone else's life.

As I looked down at an unconscious Andros, I didn't know what the better outcome would be: him, gone from their lives for good, but leaving Sloane with the weight of his death on her shoulders; or him surviving and posing a threat to her peace of mind for the rest of her life.

Neither seemed right.

It should have been me. That bullet in his thigh should have come from me.

I'd failed her.

TWENTY-EIGHT
WALKER

"You canceled our last session," Rich said without preamble as soon as his face appeared on my laptop screen.

Agitated, I scrubbed a hand over my beard. "Didn't feel like talking."

My therapist frowned. "Has something happened, Walker?"

Aye, something had happened. Two weeks. It had been two fucking weeks since Andros kidnapped Callie and then Sloane and almost bloody killed her.

Two weeks since I failed to protect her like I'd vowed.

"Walker?"

"Something happened the day before our last session was scheduled. It was still a bit raw," I admitted. "I needed time before we talked."

"Do you feel like telling me what happened now?"

No. But it was eating away at me, so I knew I should. Over the next few minutes, I relayed the story about Andros.

"Sloane sounds like a very strong and capable woman."

I nodded, my throat thick with the strain of mixed emotions.

"How is she coping?"

"I don't know." Guilt twisted in my chest, and I shifted uncomfortably on my couch. "I've been keeping my distance."

Rich's shrewd gaze narrowed. "Why?"

"I ... I promised her that bastard wouldn't hurt her or Callie, and now Callie is traumatized, and Sloane almost killed Andros to protect herself. I broke my promise." I huffed in self-directed disgust. "You know, when this shit was all starting, I actually told her there was no one better equipped to protect her than me. What a fucking joke."

"How so?" Rich frowned. "You've dedicated the last few months to Sloane and Callie's safety. You were the first on the scene."

"Callie should never have been taken in the first place."

"Circumstances were such that it was out of your hands, Walker. Just as Sloane deciding to go after Callie and her ex alone was. You did what you could. You tried."

"I failed."

"Sloane and Callie are both alive and the perpetrator is in prison. How is that failing?"

Frustrated, I wondered if Rich was being deliberately bloody obtuse. "None of that changes the fact that this has marked both Sloane and Callie."

"It always was going to. Nathan Andros is a dangerous man, and unfortunately, Sloane and Callie were his targets. If you weren't in their lives, if you hadn't arranged private security for them, who's to say he wouldn't have made his move weeks ago? For all we know, this could have ended very differently, and badly, for Sloane and her daughter if you weren't in their lives."

Rationally, I knew he was right.

"Sloane isn't Iona, Walker," Rich added carefully.

My gut tightened into a knot. "I know that," I gritted out.

"Do you? Last time we spoke, you mentioned old nightmares had resurfaced. Have there been any more?"

Fuck.

I nodded.

"Could it be possible you're conflating your feelings of guilt, of failure, regarding Sloane based on the past trauma of losing Iona the way you did?"

I let his words settle on me. Let them percolate as he waited quietly, patiently. The knot in my gut eased. I had thought it strange that those nightmares had restarted. Maybe the stress of protecting Sloane *had* resurrected some old ghosts. "Perhaps," I admitted.

Rich nodded. "Has Sloane made you feel like you failed her?"

"No." I shook my head. "Worse. She thanked me."

The corner of his mouth lifted. "Sloane clearly doesn't think you failed her."

I shrugged.

"We've already established you have a deep-seated fear of failing people, Walker. Especially women. Don't you think it's possible that your fear is clouding your perspective of the situation with Sloane and Nathan? *I* don't think you failed. More importantly, Sloane doesn't think you failed her."

I gave him a nod to let him know I was listening, processing.

"Over the next few weeks, I'm going to ask you to examine the events leading to the attack and really come to grips with the elements of the situation that were outside your control. Mostly, I want you to focus on the outcome. Sloane and Callie are safe. I think a good way to concentrate on that part is to spend time with Sloane again. Distance between you will only exacerbate your feelings of failure."

"I ... I'm not sure I'm ready for that." The more time I

spent with Sloane, the more chances I had to fuck up where she was concerned.

"Well, I can only ask you to try. From what you've told me of Sloane over our last few sessions, she believes in you a great deal, Walker. And I think you need that from her to help you overcome your fear of failing her. You need to feel capable, and you need to believe in yourself, and yes, absolutely, we still have to work on you getting there on your own. But right now, I think Sloane is an integral part of overcoming your feelings of failure about this particular situation."

I heard him, and I understood.

But I didn't know what I wanted from Sloane right now. "I need time to think about it."

Rich nodded, knowing well my need to process things for a while. "Okay. You take some time. We'll talk again."

Twenty-Nine

SLOANE

What *a difference a month could make*, I thought to myself as I hummed along to music on my phone and readied myself for parents' evening at the school.

Arro and Mac had fixed up the cottage on insurance money. Apparently, all the Adair family had pitched in to put our home to rights, including Arran and his girlfriend Eredine. Eredine worked as a yoga instructor on the estate but we hadn't had the opportunity to spend much time together. That two people, who didn't know us well, would pitch in to help put our home back together, reminded me there was good in the world. That what happened to us wouldn't change me for the worse.

Callie and I moved back in a week after Nathan's attack. They'd been overly generous and replaced the smashed TV with an even nicer one, and snuck in a KitchenAid mixer and other little bits and pieces we didn't have before. This was on top of the hugely discounted rent they charged for the cottage. I honestly didn't know what I'd done to deserve such kind people around me, but I'd never take them for granted.

Strangely, however, both Callie and I missed Aria, and if I

hadn't been mistaken, she'd been sad to see us go too. She hugged me extra hard the day we moved out of her family home, and I decided then not to let the genuine friendship that had sparked between us fade. Yes, she was my boss, but she was also a really good human whom I worried was lonely. I'd already invited her to have dinner with me and Callie next Sunday, since that seemed to be her quietest day on the estate.

I took time with my hair and makeup, even though it was only parents' evening. It was one of only a few occasions lately where I'd gone anywhere other than grocery shopping or delivering bakery orders. Callie and I had been invited to family dinner with the Adairs twice since the attack, but otherwise, I hadn't really had the opportunity to make myself feel pretty.

Callie was with Lewis, and Arro and Mac were watching them so Regan and Thane could attend parents' evening too. Lewis loved his aunt and uncle so much, he'd asked if he could sleep over with them. They'd said yes and invited Callie to the sleepover. It would be her first since she was taken by Nathan, and while I was nervous about it, I also wanted her to have normality again. Plus, Mac Galbraith was as tall and built as Walker, and a badass martial artist, too, so I was reassured, knowing he could protect my kid. I didn't know how they were going to manage watching two preadolescents along with their baby girl, but they offered, so ...

Another offer had come from Walker. To drive me to the school. Walker had insisted on escorting me everywhere until Nathan was extradited. Considering extradition could take months, if not years, it sounded ludicrous that Walker intended to guard me until then, but I wasn't in the mood to argue with him. I wasn't in the mood to talk with him, period.

He hadn't touched me since the day of the attack.

He'd barely spoken to me. In the mornings, he collected us and talked to Callie, his gaze assessing her with every conversation. After the trauma of being kidnapped by her father, the police had referred the case to social services, and they recommended Callie speak with a psychologist. I'd been all for it because Callie had been so subdued afterward.

It was the psychologist's opinion that my daughter should attend some therapy sessions because she was carrying a lot of guilt over me being taken by her father. *We* talked about it instead, me and Callie. I assured her from the bottom of my heart that she had nothing to feel guilty about and that it had all turned out all right in the end.

Perhaps I was wrong to put the decision in her hands, but I had a smart, thoughtful, mature kid. I asked her if she wanted to continue talking to a therapist, and she said no. I didn't want to put her through a process she didn't want after she'd already gone through so much. We'd revisit the idea if I felt she was withdrawing again, but over the last week, I'd noticed a marked difference in her. Callie was laughing, teasing, fighting with Lewis, and doing all the things that made her happy.

I was keeping an eye on her, and I was impatient to hear what her teacher observed when Callie was in class.

As for me, I'd come out of the whole thing feeling empowered. That might sound crazy to some. But I had won. Nathan had terrorized me for years, and I'd gotten the better of him not once, but twice. I wasn't afraid for myself anymore, but I was still afraid for Callie. If the cottage made a sound during the night, I had to get up and check Callie was okay. Then I'd check the locks and windows before I could fall back asleep. That happened more times than I cared to admit, but I think that was normal.

When we were out and about, I gripped tight to Callie's hand, even though she was ten and past holding it. I needed to feel her with me, to know Nathan had to get past me if he wanted to get to her. I knew Nathan had been transferred from the hospital to prison last week. But while he was in this world, I'd probably never stop feeling that fear.

Physically, I was much better. I'd suffered a few bumps and bruises from the car crash, including bruised ribs and shins, but they were almost gone, and my ribs felt a lot better.

A knock sounded on the cottage door, and I sighed heavily as I gave myself one last look. I recently redid my hair, my makeup gave me a healthy glow, and I was wearing a new dress I'd splurged on since Callie and I had to buy new clothes after Nathan destroyed ours. My bakery dream fund took a hit, but we needed clothes.

The dress was a fall-rust shade with tiny white leaves printed all over it. It had a V-neck line that was just a tad daring, full sleeves that tightened at the wrist, a nipped-in waist, and a long, flowing skirt that hit the bottom of my calves. I'd paired it with a pair of ankle boots and a slouchy wool coat. Deciding I looked cute enough to face him, I left the room at his second impatient knock and hurried downstairs, yelling that I was coming.

When I opened the door, Walker stood on the other side looking grim-faced and brooding as ever. To be honest, I'd been so distracted by Callie and how everything was affecting her, I hadn't had a lot of time to think about the fact that Walker had put distance between us again. However, the past week, with her improving so much, I'd been relieved enough to contemplate it. The man gave me whiplash.

I could only assume that four weeks of nothing but professionalism and sweetness toward my kid meant Walker Ironside was done with our casual sex arrangement. He was only in our lives as part of some misguided notion he needed to make certain we were definitely safe. Part of me wondered if he was upset with himself because he hadn't been there when Nathan made his move.

That was crazy, though, and I'd tell him so if he ever bothered to let me in, to explain to me what was on his mind.

His eyes lowered down my body, and something like heat flickered there for a second before he turned away. "Time to go."

The short drive to the school was excruciating.

It went something like this.

"How are you?" Me.

"Fine." Walker.

"Do anything fun lately?" Again, me.

His reply was a grunt. That was it. Just a grunt. Like he was a freaking caveman.

I didn't bother speaking after that and neither did he. Not even a grunt.

It hurt. More than I wanted it to. Which meant maybe it was a good thing it had ended between us. I'd promised, after all, to walk away if my feelings developed into something more. But I … it wasn't like I was in love with Walker, right? I liked him, and I enjoyed sex with him. The hurt I felt was what any normal human being would feel when they'd been rejected.

"Wait there," Walker commanded as we pulled into a parking space at the school. There were lots of other cars parked already.

I waited, feeling slightly impatient, as Walker rounded the hood to open my door. I got out with a murmured thanks and then strode toward the school before he could say another word.

Walker fell into step beside me, and his arm brushed mine. Even though I could barely feel it through my coat, it was enough to make me move a little away from him. If he noticed, he didn't comment or react. Once inside, we passed other parents, following the corridor toward Ellen Hunter's classroom. The school had bumped up the heating, and it was too hot. I shrugged out of my coat, folding it over my arm as we neared the classroom where parents waited outside on tiny seats meant for children or stood against the wall. I spotted Regan and Thane and hurried toward them like they were a lifeline.

"Walker's not coming over?" Regan asked, frowning at him.

I glanced over my shoulder to see he'd taken up position against the wall opposite the classroom door and was glancing slowly left and right, taking in everything.

Rolling my eyes, I turned back to Lewis's parents. "He's in bodyguard mode."

Regan smirked. "You don't look happy about that."

"He barely said a word the entire drive here. He even grunted at me."

She shook with laughter while Thane asked dryly, "And we're surprised by this? Walker isn't known for being particularly loquacious."

I shrugged, feeling that sting of hurt again. "He used to talk to me. Not lately, though."

The couple shared a knowing look, so I quickly changed the subject. "How has Callie been with you guys?"

They were quick to assure me they'd noticed an improvement in Callie's mood. I asked after Lewis, too, because Regan had told me the poor kid felt guilty for not noticing his best friend had left school that afternoon.

"He's doing much better. Watches Callie like a hawk," Thane replied.

"Yeah. Typical Adair male, overprotective of their females," Regan teased.

I raised an eyebrow. "They're a little young for it to be ..."

"Oh, I just meant in friendship with those two. But who knows?" She shimmied excitedly, her dimples flashing. "Maybe as they get older, it'll turn into more."

"Christ, she's planning their wedding already, I can tell," Thane muttered, but he was looking at her with such tenderness, I felt a pang of undiluted envy. Joy for them that they had so much love between them because they deserved it, but also envy. Longing. Loneliness, if I was honest with myself.

"I don't know about that." I smiled, shaking off my melancholy. "If Callie beats Lewis at tae kwon do one more time ..."

"Lewis is getting better at losing to Callie," Thane observed. "We had a wee talk after the last time about being a good sportsman."

"He wants to be the capable one for Callie, the protector, so losing to her is pretty hard."

I frowned at Regan. "He's surely not thinking like that at his age?"

"I'm telling you. The protective gene runs deep in this crowd." She gently shook Thane, who took her teasing with good humor.

"Well, as cute as that is, Callie will not lose to soothe Lewis's feelings, no matter what's behind them," I warned gently.

"Then she'll be no different from any of the women an Adair man cares for," Thane cracked.

Regan nudged her husband. "That's what happens when you surround yourself with strong women."

"Mr. and Mrs. Adair."

We turned at the voice to see Mrs. Hunter standing in the classroom doorway.

"That's us," Thane murmured.

"Good luck," I murmured back and watched them disappear into the room.

Glancing around, I saw an empty seat next to a guy who looked vaguely familiar. I took it, my gaze drifting over to Walker before I could stop it. He stared stonily ahead, arms behind his back, shoulders straight, legs braced like a soldier. The man did not blend, and he had no intention of trying to.

Hauling my eyes off him, I stared at my lap and let myself worry about what Mrs. Hunter might have to say regarding Callie. I hoped she'd noticed an improvement in her mood too.

"You're fairly new around here, right?"

I startled at the question and looked to my left at the parent. This close to him, I realized why he was familiar. Dr. Haydyn Barr, a parent who'd asked Monroe out last year. She'd told me all about him, how he was a professor of engineering at the University of Highlands and Islands, but dressed well and had an expensive car, which suggested he had some other income or inheritance. Monroe had thought him charming, but she wouldn't date a child's parent, even if she hadn't been hopelessly in love with Brodan for two decades.

"Yeah." I smiled at him and held out my hand. "Sloane Harrow. Callie's mom. You're Michael's dad, right?"

Haydyn gave me a handsome grin as he shook my hand. "I am. Nice to meet you, Sloane. I've only ever heard Sloane as a surname, never as a given name. Is it a family name?"

"Really? It's not unpopular in the US as a girl's given name. It's an Irish clan name that means *warrior* and it was my mom's surname. She always liked the sound of it as a girl's first name." Funny, no one had ever asked about my name. Not even when I first moved here.

"I like it." His grin was flirtatious as he searched my face, as if he liked it too. I wondered if Haydyn Barr was a player. Honestly, I didn't care if he was. It was just nice to feel attractive. "It suits you."

I smiled back. "Oh, you have no idea."

He laughed loud enough for me to see in my peripheral that Walker turned to look at us. I refused to give him the satisfaction of noticing and continued to chat with Haydyn.

"So, you work at the estate as a full-time housekeeper, you have a bakery business on the side, and you're a single mum?" Haydyn said five minutes later. "Are you Superwoman, Sloane Harrow?"

I chuckled at his admiring tone. "Maybe a little."

"Maybe a lot. You put me to shame."

"You're a single dad and have a full-time job too."

He gave me a sheepish look. "With a nanny who helps out."

"I have help," I admitted. "Friends who take care of Callie when I'm at work. They're amazing. I don't know how I survived before them, actually."

"I'm glad to hear it. Being a single parent isn't easy. And I hope you don't mind me saying this, but you must have been awfully young when you had Callie."

"Seventeen."

He shook his head in wonder. "At seventeen I was an immature moron. I can't imagine being a father at that age."

"You'd surprise yourself. Makes you grow up fast."

"I'll bet." His gaze wandered over my face again, and I flushed a little at his appraisal. There had been no judgment like I got from some people who realized I'd been a teen mom. No snobbery regarding my job as a housekeeper. Haydyn seemed genuinely interested in me. "Do you—"

"Mr. Barr."

We glanced over at the door to see Regan and Thane standing next to Mrs. Hunter.

"I'll see you in a bit," Haydyn said, like we would actually see each other after.

As he disappeared inside the classroom, Regan and Thane came over to say goodbye.

The whole time, I was hyperaware of Walker standing guard, wondering if he'd been watching the interaction between me and Haydyn.

Regan hugged me and whispered in my ear, "Barr is a catch."

I rolled my eyes but laughed at her matchmaking attempts.

When my friends left, stopping to talk with Walker for a few minutes before they did, Walker finally looked at me. My breath caught, and I wanted to go to him. Wanted him to touch me so badly. The muscle in his jaw flexed before he whipped his head around, breaking our stare.

Why did he have to be the one who made me feel like this?

Time crawled as the parents who were left either talked to one another in low tones or glanced around awkwardly, trying not to meet anyone's gaze. I noted a few of them staring at Walker in curiosity.

Michelle Kingsley, a woman Monroe had known in childhood and still disliked (but whom Regan liked because she'd once helped fend off a man who attacked Regan at the school gates a few years back) gazed at Walker like he was the sexiest thing she'd ever seen.

I decided at that moment to side with Roe on this one, even if Michelle had helped Regan.

Petty, but true.

Finally, Haydyn came out of the classroom, and Mrs. Hunter called Michelle in. Instead of leaving, Haydyn walked over to me.

"All good?" I asked.

He nodded. "Michael makes parenting easy." Haydyn reached into his coat and pulled out his phone. "If it's not too presumptuous, I would really love to grab a coffee or dinner with you sometime."

My lips parted in surprise. While, yes, we'd definitely been flirting, I hadn't expected him to ask me out. And in front of people.

In front of Walker.

I couldn't look in Walker's direction as I nodded. "Sure."

Haydyn's smile was slow and sexy as he held out his phone. "Can I have your number, then?"

I typed my number into his phone and he took it back, pleased. "I'll call you soon."

"Great."

He nodded in agreement. "It is."

As he strode past Walker with a spring in his step, he missed my bodyguard/ex-lover watching him walk away with a coldly murderous look in his eyes.

My heart raced at the rare show of emotion on Walker's face, and I instantly regretted giving Haydyn my number. It didn't matter if things were confused and weird between us right now. If Walker did that to me, it would hurt.

After a month of nothing, I thought he wouldn't really care.

But I caught his eye as Mrs. Hunter called me into her classroom ... and he was pissed.

Through the guilt, I felt a mingle of indignation and thrill shoot through me.

THIRTY

SLOANE

To my everlasting relief, Mrs. Hunter seemed to agree that Callie was coping well after her father's attack. It was weird for her teacher, someone who was kind of a stranger to me, to know such intimate details about our family, but in order to do her job well, she needed to be aware of the situation. She told me Callie had been quieter than usual for the first few weeks, but the past week she'd noted an improvement. My daughter wasn't a loud, boisterous kid, anyway, but her teacher said she was holding her hand up to answer questions again, she had more energy, she was getting more involved with their projects, and seemed overall happier and more content.

It was exactly what I needed to hear. On top of the fact that Callie's grades were great and Mrs. Hunter called her an "exemplary student," I was in an awesome mood when I stepped out of the classroom. It was only when my eyes met Walker's that I remembered Haydyn.

Walker fell into step with me as we walked away from the classroom.

To my surprise, he asked in a tight voice, "Callie all good?"

If only he didn't care about my daughter, maybe I could stay madder at him. "She's doing really well. Grades are great, and her teacher says she's acting more like herself again, which is what I'm seeing at home. So, all good."

He gave me a scowling nod. "Good."

"Yeah."

We fell into an awkward silence as we walked to his car. He yanked open the passenger door of his SUV, and when I looked at him, I found him glowering at me. A shiver rippled down my spine as I hopped into the vehicle. Then Walker shut the door, and if I wasn't mistaken, he shut it a little harder than usual. Not enough to be called a slam, but there was definitely anger behind the action.

I sucked in a breath as he rounded the SUV to get in.

As soon as he started the engine, he bit out, "Callie's staying with the Galbraiths tonight, right?"

"Right."

When he said nothing else, I eventually asked, "Why?"

He cut me a dark look.

Well, this was fun. I'd been ready to apologize for accepting Haydyn's number, but his attitude made me swallow it. Why should I apologize? Walker hadn't had the decency to have a mature conversation about what was between us, so why should I bother?

A minute later, I realized we were not driving back to my cottage. "Where are we going?"

"My place," he replied gruffly.

Butterflies sprang to life in my belly. His place? For what? "Walker ..."

I didn't know what to say. Part of me was totally indignant, and the other part that was addicted to him wanted to shut up so I could have my wicked way.

When he pulled up to the house, my indignation won out. "Why are we here?"

"In the house," he replied and jumped out of the car.

My fingers knotted together on my lap as he rounded the hood to open my door. "Why?"

He stared at me with baleful lust. That shouldn't have excited me as much as it did. Hands trembling with the thrill, I unhooked my seat belt, and Walker put his hands on my waist to help me out, even though I didn't need it. My pulse raced as my body thrummed with life at his proximity. Everything always felt heightened around him. All my senses, my responses.

Damn him.

He released my waist to take my hand in his firm grip, and a piercing score of longing cut across my chest as he led me up to his house. Walker rarely ever took my hand. It felt so damn good, I almost wanted to cry.

Alarm bells rang in my head.

This was not just about sex.

He'd hurt me by staying away.

I had to stop this.

But as soon as the door closed, Walker leaned past me to lock it and then took the lapels of my coat in hand and shrugged it down my arms. My purse dropped to the floor, I was so shocked by his abruptness, but my coat was off by the time I opened my mouth.

Then I let out a little squeak of surprise as Walker lifted me into his arms like a bride. I wrapped my arms around his neck to hold on as he marched down the hall. He walked into a bedroom that was neutrally decorated but furnished with the same sparse masculinity as the rest of his home. The bed frame was a modern take on an old-fashioned metal design and made of sturdy black metal. At the sight of it, I tightened my arms around his neck.

"Walker, we need to talk."

In answer, he threw me on the bed, and I'd barely had time

to recover from it when he bent over and started tugging off my boots.

"Stop!"

Walker threw my boots behind him and straightened. I could see his arousal straining against the zipper of his jeans. His chest was moving up and down in shallow breaths, a flush cresting his cheeks. Those vivid blue eyes were hungry, and I shivered at the desire in them.

I wanted him so badly.

I always wanted him.

But I was sick of the whiplash I suffered every time he decided he was over what was between us.

"I can't do this if you're going to ignore me for another four weeks before you decide you need to get laid again."

A muscle ticked in his jaw. "I wasn't ignoring you."

"It sure felt like it."

Walker's lips pressed together tightly as he glared down at me. Then, "I'm sorry."

I wanted to ask him why he'd been so distant, but I had a feeling I already knew, and those kinds of questions were asked between two people in a relationship. "If we do this again, no more blowing me off for weeks on end like I'm some stranger you picked up in a bar."

He swallowed hard. "I didn't mean to make you feel that way."

"Well, you did. So, what is it? Are you in or are you out?"

Walker's gaze seemed to touch on every inch of me. His hands fisted at his sides. His voice was gruff when he replied, "I'm in."

The sense of relief that came over me was another warning sign.

And I stupidly ignored it.

Anticipation filled me. "Okay."

I'd barely said the word when Walker pulled me back up

off the bed and turned me around to unzip my dress. His calloused palms coasted down my waist and hips as he slowly pushed the dress toward the floor. Cool air prickled my skin as I stepped out of it, and my belly flipped with excitement as Walker deftly unclipped my bra.

"Turn around."

I did as he asked, and he watched me as he peeled off the bra. My breasts seemed to plump for his attention, my nipples tightening into buds desperate for his touch.

"Do you know how beautiful you are?"

My eyes flew to his in surprise. He'd shown me in actions that he was attracted to me, but he'd never complimented me outright.

He observed my reaction, and as if he knew my thoughts, he frowned. At me or himself, I didn't know. Walker hooked his fingers into my panties and lowered to his knees to press kisses to my stomach as he drew the silk down my legs. After I stepped out of them, he nuzzled his face between my thighs, and I sighed pleasurably into his playful touch.

But he merely gave me a teasing lick before standing up.

I wanted to protest, yet his look was so fierce and promising that the words caught in my throat.

Walker unceremoniously lifted me up and threw me down on the bed again. I bounced, letting out a little cry, and Walker's eyes flared with satisfaction as my breasts trembled with the movement.

He was a little more hurried as he undressed before me.

Just as he peeled his boxer briefs down over his impressive erection, I commented dryly, "You know this all feels a little like you're peeing around your territory."

Walker's eyes narrowed as he understood my comment was in reference to Haydyn asking me out. He strode over to his dresser and pulled open a drawer. "And if I am?"

My gaze took in the black ties he pulled out of the drawer,

and my pulse leaped. "Well, that would make you kind of an asshole," I replied distractedly.

Walker returned to the bed, his erection as proud and fierce as him. He braced his hands on either side of my head, his delicious scent tickling my senses as he brought our faces an inch apart and murmured against my mouth, "Then I'm an arsehole."

He kissed any response I might have had off my lips, and I kissed him back, stupidly thrilled that he was jealous of Haydyn. That he wanted to prove I belonged to him.

What dangerous, dangerous ground we were on.

But neither of us could stop ourselves.

Walker's kiss was deep and possessive, and I clung to him, trying to pull his body over mine, to feel his hard chest against my breasts.

Instead, he gently unhooked my hands from around his neck and broke the kiss.

He observed my expression as he took my left wrist and stretched out my arm toward the bed frame. My belly clenched and wet heat slickened between my thighs as he knotted the silk tie around my wrist and stretched my arm taut toward the frame. Seeing my quickened breathing, Walker murmured, "All right?"

The man had been pretty dominant in the bedroom so far, and I'd loved every second, but it hadn't involved tying me to his bed. He did it with a proficiency that suggested he'd done it before. I couldn't think about that. About other women. That was the past. This was now.

And I seriously enjoyed it when Walker held me down while we had sex.

I nodded, wetting my lips a little nervously.

He noted it. "Say the word and I untie you, all right?"

"Is this ... Are you ... like ... Do you have the whole *Fifty Shades of Grey* thing going on?" Because I was into him tying me to a bed, but I wasn't sure I was up for a sub/dom situation.

"That's a movie, right?" he asked as he affixed the tie in a complex knot to the bed frame.

"Book first, actually," I muttered inanely, watching him as he tied my other arm to the bed.

I tugged on them to find myself well and truly secured. The silk material meant they didn't chafe my skin. Savage satisfaction filled Walker's expression, and he moved down the bed to grasp my hips and pulled me taut. My back arched with the action, drawing his gaze to my breasts.

I felt a luscious thrill score through me, deep in my belly.

"I don't own whips and paddles, if that's what you mean," Walker replied as he fondled between my legs, his thumb catching on my clit. "But I do like a bit of control."

"I-I already g-got that." I attempted to push my hips into his touch.

"And you like giving it up," he murmured thickly, his eyes searching my face. "You're soaked, baby."

I whimpered with need, straining against my restraints, desperate for him to do something more than tease my clit with his thumb.

Thankfully, he was done torturing me. Walker spread my thighs with a forceful jolt that made my stomach tremble, and then he braced them over his shoulders, lifting my hips off the bed.

To feast on me.

I cried out with sensation, feeling the sucking pull of his mouth on my clit and the yank of the ties around my wrists. I couldn't do anything but let him do what he wanted.

And that excited me beyond bearing.

His fingers dug into my ass as he licked and sucked. Teasing me, he stopped, only to push his tongue inside me. I tugged on my bonds in frustration. "Walker!"

I felt his smile against my skin seconds before he returned to where I needed him at that bundle of tormented nerves. Then he stopped, licking inside me instead. Then back to my clit, drawing me closer to release, only to stop again. He repeated this until I was almost crying with desperation.

My body tightened, my thighs closing in on him, my chest heaving and shuddering as the tension spiraled tighter and tighter toward relief.

"Walker!" I yanked on the ties.

He suckled harder on my clit and thrust his fingers inside me, the sensation of fullness overwhelming. That was all I needed. The tension shattered, and I screamed, raw and lost to the blinding climax. I shivered and shook against his mouth as he lapped up every drop of my orgasm.

I was still panting, stomach still quivering with release as Walker got off the bed to don a condom. He watched me as he rolled it on, his gaze devouring me spread out on his bed like an offering. His erection was so swollen and hard, it strained toward his abs. My excitement made me restless for him.

Never in my life had anyone made me feel as wanted as Walker.

And he didn't release me from the ties. He got back on the bed, face hard with need and determination, and he lifted my hips again.

His thrust inside me was powerful, hard. A pleasure pain that made me cry out and arch into him.

"Christ, look at you," he growled, his grip tightening as he pounded into me.

I was being fucked. There was no other word for it.

And it was epic.

The tension rippled down the ties as he drove into me with uncompromising power, like a goddamn conquering warrior taking his prize. His abs tensed with every hard stroke, his expression hooded and intense. He was so much bigger than me. I felt feminine and fragile in his hands. But sexy. I wasn't Sloane Harrow, single mom struggling to get by. I was just Sloane. The woman Walker wanted to fuck like there was no tomorrow.

"Walker," I gasped as the tension tightened and spiraled inside me once more.

Then he slowed his thrusts to a halt, and I stared up in confusion as he hurriedly reached over to remove the ties from my wrists. My gaze was questioning as he loosened the second tie.

"I want you on your hands and knees," he explained gruffly.

But then he was kissing me as he moved inside me again, and I groaned into the kiss, running my hands down his muscled back, feeling his strength. I grabbed at his strong ass, and he grunted into my mouth. Walker broke the kiss and suddenly maneuvered me onto my hands and knees. My thighs trembled as I waited for him to return to me. It was like he needed me every which way he could get, like he'd lost all control.

And I loved that.

It made me feel empowered.

Walker smoothed a hand up my spine and under my hair to grip my nape in his typical domineering way. He caressed me in reassurance and then thrust into me. My back arched and as he pulled out to drive back in, I undulated into his strokes. His other hand slid up my stomach to grasp one of my breasts. Walker squeezed it, and I was lost all over again.

"I can't get enough," he confessed harshly. "I can't get enough of you. Sloane, fuck."

At his words, I came. My inner muscles clamped hard around his driving cock, and Walker let out a stream of surprised expletives before his hips stuttered to a halt. And then, "Sloane!" His hips shuddered against me as he throbbed around my own pulsing release and came.

I collapsed onto the bed, and Walker fell down over me, bracing his body so he didn't crush me. He scattered kisses across my shoulder, even as he still pulsed inside me.

Then he eased out and laid down at my side. His chest rose and fell with his pants. Walker turned his head to look at me. "Never come harder in my life, woman," he admitted hoarsely.

I smiled smugly. "Me too."

His eyes moved from my smile to my wrist. He rubbed at the slight mark left by his tie. "You liked?"

"I liked," I replied. "A lot."

Walker seemed satisfied by that as he rolled onto his side to brush his knuckles down my back in a slow, easy caress.

"I won't take his call," I whispered.

His gaze flew to mine, his voice a little harder as he said, "Good." Then he pushed up off the bed and walked out of the room, those bitable, muscular ass cheeks flexing with every stride.

Good?

What were we doing?

Why was I agreeing not to date someone in return for someone who only wanted sex? And why did Walker care so much that he'd carry me back to his house like a caveman, just to prove he was the man I wanted?

He was the man I wanted.

And I wanted more than he could give, I allowed myself to realize.

After he disposed of the condom, Walker strode back into the bedroom, his eyes on me as he reclined beside me.

Despite my inner voice screaming at me to shut up, not to ruin this, I couldn't stop the words that blurted out. The words I knew I needed to say to protect my heart. "This doesn't feel casual anymore, Walker. I ... I have feelings for you. And I promised I'd be honest about that." My throat constricted at his careful expression and the words I needed to say next. "I know I asked you if you were in ... but maybe I need to be out?"

The words hung between us like an ax hanging over the invisible thread connecting us. I held my breath, waiting for the inevitable fall, the inevitable severing of our tumultuous but extraordinary bond.

THIRTY-ONE
WALKER

I studied her face, every aspect. Every curve and line. The thought of never getting to look at her like this, to lie with her, to be inside her ... I couldn't deny the panic it induced.

Just like I couldn't deny how jealous I'd been when Sloane gave her number to that arsehole at school. How possessive. She hadn't been wrong about my territorialism or the satisfaction I'd felt as she came around me. I was who she wanted, who she needed.

But—and as much as it scared the shit out of me—I realized I needed her too.

The past four weeks of staying away from her had been the biggest test of self-control I'd ever faced. Only guilt at having fucked up in protecting her and Callie from the situation with Andros had stayed the urge to reach for her. But Rich had helped me understand that my fear of failing her had come from another place, another time. I was still processing his theory even as Sloane gave her number to that prick. It came to me, crystal clear in that moment. I knew Sloane didn't see me as a failure. But if I lost her to someone else, I would have failed us both.

Fuck.

I was not a stupid man.

I knew I'd never felt about any woman the way I felt about Sloane Harrow.

It wasn't merely sex.

Now I doubted it ever had been.

At the sight of the disappointment lighting her eyes, I reached out to caress her cheek. "It isn't casual between us," I agreed.

Sloane tensed in surprise, her lips parting with the shock of my admission.

My lips twitched at how fucking cute she was, but I needed her to understand something. "I've never been in a relationship, Sloane. I don't know if I know how to be in one. But if it's enough for you to know I want to try, then stay with me."

Emotion glittered in her eyes. "We're dating, then? For real?"

I swallowed my fear and nodded.

At the grin she tried to bite back, I pulled her to me, kissing the smile from her mouth. She climbed over me, her soft, warm body lying atop mine as we kissed until I was drowning in the feel and scent of this woman. As she moved over me, taking control of the kiss, her hands stroking and searching and learning every inch of me, I let her do with me what she wanted. Usually, I needed to be in control when I was with a woman, mostly so I could decide when we were done. So I didn't have to be callous or cruel if a woman tried to take us to a place of intimacy I didn't want to go.

But as Sloane scattered soft kisses across my body, taking her time at each scar as if she could kiss the old wounds better, I enjoyed it. Any attention she gave me, I was taking it. And when she took my dick in her mouth and tormented me as I had tormented her earlier, I fucking loved every second. I watched her, my fingers threading through the silk of her hair, so turned on by the sight of her mouth wrapped around me, I felt like a bloody teenager.

She was young and beautiful and had her whole life ahead of her.

I was thirty-eight years old, set in my ways, and I didn't know if I could give her the future she and Callie deserved.

Maybe I was a selfish bastard for not giving her up, but I could live with that if it meant she was mine. She looked up from beneath her lashes as she sucked hard, and our eyes met at the same moment sensation skated down my spine.

"I'm going to come," I warned her.

But she didn't let go.

Sloane made me give it all to her.

She demanded I relinquish every inch of my control.

And for her, I did. I would.

Thirty-Two
WALKER

The lone bagpiper was in full Highland dress, in kilt and piper's plaid and all, while he played "Flower of Scotland" on his pipes. A crowd had gathered around him on the corner of Princes Street and Waverley Bridge. Princes Street Gardens plummeted behind him in a sprawl of faded greens and rusted autumn leaves, while Edinburgh Castle rose over the city beyond that. Callie bobbed on her feet between me and Sloane. "I can't see!" she complained over the mournful sound.

Sloane ducked her head this way and that, trying to find a way closer to the piper, but he was surrounded. It was one of those days. Some days, the lone piper was passed by, people too busy with their lives to stop and listen other than to throw a coin his way. Other days, the tourists descended around him like a barrier.

I lowered to my haunches, and Callie turned to me. "Want up?" I patted my shoulders. Perhaps ten was too old to be put on my shoulders, but Callie didn't seem to think so. She nodded eagerly, and I realized she'd probably never received the fatherly offer before.

Another reason to hate Andros. I helped her climb up. Holding her light weight securely, I raised to my feet, and I heard her giggle with excitement. "I can see everything up here!"

People in front of us turned to smile at her, and I glanced at Sloane.

A hard lump formed in my throat at the utter adoration in her eyes.

Fuck, I'd give anything to make her look at me like that for the rest of our lives.

I was in trouble.

Brodan had ripped the piss out of me days before because he, too, knew I was in trouble. He knew because he'd been where I was only months ago.

A week.

It had just been a week since Sloane and I made it official. Dating seemed like too tame a word. Like something teenagers did. It wasn't an easy transition. It chafed a wee bit. Not enough to make me turn back on my word to give it a shot.

And the fear was worth it to have her look at me like that.

Callie rested her hands on my head, and my lips twitched as her wee fingers unconsciously curled into my hair as the pipes swelled. Another glance at Sloane, and I noted the pipe's song had captivated her too. People either loved or hated the bagpipes. I was in the former camp. It was hard to explain, but rarely anything made me feel more patriotic than those damn mournful wails.

Seeing and feeling Sloane's and Callie's emotion as they listened filled me with pride.

Seeing them enjoy anything was worth everything.

Including journeying south with them to Edinburgh for the weekend. Sloane had taken some persuading since the trip was my treat, but I felt they needed a change of scenery. Unable to let go of the feeling that the threat toward them wasn't over, I hadn't eased up on their protection. Andros wasn't talking. He'd refused, which meant I had no other insight into his motives other than what he'd told Sloane. But it felt like I was missing a piece of the puzzle, and even with Andros behind bars, I wasn't ready to let my guard down.

This was my compromise. Showing them a bit of Scotland they hadn't seen before. And for Callie's sake, Sloane had agreed to the trip.

When the piper finished, Sloane waited her turn to drop some coins on our behalf at his feet. I patted Callie's leg. "You want to stay up there?"

"Can I?" She grinned down at me.

Laughter rumbled in my chest. "Aye, why not."

"Everything is so different up here, Mom. Walker is really tall."

Sloane chuckled as she returned to our side and then her eyes widened ever so slightly at my hair.

"What?" I asked, suddenly worried.

She pressed her lips together like she was struggling not to laugh as she reached up to run her fingers through it. Fixing it, I realized. Her perfume tickled my senses as her breasts brushed against my arm and I forced myself not to think about last night.

We had adjoining rooms at the Scotsman Hotel, Callie and Sloane in one, me in the other. But last night, once Callie was asleep, Sloane crept into my room. I'd woken up to her hands and mouth on me, and we'd spent a couple of hours demonstrating how difficult it was to come hard without making a sound.

"Baby girl," Sloane addressed Callie as she brushed her fingers down my cheek. "You can stay up there so long as you don't hold on to Walker's hair like a horse's bridle."

"Oops, sorry, Walker." She didn't sound sorry in the least.

I shared an amused glance with her mum and walked

toward the gardens. We'd arrived yesterday morning and visited Edinburgh Castle first because it was high on the to-do list. I'd then taken them on a walk up Calton Hill. By that point, they were hungry and tired, so we found a wee burger place that came recommended and took Callie back to the hotel.

Today, the girls wanted to visit the newly opened Christmas market in the gardens. It was always a bit of a crush, but we walked around the stalls for an hour or so. Sloane and Callie picked up some trinkets for friends back home and I bought them a new Christmas bauble they loved for their tree. The smell of churros was too much for Callie and we'd grabbed a few of those, Callie eating hers with hot chocolate while Sloane and I tried the mulled wine.

Once we'd seen the market, we spent some time walking around Old Town, stopping into every boutique on Cockburn and Victoria Street. Sloane commented on my patience, but I didn't mind. My job for the last decade had been guarding wealthy people, and wealthy people liked to shop.

Sloane and Callie were enjoying themselves, and that was all that mattered.

Even if I was forced into a tam-o'-shanter hat with ginger hair attached to it so Sloane could take a photo of me and Callie who wore one too. If Callie hadn't cackled so much at my expression in the photo, I'd have deleted it.

"We should probably grab lunch," Sloane said at our side. "Where do you fancy, kid?"

"Let Walker pick. We've picked everything else."

Sloane patted her daughter's leg. "You're right. Walker, where do you want to eat?"

"Wherever you want," I answered easily.

"And how did I know that's what you were going to say?" She threw me that sexy smile. "Callie?"

"There's a Five Guys!" She gestured so excitedly, I had to

grip her harder to my shoulders. "I didn't know they had Five Guys in Scotland."

"I guess we're eating at Five Guys," Sloane muttered dryly.

Callie insisted on staying up on my shoulders as we crossed Princes Street and headed up the slight slope of Frederick Street toward the fast-food place. Once inside, we placed our order and I told them to go find a table.

A few minutes later, I walked toward them with a tray laden with food I rarely ate and settled it down. I'd left them to collect napkins and condiments, and when I returned, I noted Sloane glowering at the table across from us while Callie kept her eyes on her mum.

I glanced at the table and saw it was a group of young guys, late teens by the looks of it. They were being loud.

Frowning, I turned back to Sloane. "What's up?"

She still glared fiercely at the boys. "I'll tell you later."

I nodded and we ate, chatting about what else there was to see in Edinburgh. There wasn't enough time to do everything, and I promised to bring them back.

"Like soon?" Callie asked, big-eyed.

Sloane grinned at her. "Probably not soon-soon. Christmas is less than a month away so we're going to celebrate that first. Have you told Santa what you want yet?"

Before Callie could reply, there was an explosion of laughter from the table of guys, their voices rising. "Seriously, this bitch was the skankiest fuckin' bitch ever. Ah was, like, ye want tae dae whit tae me?" One lad gesticulated with his food. "I told her she might as well fuck me up the arse!"

"Oi." My voice cut sharply across the room, and the diners around us quietened. The boys shut up and looked over at us. "Do you mind? There are children here. Take that kind of conversation elsewhere." I didn't shout.

The lad who had been speaking lifted his chin. "Or whit? Whit ye gonna dae aboot it?"

I stared at him with everything I could do to him blazing in my eyes.

One of his friends hit him on the shoulder. "C'mon, Boyzie. Let's just go."

"I'd listen to your mate if I were you."

"Aye, whitever." He lifted his chin again, but the lads all got up, not bothering to clear their table, before they wandered out, strutting like they were wee hard men.

Conversation built into a murmur again as I turned to Callie. "So? Santa?"

I felt Sloane slide her hand across my thigh beneath the table and squeeze as Callie denounced the idea of Santa, but with shy excitement told her mum she'd like a pink electric scooter. Behind Sloane's smile, I saw a flicker of worry and hated that everything was such a bloody struggle for her.

After lunch, as we waited outside the ladies' restroom for Callie, Sloane leaned into me, casually sliding her hand into the back pocket of my jeans, her tits soft against my side. I bent my head toward her as she explained, "Those guys were being disgusting while you ordered the food too."

I nodded in understanding but then tensed when she squeezed my ass before releasing me. I gazed down to find her looking at me, a hunger in her eyes.

"You just shut them up with barely a word. All you had to do was look at them a certain way, and it was over without getting out of hand," she murmured.

"And?"

"It was seriously, seriously hot." She bit her lip against a grin, and I couldn't help but smile back.

Her eyes widened ever so slightly and then she blurted randomly, "Callie cares about you, Walker."

I knew that and I cared about her too. "I wouldn't be here with you both if I intended to walk away," I promised. "I wouldn't play with you or Callie like that."

She nodded and took hold of my hand. "She asked me this morning if you were my boyfriend."

My throat tightened slightly, and my voice was hoarse. "What did you say?"

Sloane smiled. "I told her you were. But really, you're my *man*." She nudged me playfully. "You're too rugged and sexy to be my boyfriend."

I let out a small huff of amusement. "I think you mean I'm too old."

She turned more fully into me. "How old are you?"

"Thirty-eight."

"Do you really think you're too old for me?"

"Aye." I reached out to stroke her cheek. "But I'm a selfish bastard, so that won't stop me."

"Good," she whispered back.

Callie appeared out of the restroom, breaking the intense staring match between me and her mother. We strolled out into the frosty first day of December, Callie sandwiched between us. She took hold of her mum's hand and then tentatively reached for mine.

At her slight hesitation, at the reminder she'd had no real paternal affection in her life, I ignored the fear that wouldn't abate no matter how hard I tried, and I took her wee hand in mine.

Callie's sweet smile cut through that fear, dimming it until eventually it washed away in certainty. Her happiness at walking hand in hand with her mum and me was what mattered. No one knew what the future would bring. But I could give this to Callie now.

I could give them both this.

Because I wanted it too.

Terrifying to admit, but it was the truth.

Callie, a reserved child with those she didn't know, chattered incessantly as we walked along Princes Street. I was glad of it. Glad to see her father hadn't traumatized her too badly all those weeks ago. Thank fuck children were so resilient.

"Oh!" The startled gasp drew my gaze from Callie to the woman we'd almost walked into. I drew to a stunned halt. My cheeks prickled, vaguely aware of people bumping into us and muttering their annoyance as they had to go around.

Callie's wee fingers tightened on mine, but I couldn't drag my eyes off the older woman, her face familiar, but changed.

My mother's blue eyes, the same shade as my own, were wide. Her lips parted but then clamped together again.

Her gaze darted down to Callie and over to Sloane before returning to me.

When she said nothing, I gave her a brittle nod and guided Callie and Sloane around her.

I felt Sloane's questioning gaze but stared straight ahead, not looking back.

Never looking back.

I only allowed myself to look back once a year, and the week for that was not this week.

"Who was that?" Sloane finally got up the courage to ask ten minutes later as a children's jewelry section in a small boutique distracted Callie on the cobbled lane of Rose Street.

"No one," I replied. If my tone wasn't warning enough, I shot her a cool look before heading over to join Callie.

"Pick one," I said, after observing her preoccupation with a stand of bracelets.

Callie's eyes widened. "You don't have to do that."

"Go on," I insisted.

Her joy over the bracelet was a slight distraction from my mum, whom I hadn't seen in two decades. When I went to share a look of amusement with Sloane, I found her staring out of the shop window, expression contemplative. She worried her lip with her teeth.

Unease shifted through me when she finally looked at me,

and I couldn't read what was going on behind her unusually flat expression.

Then she sighed and shook her head with a smile that didn't quite reach her eyes. "You spoil her."

I shrugged, trying to shrug off my disquiet. "She needs spoiling."

Sloane nodded and gestured for Callie to follow her out of the shop. "Time to head back."

We had a train to catch and then from there, the drive from Inverness to Ardnoch. Tension radiated between us, though, and I didn't like it. I didn't want to deal with it on top of the memory of my mother's stunned face on Princes Street.

At the station, as we waited on the platform for the train to arrive, I stood behind Sloane and coasted my hand down her hip where Callie couldn't see. I pressed a kiss to her temple.

And sighed a heavy inward sigh of relief when Sloane leaned back into me and caressed my hand with her own.

THIRTY-THREE
SLOANE

We were allowed into the grading room so long as we were quiet. Walker, Regan, Thane, and I took a few seats on the bleachers of the huge gymnasium where Callie and Lewis's first tae kwon do grading would soon be underway.

Walker had smartly advised we take seats near the front because our kids' grading was up first, and we'd be leaving after that. In all the time Callie had been going to classes, I had been unable to watch one. She'd shown me her moves in the house, but it wasn't the same, and I'd been carrying definite mom guilt about my lack of presence in this part of her life.

It was the weekend after our trip to Edinburgh with Walker. All of our friends now knew we were dating. Monroe was ecstatic, Brodan needed to stop teasing Walker or he might lose an eye, and Regan had been throwing me gleeful looks all morning. The woman was a year older than me, and yet you'd think she was thirteen from the way she was acting.

Walker was on my left, Regan on my right, and Thane on Regan's right. She nudged me with her knee, and I met her gleaming gaze. She wiggled her eyebrows.

I gave a huff of laughter. "Will you knock it off?" I whispered.

"You and Walker. I knew it," she whispered back.

"Anyone with eyes knew it," Walker murmured from my left as he surveyed the grading before us.

Thane muffled his laughter, but I couldn't hide my grin as Regan smirked and faced the front.

One thing I loved about Walker was that he didn't hide from much. Even though he hadn't wanted to be attracted to me, he hadn't hidden from the fact that he was. Even though he'd never wanted to be in a relationship, he hadn't hidden from the realization that he wanted to be in one with me.

He didn't often offer information about himself, but if I asked, he'd tell me.

So the fact he wouldn't tell me about the older woman we bumped into in Edinburgh bothered me. It wasn't like Walker to avoid a truth. And the truth was, she had a remarkably similar pair of vivid blue eyes to Walker.

He didn't want to talk about it, and I was trying not to be bothered that he never talked about his family. His past.

The sight of Callie and Lewis stepping onto the mat in their little white doboks drew my focus. Their jackets were closed with a white belt, signifying they were tenth gup. I had no idea what that meant, other than that they were beginners, but I knew today, they'd be tested to see if they could advance to ninth gup. Yellow tips would be placed around the ends of their belts if they advanced.

Nervous butterflies filled my belly, and I squeezed my hands between my knees at the sight of my little girl standing on that mat in a line with her peers. Lewis stood at her side. It suddenly occurred to me I was going to have to watch her fight.

Walker's big hand covered both of mine. "She'll be fine."

I took in the tender understanding in his expression.

Leaning into him, I slid my fingers through his, and he held my hand as grading started. An instructor yelled out words I couldn't understand, and then Callie, along with her peers, moved.

I watched in awe as she punched and kicked the air, the gliding movements almost like a dance.

"It's called a pattern," Walker murmured in my ear. "They include offensive and defensive maneuvers, and they have to memorize the pattern."

I'd seen her rehearse this but hadn't known what it was called. Pride filled me as I observed a few of the other kids stumble and forget their moves. But not Callie and Lewis. In fact, they moved in perfect synchronicity because they'd practiced over and over together.

"They're amazing," Regan murmured beside me. "Our kids are amazing."

"When did Lewis get so tall?" I asked.

"He just had a growth spurt. We had to buy him new jeans, pants, shoes, everything."

The pattern ended and I wanted to surge to my feet and clap, but Walker squeezed my hand with a sexy smirk and a shake of his head.

Okay. No clapping at gradings.

"She did good, right?"

He nodded. "She did very well."

Pride was practically bursting out of me, and Walker leaned in to press a quick kiss to my lips.

There were more parts to the grading, but the worst for me was sparring. Callie was called up to spar with another girl, who looked a little older. I might have cut off Walker's circulation by squeezing his hand as the girl flew at Callie. But my girl blocked and defended and got through the other girl's lazy defense with an impressive kick to her side and a punch to the chest. The sparring went on for too long for my peace of mind, especially when the girl kicked Callie in the upper thigh, causing her to stumble.

But when it was over, Callie was announced the winner.

"She's good," Walker told me quietly. "A natural, in fact."

"I'm proud and terrified by that."

He chuckled and kissed my temple in reassurance. The man was surprisingly affectionate now that we were officially dating. I loved it.

Lewis's sparring went just as well. His opponent wasn't as sloppy as Callie's, but Lewis was fast and precise. For beginners, they really were impressive.

"Look at that intense determination on his face." Regan's dimples flashed. "My savage little guy. I could just squeeze him, he's so cute."

"I think he'd rather you didn't at this precise moment," Thane said dryly.

I choked on a chuckle. Even though Lewis wasn't Regan's biological son, you wouldn't know it. She'd been Lewis and Eilidh's nanny before she fell for Thane, and she'd loved those kids from day one. It was clear that love had grown as deep as any mother's love could.

Lewis won, and no one could hold Regan back from jumping up in her seat and whooping her delight. Thane shook his head in amusement while Lewis grinned up at his stepmom from the floor. He gave her a wave and then headed off the mat, straight for Callie, and they high-fived.

A little while later, we all watched, all of us bursting with pride we couldn't hide, including Walker, as our children advanced to ninth gup.

Callie and Lewis were hyper, swinging their belts with their new yellow tips, as we led them out of the sports center toward the parking lot. I had texts from Aria and Monroe asking how the grading went, and I quickly texted back to let them know.

Thane insisted on taking us all out to lunch to celebrate, and since it was kids' choice, we found ourselves in a fast-food restaurant again. I knew Walker, despite his sweet tooth, didn't eat junk food normally and appreciated him doing so for the sake of the children.

I watched him praise Callie until she practically glowed. I observed the way Callie chose a seat next to Walker and how he bent his head to hear her as she chatted away easily to him. His patience with her was one of my favorite things in the world. Walker would never be the most talkative man. That wasn't who he was. But he was one of the best listeners ever, and he engaged with Callie. He cared.

My heart beat a little too fast as a mammoth swell of emotion overwhelmed me.

The way Lewis was with Callie only compounded it. He teased and joked with her, but he also told her that her performance was "totally lit."

"Did you see us during the pattern?" he said to her after barely swallowing a bite of burger. "We were completely in sync."

"You were," I agreed. "It was very cool."

"And the way you blocked Amy and then landed that kick on her side." Lewis beamed at Callie like she was a superhero. "It was amazing."

Callie smiled so big it surprised me her cheeks could handle it.

And I loved every second for her.

Finally, after years of struggling, my daughter had the life I'd always wanted for her. It wasn't perfect. I still might not be able to give her some material things, but the things that mattered ... she had those now.

My eyes flicked to Walker, who observed the interaction between her and Lewis, and I felt a shiver of fear cut through my joy.

Walker was such a big part of what I'd found here.

In so many ways, he was solid and safe.

But there was a kernel of uncertainty within me. I shook it off.

I didn't want my insecurities to ruin this day.

LATER, Walker took us home and we watched a movie. At Callie's bedtime, he waited until she was upstairs and tucked in before he got up to leave.

I asked him to stay instead.

"Are you sure?"

I nodded.

We hung out downstairs for a little longer and then I led him up to my bedroom, where Walker Ironside proved once again he could make love. Slow and tender. And quiet, even though that last part was very difficult for me.

Afterward, I lay in his arms, my cheek resting on his strong pecs. I touched the scar on his upper chest that looked like the one on my arm. "Who shot you?" I whispered.

"Sniper. Afghanistan," he answered quietly, his fingers stroking lightly across my shoulder. "Not a very good one."

"What do you mean? He hit you."

"And yet I gather he was aiming for my head."

Walker said it so casually, but the thought made me sick to my stomach. "Was it awful there? Stupid question, I guess."

"It was pretty bad. They deployed us on operations, but it wasn't long after I joined 43, the protection fleet. I didn't see as much action in Afghanistan as others did."

Thank God. "And this?" My fingertips trailed over his largest scar, a gash that ran down his ribs.

"Bar fight. Sometimes moron drunks like to pick a fight with soldiers."

"Oh my God," I muttered, annoyed at the idiocy of people. "It looks bad."

"Aye, he slashed me pretty good, but I survived."

"And these?" There was a cluster of small red scars on his side.

Walker scowled. "Shrapnel. I was lucky and wasn't close enough to take much of the blast. My mate, Harry, he took the worst of it."

I swallowed past my emotion, thinking about how close Walker had come to dying. Several times. "Is your friend okay?"

"Aye, he's still alive. A few of us meet up every year and camp and fish and drink."

"Is that your therapy?"

He glanced down at me, studying my face. "Partly. But I also have an actual therapist."

Surprised by this admission, I lifted my head. "Really?"

Walker nodded carefully, gaze assessing. "Rich. He's an ex-marine."

Pride swamped me as I reached out to caress his bearded cheek. This big macho man wasn't too macho that he wouldn't seek help when he needed it. I was so used to boys pretending to be men that Walker's maturity was a massive turn-on. "You amaze me. You know that, right?"

His expression softened with affection. "Right back at you, baby."

I shivered at the words, the endearment, and lightly brushed a tender kiss on his chest before nestling back into him. His last scar, a small, jagged line low on his gut, drew my fingers. "And this one?"

Walker's entire being seemed to tense, and I swear the mood iced over in an instant. He took my hand and lifted it away from the scar. Suddenly, I was being maneuvered onto my side as the little spoon curled against Walker's front. "Get some sleep," he murmured in my ear.

Okay, so maybe there were some things he wasn't emotionally mature about.

I forced myself to relax, but I couldn't sleep. Staring unblinkingly into the dark of my bedroom, I listened to Walker's breaths even out as he eventually fell asleep. It was our first time spending the night together. And I couldn't even enjoy it.

That scar on his belly was like the woman on Princes Street.

There were things Walker didn't want to tell me, and I didn't want it to hurt ... but it did.

This man knew everything about me.

Yet there were things I didn't know about him, and I wondered if he'd ever really let me in. Why was I the first woman he'd decided to try a relationship with? What had made him remain a bachelor until me? Who was the woman on the street? Was she his mother? If so, why did he treat her like a stranger? What caused that small scar on his belly? Why did he take off for two weeks every year on the same date? And if I was so different from all the women who'd come before me ... why wouldn't he talk to me?

Why wouldn't he let me in?

I drifted off for an hour before I awoke again. Walker had rolled over onto his back. Restlessness agitated me and my toes curled with the sensation. Needing to do something, I slid out of bed and fumbled quietly in the dark for my gown. The cottage was cold at night, so I shrugged on a robe and gently pulled open a drawer to grab socks. I held my breath, hoping I wouldn't wake Walker, but he didn't so much as twitch on the bed.

Leaving the bedroom, I made my way downstairs and turned on the kitchen lights. Unable to use my fancy new electric mixer because of the noise, I took some joy in mixing the chocolate cake batter by hand. As the cake baked, I melted chocolate for the buttercream. Removing it from the heat, I switched off the stove and leaned against the sink, bowl cradled to my stomach, as I stirred out the last of the lumps, trying not to think about the man upstairs in my bed.

Just then I heard the creaking of the stairs and looked up. Seconds later, Walker appeared in the kitchen doorway wearing only his jeans. He was so tall, his hair brushed the top of the doorjamb. Leaning against it, he crossed his arms over his bare chest, and I tried and failed not to ogle him in his half-naked state.

"What's up?" he asked, voice gruff with sleep.

"Nothing." I pushed away from the counter. "Couldn't sleep."

Feeling naked beneath his perceptive, inquiring gaze, I held up the wooden spoon. "Want to lick it?"

Walker pushed off the jamb and crossed the room. He stopped to wrap his hand around my wrist to bring the spoon to his mouth. My breath caught at the intensity of his gaze as he licked off the chocolate.

A tingle of desire woke into a full-fledged pulsing.

"Good?" I choked out.

He nodded slowly, not releasing my wrist.

"I should ... I should finish the buttercream. Cake's in the oven."

Walker released me, but only to lean over and switch off the oven.

I frowned, but he took the bowl out of my hand and rested it on the counter. "I have a better use for it."

He pressed a hand to my stomach and gently nudged me back against the counter.

"Walker?" My chest rose and fell with confusion and anticipation.

Without a word, eyes still holding mine, he unknotted the tie on my robe and pushed it off my shoulders so it fell to the floor. And then he nudged down the straps of my nightdress until it pooled around my hips. My naked breasts prickled in the cold, my nipples tightening to hard buds.

Walker opened the cutlery drawer, took out a small spoon, and dipped it into the now cooled melted chocolate. Understanding made me gasp seconds before he poured the chocolate over my nipples. I sucked in a breath at the sensation, feeling it drip down my stomach.

Walker lowered to his haunches and took my nipple into his mouth. The pull of his warm mouth, sucking and licking at the chocolate, caused sensation to streak down my belly and deep to the apex of my thighs. I choked back a cry and grasped onto his shoulders, fingers biting into his warm, hard muscle as he took my other breast in his mouth. Once I was swollen and throbbing, his lips moved down my stomach, lapping up any stray bits of chocolate.

As his tongue touched my lower belly, I whimpered, and the sound seemed to break the hold on Walker's patient seduction. Suddenly, he tore my nightdress down my hips and I heard his quick intake of breath when he discovered I wasn't wearing any underwear.

He yanked my right thigh up and over his shoulder, and I had to grasp onto the counter to steady myself as he buried his head between my legs and feasted on me. I bit my lip against the groans and cries lodged in my throat, undulating against Walker's talented tongue.

"Fuck me," I gasped, knowing that word from my lips did something to him.

His grip on my thigh turned bruising as he lifted his head to look up at me. "Need a condom."

"I'm on the pill," I reminded him.

Fire blazed in his eyes as he stood to his feet, lifted me

into his arms, and crossed the room to rest my ass on top of the small table in the corner of the kitchen. Need rushed through me in desperate flickering flames as he shut the kitchen door to muffle whatever noise we were about to make.

As soon as he returned, Walker pushed down his jeans, spread my thighs, and curled them around his hips to surge into me.

The overwhelming fullness was perfect.

I rested my hands behind me, arching into his thrusts. He bared his teeth as his fiery eyes watched the way my breasts shook and trembled with every drive.

"Fuck, look at you," he gritted out.

"Harder," I panted, my head falling back as the table bumped against the wall with every stroke.

"Look at me," he demanded.

I lifted my head, eyes hooded.

Walker's face was etched with a sexy harshness that made me gasp as he thrust into me, so hard and deep, I had to bite my lip to stifle my cries.

My thighs trembled with tension and my arms ached from holding myself up against his powerful drives. Nothing else mattered. All my worries and insecurities were obliterated beneath his domineering and all-encompassing desire.

"You're mine," he growled as his hips slammed against mine. "I'm yours and you're mine. Say it, Sloane. You're mine."

The orgasm exploded through me. Goddamn fireworks lighting up my freaking eyelids kind of exploding. My inner muscles clamped down hard on Walker, throbbing around him in voluptuous tugs that made him collapse over me, his forehead resting on my shoulder as my climax wrenched his own from him.

His hips shuddered, and he pulsed and released inside me.

"Oh, fuck." Walker gasped against my skin, his grip bruising. He groaned my name as he trembled through his orgasm.

I shivered, my thighs quivering around his waist as he pressed his lips to my shoulder and pumped his hips a few more times. "I'm yours," I whispered.

He lifted his head, his face slack with wonder. "I'm yours," he promised me back.

And at that moment of blissful release, I desperately wanted to believe him.

THIRTY-FOUR
WALKER

T he school hall, like last December, was packed with
pupils, teachers, parents, and friends. They bustled
among the tables of baked goods being sold by the pupils and
their families. Last year, I'd attended because Brodan was here
to help the kids rehearse for their school play, and I was
working as his private security. Now, I wanted to be here for
Sloane and Callie and had taken the day off work to help them
set up.

I frowned at the prices Sloane was writing onto bits of
cards for each item she'd baked.

Not this again.

I held my palm out for the marker. "Give it here."

She grinned up at me. "You overprice everything."

"Woman, you underprice everything. You'll need to up
your prices once you open your own place." I took the end of
the marker between my fingers and she released it with a mock
exasperated sigh.

"A bakery isn't a school bake sale." She gaped at the price I
wrote for the cupcakes. "That's extortion."

"You get what you pay for." I propped the card next to the

cupcakes and moved on to the madeleines. "They're not buying crispy cakes. They're buying from a professional bloody baker."

Callie giggled at my side.

Sloane cleared her throat, and I glanced over at the husky sound of it as she replied, "I'm not technically a professional baker." That gleam of outright adoration in her eyes made me want to kiss her inappropriately.

"If I say you're a professional baker, you're a professional baker."

Her lips quirked at the corners. "Bossy."

Don't you know it.

Her cheeks flushed as if she read my expression and was remembering being tied to my bed the day before yesterday.

I'd eventually had to admit that it was time to ease up on my overprotectiveness. Callie had gone swimming with some friends from school and then to a sleepover. That meant Sloane could have her own sleepover at mine, but she'd gotten little sleep.

She also had her car back, and we were trying to return to a sense of normality.

"Stop making moony eyes at each other and sell some cakes," Callie teased good-naturedly.

I'd never been accused of making "moony eyes" at anyone in my life. I grunted, which only made her and her mother giggle. The sound put me in a good mood.

Fifteen minutes later, the sight of Haydyn Barr, the dad who'd asked for Sloane's number, threatened that good mood. I knew Sloane had taken his call and explained she couldn't see him because she was seeing me, but it was like my possessiveness had a mind of its own. With one hand on Callie's shoulder and the other on Sloane's waist as the man approached our table, I told him clearly I considered the Harrows mine.

He took us in and ignored me entirely.

The fucker.

"These look amazing, Sloane." Barr gestured to her table. "I've been told by everyone to come taste your wares."

The way he said that while looking at her like she was a fucking cake he wanted to *taste* was more than a dick move with me standing there. I squeezed Sloane's waist, and she shot me a confused look before she pushed a cupcake toward the prick.

"These are always popular."

He dug into his wallet and pulled out a five-pound note to match the price I'd stuck on the card in front of them. Sloane took the money with a smile, and I waited for Barr to leave.

He didn't. He stood there, eyes on my woman as he ate her cake.

I wanted to rip off his face.

Jealousy, possessiveness, was new for me.

It rode me uncomfortably.

As if sensing my tension, Callie leaned into me, cheek resting against my side. Forcing myself to relax, I smoothed a hand down her wee shoulder and gave her a soft look.

She smiled up at me, and I felt her own tension drain.

Another new thing for me to contend with was watching my body language around Callie. To be aware that she's observant and attuned to the adults around her. I forced myself to stay relaxed for her sake.

When I looked up, Barr wiped his mouth with a napkin, watching the interplay between me and Callie. Understanding seemed to dawn on his face, and he flicked a look at Sloane. "They're delicious. I can see what everyone is talking about."

"Thanks." She gave him a smile, but it wasn't the same smile she gave me.

Barr nodded, and then finally met my eyes. He lifted his chin at me and murmured, "Lucky man."

I watched him walk away, returning to his table where his son stood with an older woman.

"I'm going to see how Lewis and his mom are doing." Callie pulled away from me with a sweet smile and then left us to cross the hall to where Regan, Lewis, and Eilidh were set up.

Sloane turned her back to the rest of the room, crossing her arms as she leaned against the table and stared up at me with an unamused smile. "Even the best of men are cavemen."

Still uncomfortable with the way I wanted to snarl at any fucker who so much as blinked at her, I lifted my chin in acknowledgment. "I'm trying."

"I know." She curled her fingers around the edge of the table. Her hair was braided in a loose plait over one shoulder, and she wore a long-sleeved dress in a style she was partial to. The green of the fabric made her hair look lighter, her skin tanner, her eyes a richer brown. If I noticed everything about her before, my awareness was on another level now. You'd think it would be the opposite. That having her in my bed would dull the intensity of feeling.

But it was getting fucking worse.

She studied me thoughtfully. "Walker ... you should know you never have to be jealous. No one makes me feel like you do. I've never wanted any man the way I want you. And I know I never will."

The pulse in my neck throbbed as I clenched my hands into fists to stop from reaching for her. To stop myself from dragging her out of the school cafeteria and into the nearest room to bury myself inside her.

"I meant it that night in my kitchen. I am yours."

Exultation thrummed through me, and I swallowed hard around the emotion. My voice was gruff as I replied, "I meant it too. I'm yours."

A sadness crept into Sloane's eyes. "Are you?"

The question, the tone, was like a punch to the gut.

"Oh, look at all these goodies." A woman interrupted us, surveying Sloane's baking.

Sloane turned from me, and I felt unease creep over me at her melancholy question. At the disbelief in her voice. The unease felt a wee bit like panic. No. Not a wee bit. A big bit. Indignation simmered as Sloane was inundated with people buying her cakes. I'd never told a woman that I was hers. Ever. I finally had, and she didn't believe me?

My phone buzzed in my back pocket and when I pulled it out to see my friend Sully's name on the screen, I took the opportunity to put distance between me and Sloane while I was pissed off.

"I need to take this," I muttered to her as I passed.

I sensed her turn to watch me, but I strode out of the room, phone to my ear. "Give me a minute to get somewhere quiet, Sul."

"No probs, mate."

Less than a minute later, I was outside the school entrance, the Baltic December air cutting through my Henley shirt. "What's up?"

"Where are you?"

"A school bake sale."

His tone lilted with amusement. "How the fuck did you end up at a bake sale?"

Sully was one of my mates from school. We'd joined the marines together, and he was one of the blokes I met up with every year for fishing and drinking. That meant the guys would know soon enough about my change in situation. "The woman I'm seeing has a wee girl."

Sully was silent for a few seconds. Then, "Fuck, Walk. Never thought I'd see the day."

"Aye, me neither." I scrubbed a hand over my beard, trying

not to think about the shit moment with Sloane back in the cafeteria.

"She must be something. What's her name?"

"Sloane. Wee girl is ten. Callie. Cute as fuck."

"I bet she's got you wrapped around her finger." He chuckled.

They both did.

"I'm pleased for you, Walk."

"Aye, aye, thanks." I sighed and stared up at the bright winter sky. "Since you didn't know about Sloane and Callie, I can't imagine they're the reason you're calling."

Suddenly, his tone was somber. "My mum got a call. From your mum. She wants your phone number, Walk. I didn't want to give it without your permission."

Fuck.

Blood rushed in my ears as I rubbed the nape of my neck and tried to control the million feelings flooding me at the news.

Her face flashed across my mind. The stunned look on it as we stared at each other on Princes Street. And if I let myself think hard enough on it, I'd seen something like regret and pain in her eyes.

"Walk? You all right?"

"Aye." I let out a shuddering exhale. "Give her my number, Sul."

"Good," he murmured. "That's good, Walk. I will."

THIRTY-FIVE

SLOANE

"Walker's house is so clean," I told Monroe as I passed a pristine and sparse spare bedroom and stopped at the threshold of an impressive home gym. "And the man works *out*. Every time I see this gym, it makes me want to do a hundred squats."

Roe's snort of amusement echoed out of the speaker on my phone. "Somehow I doubt that."

"Okay, it makes me *think* about doing a hundred squats. The only exercise I get is—"

"Is working eight hours a day in a massive castle and running around after your child twenty-four seven." Roe yawned suddenly. "Not to mention all the sex you're having at the moment. I seriously don't know how I'm going to manage returning to work, being a mum, and having the energy to jump Brodan. I mean, I look at him and, of course, I want to jump him, but I'm so tired. I'm exhausted all the time. And that's with a husband who's lucky enough to take time off work for a while. Brodan and I have had no time for each other, and that's fine because we're getting to know Lennox, but it makes me anxious about the future and how we're supposed to do it all."

Hearing the weariness in her voice, I felt a surge of guilt. I'd been so wrapped up in my stuff with Nathan and then Walker that I hadn't been a good friend to Monroe. She'd done so much for me, and what had I done in return? She and Brodan only found each other again after a bittersweet eighteen years apart! I knew they were ecstatic to be parents and Lennox was the love of their lives, but they deserved time with each other, too, after all that time apart. "Okay, this weekend, Callie and I are taking Lennox for the day, and you and Brodan are going to have some one-on-one time."

"Oh no, Sloane, I didn't say it for that—"

"I know you didn't." I turned on my heel and strolled to the kitchen. Callie was having dinner with the Adairs, so I'd come to Walker's after work and he was out grabbing us takeout from the only Chinese restaurant in the village. "But I am doing this for you, and you're going to let me."

"I don't know," she mused. "I—"

"Lennox will be perfectly safe with me."

"Oh, I know that." Roe exhaled slowly. "Okay. If you're sure?"

I grinned hard. "Yes! I'm very sure. And it'll be nice for Nox to have some time with Aunty Sloane."

"Nox?" I could hear her smile down the line.

"Oh yeah, we are figuring this kid's nickname out right now, and it's going to be the cool-as-shit nickname Nox," I insisted. "Brodan and Monroe Adair's son is not getting landed with the nickname Len or Lenny."

She chuckled. "What's wrong with Len or Lenny?"

"Len or Lenny is a sixty-year-old man."

"Fair enough. You know ... actually ... I really like Nox. It's different."

I smiled at that, happy to assist. They'd named their son

after his uncle Lachlan, whose middle name was Lennox, a Scottish surname on the maternal side of the family tree. "Nox it is. And I will see Baby Nox on Saturday."

"Are you sure you have time, Sloane? Christmas is coming up, you've got Callie, the baking for Flora—"

"I'm sure."

"Okay. Thank you. Now I know the sex is great"—maybe I'd been talking a little too much about my sex life—"but how are other things between you and Walker?"

I opened my mouth to say fine and then thought better of it. As much as Walker, who was not big on *the words,* had told me he was mine, his actions said otherwise. If he was truly mine, there wouldn't be things about his life that he hid from me. That he avoided talking about. And maybe I was asking too much of him. Just because I was an open book didn't mean everyone else was, right? But if I was becoming to him what he was to me ... why didn't he trust me enough to tell me everything?

Before I could say any of that to Monroe, I heard Lennox wail distantly through what sounded like the baby monitor.

"I'm sorry, Sloane. I have to go check on Lennox."

"Go." I gave her a strained smile she couldn't see. "I'm supposed to find plates, anyway."

After we hung up, I pulled open cupboard doors in Walker's swanky kitchen, trying to find where he kept the plates. While I'd ordered a heavy-on-the-calories sweet-and-sour chicken dish, the man had ordered a healthy, light-on-the-sauce chicken chow mein and vegetable sides. I swear, he was almost guilting me into eating better, but while I still had a teenager's metabolism, the plan was to enjoy the heck out of it while I still could.

Finding the plates, I then searched for cutlery. Nosiness, however, got the better of me. I began looking through all the kitchen cupboards and drawers. Walker cooked for himself, and he had equipment like steamers and hand mixers and juice makers stacked inside. Again, everything had order and a place. I wondered how he'd cope with living with two messy Harrow girls.

I wondered if that would ever be a possibility.

In every other way, our relationship was the second-best thing that had ever happened to me after Callie. Walker made me feel safe and cared for. The sex was utterly mind-blowing, and he was affectionate in his actions. He was a good listener, he wasn't judgmental, and he made me feel like I was the most capable woman in the world. That I was a special mom and a talented baker. The cherry on top was his patience and kindness toward Callie. Oh, and that he still gave me butterflies when he walked into the room.

But he had a wall up between us, and that wall hurt me. Deeply.

As if to exacerbate my feelings, the drawer I pulled out made my heart race a little. The drawer was the messiest thing I'd found in Walker's house so far. It was filled with bits and pieces, pens and measuring tape, scraps of paper, odds and ends.

And also photographs.

Old Polaroids.

My hands shook as I picked them up, because I knew I should put them back. Instead, I flipped through them, the blood rushing in my ears as I tried to piece them together like a puzzle. The photographs were aged, but there was no mistaking one woman in them. The woman from Princes Street in Edinburgh. The one with Walker's eyes. She was younger in the photographs, but it was definitely her. Unsurprisingly, she was attractive, and in many of the images, she was with a tall, handsome man who looked a lot like Walker.

There was also a girl in the pictures. An adorable photo made me stop flipping. The girl, pretty, with the same blue eyes as Walker, and thick dark hair, stood behind a little boy with her arms wrapped protectively around him. She'd bent her head so her cheek squished against his and he held on to her arms while they both beamed at the camera. It shocked me to recognize the shape of those eyes, the mouth ... and realize the little boy was Walker.

I couldn't believe the adorable little boy with that wide open smile and heart in his eyes was Walker Ironside.

The girl looked so much like him, she had to be his older sister.

These pictures ... I flipped through them again frantically ... these pictures were of a family he never spoke about. Why? Why had he treated his mother like a complete stranger in Edinburgh?

I placed the photos on the kitchen island, and my stomach twisted with nerves as I waited for Walker to arrive home. At the sound of the front door opening, of his casual, "Baby, it's me," sweat gathered on my palms and under my arms.

When Walker strode into the kitchen, the sight of him made me want to hide the photos, to pretend I'd never seen them, to bury my head in the sand and just take of this man what I could.

The problem, however, was that I was in love with him.

I was completely, totally, head over heels in love with Walker Ironside, and I was greedy because I wanted *all* of him.

And it turned out, I was an all-or-nothing kind of woman.

His soft expression flattened at whatever he saw on mine. He rested the bag of takeout on the island, his gaze searching before it flicked down to the photos on the counter.

Walker's expression blanked.

Queasy, I blurted, "I'm sorry. I was looking for cutlery ... no. I was being nosy. And I found these photographs."

He said nothing. He stood there, frozen like a statue, eyes blank on the Polaroids.

"Walker? Is this your family? Was that woman we bumped into in Edinburgh your mom?"

Suddenly, his features hardened and the look he gave me, like I was an intruder trespassing in his home, made me die a little inside. "It's none of your fucking business."

I flinched like he'd slapped me, but it was as if he didn't see. Couldn't see how much his words cut me.

He rested his hands on the counter, bending his head toward me. "Do I snoop around in your fucking house? Christ, Sloane, I thought you were better than that."

I would not cry. I would not let him make me cry.

Biting back the burn of tears, I lowered my gaze and stepped away. "You're right, I shouldn't have gone looking. I'm sorry."

"Apology accepted," Walker replied abruptly and strode around the island to grasp the photos in hand, yanked open the drawer I'd found them in, threw them inside, and slammed the drawer shut. "They were out of spring rolls, so I got you garlic broccoli." He moved to open the takeout bag.

I stared at him, stunned, as he removed takeout cartons.

He flicked me a look. "You don't like garlic broccoli?"

Was he kidding?

I let out a huff of disbelief and, hearing the anger in it, he stopped what he was doing. "What?"

That sharp impatience was like a hook, yanking my spine straight, forcing my shoulders back. "I want to know why you won't talk about your family. I want to know why you ignored your mom. Why you disappear at the same time every year, why you won't talk about the scar on your belly when you'll talk about all the others." I rounded the island to press my hands to his chest. "I want to know you, and you won't let me."

"Bullshit," Walker replied harshly. "You know me better than most."

"Than most?" I smoothed my hand over his heart. "You know everything about me. I've let you in to every part ... why won't you let me in?"

He curled his hand around my wrist. "I have. But there are some things I don't want to talk about. This"—he trapped my hand between his palm and his chest—"is what I can give you. That's either enough or it isn't."

I yanked on my hand, and Walker's eyes blazed as he reluctantly let me go. "So you're telling me that there are important things about your past you're never going to tell me?"

"They're not things you need to know. They don't affect us."

Was he serious? Was he really that clueless? "If we stay the course, I'm just supposed to shut up when you disappear every September for two weeks?"

He seemed surprised I'd been paying such close attention. "It's not about us so, aye."

Hurt clawed at my throat. "Are you kidding?"

"Sloane—"

"Are you telling me that if I just up and disappeared with Callie for two weeks every year and didn't tell you a damn thing about it, you'd be cool with that?"

A muscle ticked in his jaw, and I knew I had him. Yet still the stubborn bastard said, "If it was important to you to keep it to yourself, then aye."

"You're a liar," I spat angrily, retreating from him.

Walker's eyes flashed in warning. "Sloane."

"No, don't use that tone like I'm a misbehaving child." My whole body shook as an awful decision weighed on me. "This is serious, Walker. I ... How can this go anywhere if you don't trust me?"

"I could ask you the same thing. I'm asking you to trust that this doesn't affect us." He reached for me, but I retreated.

Hurt flared in his eyes and I hated that ... but he was hurting me too.

"Of course it affects us. You're a fool if you think your secrets won't affect us. They would eventually come between us. I ..." I stared at him, taking in every inch of his handsome face, hating him a little but myself more. Because hadn't I known it would end this way? "I need all of you ... I need your trust ... I don't know if that's fair or not. To want all your secrets. To know about your family, where you come from. I really don't. And I'm sorry if it's *not* fair. But just like you know who you are, I know who I am. And I know that I need all of you, and not having that will fester between us." Because it would make me question if he could love me the way I needed to be loved. I'd never been loved enough by my father; I'd been loved in the wrong way by Nathan ... My soul was battered and bruised by the men who had come before Walker. It wasn't his fault.

But the reality was, they'd left wounds, and those wounds meant I'd need the man I loved to show me in every way he could that I was *everything* to him. That I had him in a way no one else did. I didn't know if that was realistic or right, but it's how I felt. How I needed it. "So if ... if you can't give me that ..." I exhaled shakily, tears pricking my eyes. "This has to be over."

Walker's eyes widened ever so slightly, and a heavy silence hung between us as the color drained from his face. He rubbed a hand over his mouth, staring at me in stark disbelief, as the only sound in the room was the scrape of his fingers against his beard.

Finally, and just in time, because I thought I might puke with the suspense, Walker dropped his arm. Looking defeated.

He said nothing.

He didn't need to.

His answer was written all over him.

I turned as my tears fell, and the effort of holding in the sob that wanted to break free was excruciating. Even as I hurried into his living room to grab my purse, I hoped he'd call out to me. That he'd stop me from leaving.

But I got to the front door, and then I was outside.

He never called my name.

The sob I'd been holding back burst out of me as I reached my car and fumbled to get in.

I struggled to contain it, to keep the gaping hole that had opened in my chest from swallowing me. My mind went into autopilot after I decided I didn't want to be alone, but I couldn't go to Monroe because Brodan was Walker's best friend.

Instead, I drove to the estate, and the guards, faces stricken at the sight of my tears, let me in.

I parked outside Aria's and had barely gotten out of the car when her front door opened. She came toward me, wearing a thick cardigan against the bitter December air. As I climbed the porch steps, her expression softened with sympathy at what she saw on my face.

"Sloane?"

I burst into loud, messy sobs as reality crashed down on me.

It was over.

Walker would never hold me in his arms again. Never kiss me or touch me or hold my hand. I'd never see his eyes crinkle with amusement and tenderness for me. Never feel protected and needed in the way only he ever made me feel. Never smell him or connect with him or sit in perfect silence with him.

The hole in my chest cracked wide open, and Aria rushed for me, pulling me into her arms as I sobbed against her shoulder like the love of my life had just goddamn died.

THIRTY-SIX

SLOANE

S ometimes I got so used to living in Scotland that I forgot
to take in its beauty. As a distraction, the past few days I'd
forced myself to look around me. The Highlands in the
summer were lush and wild, but as winter moved in, there was
a starkness to its beauty. Emerald and olive greens gave way to
burnt umber, smoke, and amber. Clouds with heather-colored
bellies hung above a North Sea tinted by its reflection in the
sky. Mountain peaks in the distance were topped with snow.
Naked tree branches glowed copper in the early setting sun.

We get to live here, I reminded myself as I drove to Monroe
and Brodan's.

Every day I tried to remember something good.

It helped keep a heartbroken meltdown at bay.

Callie was in the back of the car, cooing to Nox as we
drove him home. It was just past three thirty and the winter
twilight was drawing in. We'd had Nox since nine o'clock in
the morning. The car had lulled him to sleep, but before we'd
left the cottage, he'd thrown a baby fit, and I deduced he was
missing his mom and dad.

"Can't we keep him a little longer?" Callie asked.

I glanced at her in the rearview mirror, knowing my smile couldn't quite reach my eyes. "Nox wants his mom, sweetie."

Two days.

It had been two days since I'd broken up with Walker. I had a good cry with Aria until it was time to collect Callie. My daughter had taken one look at my swollen eyes and knew something was wrong. I lied and told her Aria and I had watched a tearjerker together.

"I thought you were hanging out with Walker?" Callie had quizzed.

"Girls' night instead," I choked out.

I hadn't told her we'd broken up. I didn't know how to. The fact of the matter was I was furious with myself for acting so selfishly and involving Walker so completely in her life. This would hurt her, too, and was a massive lesson for me to never introduce a guy to my daughter until months into the relationship. *Months.* That wasn't Walker's fault. That was all mine.

Eventually, I'd have to tell Callie, but for now I'd made excuses that Walker was busy these past few days.

At night, I cried myself to sleep. By day, I pretended everything was all right.

Today had been a pleasant distraction. We'd taken Nox for a long walk around the village. He'd napped while we ate lunch, and then Callie had fun playing with him this afternoon until he got too tired.

"Do you think I'll ever have a brother or sister?" she asked from the back seat.

My throat closed up at the thought. It took me a minute to push away the sting of tears. "Maybe."

"Walker should have a kid, Mom," Callie advised, like she was a wise old lady. "He'd make a really good dad."

Emotion threatened to break me, so I quickly changed the subject, asking her about a girlfriend at school who'd been pissed at her because I'd bought Callie the same pencil case. Seriously, the things that set some kids off.

"We're fine now. I gave her some emoji stickers I got free in the cereal box, and she stuck them all over hers, so it looks totally different."

Ah, to be ten and problem solving on that level.

"Can we stop in and say hi to Lewis?" she asked as we drove down the narrow road past Thane and Regan's.

"It's rude to just drop by, baby girl. I'm sure they're doing family time, anyway."

"Did I tell you that McKayla told Lindsey she fancies Lewis?"

I glanced at Callie in the rearview. She was growing all Scottish on me with her word choices these days. "Fancies, huh?"

She shrugged, her eyes lowered to Nox. "It's what they call it here."

Were we at that age already where kids had crushes on each other? I tried to think back to being ten.

Yup.

I distinctly remember thinking Colt Matthews was the cutest boy in my class. He gave me a Valentine rose that year. "How ... do you feel about that?"

She shrugged, still not looking at me. "It's fine. Lewis thinks she's a pain in the butt. He ... he thinks McKayla's pretty, though."

Uh-oh. "He told you that?"

"He told Michael who told me."

"Do you ... do you *fancy* anyone?"

Callie's eyes flew to meet mine in the mirror, and she wrinkled her nose. "Boys are annoying."

I chuckled softly, relaxing. She was still too young for all that nonsense, and I couldn't be more relieved.

"But ... I wouldn't want Lewis to spend all his time with McKayla instead of me."

I smiled at her in reassurance. "Never going to happen. That kid loves you."

She made another face, but a smile curled at her lips.

My eyes flicked back to the road. We'd passed the Adair siblings' homes and arrived at the end of the lane where Brodan and Monroe's impressive, LA-style home sat.

The sight of a familiar Range Rover made my heart lurch in my throat. Blood rushed in my ears as I swung into their driveway and parked next to Walker's vehicle.

"Walker's here?" Callie asked excitedly. "I thought he was working?"

Rummaging quickly in my purse for my phone, I snatched it up to find three warning texts from Monroe that Walker had stopped by.

Shit, shit, shit.

He had not texted, called, or dropped by since I walked out of his house two nights ago.

For him, it was over too.

A lead weight sat on my chest, painful. Momentarily debilitating.

"Mom?"

Get it together.

"Coming." I gritted my teeth and jumped out of the car to open Nox's door. "Will you take him while I unclip the car seat?" I'd borrowed it from Monroe.

"Sure."

After I'd settled a still sleepy Nox into my daughter's arms, I quickly unbuckled the car seat and carried it with me as we walked up to the entrance. The door opened before we reached it, and Monroe stood there.

As if alerted to her presence, Nox woke up and started wailing.

She hurried out to take him from Callie, holding him against her and crooning as she swayed him from side to side. "How was he?" Her eyes were wide and apologetic.

"He was great," I assured her. "We'll leave this with you" —I placed the car seat at her feet—"and go."

"We have to say hi to Walker." Callie threw me a confused look before darting past Monroe with uncharacteristic rudeness.

"Callie!"

But it was too late.

She was already in.

Roe whispered, "He just stopped by. I'm so sorry."

"It's fine."

It was not fine.

She knew that, too, and patted my arm before I followed her into the house to retrieve my daughter.

We found her standing with Walker at the kitchen island, leaning into him as if she belonged at his side. "Mom, look who I found!"

I know she expected me to smile, cross the room, and press a kiss to Walker's lips like she'd seen me do a hundred times in the last few weeks. Guilt crushed me as I refused to meet his gaze. The sight of him with Callie was already too hard to bear.

"Hi," he greeted me, voice gruff.

"Hey." My attention moved to Brodan who leaned against the island, observing all. "We're just bringing Nox back."

"So I can see." He pushed off the island with a handsome grin and took his son in his arms. Nox smiled big and gummy for his dad. "I like the nickname, by the way." Brodan shot me an approving smile.

My return grin felt strained. "Glad to be of service."

"And thank you for today."

"I hope you guys had a good time." I looked between Monroe and Brodan.

My friends shared a tender look of love, and Roe turned to me. "It was quiet, but lovely. Thank you."

"No problem." I turned to Callie, still not raising my eyes to Walker's face. "But we need to hit the road, baby girl."

Callie scowled at me. "I want to stay for a bit."

"Callie—"

"It's fine," Roe assured.

"Want to say hello to Uncle Walk, wee man?" Brodan asked quietly, as he bridged the distance between them.

Walker didn't miss a beat, taking Nox in his arms and settling him against his chest like he'd done it a million times. I let my eyes finally rest on his handsome face as he stared down at the little boy with affection. "You being cool, wee man?" he asked with hilarious seriousness. "You cool for Uncle Walk?"

Nox flashed his gums again.

What was it about kids and this man? They loved him.

My heart clenched in my chest because Callie was right. He was caring, protective, invested ... He'd make a damn fine father.

That hurt too.

Lowering my gaze to Callie, my tone brokered no argument. "Callie, let's go."

Her expression was uncharacteristically mulish as she asked Walker, "Are you coming with us?"

A frown furrowed Walker's eyebrows, and then I was subjected to his scowling confusion. Realization lightened his eyes. He knew now I hadn't told Callie the truth about us yet.

"Walker's working later, so no," I lied. "Let's go. Now."

Finally registering my tone, Callie said a painfully sad goodbye to Walker and Nox, then Roe and Brodan, and followed me out of the house like I was leading her to prison.

I didn't look back at Walker, though I felt his eyes on me

until we disappeared down the hall. Monroe hugged me and murmured another apology in my ear, but I shook it off. It wasn't her fault.

Walker was a part of my friend group.

We were going to have to get used to being around each other.

Or I was going to have to get a new friend group.

That thought cut deep, too, so I threw it away.

We were barely in the car thirty seconds when Callie asked belligerently, "Why were you rude to Walker?"

"I wasn't rude."

"You were too. Is there something going on?"

"Nothing is going on," I lied. Another wrong to add to my list.

My girl grew quiet. And sullen. Because she wasn't stupid, and she knew I was lying. Guilt crushed me for not protecting her from this. From the inevitability of me and Walker's demise. She was the last person I ever wanted to hurt or disappoint. Tomorrow, when I felt stronger for her, I would tell her the truth.

THIRTY-SEVEN
WALKER

The street fair with all the fucking fairy lights, the faux snow-dusted, red-and-green stall coverings, the winter-bundled customers, and the smell of crisp, smoky air, mulled wine, and hot doughnuts should have put me in a good mood. I was not above being moved by how fucking quaint and idyllic my new home was at Christmas.

But right now, it was a vehicle of torture.

An excuse to watch Sloane like a prick of a stalker.

Her stall was set up between all the others. An array of baked goods I knew tasted almost as good as the woman who'd baked them. Callie stood at her side, adorable as ever, all bundled up in her hat and scarf.

I should walk away.

I was acting like a fool.

But I missed her. I missed them both.

And it had only been days since she told me it was over. Yesterday, she'd looked right through me in Brodan's kitchen.

It felt like fucking years.

I'd gone to Brodan's to tell him the news about Byron Hoffman. Sloane had fled the house before we could talk, so

Brodan had relayed the information to her on the phone last night. Which meant I couldn't even be there to see her relief when the news broke that Byron Hoffman faced charges of sexual assault from several women and a lengthy legal battle. One last asshole she had to worry about. I wondered how she took that news. If it brought up the attack all those months ago. If she needed someone to hold her and protect her from bad dreams.

Knowing that person wouldn't be me fucking killed. The ache in my chest was so bad I rubbed at it through my winter jacket. *Maybe it's heartburn*, I lied to myself as I stood near the coffee van, hidden by the many people who'd come out to enjoy Ardnoch's annual Christmas street fair. Last year, I'd shown up with a woman I'd slept with the previous night and couldn't get rid of. I'd noted Sloane's disappointment when she saw her, recognized it for what it was. And pretended like I didn't feel the same attraction to her as she did to me.

All that time wasted, and it was only months. How could Brodan bear the weight of eighteen lost years between him and Monroe?

I stiffened at the sight of a familiar figure approaching Sloane's stall. His son accompanied him.

Haydyn Barr.

Crossing my arms over my chest, I bobbed my head, probably looking like a lunatic, trying to see past everybody who cut across my view of them.

A few minutes passed, and he was still at her stall.

Prick.

"Is this helping?"

"Fuck," I bit out, more shocked than anything that Brodan had taken me by surprise.

I couldn't remember the last time someone crept up on me.

Glowering at the smirk on my friend's face, I glanced

down at the cup of coffee he held out. Reluctantly, I took it. "Where's your wife and son?"

"Enjoying the fair. I saw you lurking in the shadows, stalking Sloane, and felt the need to intervene."

"I don't lurk." I took a sip of my coffee, eyes returning to Sloane.

"Then you're doing an excellent imitation of it." Brodan followed my gaze and scowled. "Och, c'mon. You're not going to let that arsehole fawn all over her, are you? First Roe, now Sloane. I don't bloody think so."

Sloane was smiling at the bastard in a way I hated. Like I didn't exist. "He's a better choice for her."

"Stop being a martyr." Brodan stepped into my line of vision, expression annoyed. "Be honest with yourself. You want to kill him and any man who goes near her. Or am I wrong and you can actually stand the idea of Barr taking Sloane to his bed?"

Fury rose in me, and I clenched my hand around my coffee. "Watch yourself, Brodan."

"Considering you manipulated me and Roe into spending time together, I think this little intervention is letting you off easy." Brodan leaned into me. "Do you actually want Sloane to date Barr?"

I glanced past Brodan and witnessed Sloane laughing at something the wanker said. "I want to rip his fucking face off."

Brodan chuckled humorlessly. "And considering you've been trained to maim and kill a man in a hundred different ways, I almost pity Barr. But I'll pity you more, Walk, if you let whatever prideful thing is standing in your way get between you and what you want. Fix this. Before you lose her for good. Believe the man who wasted eighteen years of his life without the woman he loves ... whatever the problem is, it isn't worth being without *her*." He clapped me on the shoulder, hard, and then walked away to find his family.

His words knotted in my gut as my attention returned to Sloane and Barr.

For the first time in a long time, I was truly afraid. Of not being enough for her. I already failed her with Andros. I'd failed Callie too. If Sloane knew about my past, she'd know she wasn't the first I'd failed. She'd know the thing I was most ashamed of. And I couldn't bear for her to look at me the way I looked at myself.

The missed calls, three of them, sat unanswered on my phone from the past week. Missed calls from my mum. Because as much as I thought I was ready to take them ... Like confiding in Sloane, the thought terrified me. And I was afraid to be terrified. So I ignored her calls.

Like I refused to tell Sloane about my family.

But could I bear to lose her like I lost them without trying? Without trusting that maybe she'd think better of me than I thought of myself?

So lost in my thoughts, I hadn't realized Sloane had left Callie at the stall with Regan and Eilidh until I saw her heading toward me. Toward the coffee van.

She wore a cream knit beanie hat over her long hair, her cheeks pink with cold. Her winter boots flashed beneath the long skirts of her dress and her cream winter coat hung open, a heavy knit scarf the only thing between her and the winter air.

Beautiful, I thought.

Had I told her that enough?

Her gaze moved up from the ground and met mine.

Sloane halted in the middle of the bustling crowd, the color leaching from her cheeks.

Then she abruptly turned and headed back toward the stall.

To avoid me.

To get away from me.

My hands clenched at my sides, and I took a step forward before I stopped myself.

Was this how it was to be, then? To bump into her on the street and have her treat me like a stranger? Like how it was with my parents?

The thought wrecked me.

I walked away before I did something impulsive. On instinct. Without thinking.

I couldn't do that with Sloane. With Callie. I had to know for certain what I was capable of giving because they were the last people on earth I ever wanted to hurt.

Thirty-Eight
WALKER

L ife was empty. It hadn't felt that way before her, before them, but now it felt cavernous and lacking.

Sunday I took a bracing run on the beach and then worked out at home. The rest of the day I wandered around my too big house wondering what they were up to.

Monday morning, I drove onto the estate and parked next to Sloane's car. It happened as Brodan had promised. I couldn't think of anything else but her, and it was infuriating and uncomfortable and—

I needed her.

Staff members practically leapt out of my way as I marched into the castle that morning. They seemed to take one look at my face and turn on their heels to avoid me. Good. That was my preference.

However, avoiding all human contact was impossible, and I was called to a meeting with Aria and Jock. Lachlan was still preoccupied at home with his wife and child and plans to launch a whisky distillery with Brodan, which meant Aria was taking on more and more of the everyday running of the estate. She'd called us into her office first thing.

As Jock and I entered the opulently furnished room, Aria rounded the table and held out a tablet to us. Jock took it, and I read the screen over his shoulder.

It was a news article on North Hunter.

Jock muttered a curse under his breath as we read it.

Apparently, when North was thirteen years old, he and his friends were responsible for the death of a homeless man. Details were vague, but it painted North in a very bad light.

"He's here," Aria announced as we looked up from the tablet, her expression decidedly unhappy. "Mr. Hunter has chosen Ardnoch as the place to hide out during this scandal and, as a paying member, he has every right to do that." She sounded like she wished he didn't. "He arrived at the crack of dawn, and I can only assume it won't be long before the paparazzi descend at the gates."

"We'll add extra security at all entrances," Jock said. "We'll also test our drone perimeter."

"Good." Aria exhaled heavily. "More members will arrive soon for Christmas, and having the tabloids as a welcoming party wasn't really on my gift list this year."

"Some people," Jock huffed, staring at the tablet before he handed it back to her. "But he's a member, so we have to protect him."

I frowned at that, remembering the man who willingly dove in to help me protect Sloane when it wasn't his job to do so. "North was a child," I reminded them both. "A thirteen-year-old child, and the tabloids have provided no detail. What we do know is that North Hunter helped me protect a woman who means a great deal to me from a predator when it was not his responsibility. As far as I'm concerned, I owe him. I'll protect him because I'm paid to, but also because of the man he's proven to be now. We of all people should know not to trust everything we read."

Jock and Aria both look sufficiently chastened and stunned.

"I think that's the most I've ever heard you say in one go." Amusement curled Jock's lips. "And you're absolutely right." He turned to Aria. "We'll take care of this."

I moved to follow him out of her office, but Aria stopped me. I glanced back at her.

She narrowed her eyes. "A woman who means a great deal to you?"

I tensed. "Aye."

She shook her head slightly, expression somewhat exasperated. "Maybe you should tell *her* that."

"Maybe I will," I retorted without thinking.

Her eyes flared, but I marched out of the room to follow Jock.

Then I stopped, pulse pounding in my ears.

My problem had always been my inability to release myself of the blame I carried for an action that was not mine. Was I really willing to be miserable for the rest of my life because Sloane might look at me differently once she knew?

"I need your trust ..."

I hadn't thought it was about trusting Sloane. But she was right. It was. And I'd done her a disservice by not trusting her.

"Jock."

My boss turned at the top of the hall and gave me a questioning look.

"Do you need me for this, or can you do without me for a bit?"

Sensing the urgency in my voice, he waved me off. "Go do what you need to do."

So I did.

Fear and anticipation thrummed through me as I tracked down Sloane's boss, Mrs. Hutchinson. She seemed bemused when I asked which room Sloane was working on right now, but she gave me the suite number she reckoned she'd be in, and I tried to move through the castle with patience.

Not wanting to draw the members' attention, I forced my steps to be unhurried as I made my way upward and then down the hallway toward Sloane. Another housekeeper, Frannie, I think Sloane called her, was outside a suite dumping rubbish into their cart.

"Sloane in there?" I asked her abruptly.

The older woman straightened and blinked at me owlishly. "Aye, she is."

"Can you give us a minute?"

Her brow furrowed. "You the reason she looks ready to burst into tears every five seconds?"

Fuck.

An ache flared like an old wound in my chest. I nodded stiffly.

She considered me. "You don't say much, do you?"

I scowled.

Frannie chuckled humorlessly. "Fine. On you go. Tell Sloane I'm moving on to the next room."

She'd barely said the last word and I was slipping into the bedroom, closing the door behind me.

"Frannie, you would not believe what I found in the— oh." Sloane appeared out of the bathroom, her features slack at the sight of me. "What are you doing here?"

Once I was decided on something, I didn't beat around the bush. "I want to tell you about my past."

The rubbish bag in her hand fell from her trembling fingers. "Walker?"

"I miss you." The confession was rough with emotion. "I miss you so fucking much."

Tears brightened those warm brown eyes. Eyes I could drown in. "I miss you too."

"Will you sit?" I gestured to an armchair.

Her gaze darted to the door. "What about Frannie?"

"She's working on your next room while we talk." I sat down and, seeming unable to take her eyes off me, she watched me the whole time as she backed into the armchair and sunk down as if her legs had given out.

"You were right," I admitted. "I didn't know at the time, but I didn't trust you with the truth. I was blinded by how *I* feel about the truth. And I ..." I scrubbed a hand over my face because I wasn't used to talking about these things with anyone but Rich. "Fuck, I ... There's a part of me that will never forgive myself, and I thought if I told you and you looked at me ... differently ... that it would royally fuck me up."

Sloane leaned in, her beautiful face soft with sympathy. "Look at you differently, how?"

"You ... even after I messed up with Andros ... you look at me like I can fix everything. I like the way it makes me feel," I confessed gruffly. "I like that I'm that man for you. That someone as strong as you, as capable, wants me to be the man at her side."

"Walker," she breathed, tears brightening her eyes and slipping slowly down her cheeks. "You are. I do. You make me feel like even if bad things happen, they can't touch me. Not really."

Jesus. I felt winded by her words.

"Why would you think the truth would change that?"

"Because I failed someone in a way there's no coming back from."

Her gaze sharpened. "Tell me."

There were very few people in the world who knew the truth. Not even Brodan knew. Rich did. Sully too. I licked my suddenly dry lips but held Sloane's gaze. "I grew up in Portobello, just outside Edinburgh. Right on the water. My dad was an architect, a very well-paid one. We had a nice home, and I had a mum who didn't have to work and she showered me and my sister with attention."

"Sister?" she whispered.

The thought of Iona was a pain unlike any. I'd been shot and stabbed and almost drowned and suffocated. Burned and bombed. More than most men had ever experienced.

None of it compared to grief.

"My big sister." My voice was quiet, words thick with memories. "We were close. She even opted to stay at home and attend Edinburgh Uni. When I was sixteen, she was twenty and had just finished up her second year at university. She was premed." Intelligent and caring. And funny. Christ, she'd made me laugh. But I was a different person then. "She started seeing this guy who was older. His name was Tommy Dingwall. My parents didn't like him. Neither did I. He was always touching her inappropriately in front of me. Pawing at her. I hated the way he looked at her, like she was a pet he owned. I had a feeling something was going on that I didn't know about because Iona was arguing with my mum a lot. But I was focused on my own stuff, you know. I wasn't paying enough attention.

"Then one day, I cut school because I was in the middle of this video game and I'd rather be playing that than sitting in a geography class."

Sloane subconsciously leaned closer, as if she could hear that my heart rate had sped up.

"I knew Mum wouldn't be home because she went to painting class every week on that afternoon. But when I got to the house, I could hear Iona yelling at someone upstairs. Then I heard Tommy's voice." I exhaled shakily as the memory flooded over me. "Then ... her scream."

Sloane covered her mouth as if she knew what was coming.

"I raced upstairs and the bedroom door was blocked. So I

rammed against it, hearing her ..." Emotion threatened to choke me. "Hearing her scream my name for help."

"Walker." Fresh tears slipped down Sloane's cheeks.

"I got in. He'd shoved her dresser across the door. But he ... he came at me as soon as I slipped into the room. I felt a burning pain in my gut, and I looked down and saw he'd stabbed me."

Her breath caught. "The scar on your stomach."

I nodded. "I tried to attack him, but I was losing consciousness. The last thing I remembered was Iona begging him to help me." My breath shuddered as I dropped my gaze to the floor.

"Walker, if this is too much ..."

I shook my head. Determined to tell her. She wanted all of me? Well, this was it. "I came to when the paramedics lifted me onto a stretcher ... and Iona on her bedroom floor ... dead. He'd cut her throat."

Sloane cried silently.

"He killed her while I was in the room. And I couldn't save her." I laughed, a harsh, ugly sound. "The first thing my dad said to me when I woke up out of surgery was that I failed him. I failed her. He hated me for not saving her."

"No." Sloane launched out of her chair and fell on her knees at my feet. She reached for my face, and I leaned into her touch, only then realizing there were fucking tears on my cheeks. She wiped at them, eyes blazing. "You were a boy and you tried. It was no one's fault but the sick bastard who killed Iona. He almost killed you."

With a sob, she clambered onto my lap and I pulled her close, tight, burying my face in her chest as she held me. "It wasn't your fault," she said over and over. "You didn't fail her. You didn't fail me."

THIRTY-NINE
SLOANE

I thought the only person whose pain I could feel as if it were my own was Callie's. But I was wrong. In that room, holding Walker to me as he fought back tears, I felt his grief squeeze around my heart and throat. I wanted to sob for days. Instead, I trembled with the tension of holding it back in order to be strong for him.

All the things this big, capable, brave man had seen in his lifetime, and nothing could scar him more deeply than his sister's murder. How could it? No wonder he'd been able to deal with everything else life threw at him. If he could survive that, he could survive anything.

Slowly, Walker's shaking eased, and he lifted his head from my chest to meet my gaze. The tortured look in his eyes would haunt me forever. I would give anything to change the past for him, to take away this pain.

I brushed my fingers down his cheek, his beard rasping against my palm as he leaned into my touch.

"Thank you for telling me."

His arms tightened around me.

"You should know that knowing this about you only

makes me more amazed at everything you've become, despite losing Iona that way." Walker Ironside was a fierce protector of women, and maybe he always would have been if life had gone a different way, but there was no doubt in my mind that his sister's death had forged that fierceness. The reminder that his father had blamed him caused a rage to simmer low in my gut. "And your father was *wrong*."

Walker caressed my hip as if to comfort me. "I spent almost a year under his roof being treated to cold silence until I couldn't stand it anymore and I left to join the marines. I haven't seen my parents since."

In other words, his father had planted the seed that Walker had failed Iona. By his cold treatment, every day for almost a year. If the man was in front of me, I'd tear him a new one. "He was wrong," I repeated vehemently. "He took his grief out on you. But he's the one who bears the brunt of his actions ... because he lost two children."

"I ... I know rationally, it wasn't my fault." Walker looked exhausted as he leaned his forehead against mine. "But no matter how hard I try, I can't seem to shake the guilt."

"You don't have to. I'll shake it for you." I kissed his cheek tenderly. Then his other, and his nose and his mouth. A soft brush of my lips, as if every touch could extract the pain from him. "You tried to save her. She died knowing that. You're a hero, Walker." Tears slipped down my cheeks, my voice quivering around the words. "You *try* like no man I've ever met. Everything you feel is in everything you do. No one has ever made me feel so safe and essential as you do. I ... I love you."

His eyes blazed with emotion, his grip on me tightening until it almost bruised. Walker raised a gentle hand to swipe away my tears with his thumb. Then, as if something snapped, unleashed inside him, he slid his hand beneath my hair to clasp my nape. And he crushed me to him in a devastating kiss. As if to prove my point, he poured all his feelings into the kiss.

Until I was breathless and panting and completely consumed by him.

We didn't hear the knock at the bedroom door, but at the sound of a throat clearing, Walker reluctantly released me. We turned to look at the intruder at the same time.

Jock.

He wore a smirk and a raised eyebrow. "I'm sorry to interrupt but, Walker, we need all hands on deck. The paps have arrived."

Walker turned to me and, seeing my confusion, he explained, "A story about a club member broke in the news and he came here to hide. Paparazzi are at the gates."

"Oh."

"I'll tell you everything." He squeezed me. "Can I come over later?"

It was Monday, so Callie had tae kwon do after school, something I'm sure Walker remembered. "Of course. Will ..." I shot a look at Jock and lowered my voice. "Will you be okay today?"

His expression softened. "Do you love me?"

A shy smile prodded my lips. "Yes."

"Then I'm more than okay."

———

WALKER DIDN'T NEED to tell me about the scandal. Everyone at the castle was talking about how North Hunter was splashed across the papers and being ripped apart on social media for his involvement in the death of a homeless man years ago. There were lots of different takes on the wider story, but no truth from what I could see. I would not participate in the gossip. North had helped me, and I wouldn't repay him by assuming the worst. The world was doing enough of that. Rumors were

that he'd already been sacked from an upcoming block-
buster movie.

The security team was on high alert at the estate and had
been deployed several times today to stop paparazzi who'd
tried to break onto the property. The buzz of it wasn't enough
to distract me from Walker. I was still heartbroken for him,
but so relieved he'd finally confessed the truth. That he'd
trusted me. That I didn't have to spend the next lonely, miserable months trying to get over him. And I was thankful I
hadn't gotten up the nerve yesterday to tell Callie we'd
broken up.

Now I didn't need to.

Walker hadn't told me he loved me back, but I felt it in his
kiss. And I could wait for him to say the words. I knew now
that those kinds of emotions couldn't be easy for him. He'd
avoided a relationship so that he never had to feel the failure
he'd felt when he lost Iona. When he lost his parents. I could
be patient with him while he came to grips with working
through his fears.

Thinking the paps would totally preoccupy him, it was a
surprise when Walker met me after my shift.

"Don't they need you?" I asked.

He shook his head, his palm on my back as he guided me
toward our cars. He'd parked next to me this morning.
"They're handling it, and I wanted to escort you off the estate.
Those arseholes are clambering at every car that comes out."

"What about my car?" I asked as he guided me to his SUV.

"I'll take you to work tomorrow, and you can collect it
then if this circus has calmed down. That okay for you?"

"Yeah." I hopped into his Range Rover.

As soon as Walker started driving, he leaned over and
squeezed my knee. "All good?"

I covered his hand with mine. "We're all good."

His expression was suddenly so intense, it made my heart speed up. "You mine again?"

I swear my pulse fluttered. "I'm yours again. Are you mine again?"

Walker squeezed my knee once more. "Never stopped being yours."

Tears stung my nose, and he tensed at the sight. "Happy tears," I promised him.

He relaxed for about thirty seconds and then was on alert as we approached the gates. Not only had the paparazzi camped out at the main gate, it seemed they'd cornered the staff entrance too.

"Jesus," I muttered, seeing the crowd being pushed back by armed security as the gates opened to let us out.

They shoved past the team, lights flashing in my eyes as they snapped photos just in case. It stopped when they realized we weren't anybody of note, but I gaped in the wing mirror as I saw Jamie tackle paparazzi who'd run through the gate before it closed.

"Holy crap."

"Aye. They're like rabid animals," Walker muttered in disgust.

Their vehicles also lined the road along the woodlands as we passed. "How many are here?"

"About fifty."

"Poor North."

"You don't believe the papers, then?"

"I don't know what's true regarding his past," I replied. "But I know he helped me ... and I don't get bad vibes from the guy, you know."

"Agreed. Don't worry. I won't let anything happen to him."

This time I slid my hand down his thigh. "I know."

We shared a quick, heated look before his eyes returned to the road.

"I missed you," I confessed again. "It's been really hard pretending to Callie like everything is okay."

His voice was gruff. "Did you tell her we ...?"

"No."

"Good." He relaxed a bit. "That's good. Now she doesn't need to know. And I'm *in* this, Sloane. You don't have to worry about our relationship hurting Callie."

The need to be realistic after the pain of the past few weeks forced me to say, "No matter what we feel for each other, neither of us can foresee the future or what might happen between us."

Walker was silent for what seemed like too long before his fingers tightened around the wheel. "I can't imagine wanting to ever let you go."

My heart did that fluttering thing again.

"But you're right. We can't promise each other the future. No one can promise another person that. But I can promise you this"—he shot me a searing look—"whatever happens between you and me, I will always be there for you both. I will always be there for Callie."

Emotion thickened my throat as I stared at him in wonder. How did I get so lucky to meet Walker Ironside? "I'm going to work my ass off to make sure I get to keep you forever, Walker."

His lip curled slightly at the corner. "Woman, you don't need to work your ass off. I have no intention of going anywhere."

Heat bloomed sweet and hot between my thighs. "I know we should do the sensible thing and talk about our future, what we want, if we're compatible going forward ... but when we get back to my place, I'm going to need you inside me as soon as we cross the threshold."

Those flutters moved to my belly as Walker grinned, big and slow and sexy. "What things do we need to talk about that we can't sort out right now?"

"Marriage, babies." I threw them out there, trying not to be worried I'd scare him.

He shrugged. "I never thought I'd get married or have children ..." Walker glanced at me. "Until you."

My breath caught. "So, you'd want those things?"

"Aye." His voice was gruff. "I'd want those things with you."

"Good." The word sounded squeaky, even to my ears. I cleared my throat. "That's good."

He grinned again, and I wanted to jump him right there. "Then I guess we know where we stand."

FORTY

SLOANE

I tried to jump the man as soon as we got back to the cottage, but Walker gentled my kisses as he caressed my arms slowly, as if trying to soothe the fire in me.

Confused, I'd released him ... and then read what he wanted in his eyes. First, he shoved off my coat and then his.

Then Walker curled his hand around the nape of my neck and drew me tight to him. The fever that crawled through me burned hotter, a fiery need only one man had ever inspired in me. Him. Maybe I was a foolish, lovesick woman, but I truly believed only one man had been put on this earth for me. Him. Walker cupped my ass. His erection dug into my stomach, and a flush of wet slickened between my thighs. I trembled under his ardent study.

My breath hitched as he flicked open the button on my jeans. I waited in heart-pounding anticipation as he slid the zipper down and gently slipped his hand beneath my underwear. I made a guttural sound, my hands grabbing onto his upper arms for support as he pushed through my wet to touch my clit.

Walker grunted and pressed his forehead to my temple and

continued to rub my clit. "So ready for me, baby. Always ready."

"Always," I promised, panting lightly. "Always only for you."

Walker growled in deep satisfaction at my words before he covered my mouth with his, hungrily kissing me like we hadn't kissed in months. Then I was up in his arms, my legs wrapped around his waist, and he carried me upstairs.

In my haze of lust, of need, I was ready to be thrown on the bed, for Walker to take control, dominate me, and fuck me until I was crying with release.

Yet he surprised me.

He broke our kiss and lowered me to my feet beside the bed.

His hands rested on my waist for a second before sliding down over my hips. We stared at each other in a mix of longing and wonder and faith and trust. It was amazing how this deepened connection between us made my body so much more attuned and hyperaware. And ready for him.

"I love you," I declared again, voice hoarse.

Light flared in Walker's eyes as he tightened his grip on my waist. He gave me what felt like a reassuring squeeze before slipping his fingers under my sweater. I shivered at the soft caress of his rough fingertips.

"I love you too." The words were rough with disuse but sincerely said.

Joy unlike anything I'd felt since Callie was born filled me completely. "Really?"

Walker bent his head to me. "Never fucking doubt it."

I laughed softly, leaning into him as he caressed a little higher, across my ribs. Goose bumps prickled over my breasts, and they felt heavy, desperate for his hands, his mouth.

"Walker ..."

His hands came out from under my sweater to take hold

of the opening of my jeans. He dug his thumbs into the waist-band, expression determined and hot as our eyes stayed connected. And then he slowly tugged my pants down over my hips. Walker went with them, lowering to his haunches. I felt his hot breath on the lace between my legs, and I shuddered with need. Bracing a hand on his strong shoulder, I lifted one foot after the other so he could unzip my boots and pull the jeans off.

Understanding dawned as Walker curled his big hands around my calves, looked up into my eyes, and caressed the back of my legs. He was taking his time. Savoring this. Loving me.

He was making love to me.

A tug deep in my womb caused another rush of wet to dampen the material between my legs. Walker's gaze lowered there. His hands climbed higher around the back of my calves before smoothing around my upper thighs. Gliding his thumbs toward my inner thighs, he demanded, "Spread your legs."

Excitement flipped in my belly as I did as he commanded. Gently, he pushed beneath my underwear, and I gasped as two thick fingers slid easily inside me.

"Oh, fuck," he groaned and rested his forehead against my right thigh. "I've missed your tight heat."

I flushed with desire at his sexy words. "I've missed you inside me."

Walker met my gaze, everything he planned to do to me blazing within his eyes. I shuddered with desperate need but kept it together as he pulled the scrap of lace down my legs. I stepped out of them, shaking. And then Walker lifted my right leg over his shoulder, and I whispered *yes* over and over, resting my hand on his opposite shoulder for balance. He made a guttural noise of desire as he deliberately rubbed his bearded cheek along my inner thigh. He knew what that did to me.

"Fuck, yes, fuck," I whimpered.

I felt him smile against my skin, seconds before his tongue touched my clit.

Satisfaction slammed through me, and I undulated against his mouth. His fingers dug into my thigh, and his groan vibrated through me. He suckled my clit, pulling on it hard, and I panted as beautiful tension built deep inside. His tongue circled that electrified bundle of nerves and then slid down in a dirty voracious lick before pushing inside me.

"Walker!" I cried, thrusting against his mouth as I climbed higher and higher toward breaking apart.

Feeling my desperation, Walker returned to my clit and thrust two fingers inside me.

It hit like an explosion of fiery, spine-tingling stars, release sliding deliciously through me as I shuddered against Walker's mouth.

He gently lowered my quivering leg, and I swayed against him as he stood. Rather than being languid with satisfaction, I buzzed with longing. Like I was still on the precipice of orgasm.

A thrilling power overwhelmed me as our eyes locked. His smoldered, his jaw set with a ferocious hunger and love.

Walker loved me.

I lifted my arms to help him raise my sweater over my head.

My chest heaved with my labored, excited breaths as Walker threw the sweater to the floor and brought his hands to my shoulders. His eyes followed his fingertips as they trailed first to the top of my arm where my scar was. He tenderly kissed the healed bullet wound, his eyes closing as if he were in pain. And I knew what he felt at that moment because I felt it every time I touched his scars.

Fear, because the mark was a reminder I could have died, and relief, because I was here.

He opened his eyes, following his hands again as they moved with excruciating slowness across my collarbone and down toward the rise of my breasts.

Gently, Walker cupped my face in his hands and kissed me so deeply, I could taste myself. But these kisses weren't like before. Not kisses of longing and lost time. Slow, sexy, and with tender reverence that brought tears to my eyes. Walker loved me. I felt it in his kiss. My hands curled around his biceps, feeling his strength, his love, and I didn't know what I wanted to do more: take him inside me or let him hold me while I cried with pure happiness.

Walker caressed me through the kiss with light strokes. He relearned every inch of me—my ribs, my waist, my stomach—as if it had been years of distance instead of mere days. His hands glided around to my ass, and his kiss deepened, grew hungrier, and he drew me against his arousal. I could feel the war inside him as his tongue caressed mine in deep, wet strokes. It was like he was determined to take his time, but another part of him wanted to fuck me until I screamed.

As I brushed my hands down his arms, the touch seemed to calm him, and his kiss grew gentler. He nipped at my lower lip and then eased away, but only to stare into my eyes as he glided his hands up my back to my bra clasp. He unhooked it, then he nudged the straps down my arms, and it fell to the floor. His gaze slowly disconnected from mine, and I shivered as his vivid aquamarine eyes grew hooded. His grip tightened around my biceps while he feasted on the sight of my naked breasts. My nipples peaked under his perusal, tight, needy buds that begged for his mouth.

"I've missed these too," he murmured as he reached up and cupped me.

I moaned and arched into his touch. Ripples of desire undulated low in my belly as he played with my breasts, sculpting and kneading them, stroking and pinching my nipples. All the time his eyes vacillated between my face and my breasts. I thrust into his touch, muttering my love for him.

The words had barely broken past my lips when his mouth found mine. This kiss was rough, hard, desperate, and his groan filled me as he pinched both my nipples between his forefingers and thumbs. I gasped, and his growl of satisfaction made me flush with pleasure. I was beyond ready. Feeling the fabric of his shirt beneath my hands, I curled my fists into it and jerked my lips from his. "Naked. Naked now."

Walker's lips twitched but did as I asked. He quickly unbuttoned his shirt and threw it behind him and then worked on his suit pants and shoes. His chest, arms, and abs were so powerful, beautiful. The scars were permanent reminders that he wasn't invincible, but he was extraordinary. My gaze lowered. I'd seen him naked many times, but it was different now that I knew he loved me, now that I had all his secrets and trust.

Now that he was truly mine.

His thick thighs and muscular calves caused another hard flip in my lower belly. I moaned when he had to peel his boxer briefs over his erection, and once freed, he was so hard, it strained toward his abs. All of this beautiful man belonged to me.

Every part of my body swelled toward Walker as he let me look my fill. I think he saw the possessiveness in my eyes because the mutual feeling glowed in his.

He reached for me, grasping me around the waist as he sat on the edge of the bed. Then he guided me to straddle him, his arousal hot against my stomach.

We held each other's gaze and my fingers curled into the back of his shoulders as I took in his expression. So much love. Desperate love.

Tears filled my eyes, and the visible emotion made his fierce expression soften with tenderness. He slid his hand along the back of my neck, tangling in my hair to grab a handful. Walker gently tugged my head back, arched my chest, and covered my right nipple with his mouth.

I gasped as sensation slammed through me, my hips automatically undulating against him as he sucked, laved, and nipped. Tension coiled between my legs, tightening and tightening as he moved between my breasts, his hot mouth, his tongue—

"Walker!" I was going to come again with only this.

Then he stopped, and I lifted my head to beg, to plead for him to keep touching me, but halted when he gripped my hips. Guiding me, he lifted me up, and I stared down at him, waiting as he took his cock in hand and put it between my legs.

Taking his cue, I lowered myself onto him, feeling the hot tip of him against my slick opening. Electric tingles cascaded down my spine and around my belly, deep between my legs.

I'd never been so goddamn turned on in my life. Walker took hold of my hip with one hand and cupped my right breast with the other, and I gasped at the overwhelming thick sensation of him as I lowered.

"I love you so fucking much, Sloane Harrow," he growled roughly against my mouth.

To my shock, his words, the emotion between us, had me so hot that I exploded with only the tip of him inside me.

I cried out and clung to his shoulders as my climax tore through me, my inner muscles rippling and tugging and drawing Walker in deeper. Shuddering, my hips jerking, my abs spasming, I wrapped my arms around his neck to hold on through the storm. I rested my forehead against his.

As the last of the tremors passed through me, I became aware of Walker's bruising grip on my hips and the overwhelming fullness of him inside me.

I lifted my head to see him gazing at me in awe. I bit my lip against a smile before I murmured, "Guess we found a new trigger for me."

He grinned, sexy, and ... free in a way I'd never witnessed before. His whole face lit up. "I guess I'll need to say it more often, then."

"It'll get easier if you do."

"It's already easy," he promised gruffly before he launched up off the bed and turned around to drop us on it with me on my back. The motion made him drive so deep inside me, I cried out, overwhelmed.

Walker muttered a hoarse expletive and then wrapped his hands around my wrists and pinned them to the bed at either side of my head. Just how he liked it.

Just how I liked it.

He moved inside me with powerful thrusts of his hips, his eyes focused intensely on mine.

I wanted to feel him; I wanted to grip his ass in my hands and feel it clench and release with each stroke, but he held me down.

As always, it excited me beyond bearing.

The tension built in me again with every thick drag of him in and out. Walker's features strained with lust, and with one more powerful glide in and out, I came again, shorter, sharper. With one hard tug of my climax, Walker swelled to impossible thickness. He pressed my hands hard to the bed as he tensed between my legs.

"I love you!" His hips jerked and shuddered against mine. He groaned loud and satisfied as he released himself inside me, his cock throbbing and pulsing.

Walker let go of my wrists to brace himself over me, burying his face in my throat as he held his weight off me.

Freed, I wrapped my arms around him, my legs, drawing him closer as I ran my hands soothingly down his damp, warm back. "I didn't think it was possible for sex to get any better between us ... but you just proved me wrong."

Walker lifted his head to kiss me softly on the lips. Our eyes met as he drew back, his gaze low-lidded. "Give me time, and I'll prove you wrong over and over."

I grinned, undulating against him in a way that made his expression darken with want. "I think you should start now."

"Demanding wee thing, aren't you?" he murmured against my mouth before wrapping his arms around me as he fell to his side. Walker cuddled me into him, and I wrapped my leg over his hip, pressing my breasts to his chest. His hands coasted lightly up and down my back as he studied my face, like I was something he'd never seen before. Something wondrous and beautiful.

"Some day, huh?" I teased gently.

Walker nodded. "Aye."

At his seriousness, I snuggled closer. "Are you okay? After everything?"

His fingers tensed into my back, and his reply was not what I expected. "My mum has called me. A few times. Since we bumped into her in Edinburgh."

"Is ... is that the first contact you've had since ...?"

He nodded grimly. "She asked a friend for my number. I haven't picked up."

My heart ached for him, and I pressed a soft, under-standing kiss to his lips before I pulled back and asked, "Do you not want to talk to her?"

"I thought I did. I ... I'm just not sure I can bear what she has to say."

I remembered the look on his mother's face that day on the street. The way she stared at me and Callie with him. Pain and longing. "I don't think the woman I saw that day has anything hurtful to say to you. I think you should call her back. Walker ... I'd give anything for my dad to reach out to me."

His features hardened, and I realized why when he pressed his forehead to mine and growled, "Your dad is a damn fool."

I tightened my arms around him. "Will you call your mom? I can be with you when you do. Or not. Just know I'm here."

He nodded, drawing me against his chest. Above my head, I heard him murmur, "I'll call her."

"What ... what happened to your sister's boyfriend?"

Pure hatred flamed to life in his eyes. "He's behind bars. He confessed to killing Iona, and other women came forward and pressed charges against him—harassment, battery ... rape."

"Oh my God."

"The judge sentenced him to life in prison. Whole life order. That means he's never getting out."

"Good." I felt a kinship with Iona, a woman I'd never met, not only because of Walker but because I knew what it was like to be in a relationship with someone like that. I'd survived it. She hadn't. And that broke my goddamn heart. For her.

For Walker.

At that moment, I couldn't get close enough to him. I wanted to meld myself to Walker Ironside like we were two halves of one whole. This was love, I realized. This was what it was like to be truly, madly, deeply in love with someone.

It was going to take some getting used to.

But I knew I could.

Because I trusted Walker like I trusted very few people in my life.

And he trusted me.

That made me feel pretty damn epic.

"I want you again." I hitched my leg on his hip.

"Like I said," he murmured, gently pushing me onto my back to oblige, "demanding."

"You know it." I opened my thighs, inviting him in. "Good thing you've got stamina, Walker Ironside."

His grin flashed, wicked and exciting. "Good thing you do too. You're going to need it."

FORTY-ONE
WALKER

"Thank you for hiding this here," Sloane said, following at my back as I carried the large box containing Callie's pink electric scooter into my bungalow. I wanted to participate in the Christmas gift buying this year, so Sloane had reluctantly agreed to let me go halves with her on the item that was number one on Callie's wish list.

"No problem." I put it in my spare bedroom and turned to find Sloane leaning on the door frame, her expression thoughtful.

I knew why when she said, "Are you ready for today?"

Truthfully, I couldn't remember the last time I'd been nervous about something. Panicked, afraid, aye. But nervous? It wasn't in my vocabulary. Until today. "I don't suppose I'll ever be ready for it. But I'm going."

A few days after Sloane and I got back together, I gathered the courage to call my mum. She was brittle on the phone and insisted we meet to talk. At her suggestion that she come to me, I allowed it. It was not in my DNA to allow a woman to go out of her way for me, but I think I needed this from her.

And Sloane had taught me that maybe it was okay to take what I needed.

My mum had arrived in Ardnoch last night and was staying at the Gloaming. I was meeting her there soon.

Sloane pushed off the doorway and I met her halfway, wrapping my arms around her waist as she laid her hands on my chest. "If you want to be alone after, I get it. But you know I'm here, right?"

"I know. I'll come to you after," I promised.

"I'll take a ride with you into the village, if that's all right. I told Monroe I'd meet her at Flora's for a coffee."

"Sure." I pressed a kiss to her lips and smoothed my hand down to pat her arse. "Just give me a few minutes to shower and change." I'd been on a run when Sloane called, asking if we could drop the scooter off at mine.

She grinned, not releasing me. "Can I watch that?"

Amused, I gave her a slight shake of my head. "Not unless you want me to fuck you."

"Of course I do." Sloane pouted playfully. "But we don't have time. Darn it." She pushed me away. "I'll go wait in the living room."

I PARKED at the Gloaming and rounded the hood before Sloane could get out to open her door. She got out of the SUV, her entire focus on me as it had been since the moment we left my place. I knew she was worried about me, and I disliked being the cause of her anxiety. But I understood, and I could soothe it once I'd met with my mum.

Sloane leaned into me, palm over my heart. "Call me when you're ready."

I nodded and bent to kiss her. The intention was a quick thank-you, but as soon as I touched her, the yawning hunger inside me greedily demanded more. When I eventually released her, Sloane's cheeks were flushed and she was panting.

"Okay." She nodded like my kiss had been an answer to a question. Then she squeezed my hand before taking a step back. "I love you."

The words I'd thought would forever feel forced since Iona's death came easily. "I love you too."

She bit her lip against a smile, a habit she had that made me want to drag her into my arms. But she was already walking backward. "Good luck."

I nodded and gestured to the road. "Please watch where you're going. I'm rather partial to you as you are, not as roadkill."

This time, her grin was big and fucking gorgeous. With a wave of her fingers, she turned and waited for traffic to pass before she started across the street. It was then I noticed Monroe waiting at Flora's with Nox in his pram. I gave her a nod, and she grinned and waved back.

I turned around, striding toward the entrance of the Gloaming, my mind returning to my mum and the conversation I wasn't sure I would ever be ready to have.

However, just as I wrapped my hand around the door to the pub entrance, a scream rent the air.

"Sloane!"

At Monroe's shriek, alarm blasted through me in icy heat as I whirled around, already running toward where I'd left her. A blue car idled in the middle of the road outside Flora's as a man wearing a ski mask hurried into the driver's seat.

Sloane.

"He took her!" Monroe yelled at me, face red with impotent fury as she guarded Nox's pram.

No.

Roaring Sloane's name, I rushed into the street as her

panicked, fear-filled face appeared in the back passenger window. She threw herself against it, trying to open it.

"SLOANE!" Rage filled me as I hurried for the front passenger door. The window suddenly rolled down and her masked kidnapper raised his arm. I registered the gun a second before he fired.

The familiar burn slammed into my gut, and my knees buckled.

"WALKER!" I heard Sloane's terrified scream and pushed through the pain, forcing myself up.

But tires screeched on asphalt as he tore away.

"Walker!" Monroe cried, her body still covering Nox's pram but her eyes on me as I pressed a hand to the burning agony in my stomach.

"Call the police!" I yelled at her, my eyes on the blue car even as I was running, adrenaline fueling me toward my SUV.

I was vaguely aware of frightened villagers hiding behind vehicles and making frantic calls on their mobile phones as I threw myself into the Range Rover and floored it after the car.

I almost teetered on the turn off Castle Street, but I had to keep going. He'd put too much distance between us. Reaching across the passenger seat, I opened the glove box, ignoring the furious pain in my gut and the feel of blood soaking my shirt and trousers. Sweat dripped into my eyes, and black spots crowded the corners of my vision.

I yanked my gun case out of the glove box and fumbled with one hand to get my thumbprint on the lock. It opened, and I snatched it up with my free hand.

I didn't know who had taken Sloane or why ... but if it was the last thing I did, I'd see her safe.

Feeling the blood flow too fast, too free from the bullet wound, I knew with a sense of yawning regret—because I'd only just found her—that saving her might really be the last thing I ever did.

SLOANE

FEAR HAD STOLEN my rational thinking.

One second, I'd been stepping onto the sidewalk, beaming at Monroe, excited to see her, and the next thing, a stranger in a ski mask had pulled up beside me, pressed a gun to my head, and forced me into his car.

Then he'd shot Walker.

Walker was shot.

"He's a determined bastard!" my attacker spat.

The familiarity of his voice ... I knew that voice. He was American. His words registered too.

Walker.

Blood rushed in my ears as I turned around and peered through the back window. Relief flooded me at the sight of Walker's Range Rover in the distance, but catching up. Fast.

I whirled, trying to think how to distract the gunman. "Who are you? I know you, don't I?"

"Shut the fuck up!" His aggression reminded me so much of Nathan.

No way.

This wasn't happening again.

And he'd shot Walker!

Glancing back, I saw Walker gaining on us.

Sliding along the back seat, I ignored the masked man's orders to stay where he could see me, and then I lunged, wrapping my arm around his throat and hauling him back against the driver's seat to choke him.

He wheezed and raged against me, eventually dropping the gun so he could try to break my hold. His fingernails tore into my skin, but I held fast with every ounce of strength I had until suddenly we were fishtailing across the road. The force of it threw me off him.

His coughing and spluttering filled the car as I tumbled onto the floor of the back seat. He braked us to a halt, but I'd barely had a second to process we'd stopped when tires squealed outside.

"Fuck!" my kidnapper barked hoarsely. "Where's the fucking gun?"

The gun!

I launched up from the floor, ready to battle him when the driver's side door flew open and the cold wind battered inside.

Walker's voice was the sweetest sound I'd ever heard, even as he barked, "Don't fucking move or I'll put a bullet through your head."

Everything went quiet. I froze, not wanting to distract Walker.

"Now get out of the car. Slowly."

Leather creaked, and I heard footsteps on the asphalt.

"Sloane?" Walker called, and that's when I heard the panic in his voice.

"I'm here! I'm fine." The back passenger doors had no handles on the inside, so I clambered over into the front and spotted the gun on the passenger side floor. Pulling my sleeve down to cover my hand, I strained to pick it up and then inelegantly crawled out through the driver's side door.

My eyes went to Walker first. His face was pale and clammy, but his arm was steady as he trained the gun on the masked man. "You good?" he asked without taking his eyes off my would-be kidnapper.

Sirens wailed in the distance as I shut the driver's door and lifted the gun to train it on my attacker. "Shortest kidnap in history, thanks to you."

"And you," he said hoarsely. "You got him to stop."

"I choked him."

"Good girl."

My lips curled into a smile that froze as I caught sight of the blood soaking Walker's left side. Fear caused a plummeting sensation in my stomach. "Walker ..."

He blinked, wiping sweat out of his eyes, and the movement made him sway.

"Walker?" I moved toward him.

"Baby ... I need you to point that gun at the bastard until the police arrive."

"Why?"

"Sloane, have you got him?" he asked instead.

Forcing myself to face my attacker, who glared at us through the eyeholes in his ski mask, I covered as much of the handle of the gun with my sleeves as possible, clasping it in both hands as I aimed it.

"I've got him."

Out of my peripheral I saw Walker sway again and collapse to his knees. "Walker!" Terror shifted through me, but I didn't dare take my gaze off the guy who was watching everything with narrowed, calculating eyes.

"Keep on him," Walker replied hoarsely as he clutched his side.

"Is it bad?" I asked tearfully.

"Only a flesh wound, baby," he promised.

Why didn't I believe him?

Cars were slowing as they passed to get around us because we were blocking the road, but then they took off at high speed, likely upon seeing the gun. The sirens grew louder in the distance, and I willed them to hurry.

"Talk to me, Walker."

"Talk to him. Who the fuck is he?" Walker's breaths sounded shallow. Too shallow.

For his sake, I held my composure as I demanded of the man, "Take off the mask."

"Fuck you." He spat on the ground between us.

I lowered the gun and shot him in the thigh. He screamed and fell to the road, clutching at his leg and cursing me with every foul name under the sun.

"Well, that's one way to do it," Walker wheezed, and I looked at him. He was on his ass, trying to stay upright as he held the wound that was gushing too much blood. "Remind me ... remind me never to piss you off."

I couldn't laugh as I strode toward the man I'd shot and aimed. "The man I love is bleeding out right now, so believe me when I tell you I will shoot you in the face if you don't take off your mask."

A glimmer of fear shone in his dark eyes, and he raised a bloody hand to whip off the mask.

I stumbled back a step. "Brix?"

Nathan's best friend sneered at me. "I should have shot you in the fucking head on the street ... but I promised Nate I'd make it last a while."

"You're doing this for Nathan?" I asked in disbelief. "You were going to murder me for Nathan?"

"I was going to torture you for Nate." He winced as he grabbed at his bleeding thigh again. He was making a lot less fuss than Nathan had when I'd shot him in the leg. "I was going to kill you for the money."

Confusion was a cold bucket of water. I shivered with foreboding. "What money?"

Brix smirked. "Nate didn't just come here for revenge. He came because he was getting paid a lot of dough to take you out. When he failed, I stepped up. Been hard to get near you with that big fucker everywhere you go, so I had to take my shot."

Glancing at Walker, I noted how sickeningly pale he was

now, but he was listening. I aimed the gun between Brix's legs. "Unless you want to lose your dick, you'll tell me what you're talking about."

The sirens were close.

Brix laughed cruelly. "Your dear old dad is dead, bitch, and it seems he left all his dough to you. Guess your stepmommy didn't like that so much, so she called Nate and made a deal. Take you out for a million bucks."

His words slammed through me. Like brutal punches pummeling the air out of my lungs. Panic suffused me, and my cheeks tingled with the oncoming warning of an anxiety attack. My vision blurred.

Not now, not now.

Walker's murmur of my name reached through the stifling, crushing sensation gripping me, and I straightened my gun arm on Brix. "You're lying."

He shook his head, enjoying my distress. "I got receipts. Bitch thought we were two stupid thugs she could manipulate, but we got evidence she set this up. If I go down with Nate on this, I'm taking that cunt with me."

"Why?" I demanded. Brix would really try to kill me for a lousy million dollars?

Nathan, sure. I could see it.

But Brix?

He understood and curled his lip in disgust at me. "Nate is the only family I got, and you betrayed him. Then your asshole boyfriend"—he glowered at Walker—"had some guys fuck me up for information. I'm ashamed to admit, I talked. Like a little bitch. So I had to come here. I had to do this for Nate. For me. The million dollars was just the cherry on the fucking top."

The news that Walker had Brix assaulted for information wasn't surprising. He'd told me he'd had guys talk to Brix and I'd heard the implication that they'd worked him over to get to the truth about Nathan's whereabouts. Walker was desperate to protect me from Nathan, no matter the cost. He loved me. He'd do whatever it took. And I loved him. He was the only man I'd ever truly trusted. He'd taken a bullet in the gut, and it hadn't stopped him from racing after me.

Feeling revulsion and hatred for the people who had brought this on us, I heard Walker's breaths come faster and sharper as the police vehicles and an ambulance pulled up behind our cars. "You and Nathan *are* two stupid thugs. Neither of you could beat me. And if anything happens to Walker, I will spend the rest of my life making sure you never walk free again."

Orders were suddenly barked at me to drop the gun.

I held up my hands a second later and then lowered the gun to the ground as police officers surrounded us.

"My boyfriend first," I pleaded with them. "He's shot. Badly." The paramedics hurried toward Walker as the police ordered me to turn around. "Walker!"

He opened his eyes, groaning, and then rage flared in them when he saw they were arresting me. "No!"

"It's okay!" I called to him. "Please," I begged the officer arresting me. "Let me go with him. I was the one who was kidnapped! That bastard"—I kicked my leg toward Brix— "shot my man!"

"We'll sort it out at the station." The officer prodded me toward the car.

"I need to know he's okay." Hearing Walker call my name, I tried to turn around. "I need to know he's okay!"

But they weren't listening, and I found myself shoved into the back of the police vehicle, torn away from the man I loved as he bled out for me.

FORTY-TWO
SLOANE

N o one would tell me if Walker was okay.

That fear kept me from focusing on Brix's confession. What he'd said about my father. About Perry, my stepmom.

All I cared about was Walker. But the police wouldn't talk to me beyond taking my statement and then shoving me in a jail cell.

That was until Brodan Adair swept in on a wave of rage with a very expensive lawyer at his side and demanded my release. An hour later, he was still trembling with fury at "police ineptitude" as he drove me to the hospital in Inverness.

"Callie?" I'd had the presence of mind to ask.

"Safe," he promised. "She's with Regan and Thane."

Tears of utter panic choked me. "Walker?"

Brodan reached over and squeezed my shoulder, his expression grim. "Roe's at the hospital with his mum. He's in surgery."

"Is he ... will he ..."

"I don't know," he replied, his voice hoarse with emotion. "I don't know. But we need to get you checked over. That the police didn't take you to the hospital first is a fucking disgrace."

"I'm fine."

"You're not fine."

I wanted to argue with him, but I decided it was quicker to shut up, allow a doctor to examine me, and get to Walker than argue about it with Brodan.

Brodan asked questions as we drove to the hospital, and I told him what Brix had told us, as if I were telling someone else's story. It was surreal. Farfetched. Like something from a true-crime movie.

My stepmom had basically put a contract out on my life.

My dad ...

Stop.

Walker. He was all that mattered right now.

HE'D LOST TOO much blood. Walker's mom and Brodan tried to reassure me he'd be fine, but I was in a quiet, furious terror. We didn't talk about anything important, only asked around the room if anyone needed coffee or a snack, and then we sat in brittle silence. Roe had gone home to pick up Nox from Lachlan and Robyn.

By some miracle, no organs had been damaged by the bullet, but there was no exit wound and it had damaged a major blood vessel. To my relief, Walker made it out of surgery with no complications ... but he hadn't woken up. It had been nearly forty-eight hours. He'd lost so much blood before the paramedics arrived. There was a possible lack of oxygen to the brain. They said his brain function seemed fine, but they wouldn't know until he woke up.

There was something utterly crushing about seeing him in that hospital bed.

Brodan had gone home to shower, and so Walker's mom and I sat vigil.

Until the police arrived to talk to me again.

"Ms. Harrow ..." The plainclothes officer ducked his head to pull my attention back to him.

"Sorry," I muttered, pushing my greasy hair off my forehead. I needed a shower. But I needed Walker to wake up more. "You were saying?"

"The suspect, Mr. Kyle Brixton, is talking. In exchange for his confession, he's provided us with evidence against Perry Harrow. Your stepmother."

I nodded, every nerve ending jangling with the need to get back to Walker. The only thing that forced me to stay put was that I knew Walker would want me to face this.

The image of him running for me, pure fear and rage etched into his features seconds before that bullet hit, played over and over in my mind.

"It's true, then?" I murmured, feeling grief take hold. "What he said. About my father?"

The officer's face softened with sympathy. "I'm afraid so, Ms. Harrow."

I WOULDN'T LEAVE the hospital. Instead, I showered there and changed into clothes Monroe brought me when she, Aria, and Callie came to visit. Aria was watching over Callie, both of them protected by a small team of bodyguards that Brodan had insisted upon until we knew this was definitely over.

Callie cried when Aria took her away, and I wanted to promise my kid that the next time she visited Walker, he'd be awake. But the longer he lay in that bed, the deeper the roots of my fear grew.

His mom had returned to her hotel to meet his dad, who'd

driven up from Portobello. I didn't know how I felt about Walker's dad's arrival. Part of me wanted to protect him from it.

Like he'd protected me.

Always protecting me.

And because of that instinct, I might lose him.

But he was the only person I wanted to talk to about my dad.

Holding his hand, I stared at his handsome face, wan from the surgery. Dark circles shadowed his eyes, and his beard needed a trim. Walker's hand was so big. I held our palms together, and mine looked like a child's in comparison. Desperate fear clawed at me at the thought of never feeling his fingers curl around mine again.

"You have to wake up," I sobbed, bowing my head. "Everything you've been through ..." I struggled for breath. "A tiny bullet won't be the reason you leave me. It can't be. We're e-epic." My gaze came up to his face. "We don't end like this, Walker. I have a million cakes to bake you and you have a million more to convince me to overcharge for. We have a life to make. To finally *live*. We've barely even started." I leaned into him, my wrath at the idea of losing him thrumming through me. "So you have to wake up. You have to wake up!"

Movement tickled my hands, and my heart leapt into my throat as I glanced down at his hand clasped between mine. I opened my palms.

Walker's long fingers twitched and then flexed.

My gaze flew to his face, and his sleepy eyes met mine.

"I thought I was the bossy one," he rasped, a wry smile curling his lips.

Forty-Three
Walker

I t had taken a moment to process the beeping of the heart monitor, the dull pain throbbing in the lower left side of my gut, and that my throat was drier than the Registan Desert.

A hospital room.

The why of it came back to me at the joy on Sloane's face as she laughed in relief. It was nothing compared to mine at waking up to find her alive. Safe.

However, two seconds later, her laughter turned to hysterical sobbing, and when I moved to reach for her, pain in my stomach stifled the action. "Shit," I huffed. "Sloane, baby, don't cry." I squeezed her hand as hard as I could.

But then she was over me, arms around me, her cheek to my chest, sobbing so hard it jarred like a physical pain.

"Baby." I clasped the back of her head in my hand, threading my fingers through her hair. "You're killing me here."

She tried to calm. I could feel the tension in her body as she trembled and quivered and forced herself to settle. Lifting her face, I noted the red, tired eyes, the lank hair, and her snotty nose. "You're so fucking beautiful."

That made her laugh as she wiped at her nose and straightened. "Did the bullet do something to your vision?"

"Aye. Made it crystal fucking clear."

"And even in the hospital with a bullet wound, he's dropping f-bombs like he's being paid to say them," she teased and leaned over to press a kiss to my dry lips. It was gentle, only a brush, and nowhere near what I needed. I grumbled as she straightened. "I'll go tell the doctor you're awake."

"What happened?" I demanded. "I remember ... Is it ... No?" What I remembered couldn't be right. If there was some god out there, some fate, for the first time in a long time, I begged them to make my memory a nightmare instead.

Because if it was true, Sloane was ...

I saw that agony buried in her eyes and cursed inwardly. "I'll tell you everything, I promise. But first I'm going to get the doctor."

***

THE DOCTOR EXAMINED ME, and I bristled impatiently as it seemed to go on forever. I had feeling in all my extremities, my heart rate and blood pressure were good, and my memory seemed to be completely in order.

With that confirmed, I demanded Sloane tell me everything. When she looked at the doctor for permission, I wanted to roar.

"If you don't tell me now, I'm going to work myself into an agitated fucking mess," I warned.

The doctor pressed his lips firmly together and then nodded. "Fine. But afterward, I want you to rest. You're not out of the woods yet, Mr. Ironside, and if you want to fully recover and as quickly as possible, you need to let your body and mind rest."

I gave him a gruff nod of agreement.

He left, and Sloane insisted I sip at some water before she spoke. She ignored the irritation in my eyes and calmly waited. The hospital bed raised upward so at least I wasn't flat on my back. I could feel the throb in my stomach near the scar from the knife wound I'd taken as a teenager. Ironic, that. There was muscle and tissue damage from the gunshot wound. I'd have to take it easy for a while. Which meant, the threat to Sloane better be over.

"Tell me."

Drawing her chair closer to my bed, Sloane reached for my left hand, and I curled my fingers around hers. She seemed mesmerized by our entwined fingers for a second, and when she lifted her gaze, there were fresh tears in them. I gave her a squeeze in reassurance.

She sucked in her breath and exhaled slowly. "My dad is dead, Walker."

Fuck. I had heard Kyle Brixton correctly, then. I gripped her hand tighter. "I'm so sorry, baby."

Utter sadness suffused her beautiful face. "Cancer. He wanted reconciliation before he died. And he was leaving the bulk of his money to me and Callie in recompense for abandoning us." A tear escaped that she impatiently brushed aside with her free hand. "He asked my stepmom, Perry, to hire a PI to find me to bring me to him ... instead, she told Nathan where I was and asked him to deal with me."

Shock ricocheted through me, as well as understanding.

Sloane's face was suddenly hard with hatred. "When Nathan failed, Brix stepped up."

I cursed, regret and self-directed anger in the word. "Because I antagonized him."

"It's not your fault," she insisted.

"I sent men to get information from him."

"I know."

"I told them to do whatever it took."

"I know." She leaned into me. "I don't care. I don't blame you. You did what you needed to do to protect me and Callie, and I will not be angry about that. Brix came here to kill me. For money. For revenge. He's responsible for his own actions."

"Your stepmum?" The need to get out of that hospital bed and end the threat she posed was almost a physical pull.

As if reading my thoughts, Sloane gripped my hand. "She'll be dealt with. Legally. I won't let her hurt us anymore, Walker, so I'm asking you to let the police handle her."

Amazed at her strength, I tried to calm. "Your dad ..."

Her lips trembled as grief tightened her features. "I know," she choked out. "And I'll have to deal with that and process it ... but right now, I have to concentrate on you getting better. This is over. Finally. The authorities here contacted US authorities with the evidence Brix handed over—he has recordings of meetings between Perry and Nathan and himself —and Perry has been taken into custody. She thought she could manipulate them. That they were dumb thugs. She misjudged them. And now she'll pay for it. She can rot in hell for all I care."

Remembering how she'd shot Brix in the same place as Andros, I said, "I take it Kyle survived the gunshot wound."

"Yup. Now he and Nathan will have matching scars."

Awe filled me. It soothed me to know how capable she was of defending herself. "You were something to witness out there."

"I could only do it because you chased after me with a bullet in your stomach." She pressed a kiss to my knuckles.

The memory of the fear that I wouldn't reach her in time before I passed out lingered. "I only got to you because you got him to stop the car."

"Okay. So we both saved me. And it's ... it's over. I feel like we had all these puzzle pieces in our hands that finally make sense. Perry lied to my father's lawyers and told them she was tracking me down. But they were getting suspicious, and she knew she only had a short time left before they found me themselves. When Brix offered to kill me for the money instead, she jumped on it."

The thought of her succeeding with Sloane ... "I want to kill the bitch."

"I know. Me too."

Realizing that she'd been alone while I lay unconscious in this hospital bed, and she found out that not only was her father dead but that her stepmother was trying to off her for the inheritance, ripped at my guts. "I am so sorry."

Her gaze was fierce. "You have nothing to be sorry about."

"Your dad, though ..."

"I told you." She leaned forward, bringing my knuckles to her lips. "I will deal with it. I promise. I'll let myself cry a decade's worth of tears about it." The first of those tears slid down her face. "But I need to focus on you right now. When ... when I saw you running for me, the fear in your eyes, that bullet hitting you ... I knew like I've never known but with Callie that someone loved me more than they loved themselves."

Damn fucking straight. "Good."

She smiled at my gruff response and then promised, "And you have to know that I love you like that too. That I need you to start protecting yourself, too, because I need you to exist in this world with me. Because I don't seem to work right without you now." Sloane pressed a fist to her chest. "You're an integral beat in my heart, Walker Ironside, and so I'm going to need you to live as long as I do and stay at my side the whole time."

"I'll try my very best to do that," I vowed.

Something shifted in her expression, turning it cautious. Wary.

Alert, I waited patiently for her next words.

"Your parents are here. In the waiting room. Should I ... should I tell them to come in?"

Fear squeezed my throat at the thought of my mum and dad in the same building as me. The last time I'd seen my father was when I woke up in a hospital bed. Life was fucking ironic that way, eh?

"I can tell them to leave," Sloane assured me.

Slowly, I shook my head. "Let them in. But ... will you stay?"

Sloane nodded, everything she felt for me right there for the entire world to see. "Always."

THEY HAD AGED. Of course they had.

My mother looked as she had in Edinburgh that day. Older, but still the kind of mum you never saw without her hair or makeup perfectly in place. Even now with worry and tension darkening circles under her eyes, she was immaculate. Her smart suit bore nary a wrinkle.

Reluctantly, I looked from my mum to my father. Surprised, I realized he seemed shorter. Like he'd shrunk with age. But his face, the one so much like my own, was smoother than I'd imagined. His lips were pressed into a thin line, and even as I feared what he'd say, I couldn't drag my eyes from his.

Neil Ironside, a man I hadn't seen in two decades, slowly crossed the distance between us.

The steel in his gaze collapsed beneath the weight of grief as he stared at me. Tears glistened in his aged gray eyes as he greeted hoarsely, "I'm sorry, son. I'm so, so sorry."

Emotion blurred my vision as I nodded in acceptance and gestured to the chair by my bed.

FORTY-FOUR
SLOANE

To my darling Sloane,

    If you're reading this, then I ran out of time. All my life, my actions were dictated by a drive for success. To never again know hunger and shame. To give my child the life I didn't have growing up.

    If only I'd known that time, not poverty, was my enemy, I would have done so many things differently. But mostly, I would have set aside my foolish pride and brought you and my grand-child home. When I looked for you too late and couldn't find you, I've never felt such regret.

    Time has stolen my chance for your forgiveness. It has stolen the chance for me to tell you in person how sorry I am and to see you one last time before I go. I want you to have everything I have, darling. To use it to make your life better. But more than anything, I want you to know that I love you more than I have ever loved anyone. And if there's one good thing I can leave you with, it is the wisdom of my failures. Never let pride stand in the way of the people you love. Never live a life that you'll leave in regret.

I wish we'd had the chance to say goodbye. For me to know where you are and to know that you're happy. All I can do is leave, hoping that wherever you are, you're being loved far better than I was capable of.

You'll be my last thought, my last hope, my last wish.

I love you always,

Dad

I READ my father's letter for the hundredth time since his lawyers sent it to me. The first time I opened it, I didn't think I'd recover from my grief. It was the only time in my life I'd truly lost it in front of Callie. Thankfully, Walker, even though he was still recovering, had been there to hold me through the sobs that seemed to rattle my entire being, to reassure my daughter when I could do nothing but lie in bed. Clutching the letter. Crying silent tears the whole night.

Perry had my father cremated. I'd missed his memorial. And he'd died not only not knowing where I was, but not knowing his wife had kept us apart and tried to goddamn kill me.

Every day since the letter arrived had been one of the hardest struggles I'd ever gone through. But Walker was barely out of the hospital, his reconciliation with his parents still an ongoing and difficult process, and Christmas was here.

For Callie, I needed to be strong. She'd already been through way too much. I needed this time to be a haven for her.

"I love you, Daddy," I whispered, kissing the letter before tucking it back into my bedside table. "I forgive you."

I said it to him every day, hoping that wherever he was, he heard me and it brought him peace.

The sound of Callie and Walker talking downstairs got me

up. I dragged on my robe and slippers and drew up my shoulders, preparing to be a glass half-full today.

And I was.

It was Christmas Eve. The man I loved was recovering from being shot but still insisted on staying here with us over the holidays. I'd watched him like a hawk as he got into bed with me last night, noting the tentative way he moved.

Callie's laughter rang up toward me, and as I descended the stairs, I smelled bacon and coffee. Regan had festively decorated the cottage while Walker was recuperating in hospital, and I spent all my evenings with Callie at his bedside. She'd found the cutest tree to sit by the window and covered it in pretty vintage Christmas baubles and gold fairy lights. Regan strung garlands of gold and red flowers along the fireplace and across our main wall. Mistletoe hung above the doorway between the kitchen and living room, and three stockings hung from the fireplace.

I'd never been more grateful for my friends as they rallied around us. Brodan was a constant presence in Walker's hospital room. He brought Nox with him whenever he could. I think it surprised Walker to realize how much his friend and ex-boss clearly loved him. How much so many people cared about him. In fact, Walker seemed to be the only one who didn't realize how incredibly lovable he was.

Giggles drew me to the kitchen, and sure enough, I found my daughter with Walker as he grilled bacon and stirred scrambled eggs on the stove.

"What are you doing?" I huffed, hurrying into the room to take the spatula out of his hand. "You're not supposed to be doing anything right now."

Walker gently took the spatula back as he leaned down to press a soothing kiss to my lips. "Happy Birthday, baby."

I flushed with pleasure even as I opened my mouth to

admonish him for exerting himself, when Callie threw her arms around my waist. "Happy Birthday, Mom!"

Hugging her tight, I kissed the top of her head. "Thank you, baby girl." I turned to Walker and held out my hand. "But you guys know my birthday is tomorrow, right?"

"We're making a new tradition," Callie announced decidedly. "Your birthday will no longer be on Christmas Day but on Christmas Eve so we can celebrate it properly."

"Is that right?" I chuckled.

"Yeah, it's not fair otherwise."

"Well, okay. I can do that." I turned to Walker. "But I can also make breakfast."

"It's almost done." He shrugged. "Grab a coffee."

Seeing the determined gleam in his eyes, I made us coffee and poured Callie juice and soon we were sitting around our crammed kitchen table eating bacon and eggs.

I tried not to let my eyes rest on Walker's stomach, to study his careful movements. He was off work now, but he'd be returning on reduced duties after New Year's. Walker caught my gaze, and I read his expression.

He wanted me to stop worrying about him.

Not possible.

The man meant too damn much to me.

"We have presents for you, Mom," Callie said, even as she watched me closely. She was probably searching for any sign I was going to break down again. I think she sensed my fragility, and I hated that.

"Oh, yeah?" I grinned. "So I get presents today, too, instead of all on Christmas Day?"

Her eyes lit up. "Yup! It's not fair you have to share your birthday with someone so famous."

I laughed. "I have been saying the same thing my whole life."

It was easy to be glass half-full for Callie as we talked and teased over breakfast and Walker sat in silent amusement, listening to our banter. This was how I wanted it to be. I didn't want to focus on my stepmother, who was out on bail but facing criminal charges of conspiracy to commit murder. My dad had indeed left me the bulk of his fortune and, though it would take a few weeks of legal back-and-forth, I was soon to be a multimillionaire. It was hard to wrap my head around that too. If necessary, I'd use every single cent to make sure Perry withered away in prison along with Nathan and Kyle.

The kidnapping had made the national news, and we'd been inundated with media requests for interviews. Ardnoch was now becoming known as the surprising thriller capital of Scotland, considering how many near misses its inhabitants had experienced over the last few years.

And as soon as Perry's part in that was leaked to the press, the sensationalism of an inheritance conspiracy was too much for them to ignore. The story was more widely reported in the States, but once something went online, there was no escaping it. I'd been beating off calls from news outlets here in the UK for the last two weeks. Finally, things seemed to quiet a little, but I knew it would all explode again once the case went to trial.

Among all that, Walker had spent some time with his parents, who had returned to Portobello. They'd had a few awkward phone calls since, but they were planning to visit again in the new year. I think seeing my heartbreak over losing my chance to reconcile with my dad had made Walker determined to work through two decades of estrangement with his parents. It turned out his mom had tried to find him over the years but Walker had moved around so much with his job, she'd never been successful. Then she'd discovered after our wordless meeting in Edinburgh that Walker was still in contact with a childhood friend and had used the connection to reach out. I was grateful Walker had allowed her to. His capacity for forgiveness was extraordinary and I couldn't be prouder of him.

Callie barely let us finish our breakfast before dragging me out of the kitchen and into the sitting room. There were gifts under the tree from her friends from school and from the housekeeping team at Ardnoch as well as presents for Walker and our Adair family friends. I soon learned two birthday presents were tucked behind there too.

Walker settled beside me on the couch, his arm resting along my back as I leaned into his uninjured side, and Callie brought the gifts over. One was a small, gift-wrapped box and the other an envelope.

I glanced quizzically at Walker. "When did you two have time to do this? We've barely had time to buy Christmas presents."

His lips quirked up at the corners. "Open the box first."

Callie handed over the box wrapped in bright pink shiny paper I knew Walker had let her choose. "Ooh, what could it be?" I grinned at my daughter because she looked like she was ready to explode with excitement.

To my bemusement, I found inside a door key tied with a ribbon. I gestured to them both with the key. "Explain?"

"Now open the envelope," Walker instructed.

My curiosity on overdrive, I opened the envelope and pulled out a couple of folded sheaves of paper. Scanning the contract, my lips parted in shock. "Is this what I think it is?"

Walker leaned over and tapped the bottom of the second page. "It just needs your signature."

I flipped back to the first page and read the address.

"How?" I whispered.

"There are four tourist shops in Ardnoch," Walker explained. "Two on Castle Street alone. This one on Castle Street used to be a restaurant in the '90s. There's an old kitchen in the back that needs updating, but we can do that, no problem."

"This is the tourist shop next to Morag's?" That was prime real estate.

He shrugged slightly and said, as if it was no big deal, "I convinced Gordon he'd be better off renting the place to you than competing with the other tourist stores. And everyone, including Gordon, knows you can afford the rent. In fact, I think if it works out for you, we could persuade him to sell the place."

I picked up the key with the ribbon on it, tears filling my eyes. "You got me ... a bakery?"

"Happy Birthday, baby," he said gruffly.

When I looked at Callie, her eyes filled with tears too. Happy tears. I held my arms out to her and she rushed me, almost shoving me back into Walker with the force of it. "I love you so much," I choked out.

"I love you too." She squeezed me tight before releasing me. Her eyes went to Walker. "But it was Walker who did it."

He tugged affectionately on a strand of her hair. "It was your idea, though."

I stared in wonder at this magnificent man, questioning what I'd ever done to deserve him. "I love you. Thank you." I knew it had probably taken some fierce persuasion to get Gordon to relent to this.

His eyes glimmered with pleasure. "You're welcome. I love you too."

"Okay, this is the last thing, and then we're gonna stop being mushy," Callie announced like a little adult before she stared at Walker with eyes that seemed too wise for her young age. "Walker, thanks for saving my mom's life. I love you."

My heart swelled as Walker swallowed hard. It took him a minute, as if he was beating back emotion, but then he sat forward and drew Callie into a tight hug. His voice was like sandpaper over stone as he replied, "I love you, too, wee yin."

I didn't know where to look. At the two people I loved most loving on each other or at the gift they'd given me.

"Jesus," I said to the ceiling, "I hate to break it to you, pal, but I totally won Best Birthday this year."

EPILOGUE
WALKER

Six months later

My phone rang in my pocket as I was settling Callie and the cakes into the passenger seat of my SUV. "You got them?" I asked her, pointing to the box.

She pressed her wee hands to the top of it as she vowed solemnly, "I'll protect them with my life."

I gave a huff of amusement, wondering where kids picked that shit up. "Let's hope it doesn't come to that, wee yin." As I closed her door, I pulled out my phone. It was Mum.

"Walker," I answered, as I rounded the bonnet of the car.

"I know. *I* called *you*." There was amusement in her voice that relaxed me. It had taken a while, but it finally felt comfortable between us.

"Everything okay?" I swung into the driver's seat.

"Just calling to wish you good luck."

I glanced down at Callie and the cake box. "Thanks,

Mum." I'd told her the other day about my plans, and she was pleased for me. And desperate to make up for lost time. "You and Dad are still planning to visit next week?"

"Absolutely. Wouldn't miss it. Your dad says good luck too."

"Tell him thanks." The reconciliation with my father was a bit more strained. Unfortunately, I think I'd inherited being too hard on myself from him. While I'd forgiven him for the past, he hadn't yet forgiven himself. His gruffness wasn't about me, and I knew that because I saw myself in him.

"I'm on my way there now."

"Okay, I'll let you go." I heard her sigh nervously for me. "Let me know how it goes."

Maybe it made me an arrogant bastard, but I wasn't nervous. I was 99.9 percent certain I knew how it would go.

Callie chattered excitedly about the day's upcoming events. When she began talking a mile a minute about possibly becoming a big sister one day, however, I questioned letting her eat so much of the leftover buttercream from the cupcakes. The subject didn't bother me. But her mouth was moving worryingly fast.

"Can we pass by the front of the bakery first?" Callie asked as we drove down Castle Street.

Sloane's rental agreement with Arrochar and Mac ended two months ago, and since I was a man who knew what he wanted, I asked Sloane and Callie to move in with me. Sloane was all about living without regrets these days, and she'd said yes. It surprised me how quickly I adapted to the feminine invasion of my space. How I barely blinked when a new cushion appeared on my sofa or a pointless candle showed up on the coffee table. My ordered tidiness required compromise with a preteen around. Callie left homework, books, her laptop, schoolbag, shoes, and hair accessories lying about ... I found them everywhere.

And I liked it.

Almost as much as I liked seeing Sloane's makeup scattered on my bathroom counter and her nightdresses and cardigans hanging from door handles. Despite having her own professional kitchen now, our home still always smelled like a baker's kitchen. I found flour in the strangest places.

And I liked it.

It felt like a home now instead of a house.

We drove down Castle Street, slowing past the bakery that Sloane would be readying to open in half an hour. A couple of villagers already hovered outside, peering in.

The new signage on the front window read Callie's Wee Cakery. Suffice it to say, Callie was over the moon her mum named the bakery after her. And the villagers were over the moon that, apparently, for the first time in forty years, they had somewhere they could buy fresh bread.

I guided the car left down one of the side streets that would lead me to the back of the bakery where we could park. With a tiny percentage of the money Sloane's father had left, we'd transformed the store on Castle Street. Restored the kitchens and bought everything Sloane would need to run it. Since a bakery would mean extremely early mornings for her, she'd decided it would only open three days a week. She would make up the rest of the days taking outside orders as before, but this time she could bake them in her new professional kitchen. Not that she needed to. Sloane's father had made more cake as a litigator than even I could have guessed. She was independently wealthy, and if she invested wisely, spent wisely, she would never have to work another day in her life.

But that wasn't Sloane.

Thankfully, however, my hardworking woman had also hired two shop assistants to help run the front of the store.

Pride filled me as I got out of the SUV and rounded it to help Callie. Not only had Sloane dealt with the stress of the upcoming trial against her stepmother and ex and his friend while trying to launch a business, she'd attempted to make life as normal as possible for Callie. And I realized Callie was where Sloane drew her strength. It was awe-inspiring. The woman amazed me. How one person could carry the weight of what she had to carry and do it with such optimism and hope, I'd never know. She looked at me like I could save her from anything, but the truth was, she saved me.

Every damn day.

"Ready?" I asked Callie as I took the box and she clasped her hand in mine.

"I think I should ask you that, eh?"

My lips curled. The longer she stayed in the Highlands, the more she was picking up a wee Scottish inflection from her classmates.

Striding into the back of the bakery, we discovered Sloane arranging fresh loaves of bread onto a tray to take out front.

"We've made space for it!" one of Sloane's shop assistants called from the store.

Sloane looked up to answer and caught sight of us. Her face split into a wide grin. "I wasn't expecting you guys until opening." Gaze dropping to the box in my hands, she rounded her long steel prep table to bridge the distance between us. The kitchen gleamed like a shiny new penny, except for one section where she was working on decorating a cake.

Along one wall were a few cakes in varying degrees of decoration, which I knew were from outside orders. Ovens were lit up baking fresh pastries to refresh the ones she'd already set out front. There was flour on one of her flushed cheeks and tendrils of hair loosening around her face from her ponytail. Her apron was also covered in flour.

She looked happy. Beautiful.

"It's going well, then?" I asked as she stood on her tiptoes to kiss me.

"Well, we haven't opened yet, but yes." Sloane leaned against me, even as she hugged Callie into her side. "What's in the cake box? You're not buying from a competitor already, are you?"

I shook my head at her teasing and held the box out to her. "Just a congratulations cake we baked."

Her eyes widened with delight. "You guys baked for me?"

"We tried."

She was more excited about that than I'd expected, and I felt the first wave of nerves hit me. All right, then. Maybe I was only 98 percent sure of the outcome.

Sloane took the box and laid it on one of her prep tables.

When she flipped the lid, five badly decorated cupcakes surrounded a sixth in the middle.

And in the middle one, instead of a giant chocolate button propped into its messy buttercream, was an engagement ring. The single diamond caught the light, and I watched Sloane's face as she zeroed in on it and gasped.

As soon as I'd seen it, I knew it was the one. It was a simple white gold diamond solitaire. Not fussy. Understated. Beautiful. Like the woman I wanted to wear it.

I felt Callie squeeze my hand and looked down at her. She gave me a bolstering smile. Before I released her hand, I squeezed it back and stepped forward to take the ring out of the cake. Sloane gaped at it like she'd never seen a ring before.

Removing it, I wiped the buttercream from the band. She turned to me, big gorgeous brown eyes searching my face, stunned.

I took her left hand and slid the ring on her ring finger without preamble.

Sloane gawked at it as it winked and glittered under her bright kitchen lights. Then she looked up at me. "Was there a question?" she practically squeaked.

My smile came easy. "I've loved no one like I love you,

Sloane Harrow. I couldn't live without you now." I rubbed my thumb over the ring. "And I want your promise that I won't ever have to."

Suddenly, she laughed, delight bursting from her every pore as she reached up to clasp my face in her hands. "That is such a Walker Ironside way to propose to a woman."

Wrapping my arms around her, drawing her close, I demanded, "Is that a yes?"

"To your nonquestion?" she teased, and then laughed harder at my scowl. "Yes! Yes, I will marry you!"

Her cries drew the girls in from the front of the store into the kitchen. They erupted into cheers of congratulations when they realized what was going on. But I only had eyes for my now fiancée. I kissed her until heat flooded my limbs at the realization she'd agreed to be mine forever. I had to release her before things got inappropriate.

A weight hit us, and we looked down to find Callie, arms around us both, jumping up and down. "Does that mean we can change our name to Ironside?" she practically yelled at her mum.

"Aye," I responded firmly as Sloane said, "Well, it's the twenty-first century, baby girl, so we can keep our name if you want."

I cut her a look.

Her lips twitched with amusement and then she nodded down at Callie. "Yes, since apparently Walker hasn't joined us in the twenty-first century, we can change our name to Ironside."

Callie pumped her fist in delight while I tickled Sloane under the arms in retaliation.

"Oh, Walker, don't!" Her laughter rang off the bakery walls as she squirmed in my arms.

I didn't stop until she was gasping with giggles. Finally,

when she'd had enough, I stopped and cuddled her into me. Tears of amusement gleamed in her eyes.

"I hate being tickled," she complained even as she grinned.

"I'll need to remember that next time you're restrained."

Her eyes flared at my meaning and she murmured, "Don't you dare."

"Dare what?" Callie asked around a mouthful of one of the cupcakes we'd baked. Apparently she couldn't wait.

"Nothing." Sloane slid her arm around my waist and held out her hand. "As much as I just want to stare at this ring for the next thousand years, I have a bakery to open."

"And we're here to help. Also, I have this." I pulled a velvet pouch out of my pocket and a white gold chain fell out. Gesturing to her ring, I said, "Give."

Bemused, she reluctantly took off her engagement ring and handed it to me. I slid it through the chain until it dangled from it. "To keep it safe when you're in the kitchen."

Understanding dawned as Sloane turned so I could place the chain around her neck. "You thought of everything." She turned back to stare up at me with so much love, I could barely stand it. I'd never know what I did to deserve her. But I knew I'd never walk away from this. "You always think of everything."

Caressing her cheek with my thumb, I said quietly, "No. Just everything pertaining to you."

Sloane clasped the necklace, the ring to her chest. "No one would believe you're such a romantic. I kind of like being the only one who knows it."

"I know it too." Callie finished up her cupcake and brushed the crumbs off her fingers. "Let's face it, Walker's like a Mento. Hard on the outside but soft on the inside. Anyone paying enough attention can see it. Lewis's mom said Walker's the reason Monroe and Brodan even got back together. So ..."

She gestured between me and her mum. "None of this is surprising, really."

I didn't know how to feel about any of that, but Sloane looked ready to pee her knickers with laughter. She turned to me, wide eyed and voice trembling with amusement, "Out of the mouths of babes. I think I'm going to call you my Mento from now on."

A smile prodded my mouth. "Don't even think about it." I gently shoved her toward the front of the store.

"No, I think I have to at least work it into my vows," she continued, as I guided her forcefully forward. "My love, my Mento!"

Callie giggled at her side.

"I can take the ring back."

They ignored my flat tone and empty threat.

"Ooh, maybe we should have a Mento wedding cake."

"I'm regretting every choice I've made since I woke up this morning."

Sloane snorted as she handed me an apron.

I glared at it.

"You said you wanted to help. I got a bigger one made just for you." She waved it at me. "Do you need one with a Mento on it?"

"I know several ways to kill a man."

"Does it involve Ment—"

"Don't finish that sentence."

She beamed gleefully up at me. "I love you."

"I've signed up to a lifetime of being tortured by you and Callie, haven't I?" I said in beleaguered realization.

"Pretty much." She stood on tiptoes and kissed me hard.

"Fine. I love you too." I grabbed the apron out of her hands and donned it.

Looking down, I frowned at the pink fabric with the white writing across the front that read Callie's Wee Cakery. I cursed inwardly, since I was trying to be better about not swearing in front of Callie. Sloane read the look on my face, lips trembling with laughter as she repeated, "I really do love you."

I pointed at her. "Only for you."

She was so happy, I couldn't regret it.

Even when the first bastard to walk through the door was Brodan Adair. His lips parted in a slow *O* as he came in with the small crowd, Monroe at his side, and Nox in his arms. Utter sadistic glee gleamed in his eyes as he took in my pink apron.

"Oh, how the mighty have fallen." Brodan grinned like a fucking fool. "This feels like karma." He turned to his wife, practically vibrating with joy. "Does this not feel like karma?"

Monroe smirked. "This feels like the day my husband might die if he's not careful."

He looked back at my stony expression. "This is the part where I say I told you so."

"I love her. We're engaged. Get over it. Buy a cake or leave."

"Engaged!" Monroe cried out and rushed around the counter, minding no one else, to hug Sloane.

Brodan's smile was genuine and warm now. "Happy for you, Walk. Congrats."

"Thanks. Cake?"

He snorted at my abrupt response and glanced down into the glass cabinet filled with Sloane's creations. "I'll take one of the chocolate sensations."

"That'll be ten pounds."

Brodan scowled. "It says four quid."

"She underprices everything."

"Walker!" Sloane admonished, laughing at my side. "It's Brodan."

"You're right. He's loaded. Fifteen quid."

Brodan glowered, but Nox diluted the fierceness by accidentally hitting his dad in the face as he shook his wee arms about. My mate took hold of his son's hand and kissed it. Then he smirked at me. "Does this mean you'll be adding to your wee tribe, then?"

"You're worse than a fucking woman."

"Walker."

I turned to find Sloane giving me wide "don't curse in my new bakery" eyes.

"Shit, sorry."

She looked at Monroe. "I give up."

"Roe, look at those strawberry tarts," Brodan said suddenly, easily distracted and salivating over the pastries. "Want one?"

"Uh, aye." His wife grinned as she leaned into Sloane, who was looking flustered, even though her two shop assistants were handling the other customers.

"So, two strawberry tarts?" I asked.

"Make it three."

"That'll be another twenty-one pounds."

Brodan shot me a look. "It says they're four quid each too."

I looked at Sloane. "Have you underpriced everything?"

She threw her hands up. "Okay. Apron off. Out." She shooed me toward the kitchen.

"Why?"

"Because this is not a school bake sale, and you can't overcharge my customers. I love you. Like a whole bunch." Sloane gently pressed her hands to my chest, attempting to force me backward. Her lush brown eyes twinkled with amusement but also determination. "But come back at closing, and we'll go celebrate our engagement."

"Dinner at ours!" Monroe announced loudly, sharing a

quick nod with Brodan. "Tonight. Six o'clock. The whole family will be there to celebrate. And I'll invite Aria."

"You guys don't have to do that," Sloane replied, expression tender. Appreciative.

"We want to. Unless, of course, you guys just want to celebrate together."

My fiancée looked up at me.

She wanted to celebrate with our friends who had become family to her.

I caressed her cheek. "We've got all the time in the world for just us."

Sloane bussed into my touch for a second before turning to Monroe. "We'd love that."

"Great! Well, we better get going so we can organize. But we'll take a few things from here for dessert, if you don't mind." Monroe turned to Callie and asked her for help to select some cakes.

"You really want me to leave?"

Sloane turned back to me. "Never," she promised, pressing her soft body to mine. "But you seem to have an issue with my prices." Her laughter shook through her and against me. "So I think you should either hang out in the kitchen or take Callie for breakfast."

I wrapped my arms around her waist, holding her to me. "I'm proud of you."

Her gorgeous smile lit up her entire face. "I know." She touched the engagement ring on its chain. "I'm proud of you. Proud of us … for getting here, despite everything."

An ache so fucking big I could hardly stand it yawned in my chest. "Me too." I leaned down to brush my lips across hers. Then I murmured, "But mostly you're just happy you'll get to take my cool-as-fuck surname, right?"

Sloane threw her head back in laughter, the bright, sunny

sound filling the bakery. Her body moved against mine with the force of it, and I couldn't hold back my grin.

I vowed in that moment to make sure I heard her laughter every day, and I'd make it happen. Because I'd promised her that I'd stay by her side for the rest of our lives.

It would be the easiest promise I'd ever kept.

Printed in Great Britain
by Amazon

45089975R00219